THE DEVILS WHO KNEW TOO MUCH

A Mysterious Comedy

Jane Gillette

iUniverse, Inc.
New York   Bloomington

THE DEVILS WHO KNEW TOO MUCH
A Mysterious Comedy

iUniverse books may be ordered through booksellers or by contacting:

iUniverse
1663 Liberty Drive
Bloomington, IN 47403
www.iuniverse.com
1-800-Authors (1-800-288-4677)

ISBN: 978-1-4502-2176-4 (sc)
ISBN: 978-1-4502-2177-1 (ebk)

Printed in the United States of America

iUniverse rev. date: 4/12/2010

Also by Jane Gillette

The Last Limerick

Author's Note

Belmont on the Mississippi is a fictional town, like its neighbors, as impossible to find as any of the characters or a pair of Beresford Boots.

ACKNOWLEDGMENT

I am grateful for the endurance, good humor, and valued assistance of my team of test pilots, who graciously read the manuscript in its warty stages…David Bednarek, Roger Miller, Ruth Kamps, Barbara Graham, Joanne Weintraub, and Nancy Christiansen. My thanks to all.

'Hang by your thumbs, everybody! Write if you get work!'

Bob and Ray radio show (1946) signature closing line
Bob Elliott and Ray Goulding

For David

Cast of Players

Archie Beresford, retired CEO of Beresford Boot

Nadine Beresford, society matron

Cyrus Armbruster, retired newspaper editor

Betty Hughes Armbruster, romance novelist

Lettice Mulroy, hairdresser

Tommy Delaney, liquor store proprietor

Admiral Melvin Moss, retired naval officer

Isobel Woolsey, real estate tycoon

Preacher Boswell, dog breeder

Marigold Woolsey, sculptress

Parnell Grant, poet

Nina Dupree, aspiring actress

Hugo Beresford, new CEO of Beresford Boot

Sheriff Charlie Lemmon of Crawford County

Lieutenant Freddy Donovan of Belmont police

Dr. Sherman Bathgart, psychiatrist

Lola Spriggs, wealthy widow

Miranda Burke, journalist

Toby Spriggs, English professor

Beatrice Wrenn, psychic

Cosmo Freese, actor

1

Coming Home

May, 1987   Belmont, a college town on the Upper Mississippi

"Did you see the Phi Beta Kappa key hanging around her neck?" Lettice Mulroy made her remark through a mouthful of shrimp dip.

"Who could miss it?" Archie Beresford replied in a wistful tone. "Lying there against those awesome orbs?"

Nadine, his wife of several decades, threw him a glance.

Archie ignored her and fixed himself a stiff old-fashioned with three cherries. He turned and winked broadly at sleepy-eyed Tommy Delaney, slouched like a rag doll in one of Lettice's worn over-stuffed chairs. Tommy was clutching a large whisky, sure to be one of his last, Archie thought sadly, if he was to believe rumors that the old boozer was really dying this time. The Irishman grinned back, fully appreciating Archie's reference to Marigold Woolsey's splendid bosom. Ah, Marigold. Archie could almost hear every man in the room sigh her name. Like a tonic, it was, seeing Marigold and Parnell Grant again after so many years. They had all witnessed a wedding that afternoon. But, it was the return of The Prodigals that had drawn the most attention. Most of the older guests were delighted to see the long-absent Grants.

Archie, for one, was grateful for the diversion, now that his only son was back in the territory too. Archie had retired from Beresford Boot and Outerwear to hand over his enormously successful operation to Hugo, a boring lad with a good head for business and little else. It had been a month since Hugo waltzed into town, surprising the lot of them by bringing with him Miss Nina Dupree, a beauty from New Orleans who was supposed to become Mrs. Hugo Beresford, in due time. Archie was finding Miss Nina damned near irresistible, to say nothing of off-limits. But, Archie did like to skate on thin ice occasionally, blessed as he was with a tanned, aging cowboy's face and a nicely tuned up physique, all quite essential when pursuing the ladies at his age. He liked to think his skates were still sharp.

"I think I'd take my chances on everybody thinking I was stupid," Betty Hughes Armbruster was saying, her mind still working on the Phi Beta Kappa key. A striking beauty herself at sixty and still cranking out romance novels that sold like white bread, Betty Hughes (who insisted upon using her given and middle names in harness) tossed two ice cubes into a glass and filled it with Lettice's generic gin, their hostess's badge of poverty, Archie liked to say. He stood to the side to watch and listen to the chatter and sniping; it had been going on since their youth. They could speak for each other and then go on to argue what had been said. Old friendships were like old marriages, not always pretty or well-oiled, but amazingly solid.

Nadine and Lettice were laughing. Betty Hughes was sure to keep the infamous Marigold on her toes. The ladies resented Marigold's intrusion after so many years. A sculptress with an awesome figure and a reputation for encouraging young talent, meaning a penchant for inviting willing studs into her bed, Marigold was beloved by the men and nearly feared by the ladies. Archie snickered. Oh, how he loved Marigold.

"Why on earth come back here after decades in Paris? Or, was it New York? I always forget," said Nadine, as she peered down her aristocratic nose at one of Lettice's trays of appetizers, soggy crackers spread with a brownish paste. "Very suspicious. Could be they've finally run out of funds." Nadine picked up a cracker and put it to her nose. "Liver sausage," she muttered aloud. She put the canapé back and selected a handful of nuts.

"I'll find out," drawled Betty Hughes with a wink. A native of Alabama, Betty Hughes had clung tenaciously to her soft accent, referring to it as her life-line. "Parnell says he needs to smell the earth of home. Earth, my foot. Probably needs a transfusion of Woolsey money." Giving her cantaloupe-tinted hair a fluff, Betty Hughes chose a place on the lumpy sofa next to Nadine and settled in.

Archie listened with his usual casual interest and sipped his drink, seriously considering getting drunk. Apparently, his wife still envied Marigold's admittedly titillating attributes. Odd, how these resentments lingered. He wondered if she continued to lust after Parnell, too. Parnell Grant, poet laureate of Fifth avenue or was it the Rue de la Concorde, was Marigold's long-time companion. The man would never be published in any college anthology, to be sure. He and Marigold were Bohemians of the old school, artistes who'd been living off inherited money and their wits for nearly half a century, often accepting invitations to dwell for lengthy spells with minor European aristocrats and has-been film stars who needed to fill up their grand and decaying castles or simply longed for charming company, even among strangers. Had Marigold and Parnell ever married? No one knew. Betty Hughes could find that out too. As he stood in his corner analyzing his old friends, Archie recalled that one or two wedding guests that afternoon had hinted that the campy Parnell was actually a fruit! Archie wasn't so sure about that, not with the poet's astonishing record of female conquests. Besides, Archie would have known. Any real man would.

"That wouldn't be too difficult," Cyrus Armbruster was heard to remark from a few feet away. Cyrus was seriously engaged in stuffing smoked trout between two pieces of party rye. He had thrust the tip of his tongue between his front teeth in utter concentration. He was a wiry, precise man, a double for William Powell of the old Thin Man films, and shared Nick Charles's passion for martinis and getting at the truth.

"What's not too difficult?" Betty Hughes demanded of her spouse in a sharper than usual reaction, half-anticipating what was coming. She pushed off the sofa and headed for the drinks table again.

"Thinking you're stupid." Cyrus stuck out his tongue at his wife and sniggered like a kid as he slid out of his suit coat, deftly switching the fish sandwich from one hand to the other while completing the task.

He dropped the jacket to the floor without thinking. Archie picked it up and arranged it on the back of a chair.

"Very amusin',Cyrus Armbruster. As if your left brain knows what your right brain is doin'." Betty Hughes splashed a good measure of gin and olive juice from the jar into her glass and narrowed her eyes at her husband. He was driving her nuts. Here they were at a marvelous age, with no financial worries, about to move into Meadowlark Retirement Village, and Cyrus was more trouble than ever. Some days, she felt as if she were crawling on foreign soil. He forgot things, rambled on about the war, and occasionally couldn't even dress himself properly. Lettice had suggested they see a doctor, hinting that Cyrus might be getting senile. Betty Hughes told her Cyrus just liked to be difficult. It gave him something to do.

As he listened to this all too familiar exchange of barbs, Archie decided that Betty Hughes' reactions to Cyrus's peculiar outbursts might sound harsh to an outsider's ear, but he understood her irritation. Whether she admitted it or not, Betty Hughes was lashing out at the husband she was losing, the strong man who had suffered her jabs for years, the sharp newspaper editor who knew how to get a tough job done. Archie could see that Cyrus was failing here and there, that his mind was slipping. And, he understood that the Cyrus who would replace him would never understand the pain of his own illness. Cyrus was his dearest friend, a witty, intelligent man, who seemed to be disappearing from the world and himself. Archie swallowed hard against an almost violent urge to weep.

They had just come back from Judith Pardee's wedding. Another. Must be the third or fourth. This time the woman had corralled a stock broker from St. Louis. Unfortunate goat, Archie decided conceitedly, helping himself to salsa and chips, waiting for the usual numbing of reality that came from drink. Jumping Judith, they called her, for her apparent marital stamina and her adroitness in locating an eligible, well-to-do mate so soon after the demise of the last. Judith was Claire Armbruster's mother, and Claire was married to the Armbrusters' son, Duncan, a dour middle-aged man much like Hugo. Archie often wondered if Hugo and Duncan might just belong to two other couples. Poor Hugo. He had turned out to be a handsome man with no discernible personality or sense of humor. In his forties now, Hugo would rather pinch pennies than women, Archie liked to joke, when he could joke about his only son. Most of the time, he and Nadine worried that they may have brought another bore into the world. Archie realized he'd just wrinkled up his nose thinking about Hugo.

"Oh, shut up, you two," Nadine scolded. "Who cares *what* Marigold Woolsey hangs around her neck? The real story is *who* is hanging around her neck." Her owlish expression made a clear reference to Marigold's agreeable nature when it came to men. The prodigal Grants, who very likely had been living in sin for more than forty years, would come under close scrutiny for manifestations of their now familiar behavior, conduct the Old Devils found refreshing, but a way of life their wives knew to be unreasonably naughty. For the Old Devils (as they were called) Marigold might inspire delightful daydreams, but it was Parnell who was held in amazing esteem. Here was a well-off man of some sixty years, content to live for decades on his chocolate company inheritance and the generosity of strangers, a gentleman seemingly undisturbed by Marigold's frequent excursions into other men's beds. The Old Devils liked to say that it took a special brand of courage to allow one's wife this kind of maneuverability. Was that the right word? Archie refreshed his drink and tried the smoked fish. Bland and oily.

"Headache, my foot!" Lettice remarked, sharply, referring to Marigold's excuse for skipping the post-wedding gathering in her rooms at the Golden Horizon Apartments for Seniors, a kind of pilot program in Belmont for retired folks with limited incomes and an aversion to living with their children.

"Ahhh," crooned Archie agreeably, unwilling to make too many enemies of the ladies tonight, "that's what I was thinking. That fellow with the moustache who kept bringing her punch...he will bear watching. A foreigner, you know." He was feeling oddly protective of Marigold. Old feelings died hard, he supposed.

"You're suspicious of anybody who isn't white, Anglo-Saxon and Republican," Lettice snapped back, perfectly willing to remind her guests of her liberal bent.

At this moment the doorbell chimed and Isobel Woolsey let herself into the tiny, cluttered apartment. Compared to Lettice, Nadine, and Betty Hughes, admittedly handsome women with perhaps an extra pound or two on the bones, Isobel swished into the room like a French mannequin. Her freshly tinted auburn hair was tucked neatly beneath a luscious little cocktail hat, her long exquisite legs in black hose, and the rest clothed in Anne Klein. For a woman over sixty, Isobel was pushing back time with only one hand. Archie had always found the woman tempting and absolutely delicious to look at, but a woman impossible to try…..like a cream pastry you're pretty sure has gone bad.

"What have I missed?" Isobel asked in a contralto that begged their attention. After tossing her handbag into a chair, she dutifully pecked Tommy Delaney on the cheek, greeted the others, and marched over to the drinks table where she poured herself a white wine.

"Examining Marigold and Parnell under the scope," Archie answered brightly. Isobel would spark up the conversation; the woman acted like the chairman of Ford Motor, but she did prod them all along.

"Good place for them. The nerve, coming back here." Isobel looked around for a place to sit. Lettice's living accommodations were beyond explanation. Too many curio cabinets and those old lady spider plants, her eyes seemed to be saying.

"We think they've used up their money," said Lettice, not really believing it.

"They're not getting mine!" puffed Isobel. "My dear husband didn't kill himself working so his silly sister could buy herself another gold turban. Did you see that thing? I thought I'd fallen into the Arabian Nights!"

The Old Devils rewarded her with a good laugh.

"Marigold thinks she's Coco Chanel. Nothing but gold will do." Nadine crowded in next to Betty Hughes on the couch and nibbled from a dish of salted nuts.

"Women over fifty should mind their cleavage," Isobel commented acidly while smoothing her skirt. "No one likes looking at boobs with wrinkles." No one had ever seen Isobel's cleavage. She and her three sisters were beautiful and prudish.

"I thought they were lovely," cooed Tommy, coming to life again at the mention of Marigold. He could say what he liked; his wife had stayed home.

More laughter. When it came to Tommy and other women, a certain latitude was allowed. He'd been luring females to bed most of his life, much to everyone's amazement. Lettice said it was his Irish charm. Archie said it had more to do with anatomy.

Tommy was enjoying himself, still surprised, he'd said earlier, that Lettice had failed to invite Father Dunn to sprinkle holy water on him, since most of Belmont was expecting him to expire any day and then float to heaven for their amusement. Too soon for that, he'd told them. Now with Marigold back on the scene, he would defy the doctor's odds a bit longer.

"Parnell still looks as divine as ever," said Nadine, surprising herself and the rest with such candor. She could see Archie strain his neck above his collar, like he did when he was bothered. She didn't mind giving him something to worry about once in a while.

"Too thin," put in Cyrus, staying with them so far.

Lettice began circulating with a tray of crackers and assorted cheeses. "This is that old cheddar from Montrose," she told Isobel. "Damned near as old as I am."

"In that case, I'll try the baby Swiss," replied Isobel with a tight smile. She wasn't comfortable making jokes but tried occasionally. "Patrick must be spinning in his grave," she said, politely sampling the cheese. When Lettice wasn't looking she put the remainder into her napkin. "It's time Marigold grew up. Her renegade black sheep act is getting old. Like the woman herself."

"Looks good in black, she does," croaked Tommy, his bloodshot eyes twinkling. "About as good as she looks in nothin'." He crowed like a rooster this time and everyone laughed, except Isobel. He waved his empty glass at Archie for a refill. Archie willingly obliged. What harm could it do at this point?

"So what," Betty Hughes answered irritably. "Isobel, she's your sister-in-law; why have they come back?" Betty Hughes slipped out of her high-heeled shoes and wiggled her toes beneath the coffee table. Lettice wouldn't mind; she was Irish.

"Hasn't told me a thing. Likes to be mysterious. Part of her act. Says they plan to stay on...for good. Says they're having too much fun to leave." Isobel pursed her thin mouth in disapproval. "I don't think men and women our age are supposed to be having a good time." She paused. "With other people's spouses."

"Jesus, Isobel, we're not dead yet!" chimed in Archie without thinking. Ashamed, he quickly glanced at Tommy to see if the old boy had caught the remark but Tommy was dozing again. Damned silly thing to say, Archie warned himself. Poor old Tommy, so close to death's door.

There was a murmur of concurrence among the men, who were considering the source...Isobel was such a cold fish. Archie was reminded that a few of the party guests were no different than the Grants, simply more secretive. After forty years of friendship there weren't many infractions of the rules that remained a mystery in a town like Belmont. Frankly, he didn't give a damn, never did.

Cyrus was wandering the room nibbling on a third trout sandwich. He suddenly announced in a loud voice that his doctor said he should drink red wine, and he held his glass aloft. "Good for the arteries," he said. "It'll turn you into a raunchy Frenchie," he remarked and then leered at Lettice, who giggled. With her comfortable, round face and gray hair, Lettice wasn't often teased or approached by men.

"You old sexpot, you," Lettice said. "You're sounding quite yourself tonight." She prayed he wasn't losing his mind. She prayed none of them would. Feeling a pang of fear, she wondered why Admiral Moss had failed to show up.

Then, stopping abruptly in the middle of the room, Cyrus stared directly at Tommy and said commandingly, "Tommy, you said the party had an eleven in it...either an eleven course dinner, or, we could stay until eleven o'clock!" Finding this hilarious, Cyrus hunched over and laughed and laughed, hanging on to his belly as if it might fall off. "I told Betty Hughes we couldn't remember which!" He let out another howl and shoved the remaining fish treat into his mouth, not minding that no one knew what he was talking about. His story told, Cyrus found a chair near the windows and peered outside at the setting sun.

"What was all that about?" Nadine asked Lettice, never quick when it came to diversions.

"Some kind of memory flash, I suppose. Jesus, Mary, and Joseph." And Lettice automatically crossed herself, a gesture which irritated Nadine, who was an atheist. "I think Cyrus is slipping," Lettice whispered in Nadine's ear; tears had sprung up in her eyes and she sniffed loudly. Nadine patted Lettice's plump hand and said Cyrus was just pulling their legs. She didn't sound very convincing.

Archie shook his head at Cyrus's joke and headed for Lettice's bathroom. Cyrus's outbursts made him jittery, and when he was jittery he couldn't stop peeing. Damn, this getting old was a crock, he grumbled. Funny, it wasn't bothering Marigold or Parnell. Fit as fiddles. He couldn't stop thinking about the woman but felt betrayed by her, too, after seeing her at the wedding. He sensed she wasn't as charmed by him as she used to be. He zipped up and decided he'd call her anyway.

When Archie returned, the Armbrusters were getting set to leave. Betty Hughes was helping Cyrus with his jacket and trying to find her handbag, and Lettice was standing near the door, still holding tight to a martini, keeping it remarkably level, something she did expertly.

"Take care of yourself, Tommy," Betty Hughes called out. "Don't forget, we're playing bridge next Friday at our house.

Tommy was nearly asleep and blinked a few times before raising his glass to the departing Armbrusters. "Bridge it is, Betty Hughes." Peculiar custom, he thought, to call yourself by two names. Daffy Southerners. "Let's hope I can roust Evette for the big night." His wife didn't like drinks parties and hated bridge even more. It was unlikely she'd go to the Armbrusters. Evette had learned to stay at home after years of pub crawling with Tommy.

"See that you do," said Cyrus, apparently back in the realm of reality again. "Where in the hell is the Admiral, Lettice?" he asked seriously, poking her arm with one finger, like he often did. "I wanted his opinion on some stuff I've been reading on D-Day." Cyrus squinted up into Lettice's face. All the Old Devils had fought in the war. He and Archie had landed together at Normandy. Odd, how they'd all survived when so many died. Cyrus would never get over the miracle of it. And, he still carried the guilt of living.

"Whooping it up at the country club, no doubt. He should have come to the ceremony." Lettice sounded miffed. She and the Admiral, who lived across the hall, had been sharing supper and Sunday breakfast the last few months, and she enjoyed his company.

"He wasn't invited," blurted out Tommy, struggling to get out of the chair. He and the Admiral had hoisted a few at O'Reilly's that Friday night, as they often did. "Hell, Judith didn't invite me either, but I showed up, just to get her goat." He giggled and then coughed until he almost choked. Isobel thumped him on the back and then patted him on the head like a child. Archie handed him a glass of water.

"Who the hell cares?" declared Archie, hoping to quash bad feelings and an argument. "One wedding's pretty much like another. Besides, we've been to how many now for Judith? The woman sure knows how to kill off her spouses!" That cleared the hurt egos, and everybody giggled.

"Four," replied Isobel. "I told her this was quite enough. That none of us would come to another."

Isobel, keeper of records, overseer of morals and manners, Betty Hughes sourly observed. "More power to her," Betty Hughes crowed and tried to open the door. "Could be our Judith marched down the aisle again just to get *your* goat, Isobel!" She smiled. "Come on Cyrus, we're going to be late." And she reached for her husband's arm.

"Why don't you call Claire and say we're *very early*, but can we come over now anyway." Grinning like a bad boy, Cyrus jabbed Archie in the ribs with a bony elbow.

"Claire won't get it." Betty Hughes wasn't sure she did.

"She'll get it," Cyrus snickered, "but, she'll blame Duncan for getting the time mixed up!" He cackled and held on to the front of his trousers, suppressing his bladder. Making fun of Duncan and his prickly wife made him feel good, made him feel like he was still attached to the world.

Archie clapped Cyrus on the back. "That's my man!" They all cheered, grateful for Cyrus's good humor, grateful he wasn't wandering in a fog again. Archie reminded himself to treasure every sane, funny moment from now on.

They bid the Armbrusters a good evening and watched them totter and sway down the walk to the car. Betty Hughes was insisting in a loud voice that she drive and soon took off down the street with a violent lurch.

Archie shuddered. God, life terrified him these days.

Twenty miles upriver from Belmont in the lake country, near Sandy Hook, Butch Flynn eased his backhoe along Pike's Wood road. His partner trailed in a dump truck. Sandy Hook was one of a dozen dilapidated river towns that clung to the banks of the Mississippi out front and nestled their rears into the forests out back. Folks around these parts survived on tourists and fish and not much else. On this warm May morning, power saws buzzed and hammers cracked through the balmy air, a sound still so brazen and unfamiliar that Flynn was having a hard time believing the current building boom.

His machine lurched over a network of ruts and potholes that should have been paved years ago, except that nobody who summered up here wanted to pay the bill. These old-timers, mostly from Chicago, had been opening their cottages in May and closing them down again around Labor Day since after the war. The weathered shacks that ringed Arrowhead Lake or huddled in the pine forest above the river were as primitive as pup tents by today's standards. Like everybody else, Flynn preferred indoor plumbing and TV after supper. The day of the outdoor toilet was gone and nobody was crying.

An Illinois developer named Kornmeyer had bought up the last of the log and shingled summer houses in Pike's Wood. He'd contracted to build twenty luxury summer homes on these quiet thirty acres. Another twenty 'villas' were scheduled to go up on the northeast end of the lake just a few miles inland. The land had turned to gold; Sandy Hook was getting ritzy. Corporate executives and their families were demanding more than a view of the Mississippi or lake frontage. They wanted tile in their bathrooms and microwaves in the kitchens and fancy restaurants in town.

One retired guy on the north end, who'd vacationed here for over forty years, was enjoying his last hurrah on the river with his grandsons. Perched on stilts, his shingled three-room cottage with its screened porch had a dainty look, Flynn thought, like a girl lifting her skirt over a deep puddle. The old man had confided to him that the property had brought him a small fortune. He and the missus, he said, were moving to Tampa.

The grandsons waved Flynn along the path, eager to watch the day's excavation. Next door, ten old pines had been cut and removed to make room for a 'villa' with two baths and a sauna. Kornmeyer was calling the development Pine Hill Park. Flynn's wife was calling it La De Da Estates.

"Morning, boys," Flynn called to the twins, skinny eight-year-olds with baggy shorts and dirty sneakers. They'd miss the fishing in years to come, but, right now, supervising the carpenters had taken their minds off all the changes.

"You starting the next one today, Butch?"

"Yep. Just keep back. Don't want to run over your toes." Flynn grinned and the boys grinned back. They'd been supervising hole digging for three weeks.

Flynn aimed the machine toward pale wood stakes flagged and pounded into the

ground. He planted the teeth of the hoe into the sandy earth and began excavating footings for Villa Number Three. His partner marked time in the truck with the engine going and the radio playing soft rock.

Not five minutes into the job, one of kids let out a scream. "Stop! Something's down there!"

Jesus! Flynn's heart almost stopped. He slowed, slammed the hoe into idle, and then swung down to the ground.

"What is it?"

"There, there!" the taller boy cried. "A foot!"

Jesus! Flynn crouched near the long narrow hole and looked down. It *was* a foot. Attached to a leg, attached to a torso. Holy Mary! Scraps of rotted clothing clung to the bones. A dirt smeared skull stared up at them, the mouth agape, a gold tooth just visible on the top row.

Flynn rose to his feet and drew the boys away from the sight. "You don't want to see any more, kids." He took a deep breath and noticed that his hands were shaking. "We'd better call Sheriff Lemmon." Out of the corner of his eye, Flynn could see his partner jumping down from behind the wheel.

More excited than scared, the boys ran ahead to the cottage yelling, "We found a body! We found a body!"

Their cries echoed among the thick trees like shrill bird calls.

"Some kids and a construction worker found …ahh, *IT*, …in Pike's Wood yesterday morning. Heard it on the radio on the way over." Cyrus, a retired newspaper editor still in love with a good story, stood close to Archie, as if surrounded by eavesdroppers. Cyrus continued in a loud hiss. "Foot bone popped up first." He quite nimbly raised his own foot in illustration. He was wearing a T-shirt and red boxer shorts.

Archie sat down on the long bench to tie his golf shoes and slammed the locker door from where he sat. "Have you talked to anybody about this?" he asked, nervous already.

"Hell, no! Why would I do that?" Cyrus began pulling on green plaid trousers and then zipped up. "All I'm saying is that one bone led to another, and now Sheriff Lemmon has the whole damned skeleton in the morgue up there."

"Damnation! What is Lemmon saying?" Archie reopened his locker and dug out a pack of cigarettes and offered one to Cyrus. They lit up, in violation of country club rules, but Archie and Cyrus rarely followed the rules.

"The remains of a body were found and an investigation is underway. The usual crap." Cyrus inhaled and proposed they have a drink in the bar to steady their nerves.

"In a minute. Put on your shirt. We have to keep quiet on this. Understand?"

Cyrus nodded. "Yeah, Archie. On my bad days, I'll hide under a blanket. You won't hear a peep out of me." He grinned, but it was shaky.

Archie hated to scare his old friend, but Cyrus did have a problem remembering things lately. Senility at 60? Hardly an option for Cyrus or anybody else, Archie told himself. They were too young. Archie patted Cyrus on the back. "We'll have to warn the Admiral and Tommy."

"Righto, Arch. You know, I've dreaded this day for over forty years." Cyrus sat hunch-shouldered on a long narrow bench that ran the length of the locker room.

"We've been lucky."

"Damned straight. We survived Normandy, Arch."

"Give me a hand, for God's sake," Archie said. "I can't lift him by myself."
A small plane buzzed through the night sky.

"Get hold of him under the arms." Cyrus crouched to lift the feet while
the other two men stood back.

In the end, the four of them carried the dead man through the dark
wood with the girl leading the way, carrying the shovel. The single yellow
disk of light from her flashlight bobbed and weaved among the branches and
pole thin pine trunks. A bank of low clouds intermittently hid the moon,
and they all jumped when a frightened deer plunged deeper into the forest.
The bearers stumbled through a quarter mile of scratchy brush before the
girl pointed out a small clearing on high ground. From where they stood
they could smell the river churning through the channel.

The earth was easy to dig, and by taking turns the four men excavated
a long, narrow trench about a yard deep. They rolled the heavy body over
the edge and into the pit where it landed with a thud on the damp ground.
Two of them filled the hole and covered the freshly disturbed soil with fallen
branches.

The girl never spoke and she never cried.

Archie awakened in a sweat and sat up in bed. The dream, the nightmare, whatever he wanted to call it, was back. Vivid details of the night in Pike's Wood all those decades ago were so real that he could still smell the freshly dug dirt and the fruity scent of the girl's cologne. He could hear again the rush of river water and see the white haze veiling the moon. He could feel the oiled leather of Buzzy Turk's boots left to decay in the dump where they had tossed them. His fingers recoiled from his bed sheet at the memory of a sticky trickle of blood that ran down the dead man's stubbled cheek.

Nadine slept on in her own bed, in her own room across the corridor, untested by such misadventure. The body buried in the wood was a secret known only to the five people at the grave.

Months would sometimes go by and Archie would be free of memories. But, now, the remains had been found, like an ugly lie revealed. An exhumation, a resurrection metamorphosed overnight into a news story and an investigation.

He supposed it was his punishment.

Sheriff Charlie Lemmon didn't get many homicides in Crawford County, and he'd never seen a forty-year-old skeleton. But, experienced or not, Lemmon was in the thick of it this time. Rotund, short, and not even close to pretty, Lemmon wore Smoky the Bear hats and drove his Jeep like a stock car. He'd been elected because his old Dad had been sheriff for thirty years. Name recognition, Lemmon liked to joke, was just about everything in Crawford County. When Charlie took the oath ten years ago, he was given an opportunity to prove himself the first week when a taxidermist shot a beer salesman at Smitty's Loon Lake Bar on route AA. It was a simple case of too much booze and two men fighting over one woman. Fifteen witnesses made it all remarkably easy. Luckily for Lemmon, nobody in Crawford County had seen fit to kill anybody else since. Not where anybody could find out about it.

On Saturday morning Charlie Lemmon read the coroner's report for about the tenth time. It stated that the John Doe unearthed in Pike's Wood had sustained a severe blow to the head, a crushed skull, which was most likely the cause of death. The fact that the remains were found in a primitive grave pointed to foul play. And, to make it worse, the D.A. of Crawford County wanted Lemmon to identify the victim and the person or persons who put the unfortunate man into the ground.

Lemmon had known Freddy Donovan, a lieutenant with the Belmont police department, for twenty years. A few times a season they fished the sloughs around Sandy Hook and got royally drunk doing it. After some serious soul-searching Charlie Lemmon decided to call Freddy. The sheriff told him he wanted to run the case past him. This wasn't exactly an admission of ignorance and failure, but Lemmon did concede that Donovan knew more about dead bodies than he did. Of course, Belmont cops didn't have to solve a dozen homicide cases a year, but Donovan had investigated one or two in his day. Donovan's reliance on a little outside advice was generally kept quiet.

"We don't have much, Freddy. No wallet, no watch, no scraps of clothing that tell us much. Just an old leather belt and one gold tooth. Still in his mouth, of course."

Donovan said Belmont was suffering a crime slump due to the heat. Nobody had the energy to be really bad, and the genial Irishman offered to have a look at Lemmon's so-called 'crime of the century,' as it was described in the *Crawford County Gazette*. Must have been a slow news day, Donovan figured, to print a line like that in bold face.

When Donovan arrived at the sheriff's station in Sandy Hook, Lemmon greeted him with a hearty handshake and a cup of fresh coffee laced with bourbon.

Donovan read over the coroner's report, examined the photographs, and then perused the physical evidence that lay in clearly marked plastic bags on a table in Lemmon's office. It didn't amount to much…bits of rotted fabric and a leather belt. The shoes were missing. Donovan thought that was significant and said as much to Lemmon, who hadn't noticed. Lemmon said they'd stop by the coroner's office later to check out the skeleton with its nice gold tooth.

"About the most interesting thing is that belt," Lemmon said, adding a drop more bourbon to his own coffee. "Dental records might be tricky to trace after all these years."

Donovan put on reading glasses and took a closer look at the belt. "That's a special buckle, Charlie. Looks like an animal on it." Donovan squinted and bent closer. "Could be a badger."

"Could be. Hard to say."

Donovan said, "He was a large man…that belt must be a 46." Donovan took a chair and stretched his legs. He, too, was a large man, barrel-chested, beer bellied, his face hidden behind amber whiskers. "How many years has he been down there?"

"Coroner isn't too exact. Probably forty or so."

Donovan did the math. "Puts it during the war then…or after. Could have been somebody too old for the draft. Check the missing persons reports. Can't be too many."

"Right. Few of us ever leave paradise," Lemmon said with a grin. In reality, the young folks were skipping out after high school and heading for the big cities. Tourism was about the only real industry in Sandy Hook, and it was in a boom period right now. "The files are stored in the courthouse basement."

"Funny, his shoes being missing. Whoever buried him must have removed them. He wasn't buried naked."

"Could be they were heavy. Like construction boots."

"Could be," said Donovan, savoring his doctored-up coffee. "Maybe he was carried quite a distance through the wood and his pall bearers wanted to lighten the load." He twinkled a little and reached for Lemmon's bourbon bottle. "Mind?"

"Hell, no."

"Let's have another look at that coroner's report."

Lemmon handed over the folder and Donovan read it a second time.

"Says here our shoeless lad had one leg two inches shorter than the other." Donovan slid his glasses to the top of his head and focused on Lemmon. Charlie was not Sherlock Holmes.

"So? What do you make of that?"

"He might have missed the war because of it. Probably limped. Might help you ID the guy. Somebody might remember a gimpy guy who suddenly disappeared forty years ago." Donovan was getting interested now.

Lemmon's eyes brightened. "Might have worn corrective shoes."

"Bingo. Check the moccasin factory in Lynton Station. They do custom work. And Beresford Boots in Belmont."

Lemmon made a note on a big yellow pad. "How about another drop?" The sheriff picked up his bourbon bottle.

Never a man to refuse a free drink, Donovan held out his mug for more. "Helps keep the cells working smoothly," he said. He sat quietly a while thinking about the dead man. Gimpy, big, maybe nasty enough to get himself conked on the head. And, for some reason buried in the wood. There had to be more than one person involved. He was too big for one person to carry. Unless he or she used a wagon or a wheel barrow. And that would be damned near impossible in these woods up here.

"Who would take the time and energy to bury this guy in a secret grave? Why not leave the body where it was? A fractured skull doesn't necessarily mean homicide. It could have been an accident." Donovan was full of questions.

"He could have fallen and hit his head," Lemmon pointed out.

"But, why bury him? Could have been a black magic ceremony."

"Nah. He probably wasn't killed in the wood," Lemmon reasoned soundly.

"His killer would have needed a shovel and some help. He was a big bruiser."

"Odd, too, that having the guy disappear was better than leaving the body and running off."

Donovan grinned. "Good point. This man vanishes. You'd need a good cover story for that. Wouldn't his friends, family, neighbors ask about him? Must have been a damned good reason to hide his body."

"He could have been a tourist. Fisherman, hunter from the city. Gets in a brawl with some guys. They get rid of the body and drive off."

"Never thought of that." Donovan felt stupid.

"We're checking the older cottages near the grave, Freddy, the few that are left. Most of those shacks have been pulled down. New houses are going up faster over there than taxes. So far, nobody remembers a man gone missing at any time."

"Check real estate records, Charlie. Find out who lived nearby and if they're still around." Donovan's mind returned to the belt. "You think that's a badger on that brass buckle?"

Lemmon frowned. "Badger, raccoon. Who cares?" He handed Donovan the evidence bag with the belt in it. Donovan put it under a strong light on Lemmon's desk.

"It's well-worn. Got a magnifying glass?"

Lemmon dug one from a desk drawer and handed it over.

Donovan scrutinized the buckle again. "I think it's a lodge insignia. You can just make out some numbers or words at the bottom. Probably a lodge number."

"A Badger Lodge?" Lemmon scoffed. "Never heard of it."

Donovan said he hadn't either. "Ask around. Might be some defunct organization popular in the thirties and forties. Might have died out during the war or after." Donovan stood.

Lemmon nodded and jotted down more notes.

"Jesus, you old flatfoot," Lemmon said with a grin, "you've given me a leg up on this damned thing." The sheriff hoisted his squat body from the chair with a grunt and clasped Donovan's big freckled paw. He stood a head shorter than the Irishman.

Donovan was surprised by Lemmon's effusiveness. Charlie rarely gave credit to anyone but himself. He figured Charlie was real nervous.

"Maybe just a few leads going nowhere," the Irishman replied modestly. "Don't forget your local dentist now. He might get real excited helping out on a murder case. Those poor guys spend their lives poking around in people's mouths. What a way to make a living." Donovan smiled. He was terrified of dentists. He headed for the door while Lemmon grabbed his Smoky the Bear hat from a hook on the wall.

Lemmon laughed and said, "Let's drive over to the coroner's office and take a look at that pretty gold tooth."

Billy's Bar & Grille on Main wasn't crowded. The regulars, mostly retirees escaping their wives and old men of few means trying to kill time, perched expertly on chrome-legged bar stools. Archie thought their nearly perfect line of curved backs and bent elbows would have made a good black and white photograph. Judging from their solemn expressions, the eight men at the bar might have been contemplating the weightiest matters of civilization, like a panel of esteemed justices. The rest of the place (about as charming and as wide as a box car) sat empty of customers.

As Archie sauntered up to the bar, he called out to Billy for a beer. Several regulars turned on their stools to greet him. He shook hands with one or two. Archie prided himself on knowing nearly everybody in Belmont. Many either knew him or worked for him. He was a big shot, but he liked to think he was a nice big shot.

Archie had insisted Nina Dupree meet him here. Billy's, he said, was the town's most notorious watering hole, occupying the number five spot in the Belmont Tourist's Guide Book, right after steamboats docked at Wrenn Park and one slot before the Depot restaurant. She had to see Billy's. Archie was still escorting his future daughter-in-law around the territory, encouraging her to appreciate the finer things in God's country.....the great muddy river, stubby bluffs cut through by deep coulees, red barns stuck like magnets to hillsides, black and white cows grazing on the nearly vertical pastures, and the joy of riding horseback on narrow wooded paths. Peaceful marshes and catfish dinners stayed near the top of his list of favorites too. It was the best excuse he had for keeping company with a pretty woman without anybody suspecting another motive. He said he was taking over for

Hugo, too busy these days with business to show Nina Dupree her new home. Archie maintained privately that Hugo might be a damned fool, but a lucky one.

Behind the long varnished bar stood Billy, pug-faced and squat, attired in a greasy apron that had never seen Tide. He was skillfully drawing tap beers and frying entrees with his ubiquitous cigar clamped between uneven teeth. The smell of seared sweet onions and beef was as powerful as the cigar smoke. Positioned on the wall behind the bar was the legendary painting of Miss Raven, Belmont's black-haired beauty, a voluptuous female reclined on red satin pillows and attired mostly in gold bracelets. The regulars had memorized every brush stroke and curve. Sixty years ago Billy's grandfather installed the painting in its heavy gilded frame in defiance of the local W.C.T.U., and to its credit, the painting now commanded five lines in the guide book. As he gazed upon Miss Raven's obvious attributes, Archie concluded that the painting was quite good and wondered idly if Billy had it properly insured.

Few females frequented Billy's twice, finding the dinge too great and the company moribund, as Nadine put it when she walked out of Billy's door years ago, never to return. Betty Hughes was one of only a handful of women who frequented the saloon without too much of a fuss, always with Freddy Donovan from the village police department. She and the lieutenant were old friends, drawn together by their love of golf and old St. Hyacinth's Church. Archie had known Freddy most of his life. They fished bass together.

Archie took a table by the window, its skin of nicotine the color of old amber, and ordered a bag of pretzels from Billy's odd nephew, a thin kid done up in black and sporting one silver earring. Overhead, suspended from the embossed tin ceiling, metal hooded lights on long rods sputtered feebly in the gloom.

A few minutes later, Nina stepped over the threshold, like summer's first light, so out-of-the-ordinary that one shriveled gentleman with ketchup on his tie whistled sweetly while his pals simply gawked. Nina smiled. She was accustomed to whistles and compliments.

Spotting Archie at the window table, Nina headed his way with her loose-limbed, long-legged runway gait. Archie's heart lurched. Jesus, he was in big trouble.

Nina touched his shoulder and kissed his cheek very lightly before sitting down. Her perfume caused Archie to go lightheaded for a moment. And, those deep blue eyes nearly swallowed him up. Yes, he was in big, big trouble.

"Welcome to Billy's, one of my favorite haunts," Archie said first off. Keep this light, old man, he told himself.

"Just like you described it. Maybe better. It's hard to define what I like best….the cheap cigars, the fried onions, the smell of stale beer? It's sublime." Nina grinned. "I can see why you love it. Billy's is a honky-tonk."

Archie laughed. "It's the real deal! Wait until you try the brats." He kissed his fingertips like an Italian might salute a fine pasta dish. It was then that he noticed how worried Nina looked beneath the good-natured smiles. Or was she sad? No woman this gorgeous and who smelled like heaven should be unhappy. He asked quietly, "Is something wrong?" Then, he wagged his finger at the waiter for two beers.

Nina hesitated, as if debating what to do and what to say. She finally whispered, "It's Hugo. We're not getting along."

Archie detected a quaver in Nina's voice, but said nothing. He should have guessed it would be Hugo. From the first day in Belmont, the two of them had been at odds. It had started with the house, an ultra-modern glass cube stuck on a cliff in the bluffs, a house purchased by Hugo without a word to Nina. She had taken one look at it and bolted, finding seclusion and peace of mind in a charming, high-ceilinged old flat at the Beacon Street Arms downtown. Said it reminded her of historic New Orleans.

"Your boots are running his life. And, mine too," Nina was saying.

Archie leaned forward and patted Nina's hand in what he hoped was a fatherly gesture of consolation. He wished he could hire somebody else to do this kind of thing. Seduction was more his game. He said, "Now, now, you'll work things out. Hugo has business on the brain." He grinned encouragingly, and Nina managed a smile.

The skinny kid set down the Pfeiffers and sidled away.

"He's terribly preoccupied." Nina sniffed discreetly and added, "And, I'm betting it isn't about a new line of ski pants."

"What do you mean?" Archie was paying strict attention now. "I stop by the office every morning. He's a general on the day of a major offensive." A gorgeous female in distress on a warm summer afternoon. Jesus. Cyrus always said these were the elements scientists stuffed into atom bombs.

Nina looked directly into Archie's eyes and said, "I think he's seeing another woman."

Archie was stunned. Another woman? He was still amazed the kid had snagged a prize like Nina…without help. Could the kid be a chip off the old block, after all? There were rumors to that effect, but he had ignored them. "Who, for heaven's sake? He just got here."

"Who knows? I don't know anybody here." Nina pulled her fork tines roughly across a paper napkin, shredding it, no doubt getting back at Hugo's phantom mistress.

Archie scoffed, but privately conceded that Nina might be right. Hugo could have hitched up with one of his old flames. There was Miranda Burke, a comely newspaper reporter, known for her love of a dry martini and a good-looking man. But, where was the chemistry? He couldn't see Hugo and Miranda Burke as secret lovers. Miss Burke made no secret of her appetites or her lovers. Of course, they had once been engaged.

"I'm sorry to bother you with this, Archie, but, frankly, you're my only friend up here." Nina still referred to the state as 'up here.'

Archie laughed. "Up here. Poor darling. You miss your friends, your family. But, you can always come to me. About anything." He squeezed her hand again. Her skin was pure silk.

Nina looked seriously into Archie's face for a moment and then said, "Let's order. I'm starved. And, I'm tired of talking about Hugo." She stuck on a cheery face and looked over the world's shortest menu. "Are you and Nadine going to the Armbrusters' Famous Characters costume party?"

"Wouldn't miss it. Naddy ordered the costumes weeks ago. King Henry number eight for me. Naddy'll reign as one of the French queens. How about you?"

"We'll be there. I'll surprise you." Nina laughed, sounding more like her old self again.

Archie was relieved. He couldn't bear to see Nina miserable. Archie ordered a cheese sandwich for Nina and the brat special for himself and suggested a boat ride after lunch. Nina thought that would be perfect.

When Archie looked up again, he found Nina staring at him. He recognized the look. It was dangerous. Cyrus was right about the atom bomb.

2

Flying Fish

Archie entered his house on Washington Circle promptly at six Wednesday evening. Nadine's white Mercedes was parked in the drive. A promising sign. They'd quarreled the day before, and Nadine had threatened to visit her aunt in Chicago. A change of heart appeared to be on the horizon, a rarity in itself.

The foyer smelled of freshly applied floor polish, and Archie could see that the housekeeper had buffed up the place like a freshly minted coin. No disruption. No mess. The large, airy rooms were sun-filled and peaceful. Clutter annoyed him, and lately, noise hurt his head. He could have lived in a more contemporary environment, but Nadine didn't share his enthusiasm for simplicity. Years ago she had made it perfectly clear she preferred the eighteenth century to Archie's Brave New World. Antiques and oil paintings, Persian carpets and old silver were her thing. And, very complicated murder mysteries. Those were the key elements. Archie found it all daunting and beautiful and expensive. But, he'd learned to say no more. He managed to have his own fun, in his own way.

"Nadine," Archie called, "I'm home." He deposited his golf clubs in the hall closet. The only reply to his greeting was a door slamming upstairs. He drew a deep breath, sensing unrest in the castle. Nadine was still pissed. They'd been at cross purposes for years. Served him right for marrying a strong woman with a mind of her own and her own bank account. What did he expect?

Of course, Archie, too, knew his own mind. He liked a certain amount of freedom, as well as order. He knew his bank balance to the penny, wore the same brand underwear he'd selected three decades ago, and understood the ins and outs of running a corporation, his own, the now famous Beresford Boot and Outerwear, one of the biggest catalogue companies in the country. Hugo had taken the helm with ease and was showing great promise. He had already initiated a home furnishings catalogue division. Archie said he was damned proud of him and hoped they'd make another fortune, together.

But, Hugo's homecoming had caused his father a peculiar kind of unrest. It was as if Archie's normal serenity had sustained a rent in its smooth surface. He was feeling that same unrest now, there in the hall with the scent of wax tickling his nose. Or, was this prickly sensation a craving, like his passion for candied orange slices when he was a boy? Archie was not clear on this, but he was fairly certain the disturbance in his disposition had started the day he first set eyes on Nina Dupree. Unrest for Archie generally had to do with females. But, this time, it was different.

"It's me!" Archie sang out as cheerfully as he could. He needed a scotch or maybe a double martini. He'd been on the go all day….. showing Hugo the ropes that morning and golf with Cyrus in the afternoon after a quick lunch with Nina.

As Archie entered his bedroom on the second floor, a neutrally colored cave where nothing jolted the eye, he could feel tension. Nadine was across the hall in her bedroom. She disliked his quarters, said it had all the charm of a prison cell and the warmth of a refrigerator. She said she would prefer making love at the Mayflower Hotel downtown with its faded rose carpets and fringed lamps. So far, Archie had ignored her suggestions, and they made love in his room, though not as frequently as they had in the past. He blamed it on their long marriage.

"Are you in there?" Archie called again, across the corridor.

"I'll be out in a second." Nadine sounded irritated. Another door banged.

"I'll change. I thought we'd eat in tonight."

Nadine emerged from her bedroom in a pink satin robe; her face was flushed. She'd been working out in the exercise room downstairs, she said, and then showered. She said she had used his new luxurious bath, somewhat fancier than her own. It had given her great pleasure to leave water spots on the shiny chrome and glass. Archie flinched. His bride was in a terrible temper.

"And, we are eating OUT." The tone remained unfriendly.

In spite of the unfriendliness of their encounter, Archie remained rather stirred by his wife's beauty. Even at her age, she remained a very pretty woman. He'd fallen in love with her instantly at a charity party when they were seniors at the university. Soon after, he had presented her with a Tiffany diamond so dear he actually felt giddy and sick whenever he saw it on her finger.

"What is wrong, Naddy?" Archie pulled out his wallet and change from his pockets and placed it all in a leather tray on his bureau.

"What could possibly be wrong?" Nadine's monotone suggested a recent visit from the IRS or the unexpected arrival of someone who knew all her secrets.

Archie rubbed her shoulders. "You've overdone the exercises again, Naddy." He took away his arm, kicked off his shoes and loosened his tie. He'd left his golf clothes in his locker at the country club.

"This has nothing to do with exercise."

"What is it then?" Archie asked this reluctantly. He hated getting into things that bothered people, like heartaches and backaches.

"I overheard a conversation at the Half Moon Luncheonette this morning." Nadine narrowed her eyes, as if to prepare him for unsavory details. "Two members of my Mah Jongg club were talking. They didn't know I was sitting behind them in another booth."

Nadine was gathering steam. Archie braced himself.

"Phyllis Rathbone was talking to Trudy Forrest about a certain woman, whose husband supplies the country with parkas. She had concluded that this unfortunate female would be wise to look sharp and keep tabs on her territory, because a certain femme fatale had come home to take over the snow suit kingdom and its retired CEO." Nadine sat down on Archie's big bed and leaned back on her elbows where she gave Archie a speculative gaze as he started to pull off his trousers. "Where do you suppose this little story got started?"

"Ah, ah....how should I know? Who the hell are they talking about?" Archie was annoyed and a bit nervous. Nadine had this effect on him when she shifted into her inquisitive mode. "Femme fatale? We don't have any in Belmont."

"Playing dumb never works, Archie. It's quite obvious the femme is Marigold Woolsey, and you know the rest of the cast. Phyllis suggested, rather boldly, I thought, that Marigold stop drooling over you, dear heart, and concentrate her romantic energies on her adorable husband." Nadine was seriously scowling now, as if she'd just fallen in with a cast of Hollywood villains.

"Phyllis said that?" Archie stood in the middle of his bedroom floor, obviously distressed, with his pants around his ankles, a pose that made him look and feel foolish. He had no idea the women of Belmont paid such close attention to him or to his likely paramours.

"She is not one of my favorites. Wins far too often at Mah Jongg. And, tries to cheat. And, she most certainly doesn't know Marigold very well. Marigold does not drool."

"I tend to agree, Naddy." In his haste to escape the fury in his wife's eyes, Archie tripped on his pants as he pulled them over his feet. He recovered nicely. "But, maybe you misunderstood. Marigold isn't setting her sights on me or anybody else. This is a joke, Nadine. A huge joke. The two babes knew you were listening!" Archie fled into a commodious lighted closet and hung the trousers on a hanger. Women were so damned touchy. Best change the subject. "How about hamburgers?" he said, coming out with fresh clothes over one arm.

"Hamburgers! Have you been listening to me?" Nadine's face was pinker now. "What about Marigold? What about the snow suit kingdom? You have nothing to say about that?" She sprang to her feet, fists clenched, and met Archie's bewildered eyes. "And, furthermore, my sweet, I don't eat beef!"

With that reminder stinging the air, the former Homecoming queen of Belmont High retied the sash on her robe and headed determinedly downstairs, feathered mules clapping softly on the treads. "After my kingdom. Indeed! The nerve of the woman! She has more nerve than good sense. Marigold's on the loose and all you can think about is your supper!" Nadine interrupted her flight down the stairs to shout, "To think my Mah Jongg friends are secretly speculating about my private life! And, furthermore, Archie Beresford, who needs your money? I have my Granddaddy's!" Nadine's final words trailed off as she completed her descent.

"I forgot about the beef thing!" Archie yelled after her. He doubted she heard him. He returned to his bedroom and prayed the two women at the diner were just pulling Naddy's leg. They probably knew she was sitting behind them the entire time. Probably a poorly executed prank. And, Marigold! Well, they had exchanged a few glances since her return. But, hell, he'd always flirted with Marigold, whether they were fooling around or not. Any man would!

Archie buttoned himself into khaki safari shorts and a designer T-shirt bought for him by Nadine. He took a moment to examine his face in a wall to wall bathroom mirror ringed with round white light bulbs. He looked pretty good, for a man in his sixties, he decided cheerfully enough. His thick hair was mostly gray now, but a nice gray, his barber insisted. His lean face had grown a trifle heavier, he supposed. Damned gravity effect. His deep-set brown eyes did look tired. Hell, it had been a long day....and it wasn't over yet. Or, was he troubled? His thoughts strayed to the lovely Nina. Jesus, he must be crazy. Perhaps he needed vitamins. His secretary tirelessly extolled the virtues of B, E, and C. But, hell, she didn't look that good.

After turning out the light, he headed for the stairs, wondering once again if the male animal was really cut out for marriage.

Downstairs again, Archie found Nadine in the vast restaurant-style kitchen digging through the freezer. A bag of leaf lettuce lay on the counter like an ornament. Archie figured she was playing martyr, given her natural flair for the dramatic. She had studied theatre at college. Oddly enough, so had Nina....he'd just learned that today. Nina's mother, Belle, still managed a small theatre in New Orleans. Jesus, was he surrounded by temperamental thespians?

"I'm sorry, Naddy," Archie cooed and tried to put his arms around his wife's waist. "People say unkind things just to make themselves feel better. We'll get supper together." He tried to kiss the nape of her neck, but she drew away. She was pissed. "How about those fillets?" He pointed to a package of frozen pike he'd caught in Canada.

"Fine." Nadine yanked the package from a stack of neatly wrapped and clearly marked entrees. Turning abruptly, she bumped into Archie. "Really, I can hardly cook if you're hanging on me." The tone was as frosty as the fish. Nadine unwrapped the fillets and left them on the granite counter to thaw.

Archie backed off and said nothing, but took out a bottle of Beefeaters. Thank God for gin. The restorative balm. And, don't forget scotch. His old dad understood its value, especially after a few decades with an imperious wife. Archie wondered idly if Nina might be very like Nadine and his mother, a common enough circumstance which seemed to fascinate psychologists and therapists. Did humans choose the same mate time after time? All three females were strong-willed. All had similar names...Nadine, Nina, and Nora. Archie shuddered at this whole train of thought.

"Want a drink?" he asked politely, keeping a safe distance from the cook.

"Red wine." Nadine tore viciously at the lettuce, throwing pieces into salad bowls. She slammed a saucepan of water on to boil and pulled a box of rotini from the cupboard.

Ignoring the culinary melodramatics, Archie opened a bottle of good California cabernet, made himself a double martini with four olives and set out plates and cutlery on the marble-topped table set into a bay facing west. The early evening sky was a luscious rainbow sherbet. He loved it here, near the great river, near the comforting bluffs. He'd lived in this pretty, historic town all his life. He couldn't imagine existing anywhere else.

Archie eagerly sipped his drink and asked, "How are the short stories coming?" His bride of forty-odd years had taken up Betty Hughes's vocation in life, fiction writing. Preposterous notion. For the past ten years Betty Hughes had enjoyed phenomenal success with her romance-adventure novels, a feat which still amazed the Old Devils, who tended to be less creative than their wives. Just yesterday Nadine had told Archie she was working on a new story with roots in the South, but, nicely transplanted, she added mysteriously, into a humorous piece set in alien territory. Archie remained confused about her choice of subject. Aliens? Personally, he didn't much care for science fiction, but didn't tell Nadine that. Frankly, he was perplexed by the explosion of lady writers cropping up in Belmont…Betty Hughes, several novelists at Ashbury College, and now, Marigold, who was writing a play for the local college competition. Who was next? Lettice Mulroy, scratching out poems at the breakfast table?

Nadine seemed touched that he remembered her new hobby. She said, "You know O'Neill Spender, don't you? Betty Hughes's agent? Born in Kentucky, which certainly explains his fine manners." Nadine paused here and began chopping carrots for the salad.

"Sure. Never says anything."

"He does too. Well, I bumped into him at the library today, and he said he'd be happy to give me a few pointers. I let him read the first draft." Nadine smiled for the first time since Archie walked in the door. "He said the story was quite good. Isn't that a hoot?" She raised both eyebrows in a comic expression. "I bet you and Cyrus never dreamed I could write anything but checks."

The testiness of the remark warned Archie to be careful. Nadine wasn't through punishing him yet, and her dislike for the antics and opinions of the Old Devils wasn't likely to diminish with one glass of red wine. They were now within the boundaries of what Archie called the Great Snub, Nadine's contention that a good many ladies were too often patronized by the Old Devils and by males, in general, whenever they flapped their wings and tried to branch out. She and the other ladies were sick of it, she said.

"Where did you get that idea?" Archie felt helpless when it came to the Great Snub.

"You and Cyrus tell off-color jokes about females, make fun, and snub us. You would think we were silly teens." The resident teen queen fussed with the salad greens. "The male animal suffers from a poorly grounded superior attitude!"

Ouch. Archie refused to counter-punch that one. The exact day the Great Snub erupted or how it operated remained a mystery, no surprise to the ladies. Archie and the Old Devils were not about to pursue the question seriously. As always, they hoped it would blow over without any escalation of fuss.

Nadine perched prettily on a tall stool and waited for Archie to defend himself.

"Don't be silly, Naddy. The Old Devils wouldn't survive a week without you gals. Don't we support all your charity projects? Didn't I tell you how proud I am about your short stories? The new one sounds... ahh... very Southern. People love Southern writers, don't they?" He'd read that somewhere. Archie laughed agreeably and added fresh ice cubes to his drink and poured her more wine. Especially, if the plot and dialogue sound like they've been lifted from Faulkner or Tennesee Williams. How did aliens fit into this? Archie imagined Nadine's prowess with the written word might be akin to her skill with a frying pan. She might hire it done, like everything else, he supposed.

"What about the title?" Nadine asked levelly. *"Precious Little."* She slid from the stool and pulled out a carton of English water biscuits and turned down the boiling water.

"Ah, yes. Very nice." Archie gazed quizzically at the ceiling, as if giving the question his deepest consideration. "Utter perfection," he responded firmly. What had caused his very efficient wife to think she could write stories, for God's sake? Archie was unaware that she read anything except *Vogue* and *Antiques* and Betty Hughes's romance novels. Archie offered the resident scribe a generous smile.

Nadine smiled back appreciatively and nibbled delicately on a cracker. "Mr. Spender says I'm a natural. The next Mary Wesley, or maybe Barbara Pym."

Archie took a chance and asked who this Miss Pym might be.

"She's British and highly respected. Dead, of course."

"Well, if this Spender handles Betty Hughes, he must know. She's made a fortune on those damned romance books."

"At least she has gone well beyond Marigold Woolsey's nude sculptures.....nothing more than an attempt to titillate." Nadine sipped her wine. "Trashy."

She was lifting her chin a bit loftily, Archie thought, for an unpublished author.

"I like Marigold's sculptures," Archie countered. The gin had loosed his tongue. "Great bodies. Nudes have been around for centuries."

Nadine flashed Archie a look that reminded him instantly of Sister Mary Raphael at St. Andrew's Grade School, who'd wielded a ruler like no other. "Well, well, well, I had no idea you were such a fan of Marigold's so-called art." Nadine was swinging her leg peevishly. "What else do you like about Her Majesty?"

Knowing full well what Nadine was up to....casting out the poisonous worm for him to bite. Archie nearly burst out laughing. Cyrus often called Naddy the Master Baiter. Bad, bad, bad. Reddening slightly, he bit his tongue and wasn't sure who had fallen into whose trap.

"Gorgeous woman," he pointed out. "Terrific figure." Archie grinned and began striding about the room in an expansive fashion, suddenly feeling invincible. Nadine was obviously itching for a fight. He would oblige. He wondered if gin might be a primary instigator of domestic violence. "She's quite well read. Likes devious plots."

"Going to fat," replied Nadine without missing a beat. "She'll be a blimp in five years." She hopped from the stool again and began chopping tomatoes for the salad. One wedge squirted past her and landed on the floor. She made no move to pick it up. "Like your Aunt Kit. Women with figures like that tend to look like sausages when they're old."

This offhand and heartless remark about Marigold and his Aunt Kit made Archie flinch. He barked, "What a horrid thing to say about my auntie! And Marigold!" He gulped the rest of his drink; he would need fortification in the ensuing battle.

"Face facts, Archie." Nadine smiled a little. "Women know about these things."

"Neither one even comes close to resembling any sausages I've ever seen." Archie's boldness surprised him, and he stopped pacing to polish a smudge on a chrome chair with the edge of his shirt.

"I bet they're on the cabbage diet every other week." Nadine's eyes flashed wickedly.

Archie countered, "Nonsense. Marigold is like me. Fit, trim. We can eat anything." He smirked and rolled three olives from the jar and defiantly threw them into his mouth. Nadine was coming up on the boil. Why did he want to make her angry tonight? Why were they pecking at each other? Were they one of those pathetic couples who required warfare and reconciliation between the sheets to keep their relationship viable?

"Marigold could have any man in town, if she wanted!" Archie pointed out. As if to say, I'm popping over to see her after supper. Jesus, he was tight. Nadine would kill him.

Spinning deftly on her toes, Nadine now faced Archie with an almost blinding savagery. His faculties miraculously sharp now (the gin buzz considerably diminished by imminent danger), Archie could see that his bride was brandishing of all things....the frozen pike! The fish had taken on an eerie menacing quality, its bluish scaly back as hard and shiny as a hunting blade, its noble head firm, the eyes starring fixedly upon its target.

"Terrific figure? With devious plots?" Venomous drops from sneering lips. Nadine, Archie silently noted, had gone beyond mixing her metaphors; she'd stirred the curves in with the characters, but he didn't dare point this out right at the moment.

"Now, Nadine," he growled, slowly backing up, holding his glass in front of him like a shield. "Don't upset yourself over nothing." He flattened himself against the wall next to the Sub-Zero.

"Nothing?" Nadine's expression was frighteningly irrational, and Archie knew that no matter what he said, it would be wrong and quite possibly dangerous. Narrowing her eyes (she was slightly nearsighted), Nadine held the pike aloft like a spear and took aim. "How is this?" she yelled hoarsely, "For upset!"

Archie saw the fish coming; after all, he'd been paying rapt attention to all the preliminaries. And, he knew Nadine would throw *something* in a spat. In his experience, most women did.

The pike sailed through the air with remarkable speed. Nadine had more of an arm than she knew. Completely clear-headed now, Archie ducked just as the fish bombed the wall, inches from his left ear and the Sub-Zero. He watched his dinner boomerang off the plaster, take a serious nose dive, and finally come to a rest at his feet after a dainty spin on the slick floor.

Neither Archie nor Nadine said a word. They both looked down at the fish, Nadine's most novel weapon, Archie had to admit. The first week he'd known her, she'd thrown a bottle of expensive perfume that stank up the carpet for weeks, and just two days ago she'd tossed a head of broccoli at him when he suggested she not overcook vegetables. Archie could hear her breathing.

"Are you quite finished with this silly tantrum?" he asked with some pluck, after making sure there were no other projectiles within easy reach. "You could have killed me with that damned fish. It almost took off my ear!" The new plaster was deeply pitted where his supper's snout had made its mark.

"Archie Beresford!" Nadine howled, fists tight, arms stiff at her sides, "you are the most insensitive, pitiful.....obtuse man on the planet! I hope you choke on those, those.... very, very fattening olives." And with tears streaming down her face, Nadine ran from the room, her satin robe billowing like a spinnaker.

Archie exhaled and stayed where he was. Obtuse? He was lucky to be alive, and there was no point in going after her; she'd stay mad for hours. As he listened to doors slamming and water running, he happily went about fixing himself a fresh drink, relishing the solitude. He was no longer hungry. He went a step further and lighted a cigar, from his secret box in the back of the cupboard. Nadine had vetoed cigars in the house. Well, to hell with that.

Standing there on the cool tiled floor, in his remodeled kitchen with its shining chrome fixtures, the rarely used expensive pots hanging from a steel rack, he realized that he'd never really understood women, Marigold included. Females were a mystifying phenomenon, as mysterious as the pyramids.

With the cigar clamped between his teeth and a very dry martini with extra olives in hand, Archie took a seat at the table. As he gazed across the darkening yards, he caught a glimpse of his neighbors moving about their kitchen next door. Had the husband come close to being impaled by a pike tonight? Archie giggled, feeling the earlier gin again, now that the adrenalin rush had subsided. He and Nadine had lived here for over thirty years; he knew which neighbors were ferocious scrappers. But, two pikes flying on the same night? Probably against the odds. It didn't matter. Archie grinned and then laughed out loud. Almost any crisis was worth the grief...if you could get a good story out of it. And, Cyrus would love it!

3

Consequences

"I never thought I'd need a shrink," Archie told the doctor, quite bluntly. Dr. Sherman Bathgart didn't seem to mind the remark, and Archie assumed the psychiatrist had heard it all before.

"Sit down, Mr. Beresford. I'm here to help. The whole procedure might not be as painful as you think." Bathgart was a short, slight man with very white skin and large, liquid brown eyes. He smiled easily, an obviously calculated tactic to put his patient at ease. He tidied his blue and white dotted bow tie, which Archie noticed was the real thing.

Bathgart, like any good shrink, understood that few people think they'll need a psychiatrist. He sometimes allayed his patients' fears by telling them that shrinks have their own shrinks. Of course, he did run the risk of scaring off timid souls. Bathgart didn't believe Archie Beresford was a timid man.

Archie nodded and took a seat in a pull-up arm chair across from Bathgart's highly polished desk. Its only ornaments were a telephone, a calendar in a brass holder, a steno notebook and an expensive looking stainless cased pen. The psychiatrist sat behind it in a high backed chair of burgundy colored leather. He was dressed in a well-cut navy suit and fine leather shoes of a deep caramel color. As a merchant of boots and clothing, Archie had noticed the doctor's footwear when he walked in and immediately concluded that Bathgart was a man who preferred his patients admire his wardrobe rather than take too much interest in him as a person. Archie assumed the psychiatrist was intensely private, and he liked that.

The room was large and airy, lighted by three windows with thin blinds. Bookcases occupied two walls; a tufted leather couch sat against another, and Bathgart's medical certificates decorated the short wall next to the door. On the floor lay a fine subdued Turkey carpet that was very expensive. There was one painting in the room, over the sofa, a particularly good mid-nineteenth century landscape oil of a grove of trees near a river. There were no people in it.

"Now then, Mr. Beresford, how can we start?"

Archie shifted positions in the chair; he didn't know where to start. He wondered if wiggling had some great psychological significance. Probably. These guys read volumes into everything from your haircut to your shirt color. What was he doing here?

"Just tell me what's bothering you." Bathgart leaned back as a man might make himself comfortable anticipating a good story.

Archie paused only briefly and then replied, "It's women, Doc. It's always women." He shook his leonine head as if ashamed of himself. Was he? He supposed he was or why else would he be here?

"What about women?"

"They're everywhere." Archie sighed and then smiled a little. "Pretty ones, nice ones, tall ones, plump ones." What was he saying? The Doc knew the world was full of tempting women.

"I take it you like women."

"You bet. Too much. And, sometimes it's not good."

"How is that?"

"I'm in love with the woman my son plans to marry." Archie closed his eyes after he said this, as if not wanting to see the results of his confession in Bathgart's kindly eyes.

"Ahh," replied Bathgart. "That could present problems. Tell me how you feel about this."

"It happened by accident; I swear! Hardly an excuse, but it's the truth." Archie waited for Bathgart's reaction; there was none. "Hugo…. my son….returned home recently and brought along this woman….. Nina…. he met in New Orleans. She's a knock-out, Doc." Archie looked plaintively at the psychiatrist, as if hoping for absolution on Nina's beauty alone. Bathgart just smiled benignly and motioned for Archie to continue.

"We get along famously. Love talking to each other; I take her places. She's new in town. Somebody has to help her settle in." Archie grinned a little. "Nice excuse for me. We laugh at the same things. Hugo has no sense of humor." He sounded apologetic, as if his son's lack of wit was somehow inherited. "I'm forty again."

Bathgart nodded appreciatively.

Archie went on more quickly, having caught on to the psychiatric confession technique. "She's a stunner. A babe. And, she needs a friend. Hugo's pals are stand-offish." Archie was thinking of a few he knew rather well. "Small town cliques are hard to crack. Besides that, Hugo works long hours; he's running my company ....Beresford Boots." Archie tossed this off. Everybody in the state had heard of Beresford Boots. Everybody in the country, for that matter.

"I read about it in the paper," Bathgart replied. "I have a pair of your hiking shoes. They're very nice."

Archie nodded. Who didn't own a pair? He was stinking rich because of those boots.

"So, what have you done about your interest in your son's intended?" the doctor asked very politely, even choosing a formal word from the past.

"Nothing. If you mean, have I taken her to bed?" Archie threw up his hands a little. "But, I'm getting close. And, that's what's scaring the hell out of me. Well, one of the things."

"Would she go with you?"

"I think she might. She gets a look in her eyes sometimes. You know that look, Doc?" Archie wasn't sure Sherman Bathgart did, but it would have been impolite to dismiss the man on this particular point.

"I know what you mean." Bathgart nodded and stared at something just past Archie's shoulder, as if a certain somebody might be standing behind him. "Try entertaining her in groups," he said. "Perhaps, that would help when you feel tempted."

"I could do that." Archie stared at the floor. He didn't want to see Nina in groups.

"What is the other thing that's bothering you?"

Archie paused a good fifteen seconds. "It's Marigold." He shook his big head again. "She's back. And, Doc, Marigold Woolsey is a Biblical temptation. She's not like Nina. Marigold's my age. I've known her for years. She's a classic, Doc. A free spirit. An expatriate who's been living it up in Paris for thirty years! Just what Belmont needs." Archie laughed heartily at this. Bathgart smiled, knowingly. It was generally accepted that Belmont was not New York or Rio.

Bathgart leaned forward slightly. "And, you love this Marigold, as well?"

"In a different way." Archie rose and began walking the perimeter of the old rug. He had one rather like it in his library. Bathgart had good taste. "I'm suffering here, Doc. Women are a hobby; I collect classic beauties like other guys collect antique fishing rods." He laughed a little. "Nadine, my wife, doesn't pay any attention." Archie took another look at the painting over the sofa. Now, that was something Nadine would pay attention to and then offer Bathgart a tidy sum for it.

"What would you like me to tell you, Mr. Beresford?"

"Call me Archie. I want you to tell me to behave myself, I guess." Archie turned from the painting, looked at Bathgart and burst out laughing."

Bathgart laughed too. "I'm not your father or your priest. I'm not your conscience. But, I would advise you to think about what you're doing. You might hurt your son very deeply. Does that worry you?"

"No." Archie sat down again. "That's bad, isn't it?"

"It's not bad or good. It's just the way you feel about it. I'm guessing you think Hugo doesn't deserve this pretty woman and you do."

"I think that's it. He doesn't. Nina should have the best."

"What about Marigold?"

"Marigold would be my friend no matter what."

"You must think of the consequences, Archie. Will Nina be happy with you or with Hugo? Will Marigold be happy knowing you love Nina? Why don't we talk more next week?"

"Fine, Doc. I'll be back."

Bathgart asked Archie several background questions about his health and wound up the session by confirming the next appointment.

At the door Archie shook the doctor's hand and said, "There is one more little thing." He was thinking about the skeleton in the morgue up in Sandy Hook. "But, hell, it can wait. It's waited this long."

"You aren't goin' to faint, are you?" Betty Hughes Armbruster asked, as she thrust out an arm to steady the young cop, who was starting to look gray beneath a spray of freckles.

"No, I don't think so, ma'm." Harley Flood took a deep breath and edged into the large, windowless closet. There were wooden poles on three sides with dozens of dresses arranged on pink satin hangers.

Betty Hughes kept an eye on the officer; he was so young. The smell was terrible. She tried to move ahead as bravely as she could, but her knees wobbled, and the sound of rushing water filled her ears. Inexplicably, she kept wondering what Cyrus would do if he'd just found a dead body. He'd been so brave during the war. She had discovered the body. After bridge club that afternoon, she'd popped in for a visit. Not finding anyone downstairs, she'd gone upstairs, thinking her friend was probably fussing with the redecoration of the bedrooms. The closet door was open a crack.

"Sorry, ma'm, if I'm a little shaky, but I've only seen one dead body before. My Uncle Louie, all stretched out in a bronze casket. His cheeks were real pink and his hair was combed in the wrong direction. It made my aunt real mad."

Betty Hughes nodded sympathetically. This was a first for her too. But, this dead body was wound up in bright red cloth and left propped in a corner next to a rack with shoes tucked on wire loops. The body half sat and half reclined, as stiff as a rolled up rug or a badly wrapped mummy. The shoeless feet poking out the bottom were pointed in two directions. With another tentative step closer, Betty Hughes saw again the face of her friend. The head was tipped back against the wall with the top half of the face exposed above the velvet. Her light blue eyes were wide open and scared, and her long nose rested on the edge of the peculiar shroud as if she'd been trying to take one more deep breath before death. Buried below the folds were the mouth and chin and all the rest. Betty Hughes had to wonder if the poor soul had her clothes on. Her skin seemed to glow fluorescent blue-white in the closet light, like a tropical fish she'd seen once. To make the scene worse, the killer had stuck a tiny pink lamp shade on top of her head. Betty Hughes found it more offensive than the shroud. Officer Flood's youthful face registered disgust, as well it should, as if the humiliation of murder should have been enough punishment for the poor woman.

Several rolls of new wallpaper rested on the floor of the big closet next to four bolts of fabric propped against one wall. Their unpleasant chemical odor had combined potently with the sickly stink of death. Betty Hughes prayed she could keep down her lunch.

"Aren't you goin' to call the police chief or the coroner?" Betty Hughes asked. "I'm no expert on homicide, honey, but I think this is where you get hold of the man in charge."

"Yes, ma'm, I'll radio Lieutenant Donovan and the Chief." The officer took an eager step backward and bumped into a stack of shoe boxes, which clattered to the floor. "Geez, ma'm, I'm sorry." Flood hurriedly re-stacked the cartons and asked, "Are you sure she's dead?"

As the two of them fled the closet, Betty Hughes nodded adamantly and replied, "Yes, Officer, Lola Spriggs is quite dead."

"Murdered?" Nadine repeated the word in astonishment.

"Hit on the head." Betty Hughes was phoning from home. "All wrapped up in a bolt of Clarence House velvet....like a dead Egyptian Pharaoh. Queen." She filled in the sketchy details; the case was only a few hours old. "And she was wearing a silk lamp shade for a hat."

"How macabre!" Nadine gasped.

Betty Hughes smiled a little. Nadine's new word for the week. "Weren't you helping Lola with the redecoration of the bedrooms?"

"Yes. She wanted to redo the second floor. Lola tears everything apart every six years like clockwork." Nadine was getting ready for bed as she talked and struggled to pull an arm from a sweater sleeve. She'd managed to twist the phone cord around one leg. "So, who do they think killed her? Lola was such a pussy-cat. Was it robbery? She did have some lovely baubles." Nadine quickly slipped her leg from its noose and listened for Betty Hughes's reply.

Rain was stinging the windows and the lights dimmed. Betty Hughes dropped the blinds over the dark panes next to her desk. She didn't like sitting in a fishbowl. She said by way of comforting herself, "Nobody knows. I hate thunder storms. Cyrus just ignores them and sleeps like a baby."

"Archie's out. Playing cards, I think. My lights keep flickering. I set the security alarm and I always stick a pair of sharp scissors under my pillow when he's gone. Isn't that silly? I guess I'll never grow up. I thought I'd watch on old movie."

"Sounds divine." Betty Hughes sighed, thinking again of the unfortunate Lola Spriggs. Dead at sixty. Hardly old these days. She, Nadine and Lettice had played bridge with Lola for thirty years. She said, "All that gimp and gold fringe gone to waste." Lola's huge Tudoresque pile of stone and brick with seven bedrooms and ancient plumbing was a showplace of lurid extravagance. Overdone and overwrought, as Lettice Mulroy always described the place. Of course, poor Lettice hardly knew the difference between lurid and just plain awful, a term that might be used to describe her three rooms at the Seniors' Boarding House.

"Lola liked things showy," said Nadine. "Bless her heart. She did keep me hopping. Now, I suppose, she'll be accused of overdoing her own death. I can't believe you found the body."

"Yes, stopped by for a chat and ended up finding her in the closet."

"Dear heaven! Like a horror movie with Joan Crawford. Freddy Donovan will have his hands full with this one. Rich widows should get priority."

"Well, I told Freddy that I expected his full attention to the matter. And I told him I didn't want that insufferable police chief anywhere near the case. The Chief never got out of eighth grade." Betty Hughes and Freddy Donovan co-chaired the St. Hyacinth Church rummage sale each year, a responsibility that had created a fast friendship and an expectation of assistance if something went wrong.

"You show me a male animal who has gone beyond the eighth grade." Nadine remarked sassily.

"Yes, my mama always says boys are just a trifle behind in the civilization department."

"How did Lola expire?"

"They think she was hit on the head with a marble obelisk. Such an odd object for dear Lola to have, don't you think? They found it on the bedroom floor. Lots of good blood stains on it, and they're checking for prints." Betty Hughes trotted out the facts as she knew them. It was one thing to make up details for a novel, but, this was a woman she knew. Betty Hughes's appetite for supper had disappeared.

Nadine finished dressing for bed. She asked, "Any suspects?" She plunged her feet into slippers and threw a robe around her shoulders. A crack of thunder ripped the sky and made her jump.

"Couldn't be too many. Lola was a lamb. The body's been in the closet almost forty-eight hours, the coroner figures. A bit ripe, as they say in the trade."

"Good heavens!" Nadine groaned. "I saw her Thursday about six. Nobody reported her missing in all that time? What about Toby?"

"Toby wasn't very close to his mother. You know what a nit-wit he is."

"Why don't you drive over, and we'll watch an old Bogie film?"

"I suppose I could. Cyrus won't know I'm gone."

"Good. I'll turn off the alarm."

"Who will buy Lola's house?" Betty Hughes liked the old place.

"Walter Hargate, probably. He told me a few weeks ago that his funeral parlor on Dishy Avenue is too cramped. Lovely thought. He's been scouting the city for a mansion like Lola's." Nadine kept track of local lore. "The nicest old houses so often end up as funeral parlors. Thank God, your place won't go that route."

Betty Hughes had to appreciate Nadine's skill at not only keeping track of village business but her ability to swing gracefully from brutal homicide to funeral parlor real estate, all in one brief conversation. But, Nadine believed in positive thinking, and positive thinkers were not like other people. They were capable of pole-vaulting over life's mishaps and successes, big or small, only to land firmly on their feet like Olympians. They weren't necessarily insensitive; they simply accepted what came along and refused to dwell on the unfortunate aspects. It kept them safe, Betty Hughes supposed. Like a very expensive alarm system or a dog who barked. Betty Hughes, on the other hand, was a born cynic. Darker details always caught her eye and fueled her imagination. She was already rummaging in her memory for long forgotten bits and pieces about the Spriggs family. This was the stuff of a homicide investigation. The victim's past and the money. Freddy Donovan liked to say, "Follow the money." Not original to Freddy, but as safe a bet as Betty Hughes's preference for going back to the beginning. Maybe that was why she wrote romance novels with a touch of thriller lacing the plot.

Betty Hughes finally said, "Don't you dare start *Casablanca* until I get there."

Lettice Mulroy put the coffee carafe on the table next to the jam jar and then arranged a white paper napkin on each plate. Admiral Moss was coming to brunch. Since moving into the Golden Horizon Apartments six months ago, she and the Admiral had decided to share the Sunday *TRIBUNE* to save money. After a few weeks, she proposed they take a simple breakfast together instead of running back and forth across the hall with different sections. Neither one wanted to give up the entire paper for the whole morning, and each wanted to read the paper with breakfast. The Admiral seemed delighted to be asked. He'd never liked Sundays, he told her; it was just a lonely day waiting to be Monday. He would bring croissants.

The Admiral spooned another dollop of English marmalade on a croissant and adjusted his reading glasses. "Did you see here in obituaries that Rodney Silverman has passed on. Kidneys." The Admiral looked over the tops of his glasses at Lettice who was glancing through sports. "Donations to the cancer society are suggested by the family." The Admiral sighed and held his pastry midair. "I rarely donate to diseases," he said. "Most of the money goes to the president of the outfit and postage."

"Not Mr. Silverman?" Lettice put down her mug, her mouth slightly agape. "Lovely man. I thought he'd left early for Florida." She poured them each more coffee. "Odd, isn't it, that his assistant didn't say something? That he was so sick."

"People are funny about cancer. It's like this new AIDs disease. Or, cancer a few years ago. Nobody would say the word without whispering it. Like it might be catching if you said it out loud." The Admiral dabbed at his mouth with the paper napkin.

"You're right. People say heart attack right out loud. A perfectly strange woman will tell you in the check out at Food Fair that her husband passed away with a bad heart, but cancer still isn't spoken as loudly as heart attack or diabetes." Lettice couldn't understand this kind of foolishness. Her husband had been blown up in the Pacific in the big war. Came home in a box. Now, that was hard to talk about at Food Fair.

"I wonder if the assistant will buy the drug store?" the Admiral asked. "I'd hate to see that store close. I get my prescriptions filled there." His long, serious face grew longer.

"Mr. Silverman had no children, it says, just a brother over in Howard's Grove." Lettice hesitated, and then said, "Do you think we should go to the funeral, Melvin?"

"A Jewish funeral? I've never been to one." The Admiral looked worried again.

"Me either, but it might be interesting." Lettice smiled. "Mr. Silverman would get such a kick out of you being there in your dress uniform."

The Admiral smiled shyly. "Yes, he would. Mr. Silverman always spoke highly of the Navy."

Lettice and the Admiral agreed to attend the services and went back to their reading. Lettice handed over the obituaries and picked up the main section.

"My goodness, Melvin, did you see that Lola Spriggs is dead!" Lettice covered her mouth with her hand. "Front page, below the fold. Police are investigating, it says. A blow to the head, the coroner says." Lettice let the paper drop into her lap. She felt sick. "I've known Lola Spriggs over forty years."

"Why that's probably murder!" The Admiral's voice squeaked a little.

"Unless she fell and hit her head." Lettice pulled down her reading glasses and left them on the end of her nose. Her eyes bulged. She picked up the paper again and read a few more paragraphs. "Melvin! It says that the body was found yesterday in a bedroom closet by Betty Hughes Armbruster!" Lettice couldn't believe it. "There aren't many details. It's very short."

"Why didn't Betty Hughes call you about it?"

"That's what I'd like to know. After all, we're best friends." Lettice sniffed. Getting annoyed with Betty Hughes made her stomach return to normal.

"Could be the police kept her at the station house all night…for questioning."

"I never thought of that, Melvin. My goodness, you don't think the police think Betty Hughes killed Lola?"

The Admiral seemed to consider this and then shook his head. "Where's the motive?"

"Right you are. No motive."

"She lived alone, didn't she? Rich widow, all by herself in a big house. Nobody would ever hear her cry for help, if she fell. But, she was found in a closet."

"It was murder, I'll bet you." Lettice narrowed her eyes the way she thought a detective might look on a big case. "Hide the body in a closet. More time for a getaway." Lettice automatically put the croissant to her lips. "Maybe her boy wanted her money?" The pastry was returned to its plate.

"Possible, I suppose. But, isn't the young man a bit of a milquetoast? Not the murdering kind."

"Timid. Odd. Wears a wool scarf around his neck…winter or summer. Queer affectation for a college professor. Probably thinks he looks intellectual." Lettice pulled a pinch nosed face for the Admiral. Lola used to do the same thing. Toby was always a disappointment to her.

"Could be a serial killer of rich females."

"Belmont wouldn't have a killer like that." Lettice stirred two sugar lumps into her coffee.

"We're not immune, Lettice." The Admiral emphasized his point by uncharacteristically thumping his knife handle on the table. It made Lettice jump. Her mind flew for a moment to the news story about the old skeleton found buried up in Pikes' Wood. Violence. Death. Maybe it was closer than they all imagined.

"Lola Spriggs was a mouse. Never walked if she could drive." Lettice leaned back in her kitchen chair. "She planned her entire funeral two years ago. I helped pick out the casket and the dress. A frilly cocktail number of black organza. It's hanging in her bedroom closet with a plastic dust shield over the shoulders." Lettice paused. "She wanted to be buried in her pearls, but I told her it was a waste of good jewelry. She refused to listen, of course." Lettice shook her head and thought again about the beautiful pearls.

The Admiral looked puzzled. He said, "I've never heard you talk about Lola."

"We had a terrible row over the hymns. For her funeral. I suggested Elinor Pinzel sing the Ave Maria." Lettice absentmindedly buttered a third croissant. "Lola said she didn't care much for Miss Pinzel's soprano, and in the end, we exchanged cross words." Lettice proceeded to dunk the croissant and then dribbled coffee over the metro section. She dropped the pastry to her plate. She couldn't eat another bite.

The Admiral closed his eyes for some reason.

"Isn't that awful?" Lettice said. "To quarrel over a soprano?"

"You never spoke to each other again?" The Admiral sounded dumbfounded and rather disappointed.

"Never. When she was ill last year, her sister told me about it, but Lola wouldn't let me visit her." Tears filled Lettice's eyes, but she refused to cry.

"Well then," the Admiral said reassuringly, "you did all you could. Under the circumstances." He reached across the table and patted Lettice's hand. She felt him touch her single gold ring.

"Under the circumstances." Lettice moved on to the comics.

Early the following morning, Betty Hughes and Nadine were standing in line at the Boulangerie for morning buns. The little French bakery was crowded and electric with gossip about Lola Spriggs's death. Betty Hughes was bombarded with questions when she walked through the door until she firmly told the ladies that she was forbidden to discuss the case. Police orders, she said, emphatically. The ladies muttered among themselves after that.

It was rumored that Lola had been killed by a knock on the head. It was also rumored that she'd been found wearing a lampshade like a hat with her thin body wrapped in red velvet. Betty Hughes refused to confirm or deny any details.

"It's like a dirty story," Betty Hughes hissed to Nadine. "It's all over town."

"I would think so. The poor woman, turned into a clown," replied Nadine. She kept her voice down and moved up a notch in the line. From where she was standing the basket of morning buns looked nearly empty.

"A very sick person killed Lola Spriggs." Betty Hughes shuddered. "I'll have nightmares about this. It was horrid."

"The autopsy will tell more than we need to know." Nadine patted Betty Hughes's arm in sympathy. Her friend looked as if she'd slept badly.

A soft rumble of curiosity about Lola Spriggs continued to move among the customers. There were nods in the direction of Betty Hughes every few seconds. Few suspicious deaths ever came their way, and the possibility of fatal mischief in their civilized patch was understandably titillating. The story had been pushed to the top of the morning news on local TV and radio and the *Augusta Tribune* featured a more complete story on the front page. Generally, historic little college towns like Belmont were ignored by the press, unless a barge collided with a bridge or the brewery went on strike. Nadine felt nearly immune to such violence. Small towns were supposed to be safe havens.

"Who would want to kill Lola and then make fun of her in death?" Nadine wondered.

An older woman wearing a large sun hat and ahead of them ordered six buns, then turned to say, "Money. What else?"

"And, how would you know?" Betty Hughes asked sharply.

The older woman snapped her purse shut and said, "Put two and two together." Then, she picked up her pink bakery bag and waddled out.

"Have you ever seen such nerve?" Betty Hughes said. "Two and two. That silly woman couldn't make change for a dollar."

"The Know-It-All Queen," replied Nadine. "Often wrong, never in doubt. She peeks in people's medicine cabinets at parties. Lives next door to Sybil Connors."

"Who inherits Lola's money?" asked Betty Hughes.

"Toby, I suppose. I can't see that silly man murdering his mother? He'd hire a hit man."

One or two women close by heard this and gasped.

"Professor Spriggs would never take out a contract on his own mother!" This came from the matron behind them clutching the hand of a four-year-old whining for a cookie.

"When it comes to money," Betty Hughes said somberly, "even rabbits can find the nerve."

A few customers were snickering now. Toby Spriggs and his mother were well known. A man in his forties who still lived with his mother was considered odd, even in a town as small as Belmont. Durwood Spriggs, Lola's husband, had been killed by one of his own trucks at the Spriggs Moving and Storage Company; the business that had made him rich had done him in. The irony made Nadine smile. She'd never cared much for Durwood Spriggs or his son.

Nadine stepped up to the counter and found the morning buns sold out. She ordered a bagette and two currant buns and vowed to get going earlier next time.

"You really should bake more of those buns, Violette," Betty Hughes advised the clerk.

Violette nodded and thanked Mrs. Armbruster for her suggestion.

When Betty Hughes completed her order, she and Nadine left the shop and headed for Emma's Café. Summer was winding down, and the day held the promise of cool breezes and a change of season. Nadine felt energized.

"I suppose our little trips to the 'Boo' for morning buns will stop when you move to Meadowlark Village," Nadine commented as they crossed the street. The Armbrusters' decision to sell their beautiful home, nicknamed Tally Ho, just to live in a high-rise retirement apartment was unthinkable to Nadine.

"Don't be silly." Betty Hughes laughed. "We were born to eat those damned, calorie loaded buns!" She clutched Nadine's arm for a moment, as one who would not be denied the honor of buying sweets with her best friend. "I won't abandon the old gang."

"When's the tag sale?"

"This comin' week end. I'm practically sellin' my soul!"

"Do old friends get discounts?"

"Certainly. I love hagglin'."

They crossed at the light and soon marched into the café which smelled of good coffee and home-made pie. They chose a booth by the window.

"Lettice called this morning. According to her, you broke all rules of etiquette and friendship by not telling her about Lola two minutes after finding the body."

"Did she think I was goin' to call every soul I know at supper time? I was in shock. Absolute shock."

"I told her that." Nadine ordered blueberry pie. Betty Hughes settled on cherry. The waitress poured coffee immediately. "Why do you think the killer bothered to roll her up like a mummy?"

"Some awful hidden meanin', I suppose. He must have known her. Robbery wasn't a motive, so far as the police can tell."

"Do you think dear Lola ever really missed old Spriggy?"

"Not really. No one misses Durwood. He wasn't particularly likable."

Betty Hughes asked for extra cream. "Lots of people think he was run over in his own truck yard on purpose. Murdered! And now Lola's dead too. Why, Lola didn't even cry at the funeral."

"Archie and Cyrus didn't much care for him."

"Sneaky little squirt. Always workin' the angles."

The waitress dropped off their slices of pie and warmed up the coffee. The place was suddenly very busy.

"Do you think Lola had a lover?" Nadine hissed this across the narrow table.

"Lola? Never. She said she had her cats and a check book; that was all she needed." Betty Hughes giggled. "Men pestered her. She was very pretty....for her age. But, they were only interested in her money. She knew that."

"Yes. Some men do have an agenda." Nadine frowned and dug into her pie. "Frankly, I hope I don't end up like Lola.....rich and alone and terrified of men's motives."

"Let's drink to Lola. The sweet, generous lady she was. And, to Freddy Donovan, who's goin' to smoke out her killer." Betty Hughes sounded more comfortable with the whole thing now. "A hometown homicide sure is more fascinatin' than dying from a bad gall bladder."

The two friends clinked their heavy coffee mugs and sat for a moment in silence, just thinking about their unfortunate friend.

By the end of the day, the overwhelming preference among those interested in Lola's death (everybody in Belmont) was that she'd been murdered by a nut from out-of-town, a fanciful conclusion, according to Lieutenant Freddy Donovan, but not altogether far-fetched. After all, Belmont had a bus station and a train connection to Minneapolis and points south.

Malicious mischief. Murder. The public was eating it up. Were they not fed a steady diet of sordidness, sleaze, and horror on television every day? Archie and Cyrus were having a drink before dinner and chewing over the implications. "We've grown accustomed to swallowing mayhem with our meat loaf," Cyrus remarked a bit flippantly for an old newspaper man. Archie said he didn't much care for meat loaf.

For Archie, the question was simple enough. Who wanted Lola dead? And, why? Mrs. Spriggs had been a nice, wealthy widow with friends and family and a mania for bridge and cats.

Belmont's police chief had publicly announced in an interview on TV that rich widows were not supposed to turn up murdered in up-scale towns with low crime rates. After the program, the police station switch board juggled a hundred calls from citizens pointing out that POOR widows weren't supposed to turn up murdered either….and what did the police chief think he was saying, anyway?

The lieutenant continued to sift and winnow from his office chair at Billy's. He would be dealing with Belmont's elite on this one, not his favorite club, even though he counted good friends among them. A number of society matrons would have to be questioned. He was hoping Betty Hughes and Nadine and others would cooperate and get the rest to follow. He ordered a double burger with double onions and wondered if Sheriff Charlie Lemmon was making any progress on the Sandy Hook bones. He suspected the Spriggs case would be more fun.

Freddy Donovan was right about the privileged. He didn't like asking them questions and he didn't trust them to tell the truth. According to Lola's friends and family in three days of questioning, Lola Spriggs didn't have a single enemy. She didn't know any strange men. And, she didn't hire a nut to kill her, a theory put forward by one of Lola's more eccentric cousins named Tommy Lee Birch. Saner members of the family explained that Tommy Lee liked to experiment with exotic mushrooms and other drugs.

As it turned out, Lola's last will and testament became the most significant piece of evidence in the case. Her considerable fortune was divided into three parts. She had bequeathed the relatively modest sum of twenty-five thousand to each of five people, four relatives and one friend, her gardener. The rest of the money, several million, was left equally to her son, Toby, and to a man named Preacher Boswell. Boswell turned out to be a hapless and often jobless dog breeder with a ramshackle house in Fontana City, twenty miles north of Sandy Hook. Strangely enough, Preacher Boswell was running for mayor in November, given an unexpected opportunity for advancement when the old mayor fell out of his boat while fishing in Horsehead Slough that summer. Mr. Boswell was insisting that he never knew the late Mrs. Spriggs and had never sold her a hunting dog either. He said somebody had goofed.

Dog or no dog, Donovan complained to Betty Hughes the following hot afternoon that he smelled a rat. Betty Hughes agreed. She was catchin' a whiff of stink in the air. And, she said, as she fanned herself with a magazine, she found it very interestin' that Sandy Hook and now Fontana City (normally centers of such tranquility that one ran the risk of never waking up in either place) were suddenly thrust into the crime spotlight. First, the remains of a gimpy-legged male were unearthed in an unmarked grave high above the beach; then, a village mayor was drowned in a fishing mishap that could be examined from more than one angle; and now, this Preacher Boswell had been crowned instant millionaire in a bizarre murder case. Hardly run-of-the-mill incidents for two hamlets along the Mississippi, she pointed out more than once.

Donovan had called Lola's attorney, who just happened to be the Armbrusters' son, Duncan, and asked if he might like to announce the happy news to Preacher Boswell in person, while Donovan and his sergeant gave the lucky gentleman a look, as a possible suspect. Duncan

Armbruster said he would be delighted. They would drive up the next day.

Sheriff Charlie Lemmon informed Donovan that Boswell was a ragtag character with dubious pals and a reputation for serious drinking and under-the-table schemes that rarely worked out. He said Boswell would probably win the election on celebrity alone. When would a town like Fontana City ever get another opportunity to elect a millionaire for mayor? And, no, they hadn't made much progress in the old bones case. They were still questioning folks who'd lived around Pike's Wood forty odd years ago, and it wasn't easy.

Donovan assured Lemmon that homicide never was.

4

Hollow Logs

"Where's Nadine?" Nina asked, as she entered the Beresfords' grand foyer. "I haven't seen her lately."

"New York." Archie was overjoyed by Nina's surprise visit. He steered her firmly by the elbow into the vast living room. It was nearly six in the evening. A spell of chilly, rainy weather had suddenly turned hot and humid again, pushing temperatures into the nineties.

"Theatre?"

"A buying trip, she calls it. I call it plundering by checkbook." Archie laughed. His wife's passion for art and antiques was well established, and he generally bellyached out of habit. "I feel like a Viking who's just raided the south of England. Drink?"

"A gin and tonic would be nice. It's a hundred out there." Nina settled into one of two sofas, silky nests of brocade and richly tasseled pillows that faced each other across a stunning brass and glass coffee table the size of Rhode Island. "You sound like a well-adjusted Viking, Archie."

"I sound like a tyrant, but it is all bluff." Archie hurried off to the kitchen for ice and a lime and then busied himself at a small drinks table back in the living room. "Is Hugo still in Chicago?"

"Ah, hum," Nina replied. She slipped out of her sandals and tucked one nicely browned bare leg beneath her. She was wearing a yellow sundress and her pale hair piled on top of her head. The sun swept the room with an intense late afternoon light. "He'll be back Sunday night. Says the convention's jumpin'." She laughed. "I can't imagine a bunch of jumpin' wind breaker executives."

"Those conventions are killers. But, Hugo will fit right in." Archie cut the limes and spun the ice cubes through the tonic. Whatever was Nina doing here? She never stopped by without Hugo.

"Hugo loves ski mittens a whole lot more than hot sauce." Nina put her head back on a cushion the color of spun gold. "I'm sure of that."

"So, what can I do for you?" Archie asked with a generous smile. He handed over the tall, frosted glass and sat down beside her. Nina always smelled like fresh flowers mixed with fruit. He'd grown intensely jealous of his son's good fortune.

"You're going to think I'm crazy, but I'm worried about you." Nina tended to coo a little when she talked to men. Especially to attractive men.

"Worried? About me? Why, for God's sake?" Intrigued, Archie edged a bit closer. What the devil was bothering this pretty gal?

"I must admit to somethin'….I'm slightly embarrassed, but…," Nina hesitated and dropped her eyes. "I overheard you and Cyrus at the club on Wednesday." She placed her hand with its pink varnished nails on Archie's arm and spoke directly into his eyes.

"About what?" Archie liked her hand on his arm and rather hoped she wouldn't move it, but she did.

"You were so concerned about Lola's death. I had no idea she was such a dear friend." Nina sipped her gin and reached out to squeeze Archie's sun-tanned arm again. Archie was thankful that he was wearing new chinos and an expensive black knit polo shirt.

"Lola Spriggs and Durwood, her late husband, were old friends." What had he and Cyrus said that day? Damnation, he couldn't recall the details.

"Poor unfortunate woman. Such a hideous death, all wrapped up like a bundle."

"The police are investigating. Lola was a sweetheart. An animal lover." Egads, had he and Cyrus talked about that damned will? Had they said anything else? Had they mentioned Pike's Wood?

"Who is this Preacher Boswell?" Nina jingled the cubes in her glass and kept her eyes on Archie. "Why leave millions to such an odd character?" The newspapers were printing detailed descriptions of Preacher Boswell and Toby Spriggs, the most obvious suspects, so far.

Archie was trying desperately to concentrate on the murder, but his mind kept wandering to Nina's skin and her gorgeous long legs. He hadn't felt this way about a woman in thirty years. Warning lights were flashing, but his central nervous system wasn't responding. Nadine seemed to be transmitting one of her "looks" all the way from New York.

Archie reached over and placed a reassuring hand on Nina's shoulder. "Could be Lola was a smidgen senile when she signed the will. Cyrus and I think there might have been some mistake, and the attorney didn't catch on." Nina seemed to lean closer.

"But, I thought I heard you say you knew this Preacher Boswell," Nina insisted sweetly, as if she might be fishing for more information.

"Oh, hah!" Archie stammered. "We've heard the name. He's running for mayor up there. Fontana City. An eccentric! Breeds hounds." Was Nina on to them? Should he tell her the truth?

"Goodness. This whole story is rather troublin'."

Archie nodded in agreement. "Very strange. Nobody knew Lola was sitting on the edge. Of course, she did have four cats." He smiled, and Nina giggled.

"Why do people with more than two cats always end up in the pigeon hole for loonies?" Nina was half serious. "My Aunt Birdie has ten and she's certifiable!"

"If you have three dogs, nobody thinks a thing about it. They just assume you're not a very good housekeeper and let it go at that." Archie laughed. "Another gin?"

"Love it." Nina handed over her glass and sank back into the down cushions. "I haven't a thing to do tonight."

Archie's mind whipped back twenty years to another summer night, sensuous with heat, and similarly occupied by a luscious blonde who'd said those same words. Archie clearly recalled that he and the blonde had found something to do. His heart was doing double time. He threw an extra shot of gin into his glass.

"How about staying for supper?" Damnation! Had he said that? "Keep me company." What the hell? One innocent supper. What would his shrink say?

"Wonderful! How about that heavenly cashew chicken salad from Nonny's Deli? I think they deliver."

"Good choice." Archie returned with their refreshments and resumed his place on the sofa just a few inches closer to his guest this time.

"You know, Archie, I don't think you're tellin' me the whole story about Lola." Nina gave Archie a woman-of-the world smile and nudged closer to him.

"Why would I keep secrets from you?" The double Beefeaters had turned Archie into a brave warrior.

"I'm not teasin', but, if you need my help, I'd be so happy to give it. Discreet questions at the country club, at parties. I do get around, you know. Maybe we can figure out who killed Lola. Small town policemen are so inexperienced." Nina smiled encouragingly. "I would just love to play detective."

"Yes, indeed," Archie agreed enthusiastically. That's all he needed… Nina playing detective. He continued, "And, I would guess you sit on just about every committee God and my wife ever created." The Ninas and Nadines of the world ran the charities, raised the funds, kept the symphony playing, the elections honest, and poor people fed and clothed. As an irresistible female with more charm than a gypsy fortune teller, Nina Dupree could probably squeeze information out of the Almighty. Only, Archie didn't want Nina within ten miles of the Spriggs case. He would have to distract her.

"I'll tell you what, little lady," Archie whispered, inclining his head toward hers and grinning like a fool, "if you find out anything about Lola and her millions, I'll buy you a bracelet twice as nice as the one you're wearing." He grasped her fingers in his own big hand and patted the circle of diamonds on her thin wrist.

"Why, Archie! That's so sweet. But, I don't expect gifts!"

Arched prayed immediately that she didn't think he was bribing her and shook his head. "Just a friendly gesture, my dear. A friendly gesture."

"I'll see what I can do for you.….and Cyrus," Nina responded in a dangerous purr.

Archie was overcome. Without thinking, he pulled Nina close and kissed her like any man kisses a woman who is driving him absolutely crazy. And, Nina, in spite of herself, submitted with such eagerness that he kissed her again. Archie soon lost all train of thought, except the one that usually motivated him in situations like this.

Neither one of them gave another thought to chicken salad from Nonny's.

An hour later, Nina was still lying next to Archie in his very masculine bedroom on the second floor. They were sufficiently exhausted and quite naked beneath a silky green sheet the color of sea water.

"I think we took each other by surprise," Archie finally said, not fully comprehending what had just happened but inching his way in that direction. Good God, the confession he'd have to make to Bathgart this week! Good thing he wasn't a Catholic.

"Heavens, what have we done?"

It was a stock phrase. A cliché. But, Archie didn't much care and he didn't think Nina did either. She looked like a woman who'd just had great sex for the first time in a long time. Maybe he was just what she needed. He wondered, too, if she might be just a little in love with him.

"Our little secret, of course. We don't need a family scandal." Archie was lining up his kings in the back row, even though he didn't believe Nina was the kind of woman who bragged about her lovelife to girl friends. Or, played chess, for that mattter.

"Absolutely. I don't mind keepin' secrets." Nina snuggled beneath the sheets. "Do you?"

"No, my darling. And, I have kept a few through the years." Archie was thinking about the Preacher. And, the body buried for decades near the river.

It was dark when Nina drove off to her apartment in the Beacon Street Arms. Archie prayed his neighbors were too busy to notice.

"Lola left a pile of dough to Preacher Boswell!"

"I thought the Preacher was our big secret, Arch. How did Lola get into the act?" Cyrus pointed to a parking place in the first row.

"Exactly."

"I'm in the dark here," Cyrus said frankly. "Unless Lola's last will and testament was all Durwood's idea, crafty little prick. But, what's his connection to Boswell? As far as we knew then and know now, Preacher Boswell's link to pretty Sally was only known to us. Durwood had nothing to do with any of it. Back then."

Archie pulled his BMW into the spot and turned up the A.C. The engine purred and the air grew more bearable. They were early for Cyrus's appointment at the clinic, and the sky in the west looked like rain.

"I'm sitting in the same black hole you are, Cyrus. What possible business did Durwood have with Boswell? Could be a coincidence, I suppose. Maybe Boswell did him a favor or two through the years. Durwood worked some dicey deals in his life. Could be he needed the services of an iffy individual like the Preacher. Remember how old Spriggy fell off the twig."

"Yeah, suspicious as hell. Pure Mafia. I remember. But, what do we really know about Boswell….as a grown man?"

Archie could see that Cyrus was keeping his eyes on the entrance of the University Clinic. He was getting nervous. Archie hurried on with his story. "I called a friend of mine in the state capital. Asked him to do a quick background check on Boswell….as a favor to those of us who knew Lola for so many years." Archie patted Cyrus's shoulder and added, "I didn't tell him anything else."

"So?"

"He said the Preacher's birth records were lost in a courthouse fire. He legally changed his name to 'Preacher' five years ago. He's a shifty sort. Questions were raised about him when his parents died. Another terrible fire. He has money but doesn't work much. Raises dogs, I guess. Hell, he could be a contract killer for all we know." Archie closed his eyes. What had they wrought?

"Sleazy bastard. Sounds dangerous, doesn't he, Arch?" Cyrus shrugged. "He can't be swimming around in our gene pool. Must be a hybrid, huh?" He grinned at Archie, the clinic doors forgotten for the moment.

Archie smiled. Cyrus, always looking on the bright side. "You might be right about

the money, Cyrus. Essentially, this was Durwood's will. His money went to Lola and on

her death the estate would fall to Toby and he tucked Boswell into the equation when Lola

wasn't looking. He set it up for some queer reason we may never know. Could be Lola added a few beneficiaries….like the gardener…. but never really saw the will. I don't think she would have known a legal document from a hayride."

"Do you think the Preacher knew?"

"I'd bet my new best selling line of canvas boat bags that he knew something. He's the guy the cops are looking at."

"Could be Toby'll retaliate and bump off the Preacher. Maybe he's like his old man….doesn't like to share. I remember Toby…rotten little kid." Cyrus's eyes locked on the Clinic's double glass doors again.

Archie stared at the doors too. More doctors. More tests. More silly questions. What did any of them know anyway? Cyrus liked it when he came along. Betty Hughes made Cyrus nervous and defensive, and, Archie understood her fears. Cyrus was slipping. They were all afraid of what was happening, of what they might be losing. He prayed the problem could be fixed.

"Do you think Sally will want part of the fortune?" asked Archie. He could feel his palms grow damp. His nerves were jumping.

"Jeez, Arch, how would I know? What kind of a woman is she these days?" Cyrus was still keeping up today, Archie noticed. He wasn't lost yet. "Our Sally, our beautiful Betty Grable. She was a heart-breaker in the summer of '45. She might not be so agreeable now."

"She gave up the kid," Archie reminded Cyrus. "Without a fuss, too. And, made us a life-long promise. No hitches in forty-three years."

"We'll have to call another meeting of the Old Devils," Cyrus said.

"Right. Did you ever see the Preacher?"

Cyrus said no and didn't want to. "Who needs nightmares that bad, Arch?"

Archie grinned and pulled cigarettes from the glove box. The two lighted up and smoked a while in silence, like two boys sneaking cigs behind the garage. Up to something naughty, his mother always said when she caught him. Archie watched Cyrus toss his half-smoked cigarette out the window.

"I'm more afraid of going….in there," Cyrus nodded toward the clinic, "than I am of going to jail. We could be in trouble on two fronts now….the old bones and now Lola and the Preacher. Jeez. Could be the police'll think one of us killed Lola, to keep her quiet about Boswell and Sally and her grunt of a father."

Archie pressed Cyrus's left hand against the seat. Both hands were fluttering like bird wings. He said, "You let me take care of this. We'll get through it all." What else could he say or do? He and Cyrus had spent more time together in this life than two brothers.

"You'll still come with me to the docs when Betty Hughes and I move to Meadowlark, won't you? Jesus, I hate the idea of moving. Leaving Tallyho. My roses. My pals in the neighborhood. Betty Hughes says I have to sell my trophy fish at the tag sale." Cyrus was rubbing his hands together as if something hurt.

Archie reached out and patted Cyrus's thin shoulder. "Absolutely. Nobody should go into Frankenstein's laboratory alone." Archie grinned. "You'll make a hundred new friends at Meadowlark Village. The place is lousy with old farts like you." Archie laughed again and gave Cyrus an extra pat. Cyrus laughed too, but he kept rubbing his hands.

A tight spring in Archie's head rewound the time to 1945, to that wild summer party at the end of the war. Vivid, lurid details sprang up like numbers in an old cash register. The very willing Sally Turk, eager to take on victorious boys in uniform. She worked as the Spriggs's maid back then. The guys were so relieved to be home, so damned glad to be alive that they'd gone slightly crazy. Sex and booze became a kind of war-time therapy. Then, more sex and more booze. Not the cleverest celebration but common enough, he supposed.

More memories flooded back. A night weeks later, a night filled with earthier smells and gruesome sounds and the Technicolor memory of Buzzy Turk looming in front of them like Paul Bunyan. And, finally, the forced march through the wood with the four young soldier boys carrying the dead weight of Sally's mean old man.

"Thinking about that weekend, Arch? Betty Grable and all?"

It was downright spooky how Cyrus could always tell what he was thinking. Archie gave himself a little shake. "Yeh. Soldier boys back home."

"Great legs, huh, Arch?" Cyrus sighed. "Kinda like the flying fish days in Florida." He threw out an imaginary line and reeled in a big one.

These flashes of the old fun-loving Cyrus, brilliant newsman, man-about-town, made Archie's heart leap. What if Cyrus wasn't as bad off as they thought?

Archie said, "We caught ourselves some gems, didn't we?" His eyes teared a little, which surprised him. He wasn't a sentimental guy most days.

"The days when we could do no wrong."

"Right." Archie felt as though he were clinging to the wreckage, but didn't let on.

Cyrus looked at his watch again. "Time to visit Doc Frankenstein."

"Sure, Cyrus. Let's get you into the laboratory." Archie made himself sound like Boris Karloff and Cyrus giggled, like always. It helped Archie to help Cyrus through these preliminary appointments with the docs, even though they were both pretty sure of the diagnosis.

As the two stepped into the lobby of the Brave New World Clinic, Cyrus said, "We'll just sit tight on this, right, Arch? Until we call a meeting."

"We'll sit tight." And, Archie took Cyrus's arm.

"Nadine! I'm glad I caught you," exclaimed Betty Hughes. "They're goin' to buy the
house!"

"Who?"

"Marigold and Parnell."

"They're staying...for sure?" Nadine sank heavily into a frail Sheraton arm chair kept next to the phone table in the foyer. "I was hoping it was all talk." The old wood spindles creaked beneath her weight, and she made a mental note to call her furniture man and to skip lunch for the next two weeks.

"Parnell dropped by with earnest money this mornin'. They're eager to move in as soon as possible, which is perfect for us. We can get into Meadowlark Village quick as a wink. I can have my tag sale any time."

"Marigold thinks being back is like old times." Nadine let a long sigh escape.

"Our beloved prodigals. Egads, Naddy."

"I would think Belmont would seem quite dull after Paris."

"Belmont is dull compared to Milwaukee."

The ladies laughed.

"Is anybody ever prepared to go backward?" Betty Hughes asked quite seriously.

"I suppose it's less scary than going frontwards."

Betty Hughes laughed. "Livin' in the past is a foolish pursuit."

"The only foolish pursuit that comes to my mind," Nadine pointed out rather fiercely, "is my husband's inclination to run after females with marmalade hair."

"Half the time Cyrus isn't sure who Marigold is."

"Archie will remind him. Rest assured. They never really forget the old days."

"Is that a good sign or a bad sign? I'm never sure."

"I think it's a clear indication that we're not exactly kids anymore."

It was Admiral Moss's turn to host the Old Devils' weekly poker party at his digs in the Golden Horizon Senior Apartments. The Victorian mansion had once belonged to a railroad tycoon, his wife, and their twelve children, all since deceased or departed. In 1985 the relatives willed the house to the city of Belmont for the establishment of a modestly priced dwelling for men and women over sixty. The Old Devils would have preferred an evening in Archie's cherry paneled billiard room with its fully-stocked bar, but the Old Devils took turns. Tommy liked to say that poker at Archie's house went beyond cards... like a Hollywood set with mobsters running the joint.

So far, Archie, Cyrus, and the Admiral were seated at the Formica kitchen table, waiting for Tommy. Lola's murder had terrified them. Archie didn't feel well. Nerves, he supposed. His stomach gave him a nasty lurch every few minutes.

"She's trying to get us from the grave," Admiral Moss whined. His hands shook as he poured bourbon into three glasses.

"How do we know Lola even knew the Preacher?" Cyrus asked them fairly seriously. He sounded clear-headed tonight. "Could be Durwood set up the will before he died. Lola wouldn't have known about his devious plans."

Archie mopped a handkerchief across his broad forehead. His head was hot. "Could very well be," he responded, solemnly.

"Maybe Lola found out something," put in the Admiral with a half-voice. "Then, played her hand…after the fact." Thin and wiry, Admiral Moss's body had aged better than his face which was weather-worn and shapeless. His watery pale eyes watched suspiciously for mankind's infinite variety of deviations…..moral lapses, bad manners, poor grooming, badly pressed shirts. Moss was older than the rest of them.

Archie said he didn't think Lola was smart enough to pull a stunt.

"Maybe it was Toby who got impatient and did in dear old mum." Cyrus's Paul Newman eyes were bright tonight.

"Toby? He's just a kid!" sputtered the Admiral. "Lola Spriggs has left millions to a dog breeder named Preacher Boswell. Jesus, Cyrus, wake up! This is a homicide case involving a very suspicious character!" The Admiral admitted that he'd been throwing up for three days.

"Well, we know damned well who the Preacher is, don't we?" said Cyrus. He was remarkably lucid tonight. "Three wild nights with Betty Grable and we end up with a kid with four daddies. We haven't been that macho in forty years!" He slapped the slick table with the flat of his hand and managed a grin. 'Betty Grable' was Sally Turk, the maid who worked for the Spriggs family during the war, a pretty girl who never refused a young man in uniform.

Archie grinned too. "But, WHY in hell does he get almost half of Lola's money?"

Nobody had any good answers.

Cyrus began moseying around the immaculate efficiency kitchen. There wasn't a thing sitting out on the highly polished counters and the chrome faucets gleamed in the light. The tiny apartment with its tiny stove and tiny bathroom drove all of them crazy. The boys hated the place. Melvin Moss tended to be tight fisted with a dollar. Actually, the old Admiral had the first nickel he ever earned. Literally. He kept it in a small box on his bedside table. Cyrus said the old boy had a tiny sense of humor to match. Hidden in another box. Right now, the Admiral was telling Cyrus to keep his hands off the cabinet doors. Cyrus waved him off and rummaged in the cupboard for something to eat. He pulled out a jar of peanuts.

"I sure as hell hope this doesn't have something to do with that body up in Pike's Wood!" mumbled Admiral Moss, while keeping his eye on Cyrus busily scavenging for food in his kitchen.

"It has *everything* to do with the body!" Archie declared in his most authoritative voice. "If we hadn't known Sally, we wouldn't be stuck with the Preacher and we wouldn't have buried Buzzy Turk! It's that simple!"

"Doesn't sound very simple, when you put it that way, Arch," said Cyrus with his head inside another cabinet. "Sounds more criminal."

"The old bones are our biggest worry," the Admiral insisted.

"If we all keep our mouths shut, nobody will ever know," said Cyrus.

"What if Sally decides she wants some of the Preacher's inheritance….. as one of the family?" the Admiral wanted to know.

"Sally's given us her word," said Archie.

"But, big money can make some people forget their promises," said the Admiral. He was looking pale and old.

"Toby isn't going to take kindly to sharing mommy's money with some strange guy from Fontana City. He'll be asking as many questions as the cops." Archie's stomach rumbled loudly this time. "We have to sort this out."

"What the hell's the statute of limitations on manslaughter?" the Admiral asked.

"Eternity," Cyrus replied.

Just then, the doorbell rang. It was Tommy, frail and buzzed. "A man could die of thirst around here!" This was Tommy's standard greeting. He made his way to the kitchen, leaning awkwardly against chairs and walls en route. He was a dying man still capable of sniffing out a free drink.

After getting Tommy up to speed, the Admiral asked if Sally would ever spill the beans to the police....about the baby and about Buzzy.

"Nah," Archie replied with a blind certainty. "Why come forward now? She could get into trouble too."

"Money, money, money," said Cyrus, his mind clicking again.

"The lawyers'll find her. Court records. Hospital dates. Adoption papers. My wallet feels lighter already." The Admiral was still clicking too.

"Your wallet's always light," countered Cyrus. "That old courthouse fire took care of any Boswell records."

"We could sell Sally another big packet of integrity," said Tommy. "Like we did in 1945."

"What do you mean 'we.' You never paid a dime!" the Admiral squeaked.

"I was willing," Tommy said, slurring the words. "Just didn't have the bucks." He tipped his body to one side where he sat and looked properly chastised. He said, "Looks like one of us must have tattled to old Spriggy about the kid." His eyelids drooped and his hands could barely hold a glass, but the Irishman could still figure the facts.

Nobody said a word until Cyrus jumped up from his chair, spilling peanuts and causing Archie to start. Cyrus began wagging one finger at Admiral Moss. He cried out, "Spriggy found out from you, didn't he, Mel?" The Admiral refused to meet Cyrus's eyes. Cyrus put his face three inches from the Admiral's and kept going. "I warned you, Mel, that if you ever blabbed about the kid I'd make you....make you.... drink muddy water and sleep in a hollow log!"

With that, Archie and Cyrus and Tommy exploded with laughter. As pissed off as they were they couldn't help it. Cyrus sang the bluesy line to the Admiral one more time....just like Lou Rawls in concert. Teasing the Admiral with song lyrics was one of Cyrus's pet acts. The Admiral could only cringe.

"Ah, hah!" exclaimed Tommy with a rapturous giggle. "Caught!"

"You sanctimonious bastard," Archie blurted out. "Had yourself a good time forty-three years ago, but couldn't keep a secret. Thought you'd just hoist yourself right out of the fatherhood equation, huh?" As mad as he was, Archie was still chuckling over Cyrus's perfect play.

"Spriggy promised he'd never tell." The Admiral busied himself with a bag of pretzels. "He lied. The will is his way of giving us one final jab."

"But why? Why betray us?" Archie remained confused as well as angry.

"Jesus, where have you been all these years?" interjected Tommy, sounding unbelievably sober all of a sudden. Perhaps danger sharpened the wits. "Durwood was a scheming little bastard. How do you think he got so damned rich?" Tommy tilted again on his chair and then caught himself. "Pulling this stunt from the grave will make Spriggy crow like a rooster....even in purgatory." Tommy chuckled quietly.

With that, Cyrus headed for the Admiral's refrigerator, where he rummaged for something more substantial than pretzels and peanuts. With his head inside the icebox he called out, "Spriggy did like getting guys by the short hairs." He backed out with a chunk of liver sausage and a jar of mayo. He placed them on the narrow counter. "Anybody hungry for a sandwich? Where's the bread, Mel?"

"You're supposed to eat before you come over," the Admiral grumbled. He pulled a loaf of factory white bread from the cupboard.

Archie knew that the Admiral hated the mess and the expense. Who could eat now? His stomach gave him another twinge. Cyrus and Tommy were the only ones interested.

"I'll drive up to see Sally tomorrow," Archie said calmly. "I think she runs a café in Stone Bank. Next to the Mobil station."

"A real beauty, she was," said Tommy wistfully.

Archie knew they were all remembering the more racy details of that infamous weekend, after months of slogging through France and Germany. After believing they'd never return home. The celebration at the Spriggs's summer place was memorable, to say the least. "Our very own Betty Grable."

"I think we should turn ourselves over to the police," the Admiral suddenly said.

The Old Devils stared in drop-jawed amazement at the man.

Tommy leaned forward, his head heavy with booze. He put his nose close to the Admiral's and spoke so quietly it was difficult to hear the words. He hissed, "You do, my lad, and you'll get yourself ...strangled."

Nobody drew a breath. Then, the Admiral's shoulders began to shake violently. "OK. OK. I'm just rambling," he whispered. "I'm scared shitless, if you want to know the truth." He began to weep. "The Preacher could find out about us and kill us too."

"Who isn't scared?" said Archie. "But, we're staying smart about this. You understand me?"

The room was quiet. Archie had spoken. They understood. After a few minutes, Archie dealt the cards.

"I think we should go visit the Preacher," Cyrus finally said, as he fanned out his hand and secretly rejoiced at his good cards. "I'm curious about this guy. I want to see him, face to face. Don't you?"

"And, what reason do we give for marching into Fontana City?" asked Tommy, still fiddling with his cards, but pretty sure he was looking at a club flush.

"I could say I'd like to buy one of his hunting dogs, a nice pup or two," said Archie, thinking this might be a good idea. "We could all drive up there….four gentlemen who like dogs."

"Yeah, Arch, that's the ticket. All four of us. Preacher Boswell would never think a thing of it." Cyrus was beaming.

"Have a wee peek at our only mutual enterprise….so to speak." Tommy laughed and gave the Admiral a nudge.

They all agreed. Curiosity would win out, once again. Who could resist? Tommy said, giggling.

The following afternoon Cyrus called Archie. He said he was at a public phone in the lounge at Meadowlark Village with a clear view of the elevators. Betty Hughes was tailing him, he said. They were checking out their new apartment and the facilities, but Cyrus had escaped.

"Did you talk to Sally?"

"Caught up with her early this morning. She owns the Starlight Café in Stone Bank. Looks wonderful. Hair's a different color." Archie kept his voice down. Nadine was only two rooms away. "Changed her name to Sally Montgomery in 1947, she said. After some movie star."

"How about the legs, Arch?"

"One-hundred percent Betty Grable." Archie laughed. "She knows about the will and the Preacher. Says he's a lucky man. Says she wishes she'd been that lucky." That remark would keep him up all night.

"For crying out loud. What did she mean by that?"

"Your guess is as good as mine. She said she's never made contact with the Preacher. But, big money can do crazy things to your psyche and your moral code…if you're nice enough to have one."

"We'd better keep an eye on her, Arch. There could be a secret connection between her and Lola and the Preacher."

"How do you propose we do that? Hire a detective to follow the woman?"

Cyrus thought it over. "Not a bad idea."

"We'll see."

"The Preacher bumped off Lola; I can feel it in my bones."

"Sure. You have cosmic bones."

"I popped ten vitamins this morning, some stinky herbal remedy, and survived an hour of exercises in the Meadowlark gym. Free of charge, I might add. I'm full of piss and vinegar." Cyrus snickered. "Our Sally's keeping a secret."

"We don't know that."

"The cops drove up to Fontana City to question Boswell. I talked to Freddy Donovan at the golf course. He said this Boswell is creepy as hell and sly as a red fox."

"Creepy? I don't like the sound of that. Hell, he could be yours or mine, for all we know." A touch of nausea flooded Archie's stomach. Had he fathered a killer? Thank heaven Hugo was who he was. "We'll drive up at the end of the week."

"OK, Arch, but if he's creepy we'll assume he's the Admiral's offspring, right?"

"Right. The virgin father."

"Could be, the old faker. Maybe he was never an admiral either." Cyrus giggled again. "So, Sally doesn't know why Lola left the loot to Boswell?"

"It's a mystery, she says. Thinks Lola might have met the Boswells through some charity and took them on." Archie doubted this. "Sally's keeping her kings in the back row, like she always did. I let her know we'd be getting back to her."

"Could be the kid is Durwood's. Same beady eyes."

"Durwood had his own girl that week end. They were inseparable."

"Any news on the old bones case?" Cyrus whispered.

"Sally says the sheriff knows that Beresford Boots made custom shoes for a man named Willard 'Buzzy' Turk, the only guy around with a short leg." Archie sat down, suddenly feeling the weight of it again. "Apparently, the accounting department looked up files on men's custom specialty shoes made during the late forties. Turk's name came up on the old Badger club files up there in Sandy Hook. His club belt was in the remains." Archie shuddered involuntarily.

"Holy Toledo!" Cyrus cried.

"Hang on, Cyrus. Nobody's connected Buzzy to Sally. Those days she told anybody who asked that Buzzy fled to Alaska to find his fortune, like he was always bragging he'd do. They believed the story then, and she's got a new life in Stone Bank with a new name."

"No good would come of her telling the real story now, would it, Arch? Besides, she's implicated."

"Right. No good at all."

"Did she ask for hush money?"

Archie laughed. "Hush money? Jesus, you sound like Sam Spade. No. And, I didn't bring it up either."

"Got to go, Arch. My personal bloodhound's just trotted off the elevator." And Cyrus rang off.

Archie sat a few minutes without moving. Bloodhounds and sly foxes. Old mistresses, new ones. Foolish men and silly women. Old money, hush money. Gray bones and black secrets. Retired four months and his life was more complicated than *The Guiding Light*, Nadine's favorite soap. Lugging the mud of Buzzy Turk's grave and the debris of Lola Spriggs's unfortunate end was heavy work. The load might be lighter if he went back to work at the boot company.

5

In Character

"Why did you run out like that?" Hugo asked, warily. "At that party years ago."

Hugo thought he might drown in what his eyes were taking in. Miranda Burke in a skin-tight Cat Woman get-up. He was Dick Tracy in a pin-striped dark suit and a soft gray felt hat. It was Famous Characters Night at the palatial digs of Betty Hughes and Cyrus Armbruster, probably the last party they would give there before moving to Meadowlark. Nadine kept Hugo up-to-date on the old crowd.

"Run off?" Miranda answered without meeting Hugo's eyes.

She was acting miffed, Hugo realized. She'd placed one hand on one very nice hip and continued to stare obliquely into the crowded room. "Let's scout the territory," she said, as if to stall any immediate discussion of their last evening together….over ten years ago.

Miranda swung easily around knots of guests, her hips swaying in their black spandex tights, a long, slinky tail bumping gently against the legs of unsuspecting revelers. Hugo followed willingly. He had left Nina to fend for herself. She was perfectly contented with the Belmont matrons and their husbands, far more contented than she was with him these days. Their engagement was fizzling, and neither one of them found it particularly disturbing.

The big party hummed on. Each year the Armbrusters invited a hundred of their closest friends to a costume party which forced guests into ridiculous outfits for the purpose of taking their minds off the dog days of summer. No one refused the invitation. When Hugo balked at the mention of costumes, his mother suggested he grow up. Guests arrived in pain, she reminded him, in bad tempers, in walking casts, in states of advanced pregnancy and recuperation, but they got there. The food always promised to be magnificent, the drinks plentiful, and the company more fun because they all felt foolish. She had ordered her son and Nina to attend. Hugo recalled the blissful years in New Orleans with his mother hundreds of miles north. Blissful years. Life would never be the same again. Hugo sighed and felt a wave of fatigue.

As Hugo and Miranda found a place to stand in the crush, Hugo noticed his mother and Betty Hughes, all rigged out, giving him the eye from across the room. The Babes, as he referred to the two women, rarely missed a thing. And, they would be particularly interested in his reunion with Miranda Burke. His mother collected gossip like she collected good paintings….with genuine enthusiasm and expertise.

"I'm still curious, you know," Hugo said. "About why you….bolted." He was feeling braver now, as if speaking in defiance of the old guard.

Miranda turned to face him and said, "I don't recall….bolting, as you put it." Her tone made his question sound far-fetched.

Hugo watched his first love hurriedly consume the last of her martini, gin fortification, she called it, her favorite solution for dealing with pain and disappointment. Hugo's new-found spunk evaporated a little. Perhaps Miranda wasn't as happy to see him as he was to see her.

"You most certainly did," Hugo replied with falsetto cheeriness. "It was a warm summer night. We were all getting drunk in the Levinsons' kitchen and you took off…. like a shot. Ran like a rabbit and refused to ever see me again."

When Miranda didn't immediately respond, Hugo laughed and gently touched her arm. She must know he was still smarting from the rejection. It had been swift and ruthlessly delivered in front of their friends, and it had taken him years to get over it.

"Rubbish!" Miranda laughed, a throaty trumpet born of too much booze and cigarettes and too little sleep. Her fingers came to rest on Hugo's hand.

"I could round up a dozen witnesses," Hugo countered lightly, smiling.

Miranda answered with a sleepy drop of her eyes, "You will notice, Hugo, that I am standing quite still now," and she pushed back a strand of caramel hair that had crept out from under her sleek cat cap.

Hugo felt his face flush, and he shifted his weight several times, as if to drive off the heat. He quickly plucked a glass of champagne courage from a circulating waiter. "Ah! So you are. So you are." Miranda's response caught him off guard. He coughed and said, "I see your by-line in the *TRIBUNE*. Fine stuff." He was more at ease, having moved off the seduction track.

"I do all right. I imagine you're up to your ears in Archie's business these days. Making piles of money."

"Beresford Boot and Outerwear. We keep you and your feet covered." Hugo recited the company line expertly. "The president wears our mountain boots at his ranch."

"Good for Ronny."

Miranda was making fun of him again. "Does my business interest you?" Hugo asked, determined to keep the dialogue going. He selected a broiled bacon wrapped chestnut from another moving tray. His eyes watered when it singed his tongue.

"Money interests anybody who breathes." Miranda rubbed up against the smooth wood of a pretty armoire and smiled like a vixen at him. "And Nina? How does she find you and your boots these days?"

Jesus, Hugo thought, the woman hasn't changed. "Nina is Nina. Off in her own little world. She and my father have hit it off, rather more successfully than she and my mother." "You're living together?"

Hugo found himself taking a protective step back and nearly bumped into a large woman dressed as Red Riding Hood, of all things. "Ahh, yes….I mean, ahhh, no. Not exactly. She has a flat downtown. Our temporary arrangement for now."

"How very modern. Nina has her own cave." Miranda swayed to the music.

"She's taking acting classes." Hugo stepped closer again. "Can't we sit? These damned standup affairs are hell on my back. And frankly, I doubt if Dick Tracy went to costume parties." He took Miranda's arm possessively and led them into what Betty Hughes called the conservatory, a hexagonally shaped fully-windowed room sprouting a disciplined jungle of flowering plants and small trees.

Miranda snuggled into a corner of a luxurious down couch; a freshly sprayed fig tree drooped seductively over her shoulder. Hugo was nearly overcome with desire for her.

"Where is your lovely Nina?"

Hugo watched Miranda glance about, pretending to be interested in the whereabouts of Miss Dupree. He wasn't fooled. Miranda had never been interested in what other women were up to. Miranda's prime interests had always been her job and the male animal.

Hugo craned his neck and said, "She's over there, (he gestured) dressed like somebody's fairy godmother, chatting up my father, her favorite pal, so far." Actually, he wasn't quite sure of what to make of Nina's tight friendship with Archie. Hugo found himself worrying a little about it. His father was a real operator when it came to females, and Nina seemed to like his attention. But, Hugo found he was too busy to do much about it, even though it irritated like a tiny pebble caught beneath his sock.

"He's a handsome man, your father." Miranda licked her lips. She made no comment about Nina. "Too bad he isn't available." She grinned like a bad girl.

Jesus. Was she actually panting after his father? "He's a harmless spook these days.....into his dotage." This was a bald-faced lie, but what else could he say? Hugo leaned closer. "Nina isn't worldly like you," he whispered.

"Worldly? Why, Hugo, what are you getting at?"

That remark was designed to make him squirm. Hugo was well aware that he started these flirtations but often lacked the fortitude to keep the volley going. "Same old Miranda! As blunt as you are desirable." He reached for her hand and then immediately withdrew it when he noticed his mother and Betty Hughes glancing in their direction. He hissed, "You're absolutely marvelous."

"I'll need another drink, if I'm forced to pursue much more of this very exciting male-female counterpoint." And, with that, Miranda uncurled from the sofa but not before releasing a sexy, guttural meow into Hugo's ear. Then, she slunk away, leaving him to sit there like a damned fool.

Across the room a few of the Old Devils and their wives and friends had congregated by the cold fireplace. Lettice Mulroy, fancifully costumed as Rosalind Russell in a severe black suit with shoulder pads and a huge rhinestone lapel pin, was saying, "You'd think Hugo would be home resting up, getting ready to play the bridegroom. I heard just yesterday that he and Nina are to be married next month." She was a trifle put out that she'd had to learn this important news from the check-out girl at Food Fair.

"Who told you that?" exclaimed Nadine, busily adjusting a powdered wig that insisted upon tilting to the side every few minutes. She was gowned as one of the French queens.

Lettice decided to fib. "A woman at the boarding house who knows Betty Hughes's housekeeper."

"Ridiculous. No date has been set. Hugo is swamped with work, and Nina doesn't seem to care one way or the other. Not very forthcoming, if you know what I mean. She has quite unexpectedly started acting classes at the university. Needs a fresh start, she said. Who doesn't?" Nadine leaned against the grand piano, exhausted after shuffling about for two hours in the heavy satin costume and uncomfortable shoes. And, where was Archie? Her mood was dive bombing.

Standing near-by was Cyrus, all done up as Phantom of the Opera. He'd pushed his mask to the top of his head, which allowed the eerie white plastic disguise to very disconcertingly face the ceiling, a circumstance that had provoked one or two of the party's heavy drinkers to pause and take stock of their evening's alcohol consumption. Cyrus had been commiserating with a Mr. Frankenstein (Admiral Moss, resplendent in green skin and bolts glued to his neck) about the futility of dressing up like somebody else. Cyrus insisted that nobody ever listened to him, in or out of costume. Everyone laughed and agreed.

The Admiral turned to Lettice and said he was certain Hugo and Nina would march down the aisle just as soon as the Christmas catalogue was finished.

"Hugo seems to be playing more attention to his old girl friend, Miranda Burke, than he has Nina." Betty Hughes, costumed as Mrs. Miniver in one of her charming war-time hats, mentioned this, as if in passing, but they all knew Hugo's behavior had grown more suspicious as the evening wore on. "There is trouble in paradise, methinks."

Lettice said, "Perhaps Hugo has a bit of his father in him, after all. He's no doubt kept himself quite beautifully tuned over the years, down in New Orleans."

Nadine let that slide and kept quiet, fussing again with her costume.

"I think," Betty Hughes said, "that was the very reason Miranda gave Hugo the old heave-ho in the first place, about fifteen years ago, far too much tuning up?" More laughter.

"Maybe Nina will regret not choosing that Rita Hayworth get-up over there," said Cyrus, pointing to a spectacularly put together young woman with red hair and a Gilda slink. "Hell, Rita could lure Hugo into purgatory in that dress." More snickers at Hugo's expense.

In her silence Nadine was wondering just what Hugo was up to, all huddled up with Miranda Burke, no doubt industriously digging up the past. To what end? Was he about to trade Nina for this journalist with her well-known love of drink? Or, was it Miranda initiating the flirting after a half dozen martinis? The woman really needed to check into Betty Ford. Nadine was feeling out of control tonight. First, Marigold shows up; then, Hugo with Nina, a total stranger who might become a Beresford; and now, tipsy Miranda looms on the horizon again after all these years. And, wound up in the scenario was Archie, as usual. What was the matter with everybody?

"To change the subject," Admiral Moss suddenly blurted, "what in the world is Nessa Quinn wearing?" The five of them pivoted simultaneously. It was never wise to ignore Nessa Quinn, especially in costume.

The woman in question had never been beautiful, and her body would never meet a Victoria's Secret standard, two facts that had escaped Nessa when she chose to be a belly dancer. With pendulous breasts barely concealed beneath a sequined brassiere, Nessa's lower half was clothed in billowing filmy trousers that, when she stood in a good light, revealed a distressing lack of necessary lingerie.

Betty Hughes remarked very quietly that she could never create a female character quite like Nessa, not if she lived to be a hundred.

"Do you suppose she doesn't realize that we can see *through* those pants?" asked Nadine, unblinking. "She's standing in front of lamp, for God's sake!"

The Admiral made a throaty sound as if he might be sick. He sounded more disgusted than titillated.

"Nessa knows," said Lettice. "And, ten to one, Jerry put her up to it."

"He's like a pimp, isn't he?" said Betty Hughes, almost innocently. None of them had ever fully understood the Quinns.

Elaborately robed as a wealthy camel owner, some anonymous film character, Jerry Quinn stood nearby with a tasseled red fez on his large round head. He was seriously engaged in small talk with an ebony wigged woman amazingly constructed like Elizabeth Taylor in white strapless satin and a several pounds of fake diamonds. His hand, they all noticed, would occasionally slip to the woman's smooth bottom, causing the ever alert Cyrus to make a rude comment for which Betty Hughes suggested he go to his room.

"Why does she do it? Why do we invite them year after year? Remember the bikini in 1985?" Betty Hughes turned her head away.

They remembered. Nadine had gone home and thrown out her bathing suit.

"It's a secret she'll take to her grave," Cyrus replied in a somber monotone.

"Well, Cyrus Armbruster," Betty Hughes sputtered, "it's all your fault. You always insist we invite the Quinns." She jabbed at his arm with a pointed pink fingernail that caused him to flinch. She was trying a Greer Garson British accent, but it still sounded like Montgomery, Alabama.

"Ouch!" Cyrus cried. "I've known Jerry since second grade. Nessa's a trifle…ah, wanton, shall we say, but doesn't hurt anybody."

"Darlin', she turns our party into *Penthouse* every year." Betty Hughes grimaced. "How can I get them out of here?"

"We could tell them their house is on fire," said Lettice in her best Rosalind Russell voice.

"The Quinns do add an element to any party," Cyrus admitted sheepishly.

"Jerry gets her to dress that way for clients," Nadine said, quietly. "Like selling her to the lowest bidder." She often wondered what went on after those salesmen's dinners that Nessa was always cooking. She'd heard about dancing in the dark and their hot tub.

"Jerry's as subtle as a rock through a window," the Admiral remarked.

"I can remember Nessa when she wore pigtails and knee socks," said Cyrus rather sadly.

They stood transfixed by the belly dancer across the way.

"The transformation and descent of Nessa Quinn, as perplexin' as how the earth was formed." Betty Hughes, they all agreed, could be almost poetic at times.

"Nessa always seems quite happy," Cyrus said. "Her appalling reputation doesn't bother either one of them."

Nadine suggested that perhaps Nessa's hooker wardrobe and the one-night stands were her hobby.

"And, who are we," put in Betty Hughes, "to push dear Nessa into needlepoint?"

They snickered at the picture and at the odds.

Another hour later into the party found Nina zeroing in on Hugo, nursing a drink by the French doors and staring out at the lighted stone patio. He was alone.

"Mr. Tracy!" Nina called out. "Can I hire you to find my dog?" They were all getting tight. She pecked him on the cheek, and he offered her a lukewarm embrace. He smelled of after shave and shrimp Creole.

"Depends on how big he is," Hugo replied, fairly brightly for Hugo. He wasn't one for brilliant raillery.

Handsome in his forties' detective ensemble, Hugo did remind Nina of one of those heroes made eternal in old English films, like the Earl of Brickbatten, her silly nickname for him. And, there remained in her the irresistible impulse to place a hand along his cheek. If she were to be honest, there were moments when she experienced the same impulse with Archie.

"Having fun?" Nina chirped. "Bumping into old friends?" Idiotic babble, but she was curious about Cat Woman, his first fiancée. She did know that much about her. Unfortunately, at that moment, Nina was seized again by the same feeling of desperation and anger she'd felt the night Howard broke their engagement, the bastard. Had it been sheer terror on his part? Was the expectation of a life with Nina Dupree so frightening that he'd chosen to cut and run in the middle of strawberry pie? Escape was his only salvation? Nina never talked to Hugo about her breakup with Howard. He just knew there had been someone else on the agenda before he got there.

"I don't know why I didn't come back sooner." Hugo fussed with his hat. He seemed nervous and ill-at-ease, Nina thought, as if she might touch him again.

"I hear your house is being considered for the charity home tour this fall. You must let me see the finished product…before I'm forced to buy a ticket." Nina smiled laughed and tried to secure her tiara. The room was warm, and she felt warmer than a fairy godmother should. Why did she say that? She had very little interest in Hugo's space-age house that looked very much like an X-ray clinic in a sci-fi film. She didn't mention the fact that her marvelous old apartment at the Beacon Street Arms had been selected for the tour two weeks ago.

Hugo laughed politely. "Well, no need for that. Ah, ah, I thought I'd have a kind of open house for old friends. Sometime. Soon."

Nina didn't believe a word of it. Hugo wasn't a man who entertained. Too messy and too expensive. He might be damned irresistible, but Hugo was also phenomenally cheap. Poor Cat Woman, according to the gossips, had to practically pull a gun on Hugo fifteen years ago just to get an engagement ring out of him …a ring she subsequently returned by parcel post. Nina had made sure she was rewarded with a Tiffany beauty before she agreed to flee New Orleans for Belmont. Well, Nina thought, here he stood, most assuredly, the same old Hugo, your basic coward in an old but good suit. What made this man so intriguing? Nina was beginning to have serious doubts as to his qualifications as a mate.

"Maybe I'll just drop by sometime on my way to the stables," Nina was going on, undaunted by Hugo's awful behavior. "Archie lets me ride Thunderbolt, you know, out at Duffy's on Indian Head bluff." It felt good mentioning generous Archie to his pinchpenny son.

Hugo blinked rapidly and settled his hat more firmly on his head. "Eerrr, ummmm," he stammered. "Good old Archie. But, I'm not home much, Nina. You know that. I barely have time to eat anymore. Might be a waste of time." He inched closer to the only path of escape, a narrow space between the doors and a grand piano.

There was a long, long moment of silence. Nina's head cleared, as if blown out by a gust of celestial X-rays. She had just experienced a brush-off the size of Mount Olympus! In the time it took dear Hugo to flick her from his social roster and his life, she had come face to face with the truth. She'd been ridiculous and foolish to give up her life in the south. Hugo was no longer interested in her. And, if that wasn't enough, she knew in that moment that she wasn't interested in him either. Her private humiliation made her feel very hot again and she took a gulp of champagne. Nina wondered if Hugo dragged her north just to prove to his old pals, to his father, most of all, to dear Miranda Burke that he was attached to somebody! Ooohhh! She wanted to scratch his eyes out, but this wasn't the time or the place. But, she'd get him!

"Well, Hugo, darlin', I'm off to the dessert table. It's about time for somethin' sweet around here, I'd say." She laughed her best carefree laugh, but doubted Hugo noticed. Subtleties were not his long suit. "Ah, I can see that handsome O'Neill Spender headin' in the same direction. Lucky me." She gave Hugo her best nonchalant gaze and scurried off, waving her magic wand toward O'Neill as she fled.

Hugo looked faintly confused, as if he wasn't quite sure what had just happened, and scuttled backward. He then turned and headed quickly for the bar.

Later, as Nina searched for Archie midst the swarm of book and movie characters who'd come to life again that night, she was struck again by her own vulnerability. She'd never considered herself the vulnerable type. Perhaps immediately after Howard's retreat, but she now understood the heavy hand of loss and loneliness all over again. Was she meant to be a solitary soul in this life? Was this the plan? And, in spite of the warmth of people around her, Nina felt a chill. Perhaps this was her punishment...for falling in love with Archie.

"Hell's bells, Naddy, she's writin' a play! A play! And, guess who thinks it's mighty smashin'?"

"Parnell?" Nadine was enjoying Betty Hughes's self-imposed rumpus with Marigold Woolsey. While their quaint little riverside village (a bit bigger than a village) lay indolent and blistered beneath a relentless summer sun, the town's female literati (to use the term loosely), seemed to be engaged in a kind of author/playwright skirmish possessing all the capabilities of reviving even the moribund. Betty Hughes's fixation with Marigold Woolsey had gone beyond sheer female jealousies. The two women had now entered that rarefied realm (did she dare use the term?)…of *literature.* Nadine wasn't sure if this left her breathless with anticipation or simply nonplused. She, of course, had her own quarrel with Marigold, her own fear that Archie might be seeing the woman on the sly. Every female in town was worried about that. Marigold was a femme fatale of considerable proportions. But, in this case, Betty Hughes was trapped in another arena. She took herself and her work very seriously. Certainly she had no peer in Belmont when it came to creating romance novels. She did have a few peers in the best-selling chick lit market, to be sure, but Betty Hughes was accustomed to these folks. The problem was Betty Hughes did not know anything about writing plays. And, to make matters worse or at least complicated, novice playwright Marigold Woolsey had decided to step on stage as well….with just a sliver of theatre experience. One of her plays had been produced a few years ago in London with some success. It was at this wobbly juncture that Betty Hughes found herself on this hot afternoon. Nadine reminded herself that it was her delicious assignment as chief confidante and counselor to Belmont's celebrity romance author to keep her from making a fool of herself. Marigold, beware. At the moment the two old friends were packing up china and keepsakes in Betty Hughes's living room, in preparation for the Armbrusters' move to Meadowlark Village. The large, sun-filled room was filled with packing cartons and paper.

"Don't get cute with me, Nadine. O'Neill Spender said the first act was perfection! That traitorous gypsy and her damned gold turbans!" Betty Hughes's long relationship with her agent, O'Neill Spender, was sacrosanct and rather maternal, Nadine always thought. Betty Hughes treated O'Neill like a bright child whose allowance was too big.

Spender's new found fascination with Marigold Woolsey was surprising and almost out-of-character for a shy man who rarely made eye contact with females of any age. Of course, he had taken an interest in Nina, too. Perhaps he was coming out of his cocoon.

Nadine didn't reply but watched Betty Hughes open a large box of Turnbull's chocolates and sweep what looked like a mocha cream into her mouth. Betty Hughes halfheartedly wafted the candy box in Nadine's direction, but Nadine declined.

"O'Neill's persuaded Marigold to enter the Ashbury College play contest, which I might add is the very same contest I am enterin' as my theatre debut!" Betty Hughes's arms shot to the ceiling and she began prowling the perimeter of the spacious, beam-braced and cluttered room like a kid hoping to escape a playpen.

"Sweetie, you're a professional. Marigold's like… like fresh out of the oven…..with just a teeny bit of experience…..in a foreign country!" Dear God, it was London.

"This is deliberate, you all know that, Naddy. It's a shot across the bow. A warning that she's goin' after whatever she wants…..plays, Cyrus, my house! Heavens, she wants my house too!" Betty Hughes returned to her place on the couch and put the candy box in her lap. Two more creams disappeared.

"Now, now. Marigold likes to stick her finger in the frosting, have a wee taste when nobody's paying close attention. I wouldn't call that a shot across the bow, exactly." Nadine carefully wrapped a lovely old flower vase and put it into a carton with several others. She had to talk Betty Hughes out of this insane preoccupation; it might even help her heal her own devilish feelings toward Marigold.

"Don't forget to mark that box, Naddy." Betty Hughes poured iced tea from a pitcher on a coffee table and then slipped out of her sandals. "Why did you let me eat all those chocolates?"

Nadine let that pass. "Why don't you ignore Marigold."

"How can I? She's in my face. In my territory. Of her own free will." Betty Hughes was on her feet again. "She's turned O'Neill into jelly. He's smitten." Betty Hughes strode purposefully to the wing chair and picked up a stack of plates sitting on the cushion.

Nadine made no comment. Bubbles of indignation were fairly floating out of Betty Hughes's ears. Nadine was reminded of cell division in a petri dish. "We should invite her out to lunch. A nice gesture of hospitality."

"Gestures. She'll see through that before the salad."

"We have to start somewhere."

Betty Hughes screwed up her face.

"I realize this is probably going to win me a place in front of a firing squad," Nadine said, cautiously and lightly, "but, I think Marigold has every right to enter that contest. Why can't she write a play if she wants to? Who doesn't need some retooling....after fifty? Marigold's obviously trying to start over....in a small way."

"Let her do it in France."

Nadine ignored that too and marched across the room to pick up a tray stacked with china teacups. "It's not Marigold's fault that you want to try playwriting. She isn't a mind-reader." She sat down on the floor and began folding each cup in white paper. What a tedious chore.

Betty Hughes made a gagging expression and sat down in the middle of the rug. She might not take Nadine's advice, but she was still listening.

"Get over it. Compete with her on a high level. Do your best and let things fly." Nadine stopped to pick up her glass of tea. Betty Hughes remained silent.

Nadine pushed herself upright and moved across the room to an ancient but remarkably smart English lounge chair. Her back was aching. She looked around the room, messy or not it was very Betty Hughes Armbruster, author at home. Old Tally Ho, as it was affectionately called, was an historic relic for this part of the country. Built by a lumber baron before income taxes, the place creaked and groaned and drafts whipped through the halls like tornadoes, but it had character, like its owner.

"I know. Marigold's from the days when we were newlyweds. She might not mean any harm.....I say might not." Betty Hughes paused, putting her thoughts in order. "She's a babe. I grew up with southern belle babes.....they're all alike. They cause us more ordinary girls to try harder and wish we didn't have to." She giggled and so did Nadine. "I just watch her glide into the room, see all the roosters fluff out their feathers and wish she'd take the next hot air balloon to Monte Carlo."

Nadine laughed. "We all wish that. Next time, close your eyes. What do you care? You're a successful author. You've got Cyrus. Marigold just owns a closet full of gold turbans and a lovely gentleman who writes bad poetry. Why are we so damned worried?"

"Why indeed."

Later, Nadine made it her business to look keenly into Betty Hughes's face. Foiled again. The lady author was still scowling as she wrapped up an old teapot. Hopeless.

6

A Lucky Man

The ride upriver on Highway 16 always reminded Archie of a documentary on the origins of the earth. There were few places he'd been, except maybe the Badlands, where the evidence of man was less evident. Here, in this ancient river valley, the Mississippi had presumed its place and kept it for the most part, like a naughty kid who gets his own way. The water fought daily with the land to create a universe of islands and sloughs so interlaced that it was difficult to tell who was winning in some spots. It didn't much matter to Archie; it was the best war going.

Smoothly carrying its crew early that morning, Archie's new wagon wound its way along a stretch of blacktop that hugged the steep sides of the bluffs and peered with a superior eye on the river far below. He and Cyrus and the Admiral and Tommy were taking a short jaunt to Fontana City, to pay an unofficial call on the financially elevated Preacher Boswell. Fontana City, population eight-hundred thirty-seven, give or take a few dozen during the summer and winter and that included the dogs, barely deserved a blink most days. Archie didn't care much for these threadbare towns that did little more than squint into the sun. But, this burg was the home of Boswell, newly minted millionaire and a possible killer of rich old ladies. The Old Devils wanted a first-hand look at the guy, a guy one of them may have fathered. Archie would approach Boswell as a man eager to buy a good hunting dog.

"What have you found out about him so far, Archie?" The Admiral was sitting in back with Tommy Delaney, already dozing.

"Not much. According to the Spriggs family, there are absolutely no Boswells in the lineup. But, I have a pal in the courthouse going over familial ties in the records. For all we know, the Preacher and his adopted family could be shirttail cousins nobody knew about until Lola made him famous."

"Why is he called Preacher? Is he some itinerant tent cleric?" Cyrus asked.

"According to the Charlie Lemmon, Boswell's a big pontificator…. likes to spout off….especially in bars when he's had a snootful. His closest associates at Fergie's Tap gave him the name as a badge of admiration."

"Very impressive," remarked Tommy, awake as a hound again at the sound of Fergie's Tap. "Is that where we'll interrogate the man?" The Irishman sounded eager.

"Might be our best bet. He's been known to hang out there most afternoons and evenings. But, we'll try his house first. Use the hunting dog excuse." Archie passed a truck on the upgrade and then slipped back into his lane again.

"Just between us boys, I don't think Freddy's got any leads other than Toby Spriggs and this Boswell character," said the Admiral. "I'd say the one who is the greediest and most impatient gets to go to jail."

Archie skillfully passed a slow passenger car on one of the brief stretches that wasn't yellow-lined. River roads were always fun to negotiate.

Tommy and Cyrus agreed with Mel Moss, and Archie turned his focus back to the scenery. It had been a long time since he'd traveled the River Road this far north. The craggy ridges were still dolled up in thick green summer robes. Sumac clung to the lower elevations waiting to turn watermelon pink in another few weeks. Maples, ever so slightly yellow in spots and so dense they nearly consumed the firs and pines, fought with ancient gnarled oaks, their arthritic branches curling among white fingers of birch. And, far below the blacktop, Soo line tracks lay so close to the shadowy river banks that he imagined a passing freight train might topple into the murky current.

"Freddy Donovan thinks our Preacher might be illegitimate?" Cyrus was saying. "Like maybe he was Lola's little secret all these years and not ours." He groaned.

"If the Preacher was Lola's little mistake, she would have seen to his welfare long before her death. Lola was a generous lady," said Archie. "Besides, we all know who the Preacher really is. What's the damned mystery? Sally told us about the adoption."

"What if it was a lie?" said the Admiral. "What do we really know about Sally?"

"Good point," said Cyrus. "What if the kid was really Durwood's? And, he paid Sally to tell us this cock 'n bull story. Spriggy was a bastard. Remember there was some question about his so-called accidental death at the company warehouse. One of his own trucks backed over him. Rumor had it that one of Spriggy's competitors planned the little mishap. Hell, he had an army of enemies."

Archie passed a gray and red tour bus loaded with sightseers, taking in the river vistas on their way to Minneapolis. "You're right, Cyrus. I remember that. But, the police looked into it and couldn't prove foul play." Cyrus was sounding sharp as hell today.

"Boswell's running for mayor of Fontana City," said Tommy, back with them again. "I read it in the paper at the barber shop."

"Nobody's sworn him in yet," the Admiral pointed out. He lighted a cigarette and then cracked the window.

"Bet he won't run now, with all that money." This from the Admiral.

"Funny thing," said Cyrus. "Going back to the war days after all this time."

"Yeah, it's right out of the movies. All we need now is Ida Lupino," said Tommy. "Nice blonde, huh? I wonder where she is?"

"On a cloud somewhere," said Cyrus. He laughed. "Remember those old black and white movies?"

"Everybody smoked," said the Admiral. "And wore hats!"

"Hell, Mel," put in Archie, "you could've been a star those days. You and your pressed pants and fedoras."

They talked about their favorite old flicks awhile and then the conversation dropped off.

As the highway drew closer to the water, Archie could almost smell the nearly stagnant pools of lily pads. The blanket of huge scalloped leaves looked thick enough to walk on. A mile or so down the road, the rippling current would spread easily into a wider, clearer channel. Unimpeded by dams and islands, the Mississippi would rush on south, swirling gracefully beneath the rivet-blistered steel bridge at Sandy Hook before gushing past Genesee and down the great gorge toward Louisiana. He watched a trio of sleek black barges slip silently past the bluffs. The pace up here was as slow as smoke on a windless day.

Fontana City, like so many river towns, clung to the side of the bluff like a bunion on a great toe, not terribly important and not very pretty. Archie easily located Preacher Boswell's run-down frame farm house just inside the village limits. The property was undistinguished, except for a red, white, and blue striped mailbox fastened to a length of rusty pipe at the side of the road. A row of drooping sunflowers marked a narrow gravel drive that led to the house set well back from its neighbors. In the rear yard he could see a half dozen fenced animal pens and wooden kennels. As the wagon pulled closer, a chorus of baying hounds broke the silence. According to Sheriff Lemmon, the Preacher raised prize hunting dogs; it seemed to be his sole means of support, outside of a modest inheritance from his parents.

The Old Devils alighted from the wagon, armed with the well-rehearsed story about Archie needing a hound and Lola Spriggs recommending Boswell's kennel to him...before her untimely death. The three of them marched up the porch steps, warped and in need of paint, and Archie rapped on the rickety screen door. They were soon allowed inside the house by Boswell himself, a scruffy man of average height attired in dirty blue overalls and a stained baseball cap, which he wore backward. The house smelled like fried sausage and wet dog.

Preacher Boswell resumed his seat in a fake leather recliner, one of five that ringed the room in front of an oversized television tuned to a wrestling match. Curtainless windows spotlighted a scarred linoleum floor that hadn't been washed in decades. Archie doubted the place had central heating. A brown metal stove sat in a corner. He guessed there was an outdoor privy in back next to the dog pens.

The fastidious Admiral, who was visibly shocked by Lola's beneficiary and his surroundings, seemed wary of sitting on any of the man's flea market (and very possibly flea infested) furniture and so remained standing near the door. Cyrus seemed equally offended by the squalor of the place and seated himself gingerly on a wood bench near the door. Tommy took a seat immediately and eyed Boswell's beer supply on the floor next to his chair.

Archie said he'd heard good things about the Boswell hounds and asked if he had any ready to sell. Boswell said two bitches would be having pups in another week or so, then it would be another two months. He released his dogs at eight weeks, he said. No exceptions. Boswell seemed proud of his animals and the care he gave them. Archie asked if he'd keep on raising dogs now that he'd inherited seven million from Lola Spriggs.

Boswell's face remained expressionless. He reached down and stroked the ears of a great black Labrador who lay at his feet. Then, he started to snicker, a tinny almost feminine titter that caused the Old Devils to take a second look at the man. His dark jowls showed a day's beard; his small dark, deeply set eyes brimmed with cunning or was it evil? Archie couldn't be sure, but he knew he didn't care much for him. "Sure will. I'm runnin' for mayor up here too. I like raisin' dogs. Hell, that woman's no connection to me."

"Are you saying, Mr. Boswell," said Cyrus in a detached businesslike voice, "that this bequest comes as a great surprise to you?"

"Got to be a big mistake, Mister. Like I told the lawyers and the cops, I ain't never heard of this Lola Spriggs woman." Boswell grinned at his guests with a crafty smile, made craftier, Archie thought, by the absence of several teeth, a condition that played well with the frayed overalls and grimy cap compliments of 'Fergie's Tap.'

Did the man really think this was a joke? Archie was thinking. He watched Boswell take a long swig from a can of Budweiser on the floor next to his chair. It was only ten in the morning. He didn't offer his guests any refreshments.

"Here, have a look at her picture," Cyrus said. "She's a good friend of ours. My wife found the body, for God's sake." He leaned forward and handed over a color photo of Lola Spriggs taken that spring at a country club party. Lola had been a beautiful woman, in great contrast to the likes of the Preacher. The Old Devils had failed to see any obvious genetic resemblance between the two, which seemed to confirm Sally's assertion that the Boswells had adopted her 'victory party baby,' as she called him.

Boswell squinted at the likeness as if he needed glasses and then handed it back. "Nope. She ain't no long lost auntie of mine." Then, he thrust out his great barrel chest and belched.

Tired of standing, Melvin Moss finally took a seat in the cleanest of the recliners and crossed one leg over the other, his highly polished loafers so out of place in the spare, neglected parlor that Archie had to smile. Moss said, "Lucky you, you'll still get a share of her estate. Why do you suppose she picked your name out of the hat? Her husband, Durwood, owned a big moving and storage company, Spriggs Cartage and Freight."

Boswell nodded. "Yeah, yellow trucks with black letters. Had one of them toy vans when I was a kid." He patted his dog's snout and then leaned back, letting his distrustful eyes take in his four visitors.

Archie, who'd taken a seat in one of the five Lazy-boys, said, casually, "Hell, Mr. Boswell, maybe you were adopted and didn't know it."

Boswell hadn't anticipated that remark. He blinked nervously, as if to clear his head. "Doubt it. I got baby pictures. My folks woulda told me." Boswell sounded testy and suspicious. "My folks passed on in a barn fire. And I was their only kid."

"Barn fire? Sounds real bad. I'm sorry about that," said Archie. He sniffed a bit, as if smelling a bit of the old smoke.

"Yep. Five year ago. Fire in the barn. Out back."

"How did the fire start?" the Admiral asked kindly.

"Arson, the cops said. Fire trapped the folks inside. Nobody found out who done it." Boswell spoke matter-of-factly and cracked open a fresh beer. "Hell, my pa had a few enemies. Who don't?"

Archie and Cyrus exchanged looks. The Admiral said, "That's right, who doesn't?"

Archie nodded and said, "I bet the cops have been giving you the third degree, huh? About Lola's murder, I mean."

"Hell, the cops check into anybody who gets a fortune like that after a murder," said Cyrus. "Bet you had to have an airtight alibi for that night, don't you?" Cyrus sounded interested in the man and downright chatty.

Preacher Boswell wasn't surprised by this question. He set his face in a polite, emotionless expression and said he'd been listening to Buddy Caspersen's campaign speech at the Baptist Church that night. Caspersen was running against him in the mayor's race, he said. "Buddy and me, neck and neck come November." Boswell shifted his weight in the chair and the vinyl squeaked. "Mayor Figgert's dead. Fell off his boat in Horsehead Slough."

"Sounds like you've got a church-full of witnesses," said Admiral Moss.

Archie thought he was absolutely right. But, he was still having a hard time believing this man would clean up good enough to run for anything. Well, maybe a bus. But, who would vote for this guy? Could be he was real popular with the locals.

"Hell, yes. Then, me and Buddy and the guys hit Fergie's for a few brewskies." Boswell rocked gently in the recliner and focused on Archie, like he might keep his eyes on a brimming bank vault. Archie was his dog customer.

"Did you ever meet Lola's kid, Toby? He's about your age. Maybe he bought a pup from you." This came from Cyrus.

"Hell no," said Boswell. "Never sold no dog to no Spriggs."

Rising, Archie said, "Well, Mr. Boswell, I sure would like to see those nice dogs of yours. Maybe we can figure out how many I'll take…. when they're ready." He crossed the room and opened the front door to the sagging porch, eager to escape.

"Not so fast," Boswell said, getting up from his chair and coming toward Archie, who tensed at the man's abrupt move. "How many hounds you thinkin' about?"

"Two," Archie replied and felt himself relax.

The men left the house and walked around to the rear of the property where the dogs were penned in clean enclosures with large kennels. A huge fenced run nearby was their exercise yard, Archie figured. The dogs lived on a par with their owner…..nothing fancy. Actually, the dog pens looked cleaner than Boswell's living room floor. They discussed the price of pups for a few minutes, while Archie got acquainted with one or two dogs roaming in the yard. He and Boswell came to an agreement and Boswell took Archie's business card.

"When do ya think I might get my money.....from that Spriggs estate?" he asked Archie, as they all walked back to the station wagon out front. "The cops said they didn't know. The lawyers were sneaky about it." Boswell nearly touched Archie's arm.

"I wouldn't know, Mr. Boswell, but usually, estate funds are doled out to the beneficiaries in two or three amounts, until the whole thing is settled. That's all I know."

Cyrus smiled and said, "Settling an estate like Lola's might take awhile. Be patient, Mr. Boswell. You're a lucky man."

Boswell absorbed what was said and said nothing. Whatever the connection between Lola Spriggs and this character out of Faulkner, Archie couldn't imagine. He just knew that a few cool million were about to be thrown away on endless nights at Fergie's Tap. Or, worse.

Archie drew himself up to his full height, which was well over six feet and well over Boswell's head. He extended one great paw and said, "Congratulations, Mr. Boswell. Enjoy your good fortune. Let me know when we can see the pups." He clapped the Preacher on the back in an overly friendly gesture that couldn't be mistaken for genuine affection. Archie didn't believe for a minute that the Preacher was as back woods dumb as he pretended. After all, he was raising some very fine dogs and running for mayor. That took a certain conceit and a certain sense of humor, and, he hoped, a modest intelligence. But, all in all, it was damned hard to admit that one of the Old Devils, with the help of pretty Sally Turk, had sired this hillbilly. Jesus, the mystery of genetics.

Boswell's Everyman's face permitted a wobbly smile. It was the first time during the visit that he appeared vulnerable. Archie was sure that Fontana City's richest inhabitant wasn't quite as cocky now as he had been ten minutes ago. He'd let four outsiders into his house and into his confidence. If Preacher Boswell had anything to do with Lola Spriggs's death, there were four gentlemen from Genesee who had just taken his measure.

After a surprisingly quiet ride back to Belmont, the Old Devils assembled again on Archie's patio for a rehash of their visit with Boswell.

Archie dug out a large jar of peanuts and a bag of chips and passed around the drinks….it was only four o'clock.

"I think he's lying through those awful teeth," said the Admiral. "I don't believe for a minute that he's never heard of Lola Spriggs." The Admiral sat by himself in a large semi-reclined deck chair and sipped his gin. "The Preacher's a killer."

"Nah, you're dead wrong Melvin," put in Tommy, already half-way through a whisky on the rocks. "I didn't see guilt in those piggy eyes, just an eagerness to get the money." He slouched in his spot on an all-weather sofa with a pot of purple petunias sitting at each end. The patio was in full bloom, so to speak. The umbrella table and chairs anchored the other end. "He's had a spot of luck in his life. Good for him." Tommy raised his glass in a toast to the absent millionaire. "Still, I think deep down, Mr. Boswell thinks somebody made a very big error and he'll end up with nothing." Tommy sighed, as if he'd already experienced such an event.

"He did seem mighty interested in selling Arch a couple of hounds. I don't think he'd be that pushy if he thought he might be filthy rich real soon. What do you think, Archie?" Cyrus was stretched out on concrete squares with a pillow beneath his head, one of his favorite positions lately. He said it made his back feel good.

"Frankly, I don't know what to think. We can't condemn the man just because he wears dirty overalls and needs better plumbing for his house." Archie took his time and poured himself a scotch over ice. He took a long swallow. The smoky flavor created an eddy of calm inside him. "After all, our best facts on this come from Sally, and she says Boswell is our 'combo kid,' that's what she calls him. And, he was adopted, fair and square. I can't think of how Boswell would connect himself to Lola Spriggs. Mr. Boswell's real identity should be the best kept secret of the 20th century, for God's sake."

The Old Devils often deferred to Archie; they listened to him again now, willing, as always, to trust his judgment.

"How can a man who loves dogs that much, kill a nice lady like Lola…..the way she was killed. And wrap her up like a mummy?" Tommy spoke softly and sincerely, his melt-in-your-mouth Irish lilt selling the words like a pretty song.

There was a general rumble of concurrence among the boys, except for the Admiral who scowled and insisted that he still didn't like the man's beady eyes. He said Boswell wasn't a man to be trusted. Why couldn't a person like dogs and kill people?

Cyrus said he figured he'd liked more dogs in his life than he had humans. Tommy told him that he'd been hanging around the wrong bars and should try O'Reilly's. No dogs but a lovely clientele. The Admiral kept insisting that the Preacher looked as guilty as Charlie Manson. Archie remained befuddled.

The only thing that was settled among them was a renewed commitment to keeping quiet about the bones in Pike's Wood and the origin of the Preacher. They all agreed that this task was well within their realm of capability. Cyrus suggested that anybody who spilled the beans would be subject to severe penalties......like banishment from the poker kingdom and shunning at the country club. This seemed fair enough.

The old quartet sealed the pact with T-Bone steaks on Archie's new gas grill while polishing off an astounding amount of liquor for four men of retirement age. When Nadine returned from bridge club, she called them a bunch of eighth-graders, her usual comment, and offered them devil's food cake for dessert.

"I've been thinking," Nadine said, speculatively.

"About what?" Betty Hughes asked with the phone clutched to her neck. She was peeling potatoes for dinner. The kitchen was a mess, awash in packing cartons for the big move. But, they still had to eat, and Cyrus wanted fried potatoes.

"About the maid who worked at the Spriggs's place during the war. Sally something."

"Hmmm. Didn't her name come up the other night at your house? Didn't Cyrus call her Betty Grable? You have to wonder what went on those days." Betty Hughes and Nadine were always suspicious of the old days.

"My point exactly. What did go on? Did you notice that picture of Preacher Boswell in the paper yesterday? He's no Robert Redford, but he did look familiar, in an odd sort of way."

"Hang on; the paper's on the table." Betty Hughes put down the potato and the peeler and located the Preacher's photograph on page two. Toothy grin, sharp nose, close set eyes, a low hairline at his forehead. "He looks like a bat," she told Nadine on the other end. "I don't like him. You're right, he is vaguely familiar."

"All I'm saying, Betty Hughes, is that this preacher man might have some connection to that maid, that Betty Grable girl."

"You mean Durwood and the maid might have had it off those days?" Betty Hughes giggled, so did Nadine. "Could be. She was a wild one. Archie, Cyrus, Tommy, even the Admiral used to drool over her."

Betty Hughes sat down on a high kitchen stool and rested her heels on the rungs. "Those tiny eyes do remind me of old Spriggy. Homely old hound dog, wasn't he? And just as mean-spirited. It's a sure thing the Preacher doesn't look like Lola." Betty Hughes readjusted her glasses and took another confirming look. "There's a bit of Spriggs in that face."

"My thoughts exactly." Nadine paused. "I've been thinking about Archie. His behavior lately; he hasn't been himself. You know, restless nights. Acid stomach. Unexplained absences." Nadine cleared her throat. "Don't even bring up Marigold. I'm trying not to think about her. But, what if Archie and the boys know more about Lola's last will and testament than they're telling? What if they know who murdered her?"

"Lordy! Lordy! But, wouldn't Spriggy have bragged to the boys about havin' fun with the maid and the girl comin' up pregnant?"

"My nose tells me there's more to this whole story than meets the eye."

Betty Hughes giggled. Nadine's spin on English! "You mean those beady eyes in the photo?" She took a deep breath. "Cyrus hasn't said a single revealin' thing. He's as hard to read lately as a wrinkled road map." Thinking about Cyrus made her tired.

"Archie's nightmares are back."

"What are we goin' to do about all this, Naddy?"

"Sniff around. Ask discreet questions. Pay attention to everything Archie and Cyrus say on the subject. Maybe have a little chat with

Freddy Donovan. He pretends to know nothing about dead people, but I think he's brighter than we think."

"Freddy and I talk all the time. We're gettin' set for the annual jumble sale at the
church."

"Already?"

"September, Naddy. Just don't mention it to Cyrus. He's wobbly."

"Mum's the word."

7

Tally Ho

On her way to Betty Hughes's tag sale Friday morning, Nina's thoughts drifted back to the years in New Orleans and the dreadful weeks that followed her disengagement from Doctor Howard Rider, the miserable heel. Imagine, requiring a bride of forty-two to produce an heir and never mentioning this rather demanding stipulation until two weeks before the wedding? A colossal nerve. How had she missed this man's monumental self-absorption? Thank goodness she'd fled during the strawberry pie. (He'd made his announcement at dinner.) As the well-off proprietor of an upscale dress shop, Nina had been one of many young beauties thought to be simply sweet and ornamental, rather like potted begonias on the terrace, all leafed out, their pink petals attracting bees and requiring a bit of morning sun and afternoon shade and not too much water. That was how she thought about herself…a fanciful, somewhat silly young woman who circulated in a lovely sheltered society, unaware of the Howards of the world.

The reality of it all had come after nights of tears and disillusionment, and finally a full-blown plate-tossing tantrum when she understood how rude and nasty life could be. Recalling it now, as she drove down the tree-lined streets of Belmont, Nina knew that she must run her own life and do something substantial with it. She would confide in Betty

Hughes, a former beauty queen in Alabama herself, and a good friend. Betty Hughes was becoming a kind of surrogate southern mother, now that Belle was so far away.

"There I sat, season after season," Nina was telling Betty Hughes later that morning. The sun was hanging hot in the sky, and the two were cooling off with tall gin and tonics. A trifle early for a drink, but Betty Hughes figured an early start deserved an early drinkie. A half dozen ladies were picking over the remainders of the Armbrusters' years at Tally Ho, all set out on card tables in the drive. Nina found it sad. She hoped they would not regret the move.

Nina went on. "I was expected to be there, lookin' pretty, just like those damned begonias." Nina wiggled her fingers at the offending flowers on the Armbrusters' patio. "That's the trouble. The expectations were everybody else's." Nina ran a hand through her long blonde hair, perfectly cut and shiny in the light. Her good looks were second nature to her. She rarely thought about how her beauty affected those who saw her. Betty Hughes understood this too.

"Yes, honey, that's the trouble in this old world, when you let other people mind your business for you." Betty Hughes agreed in that sleepy acquiescence so easily brought on by heat and liquor. "You have to go after what you want, sweet pea, on your own." Betty Hughes was beginning to think of Nina as a daughter. "Don't worry about impressin' anybody else. That's how I fell into books. I just write what I please and, lucky for me, the stuff sells like hush puppies." She laughed heartily, still surprised by it all.

"Exactly. Maybe I'd like to be an exotic orchid." (My, what a fine idea.) "I've had it with the Howards and Hugos." Nina gestured expansively and nearly dumped over a bowl of daisies on the table. Betty Hughes barely noticed.

"Have you given up on Hugo? He certainly isn't Mr. Personality, but he is gorgeous and well-off." Betty Hughes grinned like a woman of twenty. "I'd make a play for him myself, if I didn't already have Cyrus." She giggled.

Nina laughed. Betty Hughes could be so bad, rather like Belle. "Dear Hugo," Nina said, "he thinks it's been a big thrill for me to run off to Belmont. Half the time he pays me no mind whatsoever." She wrinkled her nose a little.

"Sounds like Hugo. Right now, he's occupied with the boot business."

"It doesn't matter. I'm movin' ahead on my own. My acting classes are goin' very well. I'm to have a part in one of the plays this fall. My professor likes older women, he said."

"Hah! That's a good one. Older at forty-two. He must be about twenty himself." Betty Hughes laughed.

"No, he's my age. Very mature."

"Tell me more about New Orleans." Betty Hughes fussed a bit with her cash box, resting on the patio table and efficiently took care of three transactions with three customers. Four more women were strolling up the drive, looking eager.

"My calendar for 1987," Nina went on, "was a clone of 1986. Garden parties, Sundayswith Aunt Phoebe and Uncle Otis, meetings at Ma Jolie, my nice dress shop, lunch with salesmen selling over-priced handbags."

"Nice but numbin'. You were burned out, darlin'. You were ready to move on. You must know that whatever you want to do, Cyrus and I will bring you roses." Betty Hughes leaned over and patted Nina's perfectly manicured hand.

Nina smiled gratefully. It was lovely having Betty Hughes to talk to. She said, "On the day I left home, Belle whispered to me that life would be so much nicer if I could find my hidden talent." Nina smiled, remembering. "I figured Belle had drunk too much wine at the goin'-away party. I told her I'd give her advice every consideration. But, findin' a hidden talent at forty-two? A miracle might be easier to pull off."

"Never doubt the possibility, sweet pea."

"I'm about ready to pull out my own roots." Nina sighed. "Just for fun, I asked Hugo if orchids grow in the Upper Mississippi Valley."

"And, he said?"

"We usually rely on geraniums. He didn't get my meanin' at all. He still sees me as a begonia."

"Hugo's the wrong man to ask about orchids, darlin'. Now, let's you and me sell some treasure."

Nadine found the family situation a trifle disconcerting. Hugo and Nina, a young woman of considerably more depth than was first thought, were firmly planted on the marriage fence from what she could figure out. No date was set. No plans were ever mentioned. Very odd. Very odd, indeed. For one thing, Nina had insisted upon her own apartment from the moment she'd set eyes on Hugo's steel and glass house perched like an ice cube in the bluffs. Nadine and Betty Hughes found this refreshing….an independent woman of taste. A welcome addition to any family.

Now, of course, Miss Nina was often seen around town with O'Neill Spender, a shy fellow way over his head with a beauty like Nina, and, even more disconcerting, And, to make Nadine's mood darker, Miss Nina was spending an inordinate amount of time with Archie, who was more than happy to run around town with a pretty blonde. Did Miss Nina know what a stinker Archie could be?

To make matters worse, Nina was now openly miffed at Hugo. Rumor had it that she suspected him of horsing around with another woman. Belle Dupree, hoping to forestall any wedding difficulties of a technical nature, had offered to come up to make all the wedding arrangements. She had promised her daughter to have the entire three-ring circus ready in a week, a feat without equal, Nadine told Betty Hughes, who simply nodded and pointed out that Southern women can do that sort of thing in their sleep.

In the weeks that followed Nina's entrance into Genesee society, Nina had let her mother know that life with Hugo was not a situation comedy. She had told Nadine as much at a dull meeting of the Genesee Music Society. Just last week, she had hinted that Hugo might find her more fascinating if she were a parka. Nadine suggested she wear one to bed with nothing on underneath. That would get Hugo's attention. Nina had laughed and confessed great surprise at Nadine's sophisticated view of sex. Betty Hughes remarked that the conversation certainly made the music society meeting more interesting than usual.

"Gals should have their own domain," Betty Hughes explained in between rushes of tag sale patrons. "Look at your own Daddy. Beau Dupree played half back for the Detroit Lions for twelve years and now he has his gourmet cookie business. Belle manages her theatre. Two people. Two worlds. They see each other at breakfast and supper. In between, he's prime minister of Mr. Cookie and she's prime minister of Bright Lights. Same with Cyrus and me.....he had the newspaper; I write my novels."

Nina agreed and told Betty Hughes that she was working on her own domain in the theatre. According to Betty Hughes, Nadine continued to brood about her son.....his neuroses, his horror of clutter and dust mites, his tight grip on a dollar. He was so dreary compared to Archie. Nina confessed to Betty Hughes that men like Hugo were so simple that women had to make them complicated, just to survive their company. Maybe that was the trouble. Nina had made Hugo complicated. Hugo was like his house, a cold, efficient structure possessing little personality or warmth. When you peeked inside, not much was there.

So, there Nina sat. A woman of forty-two in a new part of the country, crouched at a cross roads, saddled with a boring fiancé, no particular career at the moment, little interest in charity work or cooking lessons, and no place to go. She'd already run away from home. Nadine and Betty Hughes felt sorry for the girl. Betty Hughes said it would be a shame if she lost that lovely Tiffany engagement ring...surely Hugo would want it back if she cancelled the wedding. Nadine said it would be hard on Tiffany's too...Hugo would definitely want his money back.

"I hear," Donovan started out, "come Valentine's Day that Archie's son will march down the aisle with Nina Dupree. It's sure taking him long enough." Donovan swigged from his mug of Pfeiffers; he could feel a chalk line of foam cling to his whiskers. "I should ticket him for loitering." He grinned.

"I'm beginning to have my doubts, Freddy. Sounds like the wedding is teetering on the brink of extinction. That pathetic middle-aged parka salesman!" Betty Hughes pulled up a chair and sat down as if she hadn't in a long time. Billy's was crowded. Must be the heat.

"Ooh, let's keep this politically correct. Boring, fortyish, sportswear executive. How's that?" Donovan smiled sympathetically.

"Very civil, sweetheart." Betty Hughes's pale skin grew pink and she drank thirstily. She had agreed to meet Donovan at Billy's, bad mood or not. The old dive was such a dump, but a half hour with Freddy should turn her around. "How's the cop business?"

"Still sloshing through the Spriggs case and taking a look at the skeleton case with Charlie."

"Sounds tedious today." Betty Hughes pretended to brush off the demands on Freddy's time and talent."Gettin' back to me." She grinned alluringly. "As if Lola's death isn't bad enough, I now have amateur competition to deal with…right here in Genesee." She rapped her knuckles against the table top.

"Competition for what?"

"Marigold Woolsey, as if you didn't know. Cyrus tells you everythin' on the golf course." Her husband and Freddy tolerated each other at the Birch Hills Country Club every week. "The great sculptress is scribblin' a play for the Ashbury College competition. Blast the woman! I'm enterin' that contest this year….for my theatre debut!"

"Oh, yes. I did hear about that." Freddy laughed.

"What is so amusin'?"

Freddy grinned and said, "You're terrible, Betty Hughes. Worse than my mother!"

"Hah! Your mama's Irish. That's even better than bein' from Alabama." They both giggled at that. "And, to make matters worse, that sherbet-haired hussy's seducin' my agent. O'Neill has turned to puddin' since he met her."

Donovan reached across the square, wobbly table and patted her hand. "Now, now, let's not get carried away. Miss Marigold's a very nice lady. I've met her." Donovan didn't quite understand what exactly lay behind the feud between Betty Hughes and Marigold and Nadine, for that matter. He figured he'd pry it out of one of them soon enough. "She is a babe. I'll give her that. A genuine babe." Donovan sat back in his chair and grinned through his whiskers.

With her free hand, Betty Hughes plucked a pack of cigarettes from her purse, which caused Donovan to sink back in his chair with his mouth agape.

"Not one word from you, young man. Not one single word. I've regressed; no argument there. I'm no better than you and those stinky cigars."

Donovan said nothing but watched his friend light up for the first time in five years.

"I have my reasons.….. Marigold's back in town, the damned play contest is loomin', a very colorful batch of losses on the stock market, our up and comin' departure from beloved Tally Ho! And, I own ten pounds around my equator I don't need, and darlin' Cyrus is treadin' the crooked path into senility. It's amateur night in the asylum, Freddy." Betty Hughes alternately smoked and coughed while Donovan kept his mouth shut. "Plus! My mother's comin' for a visit in the near future, and she's bringin' her maid, India, with her!"

"I've never met your mama or her maid," Donovan pointed out. "I'll be looking forward to meeting both of them after hearing all your stories about them. We'll bring them here to Billy's." The Irishman grinned.

Betty Hughes laughed at this. "My mama wouldn't step foot in this place, Freddy Donovan. We'll have to drive her over to Augusta for some fine dinin'.…..and that won't be good enough. My mama's difficult. And, Missy India is a woman right out of William Faulkner, honey. Positively Hollywood bound! Why do you suppose I live in Belmont?" She took another puff of cigarette and coughed again.

"Ah, the evils of smoking, darlin' girl. But, do I look like a man who would chastise you for lapsing? Would I ever bring this up at a later date? Would I ever remind you of the number of cigars I've thrown out car windows because of your sensitive nose?" Donovan raised his luxurious eyebrows in mock bewilderment and slipped the wrapper from a fresh cheroot.

"I knew I'd regret this." The regulars were snickering behind their beers. They eavesdropped like children.

The bar's only waiter, Billy's nephew, who would surely be in reform school if his uncle didn't keep him employed, strolled over and asked for their order. His sullen thin face told them how much he loved his work. Donovan ordered the usual for both of them, and the kid sauntered away as if walking too fast might loosen his earring.

"And, I don't think you're fat, just to keep the record straight on that point. And you know I never comment on what your mother is up to, unless it's criminal."

"Thank you very much."

"And, frankly, your agent could use a little seduction. Miss Marigold could seduce me any day." Donovan pulled open a bag of sour cream chips. "Why do you give a damn about that play competition anyway? You have a boat load of hits on the shelf."

"Well, every knuckle-head with eight fingers and two thumbs and a computer is writin' TV scripts, novels, and How To books. Big deal. O'Neill says Marigold's little three-act play is damned good!" Betty Hughes looked stricken. "What if I lose?" She squashed the cigarette into the ashtray. "Isn't losin' Cyrus to old age bad enough?"

"You aren't losing Cyrus. He's just having a few bad days now and then. We all forget our glasses and wonder who's in the White House once in a while."

"You think I'm jealous of Marigold, don't you? Just like Nadine."

"Jealousy's like poison. Almost as wicked as too much money." Donovan ripped open a second bag of chips and pushed it over to Betty Hughes. "Maybe you're pissed off because Marigold had upset the tempo around here. Changed the equilibrium." He offered this casually, almost nonchalantly, so as not to sound too preachy. But Freddy Donovan wasn't deaf, dumb and blind. He'd heard about the fuss Marigold and her poet hubby had raised among the Old Devils and their wives.

"Well, maybe a little pissed." Betty Hughes grinned over the rim of her beer glass.

Donovan gave her a benign smirk and congratulated himself on hitting the jackpot. Age had nothing to do with growing up.

"Want to hear my troubles now?" The cop rocked back on his chair and then swung forward and leaned toward Betty Hughes. "We can't find Preacher Boswell. Keep that under your wig, my girl."

"Can't find him? Where did you put him? I thought you just questioned him."

"We did. Told him about the will and the money. He's our chief suspect in Lola's murder, and now, he's gone...like spit in the wind."

"Probably fell out of his rowboat. Those gentlemen up river don't do a thing except fish and drink."

"Boswell's running for mayor. Special election in November. Believe it or not, Mayor Figgert did fall out of his boat a while back. Remember?"

"Foul play by another candidate?" Betty Hughes sampled the chips.

"Not a trace."

"The Preacher'll wash ashore on French Island in a few days. It's happened before."

"MacArthur, he ain't."

Billy's nephew delivered split brats on chewy buns and two more mugs of beer.

Betty Hughes sat up straight in her chair and said, "Before we dig in, I have an announcement."

Donovan cringed. Jesus, women were so damned unpredictable. This could be anything from a fatal disease to a win on the lottery.

"This is goin' to be my last brat, Frederick. It might be the best sausage God ever created, but it's the last one. Do you hear me, boy?"

"You're dying of something, aren't you?" Donovan wasn't sure he could breathe.

Betty Hughes howled. "Not at this moment, darlin'."

Donovan looked enormously relieved and took a huge bite of his lunch. "Then, have you taken leave of your senses, my girl?" A dribble of ketchup slithered down the front of his shirt, already decorated with remnants of pancake syrup. "A new starvation diet?" He'd survived many of her maximum security diets. She always came back to normal.

"I'm serious this time, Freddy. It's low fat all the way. I've been readin' up on diets. We need fiber and lots of water. We're killin' ourselves with Billy burgers and Billy brats." She poured ketchup over the sausage and rearranged the onions. "From now on it's healthy twigs and vegetables from the cabbage family. It's California cuisine."

"Ah, you've been to the doc, and he's trying to scare you." Donovan nodded knowingly. "My doc's been trying to convince me that bacon's bad. I told him my sainted mother still eats bacon fat sandwiches and she's older than God."

Betty Hughes grinned. "A foreign discipline to junk food addicts like you and me, but it's time to change. And don't even bring up lung cancer."

Donovan saw a serious glint in the blue eyes peering at him over of top of the sandwich. Above the eyes, the familiar swarm of marmalade

colored curls around an angelic face. He dearly loved Betty Hughes....
rather like an auntie or a second mother or an older sister. It was a
condition in his life he accepted as normal, like having a small space
between his front teeth.

Betty Hughes was saying, "From now on, Freddy, when you dine
at the Armbruster establishment, you'll think you've died and gone to
Napa Valley."

"Ah, hell, Betty Hughes, we always think we're going to die when we
eat at your house." As he bellowed at his own humor, Donovan ducked
the book of matches that flew at him across the table. The regulars were
having a grand time.

"Getting' back to business, why would Preacher Boswell kill the
goose that laid the golden egg and then disappear before gatherin' up
his nuggets?"

"Maybe Boswell isn't our killer. Maybe the killer got rid of Boswell
to get all the money for himself." Donovan winked.

"You think Lola's boy got rid of him?"

Betty Hughes knew Toby Spriggs; who didn't? He was a grown
man who still struck poses for attention. The silly boy wore braces AND
a belt to keep up his trousers. Betty Hughes dismissed him as silly and
immature.

"Could be. Trouble is Toby has a powerful alibi. It was book club
night for Mr. Toby and his Ashbury pals." Donovan sighed. "Maybe
it's river town politics. Maybe, Boswell is floating down river to French
Island because somebody in Sandy Hook would rather see him dead
than see him elected mayor."

Betty Hughes dabbed her mouth with a paper napkin and sat back,
leaving half the sausage uneaten. "What have you got against this
Preacher man? How about a greasy thumbprint on the lampshade he
stuck on Miss Lola's head?"

"Nothing. The lab has samples of fiber and dirt taken from his
clothing and house. We haven't a single witness who ever saw the man
at Lola's place." Donovan cleaned up his fingers and patted his stomach
contentedly. "All I have is a gut feeling."

"The judge won't like that."

"Could be Lola was rewarding Preacher Boswell for years of silence. Or, for a deed well done." Donovan sounded positive about this theory.

"Maybe Boswell bumped off somebody for Lola, or for Spriggy, when he was alive. Maybe he buried a body for Lola's husband. Occasionally, a person with the bucks gets himself into a sorry mess and hires a flunky to it clean up." Betty Hughes liked this scenario. "I think Mr. Boswell looks a bit like Durwood Spriggs."

Donovan thought this over quietly. "Could be, now that you mention it. But, he doesn't know the Spriggs family."

The two finished their lunch.

"It's just an observation, Freddy. I must toddle along." Betty Hughes stood and pushed back her chair. "If I get a flash, I'll call you." She grabbed the tab. "My treat."

Bill paid, the two stepped into the impeccable afternoon light and river-perfumed air. Donovan longed for the more crystalline breezes of November and December. Winter always beat the hell out of summer and hot autumns. He detested heat, especially along the Mississippi…. mosquitoes, damp, bugs, muggy air, bugs, bats, river stink, more mosquitoes, heat, and more bugs. The first hard frost would make him a truly happy man.

The lunch crowd populated the sidewalks. Next door, at the Downtown Diner, the window tables were filled. The special of the day was corned beef hash and organic cherry pie.

"Tomorrow, we try this place," Betty Hughes declared, pointing to the diner. "I hear they serve a great chef's salad with bran muffins."

Donovan grunted and told himself to hold on. Bran muffins would soon go the way of the wheat germ on cottage cheese. They'd be back at Billy's by Thanksgiving. He was a patient man.

Archie was reading the paper with a second cup of coffee when Nadine sailed into the room with purpose written all over her face. What now? He was living with one woman, seriously dreaming about another, and he sensed he was headed for big trouble. The earth might be revolving on its axis, but the axis was a trifle bent these days.

"What is it, Naddy?" His wife on a mission was frightening.

"Do you remember that girl who worked for the Spriggs family when you and the boys were in the war? Sally something? The one Cyrus always calls Betty Grable?"

"Ahhh, ahhh," he stammered. "Yes, I think I do. A maid. Yes, a maid." Archie's heart was clicking along at record speed.

"Betty Hughes and I think she's connected to this awful creature, Preacher Boswell, the man who inherited Lola's money and very likely killed her for it." Nadine stood in place like a conservatively dressed totem pole.

"Hell's bells, how did you arrive at that?"

"We think she had an affair with Durwood during the war, had a child and the child is this Preacher Boswell." Nadine sounded so sure of herself that Archie was hard-pressed not to agree with her.

"Who can prove that?"

"Probably no one, except the woman herself. If she's still around. But, who needs proof? We're just trying to figure out why Lola gave millions to a man she didn't know. A man like Preacher Boswell. Logic and detective work, my dear." Nadine was proud of their deductions.

"You and Betty Hughes read too many mysteries." An excuse maybe, but Archie couldn't deny what she was saying, except that he knew more about it than she did. There was no mention of Turk's body unearthed in Pike's Wood. Apparently logic and detective work had not taken his wife and Betty Hughes in that direction at this point. They had not connected the Spriggs murder with the old bones. There was still time to cut them off at the pass, so to speak.

"What are you going to do about this?" Archie asked nervously.

"We thought we'd mention it to the Admiral and Cyrus and dear Tommy. See if they remember anything. If you take a good look at Boswell's photograph in the newspapers, Archie, you'll see that Mr. Boswell looks a lot like Durwood." Nadine fluttered a back issue of the local weekly in front of him, the paper turned to a large picture of Boswell, smiling, his bad teeth lined up like so many stained crooked pegs. Archie pushed the paper away as if it smelled.

"Jesus, Nadine," Archie exploded, bouncing out of his chair, "don't go bothering Cyrus with this! He's too unsteady these days. And the Admiral? What would he know? He was never close to Durwood anyway. Besides, he's a babe in the woods about such things." Archie experienced a clear sense of doom.

"Don't be silly. How can a few questions hurt?" And Nadine rushed off to answer the telephone.

"If there were any adoption records or birth records, they were destroyed in the fire some thirty years ago," said Betty Hughes, who was letting Nadine in on the latest during their Wednesday workout at Shirley's Fitness Center. "My friend in the records department at city hall knows all of this history. She's a buff."

"You mean the Crawford County Courthouse fire." Nadine held her index finger up to her lips to remind Betty Hughes that one or two ladies nearby were eager to listen in.

"The very one. Burned to the ground in '56 and took its records with it." Betty Hughes concentrated a minute on balancing face down on a large inflated ball. Nadine told her she looked like a bad, middle-aged circus performer, who would be out of work soon. Betty Hughes suggested she work on her thighs.

"What about local hospitals?" Nadine asked, as she peddled an imaginary bicycle while lying on her back. "I feel like a dog chasing its tail. Are we getting anywhere?"

"I'm not sure, but I'm not givin' up. That Boswell is connected to Lola somehow. If he is adopted, the mother could have used a different name. Or maybe she went out of state to have the baby."

"He must have known somebody in that Spriggs family. He knew he'd inherit and killed for the money. What other motive is there?"

"Or, the Preacher is a Spriggs?" Betty Hughes liked this theory the most. "The snooty Spriggs family has been hidin' a rogue Preacher among its ancestral snapshots. I love it! This is something I'd cook up for one of my books." She began trying to rotate a small inflated ball with her feet while lying on her back. It wasn't going well.

"Are we sure we're wandering down the right path?"

"Pure speculation, but that's the best kind."

Nadine raised an eyebrow while she lifted two five pound weights up and down. "We could ask Isobel to reach into her vault of gossip. Over the years she's made other people's business her business. She'd come up with a few randy facts." She grinned. "The bridge club could cover a lot of territory during the shuffle and deal."

"I'm afraid to drag Isobel Woolsey into this. She'll want to be the general in a couple of weeks." Betty Hughes looked pained. "We don't have women like Isobel in my family. For guidance, we always rely on the rosary, Father O'Malley, or my Aunt Camilla Rose."

"Well, it's time the girls were running the show. We have the smarts; and we can talk and pour coffee at the same time. No male animal can do that."

"True enough, Naddy, but, first things first. We'll rule the world after we figure out who killed Lola. I'm sayin' the Preacher might have been given up for adoption and Mr. and Mrs. Boswell, now deceased…. and suspiciously deceased, I might add,….were the fortunate couple to get this charmin' boy child…..with the beady eyes."

"So, what you have is what you don't have. Not a tire track, not a fiber, not a hair,

not so much as a microscopic smear of dog doo from his shoes on Lola's carpet. That's what Freddy Donovan told Archie last time they went fishing." Nadine was sitting on her mat with a towel around her neck, fed up with exercises and homicide investigations.

"Not so much as a chewed cigar butt in the hedge," Betty Hughes added. She sat down next to Nadine and breathed deeply. "Freddy confides in me on the golf course."

"How about Boswell's pals at Fergie's Tap? Pour enough beer into those bozos and I bet one of them would cough up a tidbit or two about the Preacher. Like….how much he's going to spend on some female he's dying to impress. He's no monk. He'll throw the money around….he'll play the big shot."

"Freddy should send a couple of his officers up there, dressed like hunters or beer salesmen, just passing through town."

"Good idea. I'm wondering if Mr. Boswell set that barn on fire…. the quickest way he knew how to get his family's money. Went through that and then killed poor Lola for some more. Our Mr. Boswell's been alive for two interesting conflagrations in his life…the courthouse and his papa's barn. Add that to one breathtaking inheritance and you've got yourself one quite possibly clever character who may not bathe too often but still knows the value of a dollar."

Betty Hughes nodded appreciatively, the way she always did when Naddy let her mind work in its usual convoluted manner. "But, we still don't have the Spriggs/Boswell connection nailed down."

Nadine got up, folded up her mat and headed for the showers. "You would think Freddy Donovan could help us out a bit, wouldn't you?"

"You would think."

8

Maiden Voyages

The following Monday morning was perfect. No rain to ruin the slipcovers or mud to track up the carpets. Cyrus had volunteered to wash out the sinks in the upstairs bathrooms, but Betty Hughes doubted he'd remember. At the tag sale she'd found him sitting on the floor of the closet reading old New Yorkers and tearing off the covers he liked. He said he wanted his bedroom papered with New Yorker covers. Betty Hughes was reminded of their son when he was five, cutting out pictures of trucks and steam shovels from the yellow pages. To add to the general merriment of moving, Marigold stopped by for a quick peek at the house on departure day.

"We made two thousand on the garage sale," declared Betty Hughes as she tossed Tupperware tubs of leftovers into a black garbage bag. "Nothin' but a lot of old junk. People will buy any ol' thing." She laughed and pulled more bottles and jars from the refrigerator. She glanced in Marigold's direction, but the aging temptress didn't seem interested in the financial report. As the new mistress of Tallyho, Marigold had other things on her mind.

Movers in gray coveralls with their names embroidered in red thread on their chest pockets were clumping in and out the front door with cartons and furniture. One young man with a body builder's physique picked up a heavy upholstered chair and carried it above his head like a sack of flour. Marigold pointed him out to Betty Hughes and admired his muscles. Betty Hughes sighed and said they were too old to notice firm young men. Marigold kept looking.

Standing there in the Armbrusters' nearly empty kitchen, Marigold ran her eyes over the old wallpaper patterned with pots of ivy and sighed a bit. Betty Hughes was aware that the place needed sprucing up; she just didn't have the time. Writing books and watching Cyrus was a full time proposition these days. Marigold said, "I think I'll hire an artist to do up the entire place like a Tuscan villa."

Betty Hughes stopped what she was doing. "A Tuscan Villa?"

Marigold was warming to her idea, Betty Hughes could tell. The woman was opening and closing doors, examining the woodwork. "I can see the plaster walls subtly painted with scenes of swaying cypress and ancient ruins in the Italian hills," she said in what Betty Hughes called her sexy Thespian voice....half Greer Garson and half Mae West. She fingered the half dozen gold chains around her neck and wandered off into the dining room, letting the swinging door thunk back and forth behind her. Betty Hughes decided to follow along on the tour.

As Marigold surveyed the large square room which was naturally lighted by tall French windows, Betty Hughes took a last look at her broad stone terrace with the magnificent crescent shaped flower beds further out into the lawn. She would miss the garden. She would miss it all.

"I'm envisioning our maiden dinner party, Betty Hughes." Marigold swept her arm about the air dramatically. "A dozen guests around an enormous Italian marble table due to arrive from New York any day. Archie will be seated on my left, that naughty painter from the college, on my right. I must do a sculpture of him one day. Nude, of course. Men rarely refused me. And, that gorgeous Hugo Beresford." Marigold stopped to hug herself. Betty Hughes didn't know how much more of this she could take. But, Marigold was hurrying on. "I'll have Nadine at the far end. She's so judgmental. Out of earshot and next to Isobel....still lovely but such a bitch!" Marigold laughed. "You, dear Betty Hughes, will preside at mid-table where you can stimulate conversation."

Betty Hughes didn't respond. Marigold was in another world, going over her bouquet of guests. Would Meadowlark dinners be this thrilling and beautifully orchestrated?

Two hours later, as the moving van pulled away from the curb, Parnell arrived with a bottle of champagne and four glasses concealed beneath his cape. He was wearing a bright blue beret and riding boots. They would toast the Armbrusters' departure, he commanded, and wish them well in their new life at Meadowlark Village.

Betty Hughes took her glass eagerly; it had been a grueling day and she needed a drink. Cyrus was more subdued; he was missing his old house already, Betty Hughes could tell.

"Cyrus, darling," Marigold cooed gently, "you may visit any time you wish." She put her arm around his shoulders and kissed his cheek. He smiled gratefully at the old vixen. Betty Hughes wanted to push the Queen of Tuscany down the stairs.

"Don't worry, Marigold," Betty Hughes interjected quickly, "we won't be botherin' you. I plan to keep Cyrus very busy…..bridge, golf, woodworkin'. We're bound to make a horde of new friends." Her smile was deliberately disingenuous.

Marigold bristled slightly but said nothing.

Parnell, more pale and fragile than ever and more preoccupied, grew suddenly alert and said, "Cyrus, my good man, you might consider starting a retirement village newspaper." He placed one finger to his temple and added excitedly, *The Meadowlark Chronicles.*"

Cyrus nodded, as if thinking it over.

"I would be pleased to contribute the occasional verse or poignant piece of nostalgia," said Parnell. His slender hands, brown spotted now, fluttered nervously about a silk ascot looped around his neck.

Betty Hughes groaned. "Yes, Parnell, that's what we need, Cyrus at the helm of the Meadowlark Chronicles." She made the name of the imaginary newspaper sound like a high school publication. "Half the time he can't find his glasses and the other half he doesn't know why he needs them."

Parnell looked pained, which he did very well. Betty Hughes liked to say that Parnell had been playing the pained, deprived poet for over forty years….he damned well should be good at it. No one ever bought the act, especially after visiting the Grants at some spectacular villa on the Riviera.

"We're none of us twenty anymore," Marigold replied briskly. "A bit of memory loss, a little equipment failure here and there. Surely, Betty Hughes, you must be close to sixty-five, aren't you, dear?" Marigold poured more bubbly and smiled sweetly.

That was the last straw. Without saying a word, Betty Hughes marched off to check on the rooms upstairs. She took her champagne with her. Cyrus could say the good-byes.

After Parnell and Marigold departed for their rooms at the St. George Hotel downtown, Cyrus walked outside into the pinkish light of early evening. He wanted a last look around. The elderly maple in the front yard would be spilling its heavy carrot foliage without him. His favorite, the burning bushes, would show off their rouged cheeks and he wouldn't be here to see it. The crab apples bending with feasting robins and cardinals would...he couldn't go on.

Glancing back at his house, its bleached stone tinted by the long arms of sun, wavy panes glinting like ancient silvered mirrors, Cyrus experienced the first stabs of terror. He'd spent over thirty years here. He had purchased Tallyho two years after coming to work at the *TRIBUNE*. Betty Hughes's father loaned him the additional money they needed for such a grand place. Betty Hughes always insisted that it was smart to live well and a little beyond your means. It would keep them on track. Cyrus supposed she was right. His life had always clicked right along with few pitfalls or pratfalls. They had led a charmed existence filled with power, prestige, money, and two intelligent sons. And, he'd played a respectable game of golf. Until lately.

Cyrus stood in the shadows and couldn't feel the magic anymore. He tried to remember playing golf. He couldn't. Golf. What the hell was golf?

He lowered himself to the sidewalk and focused on the bare windows, about as comforting as dead eyes. Tears trickled down his smooth cheeks. He would miss the tomatoes and hollyhocks in the kitchen garden. Beans so fresh they actually snapped. And roses. Where would he grow roses?

By the time Betty Hughes found him, he was sobbing like a child, sputtering about his dog and the place in his head where asparagus grew. Cyrus had confessed months ago that his head was divided into six compartments, each outfitted for specific tasks. One was a huge clay pot used exclusively for growing asparagus. Betty Hughes told Dr. Edmunds this in private a week ago. The doctor had just wobbled his head as if just as befogged as his patient.

"The dog died ten years ago, Cyrus. Now, get up from the sidewalk. Archie will be here any minute. Do you want him to see you crying?" Betty Hughes helped him to his feet and prayed the neighbors were eating dinner. Cyrus was still going on about the chocolate lab named Godiva when Archie pulled into the drive.

Archie and Betty Hughes maneuvered Cyrus into the back seat of the black sedan and put the suitcases into the trunk. Cyrus said the car looked like a short hearse and asked if they were going to a funeral. Archie smiled. As they pulled away from the house, Archie reminded Cyrus that they were on their way to Meadowlark and a new life. "Pretty exciting, huh?" he remarked brightly. Betty Hughes knew that Archie was near tears too.

"About as exciting as taking a piss in church," Cyrus replied quite happily. "Who the hell is driving the car?"

"I'm off to the Sudan!" exclaimed Parnell Grant over the phone. His voice had a lighthearted, youthful ring to it, even at this early hour. "Wouldn't you love to say that just once in your life? Before kicking off? And, then pick up your bag and hop into a taxi?"

"The Sudan?" his friend answered hesitantly. He knew Parnell was moving into Cyrus's old place. What was this stuff about Africa? "Damned hot there, you know. Lots of natives. Rebellions and uprisings. And crocodiles, I think. Wouldn't you rather go to Paris, Parney?"

Parnell sighed, not quite audibly. "You've missed the point, old boy. Badly put, I suppose. It's only a dream, my lad, only a dream. I woke up this morning and thought that I would just have to say it once," he explained quietly. "Out loud. To someone."

After several days of vigorous telephone negotiations, Hugo finally persuaded Miranda Burke to meet him at Greensleeves, a popular roadhouse outside of Augusta. With his head filled with Cat Woman fantasies, Hugo was perhaps the only soul in town not fixated on Lola Spriggs's bizarre murder and the mystery of the Pike's Wood bones.

Hugo arrived early at the restaurant and ordered a brandy Manhattan. He took it to a back booth with a clear view of the door. Greensleeves enjoyed a notorious history, one reason for its existence. During Prohibition an English sheep farmer who owned the old house cooked bootleg liquor in his barn for Chicago mobsters who trucked it off in the dead of night. Unfortunately, the entrepreneurial farmer ended his lucrative booze business by accidentally blowing up the still with a carelessly thrown match. The explosion and fire were seen and heard for miles. With time, the old house grew wings and gables and became a kind of Bonnie and Clyde inn with creaky floors, dim lights, and a reputation for keeping its guest list secret. Hugo didn't much care for the place, but Miranda wanted to meet there.

Alternately sipping his drink and smoothing his hair, Hugo waited with some impatience. As usual, Miranda was late. As he touched his hair a third time, he reminded himself that it was good he had hair to smooth. A lot of guys his age were getting sparse and were resorting to creams and transplants. Hair aside, Hugo was jittery. What if someone spotted him with Miranda? Rumors flew like poison arrows in small towns. How could he explain a rendezvous with the *Tribune*'s political reporter? His alliance with Nina was all but over, but there were days when he wondered if he could revive it. After all, she was beautiful and well-off. He could always see Miranda on the sly. He liked to think his life needed some drama.

To be on the safe side, Hugo edged another inch closer to the inside of the booth. Fooling around was always risky….he'd always professed fidelity and loyalty to the woman he was currently taking to bed, unlike his father who collected women like stray coins. Of course, he'd always made room for an exception here and there. But, Miranda seemed to be forcing him in this direction, and Nina certainly wasn't as friendly as she'd been in New Orleans. Downright hostile since that damned costume party.

Had Archie met Marigold Woolsey here in the old days? It was hard to accept one's father as an adulterer, Hugo had to confess, even to oneself. (He slipped easily into his stuffy third person again; his brain was used to it.) Had his mother known? Maybe Nadine didn't care. She didn't seem to be a sexual person, an odd but normal thought, he supposed, to have about one's mother.

The bar had welcomed few patrons at this early hour. The bartender, a young nice-looking man, was hitting on a cute blonde twice his age. She was sipping white wine and looking eager. Hugo decided that the brandy was giving him a buzz, and as he nibbled pretzels, his mind wandered off to England where Prince Charles was having his difficulties with Princess Diana. The press hounded the couple as if they were movie stars....who wouldn't have trouble with a pack of wolves nipping at your heels every time you opened your front door? Supposedly, the royal couple rarely saw each other and didn't touch in public. Was that a House of Windsor standard or was Charles just sick of his wife? Their tribulations reminded Hugo of his weeks with Nina. Their initial rush of passion had all but died. Hugo occasionally felt helpless and sad about it, but his work and dreams of Miranda had soothed the pain most days.

Hugo was gloomily playing with a damp cocktail napkin when he finally spotted Miranda swing through the door. A sensation close to a Ferris wheel rush shot through him. God, she was fabulous. He slid from the booth and waved her to him.

"So good to see you again, Hugo." Miranda gave him a light, sisterly kiss on the cheek. She was nearly as tall as he.

Miranda's flowery scent triggered a boyish giddiness. Grinning, Hugo helped with her coat and mumbled something about feeling like he did in college.

Miranda said, "I'll have a double Beefeaters on the rocks, and the soft cheese and crackers they serve at the bar." Then, she slipped into the booth on the opposite side and folded her hands in front of her like a teacher waiting for class to come to order.

Hugo felt an immediate pang of regret. Had she misinterpreted his invitation? Or had she come simply to torment him? He beckoned the waitress and gave her the order. He did worry a little about Miranda's reliance on gin. Archie had casually suggested that the woman might have a serious alcohol problem. Hugo refused to believe that.

Miranda was amused. She'd probably noticed his nerves. Damn the woman. But, what did he expect? Look at her. The Hedy Lamar of the eighties. Hair like old sherry, hazel eyes to match, and legs he dared not think about.

"You look marvelous," he told her.

"Thanks. Fifteen years older and a hundred years wiser. Who said that?"

"Probably my grandmother. She was full of such nonsense." Hugo laughed. The waitress delivered their order. "She's dead now, of course," he added foolishly. Not the right path, old man, discussing dead grandmothers! He quickly said, "Tell me about your job. I hear you won the Pulitzer a couple years ago."

"Yes. Great story. A research project on the immune system. At the university." Miranda leaned back, at ease, obviously pleased to have Hugo's attention.

"I admire anyone who can write or paint or play an instrument. Much more so than chaps like me, who run factories and make money." Hugo hoped he didn't sound too self-deprecatory; he was sincere. Miranda would see through false modesty. Spreading cheddar on a cracker, he offered it to her.

Miranda ate the cracker hungrily. "Delicious. Come now, you used to paint. Rather well, too." Miranda smiled sweetly at him, like in the old days.

Hugo beamed at Miranda's recollection of his long forgotten artistic talent. "Haven't smelled cadmium red in years. We must see the latest show at the Ashbury gallery. You remember Harry Freese, don't you?" He made it sound as though Miranda had been away. The waitress acknowledged his wave.

"Yes, I know Harry."

Miranda's half smile bore traces of mockery. Had the lecherous Harry Freese coaxed her into his loft studio bed? Hugo had heard stories about Miranda's excesses. And who didn't know about Harry's passion for conquests? The artist's famous father had come to town recently, a New York actor eager to try regional theatre, he'd heard. Christ, two Freeses in the same territory.

Hugo said, "I suppose I could sign up for lessons with Harry. He takes on private students." Hugo didn't like the way that came out and began fussing with the cheese and crackers again.

Miranda laughed shamelessly at him. Hugo colored and hoped the flush didn't show in the dim light. "Hugo, you're such a babe in the wood….for a man who routinely seduces women. And, don't deny it. You're just like dear old dad."

"You're downright cruel, Miranda." Good thing he was as old as he was. Fifteen years ago, that little dig would have crushed him.

Miranda sighed and asked him about his new endeavor, running the sportswear empire. Hugo said it was going smoothly. In New Orleans, he told her, he'd operated a spice and hot sauce company. They laughed at this, and Hugo reached for Miranda's hand. She almost pulled away but then allowed him to take it.

Hugo recalled Miranda's in-bred cynicism about wedlock, a contract that allowed a generous latitude when it came to other women's husbands and lovers. All's fair in love, war and the newspaper business. That was her credo.

"Tell me about Nina. She's very pretty." Miranda sounded gracious.

Hugo knew that the two women met at the costume party. It was generally believed by his male and female friends that Nina was a well-fixed, lovely woman in a mild to serious panic about what lay ahead…. just like the rest of them. Why must one remake oneself at forty?

"Stunning. Sweet," Hugo conceded. "A trifle absentminded. Not a specifically talented woman like you, even though she did run a dress shop in New Orleans and acted sporadically in her mother's theatre." Hugo spoke directly into Miranda's eyes and held her hand tighter. "We're still finding out about each other. It was a shotgun engagement." He smiled a little.

Miranda said, "I've heard every explanation for infidelity any man has ever dreamed up, but your sad little story is new."

"I've been faithful to Nina." Hugo came hurriedly to his own defense.

"So, you're comfortable with each other?"

"I guess so, ahhh, maybe. Ahhh, I'm not sure." He was suddenly lost.

"Comfort isn't so bad, is it, when you're moving up on fifty?"

"True, but, one doesn't want to get humdrum."

Miranda laughed. "Hugo, you are still in love with the formal third person. I'd forgotten." She snickered again. "I might cry!" She took her hand away, as if to punish him.

Hugo scowled and then gave in to an embarrassed smile. "That's not fair. You're so sophisticated, so to speak." Miranda's face had taken on a halo of light, and with this observation came the memory of her two ex-husbands (a saxophone player and a literary magazine editor) and countless lovers. He'd gleaned most of this from his pals, of course.

Miranda didn't answer but sat back and ran her eyes over his face. Hugo felt like he was being x-rayed. She leaned toward him again and said huskily, "Remember those old Friday nights at the university?" She was serious now. "Your military regimen. Up at first light and to bed with the birds. Are you still such a strict, orderly man? Do you still abhor sin, dirt and disruption? Am I a naughty disruption in your perfect life?"

Hugo smiled indulgently. She was digging deep and cutting as well. "I do not think of you as a disruption, Miranda."

"I do not wish to be resented."

"Not a chance."

"How about dinner?" Miranda suddenly asked. "I know, I know, I said no dinner. I lied." She grinned sheepishly and slid out of the booth. "Get us a quiet table; I'm starved."

Hugo beamed like he used to on Christmas morning. "You used to say that. Remember? We'd be three sheets to the wind and you'd suddenly require great quantities of food." He shoved himself energetically from the seat. "I want us to get to know each other better....again." Then, without thinking and forgetting their public circumstances, he kissed her mouth very softly in a flurry of emotion. He was clearly remembering how they'd once amused themselves after dinner.

A fresh wave of nerves drenched him. Was he actually embarking on an affair with Miranda Burke while pretending a relationship with Nina?

"It's not always a good idea to know someone too well," Miranda gently reminded him. "You might find out things you would rather not."

And she touched his coat sleeve.

A surprisingly devilish voice inside his head was insisting that no man of adventure and no liaison worth its salt would be complete without this last item. Admiral Melvin Moss was amazed at how willingly he was obeying these outrageously frivolous commands....kill the moustache, trade the car, buy Stetson cologne! Soon, he'd be riding a horse through the park and his own mother wouldn't recognize him. He parked in Dettmeyer's parking lot and entered the department store by the side entrance.

Once in men's furnishings, which sprouted like a giant pinwheel of ties and shirts in the center of the main floor, The Admiral grew uneasy and nearly bolted. The store was crowded with shoppers taking advantage of Back at School Days; he feared bumping into one of the wives or an acquaintance from church.

He stepped up to the counter and a young man of no more than twenty asked what he needed. The Admiral said as quietly and distinctly as possible that he was interested in silk shorts. Silk undershorts. The young man took this in stride and escorted the Admiral to a display of undershorts near the main aisle. Had Dettmeyer's been HIS department store, Melvin Moss would have put men's undershorts in a more private location.

The clerk pulled out a pair of dark green satin shorts with black stripes up the sides and held them up for the Admiral (and half the world) to see. The Admiral quickly pushed the clerk's hands and the garment down to the glass counter, and asked if there were any paisley shorts in his size. The green pair resembled a prize-fighter's costume, he said with a tight snicker. The clerk smiled and dug agreeably through the stacks until he came up with three pair of paisley silk shorts in varying conservative combinations of plum, navy and brown.

"Perfect," the Admiral said eagerly, hoping to complete the transaction in under two minutes and disappear from Dettmeyer's. "I'll have all three."

"My, my, you'll look like Michael Douglas in those," came a mature female voice from behind his back. The Admiral jumped, spun, and bumped clumsily against the counter. He could hear the clerk giggle.

"Lettice!" the Admiral blurted out, far too loudly and almost guiltily. "Lettice Mulroy! How nice to see you." The Admiral extended his hand to Lettice, as if he barely knew her. Lettice accepted his greeting and squinted at him slightly, as if questioning the procedure.

"Out doing a little shopping?" Lettice nodded toward the silk shorts. "They're very nice."

"Hummpf, ahhh," the Admiral stammered. "No. No," he snickered gamely, as if he didn't know what shopping was. "A small gift for....a cousin. A bachelor party gift," he stumbled on. "He's marrying...finally. Wonderful fellow. Wonderful girl! Ahh, the wedding's in...Barcelona!" Why had he said that? The Admiral was sweating beneath his new turtleneck and corduroy sport jacket. It was a cool day. Lettice continued to frown at him.

The Admiral looked plaintively at the young clerk, who was obviously mesmerized by the Admiral's story. The clerk smiled approvingly, as if to say, you are quick on your feet, my man. Keep going!

"Anyone I know?" asked Lettice, holding her ground as if she didn't have another place to go.

The Admiral replied without much thought, "Ahh, very distant cousin....from Philadelphia." He smiled broadly. "Met his charming bride-to-be...ahh, snorkling. In the Bahamas. Small world." The Admiral laughed nervously and began gliding toward the cash register with the clerk keeping up on the other side of the counter.

"I love the water," Lettice replied. "I've thought a cruise might be nice ....some time. Have you ever thought about a cruise, Melvin?" Lettice was sounding particularly brave this afternoon.

With Lettice sticking like glue, she and the Admiral were soon standing side by side at the cash register, where she touched his arm slightly, and then repeated her question about cruises. The Admiral gasped at her boldness and moved his arm. He hurriedly pulled out a credit card. The boyish clerk computed the sale and glanced up every few seconds for fear he might miss something. The Admiral rolled his eyes at him.

"Sounds...soothing!" The Admiral was desperate. His brain was telling him to run. Instead he looked frantically around him at the crowd. There must have been twenty women hovering over a table of Gold-toe socks just five feet away. Good lord, was that Betty Hughes Armbruster among the bargain hunters? Egads! The Admiral spun back to the clerk and signed the charge slip.

Lettice said, "I suppose I'll see you Sunday morning for brunch and the Sunday paper, Melvin." Lettice smiled, daring to imagine the Admiral in his new silk shorts. She didn't believe his story about the bachelor party gift.

"Ah, absolutely, Lettice. I'll bring that new strawberry jam."

Lettice said good-bye and Melvin watched her wander off to the next counter and a display of men's shirts. The clerk smiled sympathetically.

The Admiral picked up his package and noticing the clerk's bemused expression found himself mumbling, "Barely know the woman....a distant relative...by marriage. You know how it is." He coughed nervously and slipped his wallet into a back pocket.

"Certainly, sir. I have a few relatives myself. Enjoy your new shorts sir." And, he

grinned.

Freddy Donovan was three sheets to the wind, as he often was on Saturday night, but this time he had good reason. He was explaining this to Charlie Lemmon and Archie Beresford, who insisted they were four sheets to the wind. They'd been adding up the facts in the Spriggs case, the Old Bones case, and the Missing Boswell case. There were a couple of cheery moments, but, all in all, the investigations were never going to get Donovan or Lemmon elected district attorney or governor or see Archie receive a public service citation.

First, Lemmon had uncovered the now defunct Sandy Hook Badger Lodge, active during the thirties and forties and abruptly disbanded when the majority of its members marched off to war in 1941, many never to return. So, the belt buckle on Lemmon's now well-known corpse was a Badger Lodge insignia. According to the few records available, five members of the lodge were declared unfit for military duty for medical reasons. Three of these gentlemen were still alive and two were deceased, according to one of the live ones, a retired bait shop operator. Of those two, one was buried in the Sandy Hook Cemetery overlooking the river on Sheep's Head Bluff. And, the other member, a Willard 'Buzzy' Turk, appeared to be lost to the ages, according to the bait shop man, who'd exhibited a nice flair with words, Lemmon was telling Freddy and Archie. Archie's head was whirling with alcohol, fear, and more information than he wanted to know. The old secret was clearly in danger of blowing up….on the front page, if he wasn't careful. He listened and said little.

"No grave for Mr. Turk, no tombstone, no death notice in the paper. Nothing. It's as if our Mr. Turk evaporated," said Lemmon. "Some of those words were Mr. Bait Shop, you gotta remember." Lemmon was in a particularly generous frame of mind after a half dozen beers.

"What about the gold tooth?"

"That's a lost cause. The old dentist died. Left his practice to a nephew who moved outa town and took the records and we can't find him. It's up to the fat man's belt, Freddy." Charlie Lemmon giggled girlishly. He got that way close to the end of the evening when he would start tipping over. Donovan knew this from experience.

"Our ghost…lost to the ages… is probably Mr. Turk, Charlie. It makes sense. He might have disappeared in 1945, but he's turned up again in 1987. A bit worse for the wear, but we've got him in your morgue."

"Yep. Never drafted because of his short leg, and he's not in the cemetery. Nobody remembers where he went or what happened. Mr. Bait shop says he kinda disappeared around the end of the war." Lemmon giggled again. "Into a hole in the ground." They all laughed.

"Didn't anybody wonder where he went?" Archie bravely inquired.

"Nah. This guy can't remember his own phone number half the time. He can't remember if Buzzy had a short leg or a beer belly. The guy's memory comes and goes as fast as the five o'clock freight out of Lynton Station." Charlie was giving the boys the straight story. No frills. "It don't make him dead. This Turk fella coulda moved to Wyoming for all we know." Lemmon said he believed in healthy skepticism when it came to dead bodies, even when he was drunk.

"What about family?"

"I got one old lady up there who remembers an odd jobs guy named Buzzy who was fat. That's it." Charlie poured more beer but missed the glasses and the three of them watched the beer Pfeiffers dribble across the table and on to the floor. "Jesus, did I do that?" They all giggled again.

"Charlie, for God's sake. Eat a burger." Donovan threw paper napkins into the puddle on the battered plank floor. The beer was as close to a detergent the floor would ever see.

"Beer's nutritious as hell."

"Did the old lady say he was crippled? Gimpy leg?" Archie threw this out.

"She don't remember. Hell, she's ninety, Archie."

"What about this Buzzy's kids? His wife?"

"I guess there was a daughter. The wife disappeared too."

"What about the Moccasin factory?"

"No files that go back that far. Beresford Boots made the man three pair of custom shoes in the thirties. Nothing after 1945."

The Irishman shook his head. They were close; he could feel it. "Somebody wanted this Buzzy Turk out of the way. Could be his wife smashed his head and then dragged the body into the woods. Could be she was a big, strong woman."

"Could be, Freddy. But, what the hell? If we don't solve it, who's gonna care now? His family's a mystery or gone too. The D.A.'s losing interest, if you want the truth."

"I wish I was closer in the Spriggs case," Freddy said. "We have the murder weapon and one dead widow. And, the strange will."

"So, did Boswell turn up again? I thought he'd be the next corpse." Archie was listing several degrees west. One more beer and he'd be on the floor. Donovan suggested he start leaning east. Charlie gave him a wee nudge.

"Yep. He turned up. Our Preacher went on a lengthy bender up in Minneapolis, he said. To celebrate his good fortune. Millionaires get to do that, he told me, just as smug as you please. Money gives some people an attitude…..no offense, Archie. We know you're a regular guy and you're rich." Donovan clapped Archie on the back and Archie grinned at him.

"You said it, Freddy. Some of us are all right guys…..'specially when we're full of Pfeiffers." Archie laughed at this, so did Charlie and Freddy and a few fellows sitting close by who were listening.

"Shifty-eyed son-of-a-bitch. Boswell, I mean. I drove up to see if he'd turned up at the homestead. He was back all right, sitting there in his fake leather recliner, belching. He's got a definite superiority complex to go with the most God-awful suit he bought up there in the Twin Cities. He showed it to me!" The Irishman was giggling now, which started Charlie and Archie off. There would be an epidemic soon at Billy's. "I said to him, 'Boswell, where in the hell are you going to wear that plaid suit?' Ugliest damned thing you ever saw." Donovan blew his nose and wiped his eyes.

"And?" Charlie and Archie were both swaying dangerously now and giggling.

"Said he'd wear it at his swearing-in ceremony in November. Says he'll win because he's the richest, ugliest bastard in town."

"He's probably right." Charlie sighed and made a concerted effort to sober up. He asked about the lab reports. Lemmon could do that. One minute he was as silly as a kid and the next he'd turn serious. Donovan found the process disconcerting and admirable at the same time.

"Not a hair. Must have gone into Lola's house in a rubber suit. But, I know the Preacher's our man."

"How about Lola's kid?" Archie asked, still on track, but just barely.

"Toby Spriggs has an airtight alibi. You know that, Archie. Two colleagues from the college say he was at book club that night. At a house over on Beecher Street."

"Maybe he paid some dude to conk dear old mum and then dress her up like a fancy lamp. Maybe he hired Boswell to do it. Coincidences do happen, Freddy." Charlie waded through the word 'coincidences' with big feet.

"Good point. Let's give Toby a second look when he's not looking." The lieutenant started to giggle again. Once he started his nervous system seemed to stay on auto pilot. Quite honestly, he couldn't see Toby killing his own mother.

"You're a funny man, Freddy." Charlie poured more beer and spilled it again. "Whoops! Time to drag out the mop, Billy," he called to the barkeeper. "Or, Freddy'll release Ching, killer beer dog!"

They held their sides on that one. Not all the patrons were thinking this was all that funny, but nobody wanted to criticize a sheriff, a police lieutenant, and the town's richest man, all in their cups.

"Toby Spriggs," Donovan hissed across the table at Charlie, "is an ineffectual twerp who'd be afraid to sneeze in church."

"Hell, Boswell most likely toasted up his folks in that barn fire. We always thought he was guilty but couldn't prove it."

"No proof. That's always the fly in the ointment, Charlie. The D.A. always insists we get him *PROOF*. I hate that damned word."

"Yup. We're sorry-ass excuses for cops, aren't we?" Charlie was staring into his beer like he was looking for an answer in the bottom of the glass.

Donovan and Archie took peeks into the bottom of their own glasses.

"Sorry-ass," the trio announced in unison, while Charlie slipped to the floor.

9

Private Talks

On Archie's regular visits to Dr. Bathgart, he chose to never recline on the leather couch. He explained to Bathgart that by lying down he was putting himself in the weaker position. He chose instead the Eames chair that allowed him to look into the room or at Bathgart or out the window. Bathgart said he didn't mind and often took the sofa for himself, reclining on the soft, squeaky leather cushions with his notepad and pen. The two agreed that this slightly unorthodox seating arrangement was amusing, and they laughed about it. Bathgart thought Freud might find it very interesting.

In these sessions Archie had come to know and trust Bathgart as well as any man ever knows another man (like Cyrus), and probably as well as he had ever imagined knowing his psychiatrist. And, Archie soon realized that he would never divulge these same intimacies to Tommy, the Admiral, or Cyrus. The idea of trusting a relative stranger to investigate the darkest corners in his head gave Archie a sense of security rather than the grip of apprehension. And, because of this significant trust, Archie decided that he would confide the 'big secret' to Bathgart that afternoon.

Bathgart, on the other hand, was learning that one didn't have to practice psychiatry in Chicago to find fascinating patients. A modest college town in the Midwest might have less traffic and fewer delis, but there certainly was an ample supply of neurotics and psychotics. His patient list was an entertaining and medically dynamic roster of lost and worn souls. So far, he'd collected an obsessive novelist, a talented photographer with dangerous blackouts, and a neurotic politician with dreams of celebrity. There were others, of course, suffering the usual self-inflicted delusions and fantasies. But, Archie Beresford was turning out to be one of his favorites. He found the man intriguing and complex even though he certainly wasn't seriously ill. And, it was nice to see that at the age of sixty-two, a man could still be baffled by life and by himself.

While Archie was chatting about fishing at Star Lake (avoiding the obvious for some reason), Bathgart let him carry on. The doctor let his own attention slip back to his exit from Chicago just two years ago, where he'd begun suffering from 'metropolis anxiety' (his own term)… the fear of claustrophobic traffic, indiscriminate crime, bad air, toxic water, and far too many nuts who needed him. After enduring a decade of these big city horrors, Bathgart took the advice of one of his patients and moved to Augusta, not far from Belmont and the string of other picturesque villages that made up the river population.

Bathgart did have one very private motivation for moving to Augusta in particular…the residence of one Andrea Kittredge, an old medical school friend who now practiced psychiatry at University Hospitals in Augusta. She'd been the object of Bathgart's romantic longings since college, and true to form, the man's longings still outnumbered his attempts to actually make contact with the pretty doctor. Her office was six blocks away and she was single, but he'd managed to speak to her only eleven times in two years. Bathgart was his own worst patient.

Glancing at the desk clock and then scanning his notes, Bathgart yanked himself back to the present and said, "Tell me about Marigold, Archie."

"Ah, Marigold," sighed the patient. "We touched on her last time, didn't we?" Archie clasped his hands behind his impressive head and leaned back, a smile on his lips.

Beresford was a charismatic, athletically built gentleman. Handsome, virile, smart, self-assured, Archie Beresford seemed to stand beyond the brutal strokes of age. Archie was alert to danger but still obsessed with women. Bathgart found him almost as intriguing as reading Bat Man or watching Gary Cooper in a thrilling old film. Like so many patients, Archie tended to perpetuate his shortcomings and neuroses by refusing to do much to help himself. Other than pay a psychiatrist to listen.

As a quiet, almost reclusive person, Bathgart was well aware of his tendency to live vicariously through his patients. He enjoyed Archie Beresford the most. His own therapist encouraged him to overcome this unrewarding habit, but Bathgart had had little success. Archie possessed the equipment women loved....good looks, charm, humor, money, a decent profession, and a sexuality that lay enticingly beneath the surface. Bathgart, on the other hand, knew that he possessed an intriguing skill (who wasn't fascinated by psychiatry?), but his lack of finesse with females and a deeply buried sexuality were like scars to be lived with and kept hidden. And, so, here he was. Middle-aged and still alone. It seemed like only yesterday he was struggling with organic chemistry, afraid he might not make it through medical school.

Sensing he was too easily distracted today, Bathgart forced his attention back to Archie. "Why is Marigold important to you?" he asked, keeping his pen poised over the notepad.

"She's a mystery, Doc. A beguiling mystery; no one knows everything there is to know about Marigold. She always holds back a little....like a marvelous actress. The Old Devils adore her. That's what we call ourselves....the Old Devils. You'd love her, too, Doc. Marigold Woolsey is the essence of womanhood, of romance, sex, fun. She's a free spirit, even today. As rare as emeralds on the banks of the Mississippi, wouldn't you say? Funny thing, too, now that I have Nina, I can't help wondering why I still desire Marigold too? What do you make of it?"

Archie often asked more questions than the doctor. So far, in the few sessions they'd had, they'd touched on Archie's less than happy childhood, a brother who had gone to a country club prison for fraud, his imperious wife, Nadine, and his only son, Hugo, who didn't sound much like old dad on the personality side. Add to this an admirable string of beautiful women who'd amused him through the years. Marigold seemed to mean more than the others. Except Nina.

"I have heard about the Woolsey family.....a rather large one and a successful one, as I recall." Bathgart smiled. He'd treated a few over the years. He loved the way his patients fit together in a kind of web of souls. "Perhaps you love Marigold because she is your contemporary, and you love Nina for her youth. She reminds you of when you were forty-two." Bathgart smiled with great understanding.

Archie was swiveling back and forth in his chair.

You might ask yourself the same question, Bathgart scolded himself, thinking fleetingly of Andrea Kittridge, who was probably free for dinner if he'd just call. The psychiatrist crossed his legs a third time and tried to concentrate. He wondered idly if Andrea would approve of him these days….dark suits and bow ties, a shrink who understood minds and roller bladed in the park on Sundays, a thin, precise man who washed his socks by hand and kept a well-stocked bubble gum machine in his office.

"You're probably right, Doc. The Marigold and Nina puzzles have to be straightened out by me… on my own, right?"

Bathgart nodded. The patient was learning quickly. In the end, healing and moving along were the work of the patient. Patient, heal thyself….with a nudge from your shrink. But, Bathgart could tell from Archie's expression that something else was bothering him, a larger matter than Marigold.

"Take your time, Archie, but let it go, whatever it is."

"You're right. There is one other matter." Archie was very somber now.

"And what is that?" Bathgart experienced a twinge of uneasiness. He always did when a patient moved into a new realm.

"You've heard about the body, the skeleton, found up at Sandy Hook? And, the death of Lola Spriggs?"

"Yes." Bathgart's pulse rate rose precipitously.

"Well, I'm one of the guys who put the body there."

"What do you mean?" Bathgart was alarmed.

"Not Lola! We killed the man. We, I mean, the Old Devils. Years ago. After the war." Everything was coming out in spurts. "It was an accident. The guy ended up dead."

"Tell me about it." Bathgart slowly sat up on the sofa, placed his feet on the floor, and faced his patient with a renewed professional calm. Had he run into a Heartland killing cult going back four decades? Old Devils, indeed. Had they killed Lola Spriggs too? The murder had freakish markings….like the mummy wrap and the lamp shade hat.

Archie outlined the circumstances. The sexy romps with Sally Turk, the Spriggs's maid, the weekend orgy. The booze, the sex. And, finally, the child. A male child who could be his or Cyrus's or the Admiral's or Tommy's. Archie called it the bad old days. He told Bathgart about how Sally's old man died. Buzzy Turk, a bastard of giant proportions. And, how they'd buried the body. And, how terrified they were now.

Bathgart was stunned. He'd never expected such a thing. Who would? A dead body? Old bones unearthed and unclaimed. And, the man responsible was sitting in his Eames chair, not a bad man, but a man who had covered up a death.

"And, Mrs. Spriggs?"

"Hell, Doc, we didn't kill her! But, she sure as hell was murdered. And, probably by the Preacher." Archie had been in and out of his chair about four times during this recitation.

"Tell me all of it."

"She left almost half her money to Preacher Boswell, a dog breeder in Fontana City. He's our illegitimate kid! And, we think he killed Lola for the money, even though he was going to get it anyway." Archie stood again and then sat down again.

"I'm shocked, of course." Bathgart rose from his couch and walked around the office with his hands behind his back, striking a professorial pose. "I cannot advise you on what to do right off, Archie." Bathgart had left his notepad on the sofa, along with his ability to sort out complicated messes. "Have the police any clues about this dead man, this Buzzy Turk you buried?"

"A few. The sheriff thinks the bones are Buzzy Turk. Gimpy leg, belt buckle. Like I just told you. But, nobody's real interested in finding out how he died or who buried him. It's been too many years. The Old Devils are sworn to secrecy, Doc. We just have to worry about Betty Grable…the maid…the Preacher's real mother." He smiled a little and explained about their pet name for Sally, the winsome and willing housemaid who couldn't resist a man in uniform. The maid with the long, beautiful legs. "She had the kid and put him up for adoption. The Boswells took him. The Old Devils chipped in…except for Tommy… and paid Sally for keeping the secret. Nobody has ever talked. Not about the Preacher or the dead body in the Pike's Wood."

"Your secret is safe with me, Archie. I must simply figure out how to help you." Bathgart took his seat behind his desk. "I'll need some time. Strangely enough, I've never had a patient who's confessed to killing, even accidentally."

"Sure, Doc. Sure. I'm hitting you with a lot in one afternoon." Archie smiled a little. He looked relieved for having told the story. "Don't worry, we haven't killed anybody else."

Bathgart offered up a shy grin and then tapped the face of his watch. The hour was up. His head was whirling. "Stay calm. I'd advise your friends to do the same. You've broken the law. But, it is the sheriff's job to investigate." Bathgart stood. Was this the right advice? He was utterly confused.

As was his habit after these few weeks, Archie promptly crossed the room and shook Bathgart's hand, an unnecessary formality, but a gesture that seemed to signify the renewal of a gentlemen's agreement that safeguarded the sanctity of all that was said. And then Archie departed.

With his head heavy with doubt and concern, Bathgart promptly used the lavatory, washed his hands, and tried to mentally prepare for his next patient, a new one. For all he knew, this woman might be a serial killer, stopping by for a private chat with a man who must never tell. The psychiatrist knew he must accept everything. After hearing Archie's tale of death and deception going back decades, he was fairly sure that he was prepared for anybody.

As Bathgart combed his sparse hair, he was suddenly reminded of Miss Kittredge's gold hair, which she wore in a pretty swirl on the top of her head. He needed to concentrate on beauty for a few minutes. That would put him right.

He moved back out into his office and tipped the blinds slightly against the afternoon sun. If he telephoned Miss Kittredge after this next patient, he could tell himself later that he'd begun to branch out, a quaint botanical colloquial expression that always made him smile. His heart beat faster.

"Guess who I saw buying silk underwear at Dettmeyer's?"

Betty Hughes smiled to herself. It was Naddy with one of her quiz show phone calls. She said, "Sounds naughty." Betty Hughes put down a yellow legal pad criss-crossed with complicated plot notes for the new novel and poured a cup of black coffee from the carafe. She rarely tolerated interruptions, but Naddy was Naddy.

Nadine said she was trying to open a cardboard book mailer glued together by a fiend intent on keeping the contents under wraps forever. "Guess," she insisted.

"I remain befogged."

"Our Admiral Moss."

"Melvin Moss in Fine Lingerie?" Betty Hughes sounded skeptical.

"Not women's undies, silly! *Men's* silk undershorts! And guess who was with him?"

As always, when talking to Nadine, Betty Hughes felt slightly suspended, as if the entire conversation might be one of Naddy's cockamamie stories destined to find its way into the next novel. "From the sound of your voice, I'd say it wasn't someone we would have expected."

"Bingo! Try Lettice Mulroy! My God, she had her hand on his arm!"

"The Admiral and Lettice? Give me strength. I doubt if Melvin Moss has touched a woman in his adult life. Do you think their little Sunday morning brunch has turned into a Sunday afternoon nap?" They laughed.

"Perhaps Lettice isn't as prim as we thought. Could be Lettice Mulroy's a great little warmer-upper."

Betty Hughes could hear Nadine still stabbing and punching the cardboard box.

"Good choice for the Admiral. Lettice is just as tight with a dollar as he is with a dime." Nadine gave a final whack at the carton and a book fell to the floor.

"Absolutely. He's eliminated his mustache too."

"About time."

"Lettice is pretty low maintenance. That will be good for Mel."

"I think our Admiral's caught in that scary combustion of witherin' hormones and arrested development called middle age….only twenty years too late." Betty Hughes opened a desk drawer and pulled out a package of Oreos in defiance of the Diet Gods. "But, Lordy, nobody wants to get old without goin' to jail first. Trouble is old Mel Moss isn't exactly put together like sexy Archie or my Cyrus."

Nadine said, "Mel's the kind of man who'd hold tight to his 'get out of jail free card' until he didn't need it. And, then he'd sell it to someone who did." She laughed.

"Walkin' the straight and narrow is tricky and dull, honey. And, the Admiral's the nervous sort. He's gettin' panicky in his old age. Afraid he'll end up more alone than he is now. So, he buys himself some sexy silk boxers." Betty Hughes munched on a cookie. "Who doesn't want to teeter on the brink once in a while?" She unscrewed the top of another Oreo and licked off the filling.

"Define teeter. Define brink. Watching Archie Beresford negotiate his first year of retirement and stay clear of Marigold Woolsey is close enough to the brink for me."

"Or, watchin' Cyrus put his socks on every mornin'." Betty Hughes's laugh had a melancholy tint to it. "Maybe the Admiral's stab at romance with Lettice is just an old man's sorry attempt to prove he can make the grade with any woman and at any age. He's always been out-of-sorts about Cyrus and Archie and Tommy and their way with the girls."

"Closing in on old age makes people pathetic. But, I am thrilled at the thought of the Admiral in silk shorts."

Betty Hughes giggled. "He is a stick, isn't he? Except for Lettice."

Maybe they were all a little scared. But, what if one of them fell ill to a genuine mental disease, like dementia…before cancer or by-pass surgery could topple them over? There were nights when she'd awaken with her heart beating like a bird's. Scared to death. She'd see herself and her friends, old and yet dressed like children, rolling down the other side of a steep, stony hill. She couldn't tell Naddy these things. Not yet, anyway.

Nadine was saying, "All I can see right now is the Admiral standing in front of the Golden Horizon Seniors' Boarding House. In his new silk drawers."

Thank God for Naddy. Betty Hughes felt restored to normal. For now.

Archie rolled over on his side and began a contented snore. Nina smoothed his thick hair and kissed his warm cheek. Propped up on one elbow, she memorized his profile…strong chin, fabulous Connery nose, nice ears. Hugo favored his mother with black hair and an aquiline beak. And, he didn't snore. Beneath the sheets Nina knew that Archie wasn't forty any more, but he was in better shape than Hugo. She ran her hand over his bare, sun-browned back and wondered how she'd managed to fall for both the father and the son in the space of a few months. It must be her age….a last gasp effort at romance. Or, a symptom of something far more grave? Archie and Nadine had survived years with impossible odds. Perhaps, Nadine's little shopping trips to New York, like the one she took this week end, kept the pair from divorce court.

Nina glanced at the clock. Time for a quick shower and then back to the apartment. She and Hugo were going to a Bon Voyage party for a company vice president bound for South America. Hugo insisted that they 'keep up appearances' in spite of their differences. Nina agreed. There was no point in fanning the gossip or even making Hugo suspicious about her own private life. Their engagement had never been officially broken. Belle still believed the union could be saved. She blamed the endurance of her own marriage on inertia. Neither she nor Beau had the energy to file for divorce, she'd said with a hearty chuckle. Nina was stunned but said nothing more.

Nina slipped from the bed still naked and entered the large adjoining bathroom. She turned on the taps, humming a Carly Simon song she'd heard on the radio. Just as she was wrapping her head in a towel, she heard a voice. It wasn't Archie, but it was a man. The half-opened door allowed her to see Archie stir and look around for her and then glance at the bedroom door.

"Archie! Are you up here?" came the voice, quite near now and clear.

Archie jumped out of bed and pulled on his briefs just as the door banged open. It was Cyrus. Nina pulled the bathroom door closed as quickly and quietly as she could. Then, listening carefully, she reopened it a crack.

"Cyrus, for Christ's sake! What the hell are you doing up here?" Archie met his friend at the threshold and gently pushed him back into the hall, but Cyrus insisted that he needed to sit down.

"This is important," he cried. "It's the Admiral! That miserable old swabbie." Cyrus pushed past Archie and sank to the edge of the unmade bed, oblivious to the disarray of sheets at two in the afternoon and Archie's state of undress. Nina remained frozen with the shower running in the background.

"What are you talking about?" Archie sounded provoked with Cyrus, which was unusual. "What's happened to the Admiral?"

"He wants to see the sheriff in Sandy Hook!" Cyrus was looking up Archie like a boy might entreat his father.

"What for?" Archie sat down next to Cyrus. "You must keep your voice down."

"It's about the bones, Arch." Cyrus was shaken; his leg kept bouncing up and down.

Archie put his arm around his friend's thin shoulders and tried to calm him. "It's OK. Quiet, quiet."

Inside the bathroom, Nina listened intently while steam grew around her like fog. What were they saying? The Admiral knew something about the bones? Poor Cyrus. He must be getting worse.

"I heard it on the radio, Arch. There's a body in the Pike's Wood. Geez, I'm going to pee my pants." Cyrus stood abruptly and headed for the bathroom before Archie could stop him.

Nina made a dive for the shower and pulled the curtain just as Cyrus burst in, unzipping as he trotted over to the commode.

"Hot as the Sahara in here, Naddy!" Cyrus called out. He giggled. "Caught you and Arch horsing around, huh?" He snickered again. "A nice private matinee. Don't worry; it's only me. Cyrus. Having a quick pee. I'll be out in a jiffy!" He reached around and jiggled the shower curtain just to get a reaction.

Nina yelped and recoiled beneath the spray.

"Don't worry. I didn't see a thing!" Cyrus hooted, flushed the toilet, and presumably zipped up. "I thought you were playing bridge, Naddy. Well, catch you later."

Nina stood rigidly, clutching the wash cloth to her breasts...my god, what was the man thinking? She turned off the water, stepped out, and grabbed a towel. With another quick move, she locked the door. Archie and Cyrus were still chatting, but their voices faded as they walked down the corridor toward the stairs. Archie would see to it that Cyrus left the house.

What if Cyrus wasn't talking through his hat? What if the Admiral and the rest of the Old Devils did know something about the bones in Pike's Wood? Nina felt a chill and wrapped up in a dry towel before re-entering the bedroom. The whole lot of them had been acting like twits lately.

"What in the world was Cyrus talking about?" Nina began dressing. Archie was back and pulling on his trousers.

"He's confused. Thinks the Admiral… ah, ah…is leaking some old World War Two secrets." Archie laughed and waved his arm through the air. "Bogus! All bogus. Total nonsense. He gets rattled about the war. He gets flashes. We all do. What we saw and what we had to do….. it never really goes away." Archie shrugged. "Our ghosts come to haunt us every so often." He closed his eyes just for a few seconds. Poor Cyrus was reliving that day when the report had come over the TV and the radio….about the bones. History now, but Cyrus didn't know that. He was having a bad day.

"He's such a dear. You're such a dear." Nina went to Archie and put her arms around him. "Poor darlings."

Archie kissed her and told her not to worry.

"I hate to think Cyrus imagines bad things." Nina brushed her hair and threw

her lipstick back in her bag. Archie sounded like an amateur with that cover story. She wanted to bet half her family fortune that the Devils had figured out something about the bones. For all she knew, they might know who killed Lola. They might have a few war secrets too.

"Cyrus is living in a weedy patch right now. I'm hoping the docs will make him better."

Archie grinned charmingly, the kind of smile that made Nina forget almost everything, including mysteries and bad cover stories.

"There isn't much they can do. He's just goin' to get worse." Betty Hughes whispered this sobering information to Archie after Cyrus left the room to use the bathroom.

"Probably Alzheimer's? Dementia? I don't believe it," Archie scoffed. "He's forgetful. Spouts off funny things, but, a serious condition?" He experienced a painful stab in his throat, like he did when he was a boy, fighting off tears. The official truth of it all was hitting him between the eyes. They had all guessed as much months ago.

Betty Hughes said they'd seen three specialists and gone through all the tests, even a brain scan. And told no one except Duncan, their eldest son. They would tell the younger son tomorrow. Cyrus wasn't just forgetful; the docs were sure he had the disease.

A rumble of thunder shook the walls and soon a downpour clacked against the windows of the Armbrusters' second floor apartment at Meadowlark Village.

"Only an autopsy can confirm Alzheimer's," Archie said, needlessly. He'd read that somewhere and didn't want to believe the final diagnosis.

"What about blood vessel disease that can cause similar symptoms? I read about that too. Do the docs know about that?" Archie was clutching.

"I don't know what to do, Archie. I'm scared to death." Betty Hughes sniffled and took a chair next to the fire. "We've just moved. Left behind every room he ever recognized. How will he get used to this place?" She waved her pretty hands through the air. The large living room was still stuffed with unopened cartons, paintings waiting to be hung, and furniture in place but not quite in place either, Archie noticed. Betty Hughes began to cry softly. "Marigold and Parnell love the house. They'll never give it back."

Archie knelt beside her and patted her hands, soft and slightly brown spotted, adorned with two pretty rings. What would they all do? He understood Alzheimer's enough to know that the next few years would consume the energy of the entire family and his closest friends. Cyrus would sink into a kind of oblivion, while the rest of them stewed in their own kind of purgatory. All they could do was pray the docs were wrong and pray it was something else.

"It won't matter where he lives, Betty Hughes. He'll adjust. It might take more time, but he will. It won't be so bad." Like hell.

Archie stood again; his knees were stiff. He wished he believed what he'd just said. Cyrus was too intelligent to not know what he was facing.

The two of them had faced some of the hell already, trooping in and out of that clinic for the past few weeks. It was Betty Hughes who was going to have more trouble. She was a spoiled woman, unaccustomed to taking care of details, like the bills and the checkbook. She wrote her books; that was a full-time job. She didn't do heavy lifting, as Naddy always said. But, she did drive, not very well, but, well enough.

"Poppycock!" came Cyrus's clear voice from the hall. "What a pile of poppycock!"

"What are you talkin' about, darlin'?" Betty Hughes sounded almost sweet, Archie thought, compared to her usual responses to Cyrus's nutty proclamations. Had Cyrus overheard? Did it really matter? His fate was known to him, unlike that of his cronies who could only guess what would get them in the end. Archie shivered.

"Senator Barnes! On the TV. In the bathroom. That little pipsqueak. Says the state is heading for bankruptcy. Twerp. Poppycock." Cyrus rubbed his scalp, as he always did when disturbed, causing his coarse white hair to stand straight up in a Stan Laurel thatch. It made Archie smile.

Cyrus began drink preparations at a table set up with liquor bottles, the familiar ice bucket in the form of a stainless deep sea diving helmet, still unique after thirty years, and a tray of crystal glasses in three sizes. The Armbrusters had always kept their liquor on a pretty cherry table in the living room. Betty Hughes had seen it done that way in Europe and in the movies and said it made more sense than hiding the bottles in a kitchen cabinet nobody could reach.

Another drum roll of thunder rattled the room and caught Cyrus's attention.

"Sounds like Barnes, doesn't it?" Archie responded lightheartedly, immediately cheered by his friend's steady course at the moment. "He's trying to scare us into voting for him, the bastard."

Archie joined Cyrus at the table and put an arm around his shoulders. He was six inches taller than Cyrus and right now felt as if he were Cyrus's father, a circumstance that would become more apparent as months grew into years. Until it was over. Archie was trying hard to keep his emotions buried.

Cyrus stirred the three scotches with his finger and handed them off. Betty Hughes took her drink and dabbed her eyes with a handkerchief.

Cyrus focused on the neat gas fire snapping in the hearth. It looked almost real.

"Betty Hughes told you, didn't she? I'm losing my marbles, Arch. It's off to the loony bin for me. I'll be a blathering idiot before the curtain falls." Cyrus stood still while he said this and then shook his head in disbelief, his one hand upon the mantel shelf. His fury over Senator Barnes was forgotten. "It's the aluminum cooking pots, you know. I read it somewhere. The metal comes off in your food and settles in the brain." That said Cyrus sank into a favorite leather chair opposite his wife.

"That's not entirely accurate, Cyrus," replied Betty Hughes very quickly. She'd thrown out all pots and pans made of aluminum, just to make Cyrus happy. "I think it's hereditary. Wasn't your grandfather dotty and old Uncle Albert?" Her reminders were honest inquiries.

"Grandpa Armbruster, by the end, thought he was President Roosevelt." Cyrus smiled at his memories. "Claimed the New Deal was his greatest accomplishment." He laughed out loud now. "You had to love the old guy. Died a year after Pearl Harbor. Said declaring war was the hardest decision he ever had to make. Now, Uncle Albert was my Dad's brother. Batty as hell. Thought his wife was Ingrid Bergmann. They put him in a home when he was only forty-six. Sat there for ten years, never said another word." Cyrus turned somber then and seemed fascinated with the fire, unable or unwilling to go on with the family's history of failed minds.

Archie found himself floundering. What could he say by way of comfort? Weren't there drugs to put off this kind of dementia? Was there nothing the doctors could do? His sense of helplessness and sadness was overwhelming, but he refused to break down. Luckily for them, Naddy wasn't there. Her bluntness, her pragmatism would have very likely brought them to their knees. He could hear her outlining Cyrus's care in practical terms, how they might better organize their time and efforts. Archie often thought his wife should have been a nurse in one of those awful starched uniforms.

"We'll have to tell the others...Tommy, the Admiral, Lettice, Naddy."

Betty Hughes nodded. "I wish you'd do that for me, Archie."

"Sure, Betty Hughes. And, I'll call your doctor tomorrow. Double check on any new drugs that might help. Maybe get a second opinion." Archie spoke assuredly, mostly to make himself feel better.

Cyrus was staring into the fire-light while the storm churned outside. A branch scratched its fingers across the windowpanes.

"Yes, Archie. We would appreciate your checkin' on that, darlin'. Won't we, Cyrus?" Betty Hughes glanced every few seconds at her husband, who seemed quite apart from them now. "I'll be relyin' on you and Naddy now. I can't cope alone." She stood and began poking around in one of the cardboard boxes.

"You can count on us, Betty Hughes." Archie pushed his hands into his trouser pockets, suddenly more overwhelmed than he thought he would be.

"We didn't leave any windows open, did we Cyrus?" Betty Hughes asked as naturally as ever. Cyrus looked up and said no.

Archie supposed a simple exchange like that might be the only normal thing he'd hear from now on.

He soon left them. It was the hardest parting he'd ever had to make. What lay ahead was probably worse than any cancer. He was almost worse than old Tommy dying by inches with his bad liver. Archie wished Cyrus could exchange dementia for heart disease. They fixed hearts these days. Why Alzheimer's? How? Archie rode the elevator to the ground floor. He felt ill and shaken, as if he, too, had been diagnosed. Of course, he wasn't exactly immune. Nobody was.

Archie drove home in the pounding rain with lightning tearing the blackness and thunder booms from the plains rocking the earth's crust. It sounded like an overture to a colossal opera by a heavy-handed composer. And to his surprise and dismay, Archie found that, once alone in his car, he could not weep.

10

Choices

Nina was in her kitchen grinding Blue Mountain beans. She poured the coarse powder into the coffee maker's paper filter, and while the coffee dripped, she toasted raisin bread and poured orange juice. Ordinarily, these tempting aromas would put her in gear for the day, but this morning, like mornings for the past two weeks, the coffee smelled skunky and the juice tasted sour. She poured both down the drain. Left with toast, Nina nibbled on it without much enthusiasm. This flu had lingered far longer than necessary by her standards, and she planned to see Doctor Lamb later that morning.

First, she was off for an appointment with Alexandre the Bouffant, a Seuss-like hairdresser who'd turned his beauty parlor antics into performance art. Pure theatre in black leather pants, diamond studs, and pointed Italian shoes, Alexandre (supposedly, his real name was Karl Shinglebock), drove an antique English car, wore his coal black hair in a pony tail, and kept his Afghan hound, Renaldo, with him at the studio. Flaunting health department regulations and somehow getting away with it didn't bother him or his clientele. He promoted self confidence for his 'Dolls' (patrons) much like some doctors push B-12 shots. And, his 'Dolls' adored him. Nina guessed that tips alone paid the rent.

Quite characteristically, Hugo had been less than sympathetic about her illness. Illness frightened him. Nina had learned early on that Hugo's mind was medically inert. He possessed absolutely no curiosity about disease or the workings of the body or of the mind. And since he was rarely ill, his ignorance of these matters only reinforced his theory that if one doesn't think about disease or if one knows very little about disease, then, one will not contract a disease. Hugo's love of the formal third person seemed to be catching. Nina could now think in 'Hugo-Speak.' When she suggested that he was refusing to face his own fear of infirmity and mortality, he would simply blanch and say that even the medical photos in TIME magazine made him queasy.

At any rate, Hugo had made himself scarce the last two weeks, pleading late meetings and short business trips. Nina was happier than ever that she'd taken her own apartment. She was in control of her time and space. She answered to no one, rather like the old days. She missed her family and Jessie's cooking, but, she continued to reconsider a permanent alliance with Hugo. Perhaps she was not cut out for marriage. Maybe Hugo wasn't either. Her decision to continue with her acting, to retool, as Betty Hughes was fond of calling these mid-life makeovers, automatically made her less available. She'd dropped most of her volunteer work and the endless committee meetings Nadine endured. They could live without her. Hugo had already established the fact that his father's company came first. Their course together had been altered considerably. Nina' meetings with Archie continued in a kind of naughty bliss. Neither one seemed to need anything else.

Nina threw the remainder of the toast into the disposal and left the dishes out for the housekeeper, who'd be there any minute. Still peckish, she grabbed a bag of Milanos and moved to the bedroom.

While she dressed, Nina went over second act dialogue she'd memorized the night before. O'Neill had suggested she rehearse her lines aloud, and, so far, her Mid-western accent seemed to be alive and true. Her Yankee ear was becoming more finely tuned. She was creating a sure-footed character for the University Players October production of 'Letting Time Fly.'

Nina smiled at her reflection in the mirror and put on makeup. O'Neill said he loved her take on the rich small town matron she was playing, a woman with an inbred contempt for outsiders, so like some of the matrons in Belmont. If your great, great granddaddy hadn't settled the town or run the courts or built the factories and made all the money, you barely counted in the census. Betty Hughes called it The Beresford Law of Social Order and Human Dynamics. Nina understood all about old families and their power. She was a Dupree from New Orleans.

Feeling better now, Nina ate another cookie and left for Alexandre's shop. It was magic time, as he liked to say.

"You're pregnant," Doctor Lamb announced cheerily, as if this would be the first birth on earth in quite some time.

"Pregnant?" Nina squeaked. "That's impossible. I'm forty-two!" Open-mouthed, she glared at the doctor and willed him to change his diagnosis. "I had no idea you'd done a pregnancy test."

"Not an impossibility," Dr. Lamb replied firmly, looking as pleased as the expectant father himself. Seated on his little chrome roll-about stool, a grin lighted his cherubic face. He couldn't have been more than forty-two himself, Nina thought. The Doctor Lambs of the world would never have to endure such news, personally. She hated him. She hated all men.

"I was told twenty years ago I couldn't have children. And, I never have! You've made a ghastly mistake." Nina pulled her pale blue cotton wrapper tighter around her middle and stumbled into the curtained cubicle. She began to dress.

"I'm afraid not, Mrs. Dupree. If you were told you could not conceive, the error was made by someone else. There is no mistake now." With the curtain safely between them, Dr. Lamb sounded calm and reassuring, as if having a baby at forty-two was the usual thing around here. "You are suffering from morning sickness, not the flu."

Nina stuck her head around the pink cotton drape and cried out, "Well, I just won't do it!" Her eyes were filling with tears and she felt hysterical, like the time she lost the Miss Peach Blossom pageant to Mary Elizabeth Tempest. Nina zipped up and took a seat again next to Dr. Lamb's desk. She looked down and noticed that her silk blouse was fastened one off. Phooey! She let it be.

"That is your choice, Mrs. Dupree," replied Dr. Lamb in his best non-judgmental tone. "But, if I were you, I would think it over when

I was not quite so....so, surprised," he suggested nicely. He patted her clenched fists very quickly and then stuffed his hand back into the safety of his lab coat pocket, as if he'd been through this before. Nina was sure he had. No woman could be prepared for this. "Perhaps a chat with your husband will make you feel better. Won't he be pleased?"

Nina sucked in her breath and clamped her hands over her mouth. Her eyes flashed wildly, and Dr. Lamb drew back instantly, as if she might be sick on him. But, it wasn't nausea. Exhaling with a sob, Nina knew that this incredible intimate information would remain with her. She had no idea who fathered the child. Hugo? Archie? A prank by the devil himself? She said nothing more to the doctor. This was her burden to bear, and it was nobody's business.

Without another word to Dr. Lamb, Nina grabbed her coat and handbag and rushed down the corridor.

Taking care to keep her head down, Nina crept through the crowded waiting room, praying she wouldn't bump into anybody she knew. She was oddly aware of her abdomen, a belly with a baby in it. Her limbs had apparently disappeared and she was simply floating across the carpet buoyed by an enormous stomach. How ridiculous! One cannot feel a baby at this early stage. My God, she thought, I'm sounding just like Hugo.

Nina ran to the parking lot trying to imagine what Hugo was going to say. He wasn't terribly fond of children. They were messy, loud, and took enormous amounts of time and money. Life, he'd told her several months back, could be perfectly fine without children. Hah! How had this happened? Her heart was racing and her mouth felt dry. She would simply tell Hugo (or Archie) that a diagnostic mistake was made long ago. Hugo was so unimaginative he'd never figure out the timing. Besides, their lovemaking had been hit or miss for weeks. Nobody would ever get this straight. Unless there were blood tests. There would be no blood tests. Ever! Nina would create a child and a mystery all in one swoop. She smiled. The very idea made her feel much better.

Nina started the Mercedes and screeched out of the clinic lot, just missing a UPS truck. The driver thrust a fist out the window and yelled something in Italian. She gave him the finger and sped down Weston Street. Life was about to get complicated. Nina couldn't help smiling, just a little. If she hadn't been at the center of this mess, she'd have laughed her head off.

Without thinking, Nina drove east toward the bluffs, their bony shoulders exposed now. The shawl of autumn had slipped away. According to Archie, the approaching November pot gray skies would give way to the brilliance of winter. Ahead lay Christmas and New Year's Eve and her belly growing bigger and bigger. Ho, ho, ho. Nina took in her own face in the rearview mirror. She looked tired and worried, in spite of her lovely 'do' by Alexandre. She'd have to swallow dozens of vitamins and try not to get fat. She'd have to figure out who the father might be. She'd have to break the news. Hire a nanny. Find a bigger apartment. Would she have to marry? Who? Archie or Hugo? Ooooh!

Nina swung into Kipper's Custard Stand and ordered a double chocolate cone to go. What the hell. She pulled out again and licked the rich custard as she drove. What if she had a little girl? Big blue eyes, long blonde hair. A miniature Nina. Would that be so awful? For a block or two, Nina entertained mother-daughter fantasies…..how she'd teach little Nina to buy the right clothes, give parties, and maybe become an actress, like her mother, or run for president. There would be expenses, of course. Ballet and piano lessons. Braces for her teeth and trips to New York. Private school. A convertible for her eighteenth birthday. And, there would be Hugo, sitting at his desk behind a pile of bills. She could hear Hugo roaring. Archie would never roar about a child. Would he?

Turning up Sweet Briar road, it suddenly dawned on her that she was heading for Hugo's place. What possessed her? Just as quickly, the stress of the morning and the rich custard forced her stomach into revolt. She screeched to a stop in the middle of the street, flung open the door and stumbled to the nearest patch of grass where she threw up. It turned out to be the Salantine's front yard, a perfect blanket of perfect grass sprinkled artistically with gold maple leaves. As Nina crouched there on the lawn, she vowed revenge upon the father. It didn't matter who it was; somebody would pay for this very public indignity. She soon was able to drive off, back downtown to the Beacon Street Arms.

Just minutes before, across the street, Betty Hughes was standing transfixed behind the filmy draperies in Maureen Daley's living room. Quite by chance, she had glanced outside to admire a rosy barberry bush when she happened to see Nina suffering her predicament on the neighbor's lawn. She'd heard the car screech first, and then witnessed the rest. Poor Nina. And, Richard Salantine was such a nut about his grass. She grinned. Should she run out to help Nina? Before Betty Hughes could decide and open the door, Nina had roared off down the street. Who could blame her?

Was Nina ill? Too much Chablis with lunch? How well did they really know her? She could be a secret drinker, but Betty Hughes didn't really believe that. Was Nina enduring medical treatments that made her sick? Or, bad scallops? None of it sounded plausible. Nina looked too good to be too sick. Betty Hughes said nothing to Maureen. She might mention it to Naddy. After all, Nina was almost family.

Nadine and Betty Hughes sat across from each other at the Half Moon Luncheonette the following afternoon. Lola Spriggs's death remained a topic of intense speculation. Nadine stuck her fork into Mimi's crunchy chicken salad without much enthusiasm. "How does the gardener strike you, Betty Hughes?" The salad turned out to be heavenly. "He'll be richer than when he started."

Betty Hughes fiddled with her own salad, more greens, fewer calories, and said, "Rather Agatha Christie, isn't he?"

"Very. A ghoulish murder in a quaint village by a river, a gloomy, over-dressed old house, lots of eccentric, greedy relatives, a bizarre will. A handsome gardener who inherits a bundle. Dame Agatha will be popping out of her grave for this one."

Betty Hughes stuck a dot of butter on an inch square of roll and then debated about whether or not to eat it. Sometimes Nadine wanted to scream at her or give her a smack. Betty Hughes was obsessed lately with her new diet. And, she was smoking again!

"What do you know about this gardener," Betty Hughes asked. "He is kinda cute. I bet Lola thought he was kinda cute too."

"You mean a September/May romance? Or, whatever you call those affairs with the months in them." Nadine pushed Betty Hughes's fork toward her mouth and said, "Eat!"

Betty Hughes looked properly offended and replied, "Why can't pretty older women snag young studs?"

"They can. They do. But, I don't think this guy was showing Lola a good time."

"So, what's he like?" Betty Hughes ate the inch of roll and a few leaves of lettuce.

"Thirty-nine. Loves plants. Got along splendidly with Lola. He seemed polite and quite eager to talk to me."

"And, his private life?"

"Unmarried. Lives on a houseboat. A few close friends. Dropped out of college. Likes to fish. Shocked by Lola's terrible death. I think he might be gay."

"Could be. Maybe he was more interested in Toby than Lola. Toby might be playing for the other team. But, the gardener's too much of a stock murder mystery character. He's too perfect. We're on the wrong track, Nadine." Betty Hughes asked the waitress for more coffee.

Nadine finished her lunch, down to the last cashew nestled among the greens, and turned down the offer of cherry pie. "What if the motive isn't money?" she said.

Betty Hughes's eyes widened with interest. "I could go for that. Maybe Lola wasn't as sweet as everybody thought. Maybe Lola was murdered by somebody who didn't like her very much."

Nadine watched Betty Hughes reapply her lipstick without a mirror. "Dame Agatha would be proud," Nadine said. "I'll ask my old auntie a few discreet questions. She has a trunk load of dirt on everybody in town. The J. Edgar Hoover of Belmont. I'm surprised somebody hasn't bumped her off." Nadine rolled her eyes for Betty Hughes and Betty Hughes laughed.

"Freddy doesn't want your auntie within a hundred miles of anything that might go to court."

"I know, but Freddy shouldn't be so fussy. It's almost Halloween. The natives are restless. There could be a killer out there….hiding under a devil's costume."

Betty Hughes shuddered and said, "Call your old auntie."

For the faithful in Belmont, Beatrice Wrenn's séance on Halloween Eve was a big ticket event, attracting the usual suspects (as Betty Hughes called the regulars) and a fair number of neophytes. Miss Wrenn had pared her long list of Halloween Eve applicants to an acceptable circle of ten needy and curious patrons, all financially solvent. Her séances were limited to ten, and the chosen few were commanded to arrive promptly at seven on Friday evening.

Betty Hughes insisted that Nina test drive at least one of the Beatrice Wrenn Otherworldly Wingdings, these affairs of the occult. Betty Hughes didn't take Beatrice seriously, but she did find the séances amusing and certainly informative. She told Nina that it was group therapy for the well-off but not very firmly planted. Nina said she wouldn't miss it. Privately, she was thrilled to get out of the flat, to think about something other than her 'condition.' Betty Hughes said she might be a trifle late.

As Nina parked in front of Wrenn House, she remembered driving through the neighborhood with Archie on a warm July afternoon. It was called Ravenswood, a well-groomed pocket of prime real estate where baronial piles of stone and brick were shaded by towering elms that had successfully sheltered the very rich from the not so rich since the carriage days. The old mansions weren't as old or as historic as Dupree House in New Orleans, but they did possess that hysterical, larger-than-life Victorian charm.

Nina stepped from the car and nearly fell on a skin of dead leaves sticking to the pavement. A strong north wind whined through the trees and whipped the corners of Wrenn House, a buttery Italianate with fewer frills than its neighbors. A leering jack-o-lantern glowed in each of four windows in the cupola. The faces made Nina grin; she felt like a kid. On the ground, dry leaves scuttled like mice within a tidy white-fenced garden. The setting was so patently theatrical it might have been designed by Belle for one of her avant-garde productions. High in the black sky, a sliver of ivory moon rested on its backside, as if waiting to see goblins flutter through the bushes.

Nina climbed the painted wooden steps to a wide veranda and pushed the bell. A half dozen costumed urchins raced through adjoining yards calling out their two-note song…. 'trick or treat.' Candlelit pumpkins with wickedly slashed mouths and evil eyes watched from Miss Wrenn's front windows. Glancing up and down the street, Nina could see carved faces flickering on porch rails and steps; sheet ghosts and cardboard skeletons swung eerily from low branches along the sidewalks. She loved

Halloween and wondered if the little devils weren't a trifle afraid to beg candy from a woman who routinely talked to dead people.

The double doors were suddenly flung open and Nina was introduced to Belmont's famous Miss Wrenn…attired in magenta, her signature color, and looking mildly distracted. Miss Wrenn said she wasn't quite ready, directed Nina to the parlor and then disappeared into the back of the house.

The unmistakable keyboard and sax of Brubeck and Desmond floated in from the spacious drawing room. Not bad, Nina thought, a psychic who appreciated jazz. The house was beautiful. Tarot cards paid well or nicely augmented Miss Wrenn's private income. The Wrenns were a notorious band of characters and crooks, according to local gossips, a common enough ancestral story. Who didn't own a few?

The high-ceilinged room was graciously furnished with English antiques of a period earlier than the house. The fine wood pieces were interspersed with soft chairs and couches. Parchment shaded lamps and candles provided flattering light, while a collection of exceptional watercolors in gilded frames whispered scenes of another era from subtly papered walls.

"Not the kind of room I expected. Very elegant," Nina commented aloud and to herself. She seemed to be the first to arrive.

"How true."

Nina jumped at the sound of another voice. The stagy baritone came from just behind her, and she swung around to find an imposing gentleman of roughly fifty or so (who could tell anymore?), leaning elegantly against an ebony grand piano. He was holding a glass of sherry. With his graying hair and crisp mustache, Nina fancied he'd just stepped from a production of 'Private Lives.'

"How do you do?" the gentleman asked, moving forward and extending his hand. "I am Cosmo Freese, and you are?" He took Nina's hand and lightly kissed her fingertips. "I'm sorry I startled you."

"Nina Dupree." Nina gently released her hand. The gentleman looked familiar. "Have we met?"

"No. No. I would have remembered you, Miss Dupree. You possess an unforgettable face." Cosmo Freese smiled gallantly. Nina nodded her appreciation. Freese went on, "I've just moved here from New York to join the Augusta Repertory Company." He turned to the tray of crystal cordial glasses and decanters resting on the broad back of the piano behind him. "Sherry?"

"Yes, thank you." (One small glass was allowed by Dr. Lamb.)

Freese performed his waiter's role and said, "Miss Wrenn prefers us modestly awake and sober for these ordeals of the spirit. Nothing stronger than tawny wine." He crossed one tweedy leg over the other and went back to holding up the piano.

Cosmo Freese was the very essence of English charm. "I believe I saw your photograph in the *Belmont Bee*," Nina said. Freese was good looking in an old-fashioned refined manner, a man of medium build and height and deep-set gray eyes with the very devil in them. "How do you like Belmont, Mr. Freese?"

"Call me Cosmo." Freese refilled his glass. "Marvelous. Quaint, I think you'd have to say. I'm staying at the St. George."

"And, you are an actor? My mother manages Bright Lights Chamber theatre in New Orleans." Nina sipped her wine. "You do bring Noel Coward to mind." She laughed and so did Cosmo. His voice was that theatrical mix of classical training and practiced stage diction not often heard anymore.

"How flattering! I generally work in New York or London, but, Harry, my son….he's a painter….has persuaded me to try repertory. Just for fun, he said." Freese fussed with a silk scarf knotted around his throat. "I plan to take a small place at Meadowlark Village."

"Rather stodgy for a New York gentleman, isn't it?"

Cosmo grinned in appreciation. "It suits me now. Low maintenance. A dining hall."

"What brings you here tonight?" asked Nina.

"Curiosity. Background for a part I'm to play after Christmas. Check out the local beauties." He smiled sexily.

My God, Nina thought, he's flirting. She returned the smile but left out any vital encouragement. She was in enough trouble with Hugo and Archie. "Séances aren't my usual form of entertainment either. Or, communication, for that matter." They both laughed.

Any further conversation was interrupted by the arrival of two more guests, Betty Hughes and a nervous looking gentleman with a beaky nose. On seeing Cosmo and Nina, Betty Hughes waved and approached. The strange gentleman followed at her heels. Nina could almost see his nose twitch at the scent.

The Twitch called out, "Goodness, two new faces! Intros are in order!" And, he galloped across the carpet toward them, overtaking Betty Hughes. He lurched for Nina's hand, which he shook so animatedly she felt herself go dizzy from the force. The strange man said he was Doctor Dudley Dunn, with emphasis on doctor.

Dunn's presumptuousness prompted Betty Hughes to grab his arm. "Really, Dudley!" she scolded, "men just don't yank women out of their caves anymore. Where have you been the last twenty years?"

Dudley Dunn apologized hastily and explained that he'd just been turned loose on society after years of marital imprisonment. He laughed good-naturedly and so did everyone else. The good doctor's personality might have rough edges, Nina decided, but he was not nearly as dangerous as Cosmo Freese.

"No woman is safe these days," said Betty Hughes only half jokingly and all done up in autumnal colors and her good jewelry. "We must marry you off again, Dudley."

Just then, Marigold Woolsey appeared in the doorway. She paused to get her bearings and then proceeded to join the group after first fetching a glass of sherry. Nina had to admit the worldly sculptress did make a stunning impression in her flowing silks and diamond earrings. Like an aging Hollywood temptress, Marigold carried herself as if she owned the planet.

Once again, introductions were made. Nina watched Cosmo take in the likes of Marigold; he was predictably impressed. Dr. Dunn drank in the vision, as if he had just crossed a desert. Nina found all the fuss a bit half-witted. Betty Hughes looked annoyed and defensive.

"Ah, Betty Hughes, darling," Marigold said grandly. "I had no idea you believed in ghosts." She laughed and shook her head in wonderment.

Hah! The great seductress was pulling arrows from her quiver as if Betty Hughes might pose a threat to her status. Betty Hughes stepped up on her toes like the true professional woman she was. "I am here to be entertained. Séances are like the old South, filled with Caribbean voodoo magic. Who do you talk to on the other side? One of your many dead lovers, I presume."

Nina cleared her throat. It would seem that Betty Hughes possessed a full quiver of her own. Cosmo was openly fascinated with the proceedings, and Dudley Dunn stood at full attention. Nina noticed a tiny smile shape Cosmo's lips. Nice lips.

"My lovers are very much alive," Marigold responded without missing a beat. "I'm doing research on a new play." She directed her words to Betty Hughes this time.

Nina decided that Betty Hughes was acting like a nun who had just learned she was destined for sainthood. The nun smiled sweetly and countered, "I finished my second play just this afternoon." A true competitor.

"I had no idea you finished the first one." Marigold laughed, the tinkling kind females hate. "I submitted my entry for the contest last week. And, now, I'm working on a novel ……a romance novel." Her face was a mask of serenity. "Who better than I?"

Betty Hughes drew a breath, held it, and exhaled with the control of an opera singer. "Romance is trickier than sex, Marigold. I doubt you'll ever get the hang of it." She smiled like an angel and added, "Now, if you'll excuse me, I see a dear friend across the room." And, she made her exit with a polished, sweeping turn.

That should just about cover all the rough spots for tonight, Nina thought. She felt Cosmo leaning ever so gently into her arm, as if giving her a signal. She easily returned the pressure. She felt as if she'd known this man for years. Two more guests had entered the room, diverting their attention again. Dr. Dunn hurriedly filled the dead air with a burst of conversation and then audaciously led Marigold by the elbow toward the sherry table.

Cosmo was reading the undercurrent like a pro. He stepped closer to Nina and took her arm, saying, "Let's sit by the fire. It's grown a bit chilly."

"Not surprising," Nina remarked quickly, "with Betty Hughes and Marigold going at it like fish wives." They both laughed.

Nina and Cosmo sank into a sofa near the hearth. Cosmo leaned toward her and whispered, "Tell me, if you don't mind, just how long has Betty Hughes Armbruster shared the firing range with Marigold Woolsey? He raised an eyebrow and inclined his head toward hers.

"Since childhood, I think. The Old Devils ….all the older husbands….find Marigold enticing and the wives cannot shake the jealousy. Right now, Betty Hughes is pissed because Marigold has written a play for the college competition. And, so has Betty Hughes."

"Goodness. Such intrigue in a small town." Cosmo Freese laughed. Noticing Nina's large diamond ring, he asked about the lucky fellow.

"Hugo Beresford. But, I'm pretty sure the engagement is over. Hugo has that effect on women." Nina sighed. She barely knew this man and here she was confiding in him. She trusted him without really knowing why. Poor Cosmo Freese, what would he think if he knew there were two Mr. Beresfords? "I should return it, but it is quite pretty, isn't it?"

"I see. Yes. A stunning ring." Cosmo nodded sympathetically but wisely never pursued the subject further. "Do you think Beatrice Wrenn has drowned in her tub?"

"She's great at delayed entrances, I'm told. Pure show business. Isn't everything? As a matter-of-fact I am studying acting at the University."

"I am delighted to hear it. I would think your stage presence would be fabulous! We must talk about this." Cosmo was grinning enthusiastically.

That just said, Nina looked up to see Miss Wrenn waltz into the room, an apparition in velvet. Her long embroidered gown swept the toes of what appeared to be tennis shoes. A shimmering gold scarf was wound about her unruly hair. She was a striking woman somewhere in her forties or fifties. It was difficult to tell. The psychic greeted her guests without apology and accepted a glass of sherry from Dr. Dunn, as quick as a fox when it came to females. Then, Miss Wrenn turned up the tape of Stan Getz noodling vintage bossa nova.

Nina couldn't suppress the giggles, and Cosmo shook gently with a laugh of his own. Beatrice threw them a withering glance, as if to say, séances are my gig; don't spoil it. You have your own.

The psychic asked her fellow enthusiasts to remove their shoes and to join her in the dining room at a large round table draped in black silk. Ten white tapers in silver holders flickered in the center. Ten Regency chairs circled the table. They took their seats. There were rustles and deep breaths and all eyes focused on Miss Beatrice.

And, the séance began.

"She's Nessa Quinn, Archie, only twenty years older. With better jewelry." Nessa Quinn, Belmont's favorite harlot, was not normally talked about in the Beresford house.

Archie's bride was throwing lingerie into one of two suitcases lying open on the bed. Her cosmetic bag was only half filled. She continued, "The jig is up, my darling. I'm wise to your afternoons with Marigold Woolsey. Old story. Old woman, these days. I'm surprised you didn't pick some pretty sales rep down at the office. Heavens, Tommy always finds females half his age."

"Don't be ridiculous!" Archie boomed. "Marigold is one of our oldest friends. How can you say that? How can you be wise to something that isn't happening?" He threw up his arms in a dramatic gesture of innocence and frustration. He was standing on the opposite side of Nadine's bed. He didn't often visit her bedroom these days.

"You're too fond of Marigold. Always were. It's….undignified." Nadine's lower lip trembled, but she held firm. She wasn't a woman given to unseemly emotional outbursts.

"You're being unreasonable. You're running away on false information!" Archie had never been so right. He was hoping Naddy would break down. A crying female was far more likely to listen to reason.

"Don't be a fool. Marigold will tire of you or any of the other old devils who chase her around the bedroom. She much prefers those student models from the college." Nadine raised an eyebrow and carefully folded a satin nightgown before placing it into her case.

Archie cringed. Old devils. He'd always hated that silly nickname. Betty Hughes's idea of something funny. With the bed between them, Archie watched his wife go on with her packing, composure intact, her sucker punches still deadly.

"That's dirty pool, Naddy."

"You should know. I'll be going in an hour. Western Horizon Spa in Phoenix. You

know the number. I'll be gone until I get back."

It dawned on Archie that Nadine really meant business this time. An open-ended visit to her favorite spa. Not good. To cover his regret, he walked across the hall to his own bedroom and retrieved a jacket from the closet. He returned to the wide corridor and said, "I'm going over to see Cyrus. Don't wait up." He would pretend her packing was just a ploy to get him to confess.

"Don't trouble yourself about me, Archie. I've ordered Mr. Foote's taxi."

Archie stayed put in the hall and watched Nadine stuff jars of creams and lotions and handfuls of cosmetics into her small case. She was royally pissed.

"I don't know who told you what, but I have not seduced Marigold. I stopped by their new digs last week and helped Parnell carry a rug to the attic. Very sexy. Very sinister."

He puffed out his chest as if he'd just won a race. "No liquor was consumed. The lights were on and everybody had their feet on the floor at all times. Your spies are filling you full of hooey." He worried that Naddy's spies might find out about Nina.

Nadine was hurrying between the bathroom and the bedroom, fetching and carrying, not giving Archie her full attention. Archie finally gave up and skipped downstairs.

"Ah," he called pleasantly but loudly from the foyer, "the desert should be beautiful this time of year." Maybe he'd shame her into staying, but silence was the only response from upstairs. Oh, to hell with it. Cyrus would have a few stories to tell. Spats with Nadine were ancient news. The spa couldn't hurt. A few days of steam baths and radish salads might shave some pounds from those thighs. Archie was suddenly feeling mean.

As he picked up his car keys from the foyer table, Archie made it a point to whistle rather shrilly.

"Have a nice time, dear!" he sang out at the foot of the great curved staircase.

"Don't worry, Archie," came the reply. "I'm going to have a better time than you imagine."

11

Funny Fellows

Cyrus chalked his cue a third time and then positioned himself at the side of Archie's antique billiard table. Nose level with the cushioned edge, he leaned in to examine the field of colored balls scattered over the green baize, as if sighting the lay of the grass before sinking a putt.

Archie sighed audibly but said nothing. Admiral Moss busied himself with ice cubes and scotch. Tommy Delaney, dozing nearby in a tweedy recliner, was spared the performance. Archie reasoned that Cyrus had his own way of shooting pool these days, and there was no sense in asking him what he was doing. Half the time he didn't know.

"I have this hair in my nose, Archie," Cyrus suddenly announced out of the blue, pulling himself upright again and forgetting altogether to take his shot.

"So?" Archie answered patiently, wishing he could bellow like a bull. "We all have nose hairs."

"Before I go, Archie, I want somebody to get rid of it!" Cyrus tapped his cue against the side of the table with each word to show he was serious. The boys noticed that he wasn't flashing his famous 'gottcha' grin this time. "Before I croak!"

"Jesus, Cyrus, just clip the damned thing out. Let's play!"

"Get me a scissors, Arch. You can do it, can't you?" Cyrus tapped the side of his nose this time to indicate the offending nostril.

"For heaven's sake! Have Betty Hughes help you when you get home. Shoot. Shoot!" Archie closed his eyes and counted to ten before taking another look at reality. He must remember to treat Cyrus like a little kid who's still learning how to behave. That's what Nadine suggested they do. Of course, Nadine was lying on a beach towel in the desert; easy for her to say.

Cyrus now appeared bewildered by what Archie had said, as if someone else had brought up the subject of undesirable nose hairs.

"You don't have to get testy about a game of billiards, Arch. It's supposed to be fun. And who wants to hear about nose hairs?" Cyrus took his shot and miraculously socked the seven ball into the side pocket. He raised an arm in victory and the boys shook their heads in astonishment. Archie said he'd let Cyrus play alone for a while.

The Admiral took orders for fresh drinks and put them together at the mahogany bar in the game room, the only first-class billiard room in town, and it wasn't located in the basement either.

Tommy was snoring softly, unable to play but willing enough to hoist a few, he'd said. "Cyrus has good and bad days, mostly good though, when you count them up," the Admiral remarked quietly to Archie who slid onto the adjacent stool. An old Artie Shaw recording was playing in the background. The big band beat, the Admiral said to Archie, always reminded him of the war. Brought back memories of the officers' club in Hawaii, where he'd been stationed briefly.

"He's failing, kind of hit or miss," Archie whispered back. "I've come to appreciate Tommy's reliance on the sauce….when life gets rough."

The old Navy man nodded, and the two sat quietly together, each reminded of his own frailty, their own mortality.

"He'll start a new medicine this week. Some experimental stuff from the University Med School. Let's hope it works!" Archie sounded optimistic. The Admiral agreed.

"Isn't Parnell supposed to show up?" called out Cyrus after sinking another ball. "Hey, you old coots, I'm beating the socks off my phantom opponent here!" He giggled and poised himself for another shot. "Who started calling us the Old Devils?" he asked quite sanely.

"Your dear wife. Said it's what Kingsley Amis called his over-fifty characters in one of his novels." Archie still didn't like it. They might be devils, but he didn't like the 'old' part.

"Parnell should be here about nine," said the Admiral, in answer to Cyrus's question. "He's helping Marigold with some curtains."

"Very domestic fellow," Archie said. He'd known Parnell for years, well before he and Marigold fled the provincial boundaries of Belmont for the Continent, as they preferred to call Europe.

Cyrus joined Archie and the Admiral at the bar.

"Parnell's a bit fruitier this trip, isn't he?" said Cyrus without meaning any harm. "The wrist is limper than it used to be." He shoved a handful of mixed nuts in his mouth.

"You mean Parnell's a homo?" The croak came from Tommy, who'd awakened suddenly.

"Rubbish!" thundered Archie. "The man's an artist, a poet! He's supposed to wear capes and berets. It's part of his....persona." He gestured broadly like Parnell. The very idea of Marigold living with a gay man all these years sent Archie's mind reeling.

"He's got a hell of a reputation with the ladies," Tommy said, pushing himself straighter in the chair. "Hell, he's just artistic, Cyrus. We must make allowances." Tommy lighted a cigarette and took a drag that sent him into spasms of dry hacking.

Archie hurried to his side, thumped him on the back and insisted he drink cold water. Tommy obeyed as best he could. Winded and weak after the seizure but still clutching the cigarette between yellowed fingers, Tommy said, "I know. I know. I should give up the Marlboros. They'll kill me before the booze."

"We're dying of second-hand smoke, Tommy," grumbled the Admiral, who'd smoked for years before quitting.

"Too late now. My way to heaven's been paved with enough Brother Beam and cigs to get me there and back a couple times!" Tommy laughed, a wheezy, belabored effort but hearty enough to avoid a call to 911.

"Jesus, you old fart," snickered Cyrus. "You don't think you're coming back, do you? Surely, the Blessed Virgin'll keep you there, won't she? You need remedial work, my boy. A couple centuries of remedial work. The BV's got her work cut out with you up there on your very dingy shamrock cloud." Cyrus giggled softly. He was good at teasing Tommy and Tommy ate it up.

They all laughed, including Tommy, who talked about heaven a lot these days. The picture of Tommy Delaney confronted by the Blessed Virgin was almost too much for Archie and he laughed until tears dribbled down his cheeks.

"I'm thinking the BV might be a real beauty, a lithesome lass with long black curls. Ahh. It might be kinda nice up there, my lads. But, you'll be joining me soon enough. We're none of us even fifty anymore." Tommy appeared wistful and then closed his eyes for another wee nap, as he called these all too frequent recesses from life.

Archie walked over to Tommy, eased the burning cigarette from his fingers and snuffed it out in the ashtray.

"I want a hand dug grave, you know. I'm putting you guys on notice," declared Cyrus. He was serious and sane again.

"Hand dug?" sputtered the Admiral. "Where'd you get such an idea?" He opened a jar of roasted peanuts and sniffed them for freshness. "Nowadays, cemeteries use machines, like small steam shovels."

"No John Deere back-hoes for me," said Cyrus adamantly. "If you fellas can't do it, get Duncan and a couple of young reporters from *Tribune* to shovel the dirt. They've been dying to do it for years!" He giggled.

"OK, OK. But, what if it's winter?" asked Archie.

"Nobody digs graves around here in winter," said the Admiral, matter-of-factly. "They wait until spring. They'll store you in a refrigerator until April."

No one said a word for a minute, remembering the truth of bodies shelved in bins like venison steaks.

Not finished with his list of final demands, Cyrus said, "And, I want real pall bearers to carry the casket. On their shoulders. Proper. You and the other boys. Don't you dare wheel me in on one of those casket dollies." He made a face.

"It will be arranged, Cyrus. You can do the same for me." Archie patted his friend's bony back. "How about a flag? How about Arlington?"

"Damned straight. I fought for my country. Jesus, Archie, we survived Normandy together." Cyrus got up and put his arm around

Archie's massive shoulders. "We made it. Why do you suppose we did? I've asked myself that question every morning since the war." His lower lip quivered. The Old Devils knew what he was talking about.

"We were meant to stay here to..." Archie paused, trying to think of what they had been destined to become. "To drive the girls crazy, I guess!" He giggled and Cyrus perked up again and then sat down.

"And that we've done!" cried Tommy, among the living again. He struggled to sit up straighter in the lounge chair, somehow always sensing unconsciously when it might be fun to be conscious.

A singer on the CD player was warbling 'Poor Butterfly' and Tommy began to sing along in a tremulous tenor. The rest slowly joined in until they had a respectable chorus going. Cyrus attempted harmony on the last few bars of the old tune. The recording slid over to 'Body and Soul.'

'I remember a gal in Hawaii," said the Admiral, "at the officers' club, it was. Right before Pearl Harbor. Wife of some general, I think. Anyway, she'd get too many martinis in her and always wanted to sing 'Poor Butterfly' with the little combo they had on Saturday nights." The Admiral was miles away in Hawaii.

"And?" coaxed Archie.

"And, they always let her." The Admiral smiled crookedly. The boys nodded. "It's the only nice memory I have of the war," he said, a rare thing in itself.

The general melancholy of the moment was suddenly interrupted by the arrival of Parnell Grant, who swirled into the billiard room with his ubiquitous cape aflutter. "Let the games begin!" he cried out dramatically. From beneath his cape he offered up a lasagna in a gleaming white porcelain casserole, straight from his oven, he crowed proudly. He was into cooking, he told them. "I'm thinking about starting a gourmet cooking program for television. *Continental Cuisine with Parnell Grant.*" He beamed and began calling for plates and silverware. The devils eagerly sampled his lasagna and then suggested not too politely that he keep writing poetry.

"TV isn't ready for you yet, Parnell," said Tommy with a twinkle.

The Admiral, in an attempt at humor, passed around a roll of Tums.

An hour later after more billiards, Parnell approached Cyrus and whispered in his elaborate fashion, "I've written a modest poem to commemorate our homecoming and I'd like you, Cyrus, to give it a once over before I read it at Thanksgiving dinner." He pulled a folded sheet of paper from his vest pocket.

"A Harvest Ode?" read Cyrus sleepily. "A turkey sonnet, you've got there. How about I give it a go in the morning, old friend. When my head's dried out." He smiled nicely at Parnell. "If I remember correctly, you penned a few couplets to Belmont when you departed with Marigold twenty years ago."

Parnell seemed not to hear him and said, "I'd be most grateful, Cyrus. Marigold has too much on her mind right now with the redecorations." The poet of Paris fell into the depths of the leather sofa where Cyrus was lodged into a corner, unable to move. "Your abode, my dear fellow, is being transformed into a Tuscan villa. We have swaying cypress painted upon the walls, sun-bleached tiles on the floor and sun-baked urns in the garden. Marigold is positively inspired!"

Parnell was making the usual sweeping motions with his arms, the full sleeves of his silky shirt wafting close to Cyrus's nose. Cyrus sniffed the sweet cologne, as if somehow testing the notion of Parnell's possible preference for men. He soon cuddled up in his corner of the couch and relaxed, unafraid of any advances upon his person by the old bard.

With renewed enthusiasm Parnell expounded in great detail on the redecoration of Tallyho until Cyrus sat up with an expression of great bewilderment on his face.

"Tuscan villa?" Cyrus asked, confused and frightened. "Have we been shipped to Italy, Arch? We've just barely made it up the cliffs at Omaha Beach." Cyrus stared at Parnell as if he'd never laid eyes on him before.

Parnell, nearly in the arms of stupor and sleep, managed to say, "You've slid back to the Normandy beaches, old boy. To the awful hedgerows. Not to worry, my friend, not to worry. You're safe with us." Parnell looked around to see the Admiral snoring on the top of the billiard table. Tommy lay on the carpet with his coat as a blanket.

Archie was attempting to clean up. When Archie heard Parnell's words, he said, almost to himself, "Yes, the war. Maybe a safer place for Cyrus than the dark hole of dementia."

Parnell, alert enough to hear Archie, said quietly, "I wonder if Marigold and I have made the right decision. To come back, I mean. It will be a sadder time now. We'll be watching each other fail and eventually die."

Before Archie could answer, he watched Parnell slump against the cushions and drop off to sleep. Would age make them stronger or more wretched? Archie felt slightly ill and didn't have an answer. He doubted anybody did.

"What does she do all day?" asked Lettice. "Sleeps late, I would imagine. No wonder her skin shimmers. So would mine, if I napped and had a housekeeper." She washed her hands and picked up a folded, rose-spattered paper towel from a little basket next to the sink. She was in one of her cross moods and seemed eager to criticize Marigold today. Lettice still had trouble dealing with friends who were better-fixed, as she called it, than she was.

Betty Hughes listened and examined her reflection in the ladies room mirror. Their case against Marigold was always under construction. But, Betty Hughes was realizing that the foundation remained wobbly…not enough cement in the concrete. "She claims to be writin' a romance novel now. A dig at me, of course." Betty Hughes didn't feel as vitriolic as she usually did when discussing Marigold's exploits. Their quarrel was growing stale.

The ladies were lunching with Marigold and Isobel at Eugenia's, a new eatery on Rose Street, all done up in emerald paisley paper and antique French prints. The cafe existed in sharp contrast to its forerunner, Bruno's, where washroom walls had worn low-brow graffiti and lipstick kisses. Besides flowered towels, Eugenia's specialized in California cuisine and long wine lists. Pan-fish and French fries had been replaced with caramelized onions over fettuccine and raw artichoke-mushroom salad, a clear indication of the town's new sophistication. The mayor's new unofficial motto was: 'Rejuvenate and restore or move to Stone Bank…..' where life was pretty much as it had been fifty years ago.

"Shimmering or not, Marigold seems to have lost her appetite for shrimp tandoori," remarked Lettice, as she applied fresh lipstick. "She does have a certain look about her these days."

"Marigold looks like an elderly *Vogue* model who has taken a taxi into the wrong neighborhood." Betty Hughes ran a comb through her hair. Spotting a gray sprout, she leaned toward the mirror and plucked it out. "Damn things. They pop up like toadstools."

"She missed bridge club last week." Fearing they might have company, Lettice took a belated peek beneath the stalls. They were alone.

"I wonder if she's taken a new lover. Other than one of the Old Devils? Belmont nowadays is fresh territory for the old girl. Great skin can mean great sex." She smiled at Lettice, rather hoping Lettice might confide in her about Admiral Moss, especially after the silk underwear episode. Were they an item or not? So far, Lettice had kept her friendship with Melvin her own business. And, she never mentioned the underwear either. Betty Hughes fluffed her hair.

"Who would she be seeing? O'Neill Spender?" Lettice had disregarded all diplomacy this time. She knew how protective Betty Hughes was about darling O'Neill. "Frankly, I can't imagine O'Neill without his clothes. I bet he does it with his socks on."

Betty Hughes was rather shocked at Lettice's turn of phrase and her boldness about Belmont's shy literary agent. She laughed and said, "I must admit O'Neill doesn't have Archie's charms. But, an affair with Marigold? That shark? Heavens, Lettice, O'Neill's still adjustin' to his cat. He doesn't even date." Betty Hughes's bachelor agent lived in a modest flat over Eggert and Fry, a law firm with attorneys as old as the constitution. "Of course, Cyrus always says, watch out for the quiet ones."

"It has to be somebody." Lettice applied powder to her nose and tucked in her blouse.

"So, after BLTs at the Half Moon Luncheonette, O'Neill and Marigold rush back to his apartment and tear off each other's clothes? And, this explains the glowin' skin and a lack of interest in shrimp? That woman's old enough to be his mother!"

"I bet Miss Magnolia cooked up little O'Neill like a three-minute egg." Lettice put on lipstick and smoothed her eyebrows. "Men cut off their ears for babes like Marigold."

"O'Neill didn't know he had ears before Marigold came along." Betty Hughes adjusted her earrings. "If I didn't know better, I'd say she's in love or worried about something. It's hard to tell the difference….. the symptoms are the same."

"Hah! Wouldn't that be justice in a perfectly pressed black robe?" Lettice laughed, as if she might believe it. "She's always liked well-muscled life guards." She opened the rest room door and they moved into the corridor.

"That woman is absolutely exhaustin'."

It was a week after the séance, and Nina was a wreck, and she rarely was. The smooth-running Rolex days were over, she told herself. During the past year she'd endured a broken engagement, an uprooting, loneliness, boredom and now…*this*. She automatically patted her tummy, slightly larger but not noticeably so. Belle and Beau, the soon-to-be grandparents, would have to be told. She would wait until she was tougher.

Pregnant at forty-two and unclear on the paternity. Guilty of cheating on her husband-to-be while he was busy cheating on her. Tip-toeing around a lover who may or may not be interested in fatherhood. And, all the while trying her hand at acting again, something her mother had proposed she pursue years ago. She did seem to have a gift for reading a line. Her professor was quite impressed and had cast her in a play at the university. He had so few forty-something actresses that he fairly swooned when she entered his class. Her resume might be getting worse, but it certainly had depth. Was there no one she could talk to? Belle, as centered as she was, would faint if she knew about the baby. Nadine was hardly confidante material at this point, which left Betty Hughes, a woman who might be more sympathetic than judgmental. Nina smiled. She might find it terribly amusing and advise marriage to insufferable Hugo and to keep her secret lover on the side.

Adrift in her bed, Nina wasn't terribly comforted by her options. Who was pulling the strings these days? Maybe she could use all of this experience when playing a complex character some day. Not any time soon. Nina pulled the sheet over her head.

Just a few blocks away at the St. George, Cosmo Freese lay asleep on his back, a position that generally brought on nightmares. Not knowing he was on his back, and snoring besides, was one of the downsides of the single life, he'd found. At present he was without that ever vigilant female who might choose to lie beside him in the dark, that lovely, watchful creature with hearing so acute that it astounds, who easily awakens at three in the morning to the merest snort or innocent dreamy whine and eagerly nudges or kicks him into half consciousness, where he'll know he must roll over and start again. In the past one or two of these alert ladies had requested that he sleep on the sofa. These liaisons did not last long.

So, with conditions as they were, Cosmo slept undisturbed and his brain launched into one of those peculiar surreal episodes, no doubt loaded with great significance if only one could remember it the following morning.

Cosmo saw himself flying like a comic book hero, gliding through the air slowly, gracefully, and at an alarmingly low altitude right over New York City. Skyscrapers skimmed silently past, an arm's length away, so close that Cosmo glimpsed a secretary here and there working at her desk. He window-peeked on twenty gray-suited men seated around a polished table, each with his portfolio and each with an identical bottle of mineral water. On top of each portfolio was a brown sack lunch.

Looming ahead was a tall building composed of nothing more than windows in steel frames. Attached to a pane on the fiftieth floor was a large hand lettered sign. Cosmo banked his body expertly like a pilot propelling a plane or a taxi heading for the curb. He came up to the skyscraper, close enough to smell the window cleaner.

Cosmo adjusted his glasses and hovered near the window where he could read the sign. The crudely lettered message read, '*BEWARE OF WILD BORES!*'

Cosmo banked again and flew to the top of a nearby office building where he landed on both feet and then burst out laughing. Looking over the roof-top garden arranged with umbrella tables and populated by young men and women eating their sandwiches, Cosmo found it strange that all of the office workers looked like his old friend, Montgomery Zwick, a successful Broadway impresario. Zwick was a short, bald, paunchy gentleman who sported a gray goatee and stood on very bowed legs. Cosmo loved him like a brother.

When Cosmo awakened an hour later, he felt remarkably refreshed. And, oddly enough, he remembered the dream. *WILD BORES*! Indeed! He had no idea he was such a funny fellow. And, he wondered what it all meant.

Not too many days later, Cosmo Freese moved into Meadowlark Village. It was a cold, bleak morning in November. After supervising the movers and doing a bit of organizing and shoving about, Cosmo rode the elevator to the lobby in search of a newspaper and a cup of coffee. The Meadowlark administrator, a crisp fiftyish woman with fishy eyes, informed him that complimentary coffee could be found in the 'parlor.' Cosmo didn't much care for the woman or her turn of phrase, and excused himself quickly. That done, he looked across the so-called parlor and spotted Nina Dupree hurrying through the foyer doors.

Not one to waste an opportunity, Cosmo moved quickly. "Nina," he called out to her. As they met, he reached for both her hands in an elegant greeting which caused Nina to respond with a brilliant smile.

"How wonderful to see you again, Cosmo. I love our little phone chats."

"So do I. By the way, I've just joined the club here. A small apartment on the fourth floor. Coffee?" Cosmo led the way.

"I'm here to visit the Armbrusters. They're in a residents' general meeting."

"Oooh. Rather like board meetings. Or, listening to a lecture from your mother."

Nina laughed and said Betty Hughes calls it the Windbag Association. She looked up and said, "There they are now. Goodness, Cyrus looks like his hair is on fire."

Introductions completed, Cyrus launched immediately into a comic review of the Gathering of the Gestapo, as he called it. "This place will make you jump off the roof after dinner," he said with a boyish snicker. "A lot of old poops whining about bad coffee and whether or not they're allowed to keep a pistol in their sock drawer." Cyrus sank into an arm chair next to the coffee machine and planted his feet on the coffee table.

Betty Hughes told him to get his shoes off the furniture, but Cyrus just laughed. She said, "We'll shape them up, Cyrus. Just give me a month or two. Of course, the entire staff will have to be replaced." She smiled and sat down next to Nina and whispered that Cyrus's new medicine seemed to be helping him enormously. He was just as naughty as ever.

"It's a rebellious bunch," Cyrus went on. "Unafraid of authority. The sad-sacks who run this joint hate old people. You can see it in their eyes." Cyrus narrowed his own like a movie villain and everybody laughed.

"Must I move back to New York?" asked Cosmo, lightly.

"Welcome to the Land of Nod. It ain't the Ritz."

Cosmo wondered fleetingly if he'd made the right choice. Perhaps he should have rented a flat. He looked over at beautiful Nina, all ivory and silk. A gorgeous lady who needed space, he'd found. She had her own flat downtown.

"Do they treat you like children?" asked Nina.

"Rather," replied Betty Hughes. "Heavens, I don't need somebody to cut my meat."

"Getting old sucks," said Cyrus. He reached down, took off his shoe, scratched the bottom of his foot and put the shoe back on. "How old are you, Cosmo?"

"Fifty-nine. Divorced three times. Wives and the theatre don't mix well. But, it's fun to keep trying." Cosmo didn't look at Nina when he said this. It would have been unwise.

Cyrus winked at Cosmo.

"The ladies here will be after you like flies at a picnic, darlin'." Betty Hughes patted Cosmo's arm. "You'll have to carry a gun."

"Or, a fly swatter." Cyrus was quick today.

Cosmo laughed and impulsively invited them up to his new digs. "It's boxes and more boxes, but I know where I can find the ice and refreshments." He stood and took Nina gently by the arm.

"Who needs ice?" said Cyrus, and led the way to the elevators like a spry gentleman of forty.

After the departure of his guests, Cosmo put on his robe and slippers and found himself a comfortable chair midst the clutter. He adored women. Was on good terms with all his wives, and his son seemed to be carrying on the tradition. Cosmo was proud of the boy. Loving a woman, he often reminded him, was as fine an art as playing King Lear or creating a marvelous painting. His son knew all about paintings. Sadly, Cosmo was currently without a woman to adore, and this was bothering him more than the chaos of moving.

He turned on an old Bogart film and nibbled on the rest of the cheese and crackers Betty Hughes had brought over. But, soon, Cosmo was pacing his quarters with its jumble of furniture that had once neatly graced his New York flat. Everything was out of place. He was living alone. His world needed order. He needed a companion. A problem to be solved, something he liked to do. Cosmo was a decision maker, a puzzle solver. How to get the part, how to play the part, how to seize the heart of it, how to make his performance indelible. Thirty years of creative decisions in hundreds of productions had made him astute about the theatre, plays, and human nature. And, about himself, he duly noted.

But, his problem now had nothing to do with the theatre, and everything to do with Nina Dupree, clearly a woman in distress.

Cosmo ran down the woman's obvious attributes…..beauty, youth (relative), money (not particularly important, but there), and a new-found ambition, which he found terribly exciting in a woman of forty-two. And, she was bedeviled. Cosmo's intuition suggested he find out why. He grinned, imagining what he and Beatrice Wrenn might accomplish if they teamed up. He polished off the last bite of cheddar and flung one arm behind his back. He strolled about his new flat, small but new and immaculate, and outlined the Nina Project. Point one, she needed someone's help. Point two, she was modestly attracted to him; Point three, he was most attracted to her; Point four, her engagement was said to be a mistake; Point five, he didn't think Nina trusted too many people. This was the card he would play. He was good at playing the confidante. Enough said.

The actor poured himself a large glass of ice water and reached for the phone. "Cosmo to the rescue!" he trumpeted softly, with the kind of joy that made his toes wiggle.

"Lettice, if you're there, pick up!" Betty Hughes cried into the phone. Answer machines. She knew Lettice pretended to be out just to avoid nuisance calls. Betty Hughes left a curt message. *'I'll call back, if I have time...'* Rather snotty, she supposed, but she imagined they all sounded lofty at their age, what with the imposition of answer machines and bad TV.

Betty Hughes and Cyrus had just returned from Cosmo Freese's apartment after a nice visit. He seemed like a lovely man, quite charismatic. No wonder he'd had three wives. Betty Hughes mused about who might be his next. She had caught him glancing at the lovely Nina every few minutes. She must keep her eye on Cosmo. Then, she remembered why she was calling Lettice a second time.

"Lettice, I know you're there!" Parnell Grant had called with the news.

After waiting for the silly beep, Betty Hughes proceeded to tell Lettice that Tommy Delaney had been taken to the hospital that afternoon. No hope for recovery this time. He was gone, dear lad. And, no closer to home than usual when he died, she said with mischief in her voice. Tommy had taken his last breath doing what he liked best. Betty Hughes smiled to herself. She would let the story dangle, just to tease Lettice into calling back.

Finally, she caved in to the deliciousness of the tale and said, *"Our Tommy collapsed in Marigold's bed!"* This juicy tidbit fairly sang from her lips. Tommy would have loved it. Surely, he was 'up there,' on his cloud with a mist of Irish whiskey around him. *"Parnell called a few minutes ago."*

Betty Hughes couldn't help but laugh. Tommy as an angel. It did provoke a thousand funny pictures in her head. "Well, not one of us'll be leavin' this earth the way we'd like, I suppose," she was telling the machine, forgetting for the moment that Lettice wasn't there. "But, our Tommy seems to have accomplished a most happy exit." Her Cyrus would probably drift away years from now, a different man; and he'd never know he was leaving. If Tommy expired in Marigold's arms, he'd be the envy of the Old Devils for eternity.

By now, Betty Hughes was laughing and crying at the same time. Men did have such silly fantasies. What woman would dream of dyin' in a man's bed? Most of her lady friends preferred a quick heart attack while watchin' a handsome man deliverin' the news on TV. Not much romance, but the deed would be done. When and where she wanted to leave the world was still Betty Hughes's secret.

She reminded Lettice to call back for details and rang off. She would let Archie tell Naddy, all pummeled and rested out in the desert.

12

Telling the Tale

'Nina, dear, it's Betty Hughes here. I know you're up to your ears memorizin' that new part for the play, but I think you should know that Archie's in bed with flu and won't call the doctor. He calls Cyrus six times a day, but what can poor Cyrus do? I can't get over there today because I'm due at the hairdresser. Soooo, could you take a teeny break and drop by with a bowl of soup? Men are so helpless. Archie will love to see you. Didn't Nadine pick a marvelous time to fly to the desert? By the way, darlin', Tommy's funeral is Saturday at St. Hyacinth's. We're all devastated, of course. And, Thanksgivin's been switched to Nadine and Archie's place. Everybody usually comes to our house, which is like takin' a walk on the wild side, but we can't do it this year. This new place just isn't big enough. Just pray Naddy doesn't ask me to make sweet potatoes....I have a mental block about that vegetable." Betty Hughes laughed. *"Do let us know how bad old Archie's doin'. Bye, bye. Don't forget lunch on Thursday.'*

The message, which reminded Nina of a comic monologue, came to an end and she sank gratefully into the sofa and put her feet up. Poor, dear Archie. She had no idea he was sick. He hadn't called in two days, and she'd been busy with her classes and rehearsals for the play. Her dear Archie, abandoned on all fronts.

As she prepared to leave the apartment, Nina thought about holidays. Thanksgiving? Already? Another holiday that revolved around food. Didn't they all? With some unfortunate female at the center, aproned and rosy cheeked with her head in a hot oven (mascara melting and gluing her lashes together), prodding a large chunk of beast or fowl with a long fork. Wasn't there another way of celebrating? Why not Chinese take-out? Or just desserts? Or just drinks? If she were home in New Orleans, Jessie, their cook of 500 years, would be outdoing herself... roasted turkey, chestnut stuffing, corn bread. Sweet potato pie. She doubted a dozen Yankees could tease twenty people into a dining room the way Jessie could.

Back to Archie, off his feed and probably grouchy. And, attemptin' to fend for himself. Pitiful. She'd stop at the deli for soup…that would cheer him up. She called to say that lunch was on its way. Archie said he wouldn't eat a thing if she made it. Very funny, she responded, and hung up.

The day was gray as laundry water. November in the tundra. Nina touched up her makeup and rode the elevator to the parking garage. This might be the perfect time to tell Archie about the baby. Bedridden, weakened by flu, as vulnerable as a newborn. There might not be a better time. Hugo could wait.

Nina drove to Ed's Deli on Cass Avenue, ordered a quart of his specialty and headed for the Beresford house about six blocks away.

By noon Nina was sitting at Archie's bedside ladling Ed's version of chicken soup into a bowl. Small green globes splashed into the dish along with a yellowish broth studded with carrots, celery, and red disks that looked suspiciously like radish slices. Ed was getting fanciful. It wasn't handsome, Nina pointed out, but it was hot.

"What the hell are those?" Archie barked from his mountain of wrinkled sheets and blankets and far too many pillows.

Nina spooned up one green sphere and announced, "A tiny brain, darlin'. That's what we always called them when we were kids. Brussels sprouts. Not my first choice but they're nutritious."

She leaned forward and tucked a large paper napkin into the neck of Archie's pajamas. He looked terrible. His face was the color of pie dough; his hair was standing on end in various spots where he'd slept on it; his beard stubble made a salt and pepper arc from one ear to the other.

"I won't eat those. Sprouts give me gas. Is this really from the deli?" He gaped at his lunch with a fishy eye and then slouched into the heap. "Just give me soda crackers from that box." He pointed to the foot of the bed, a private jungle of junk food.....a half eaten bag of pretzels, a can of spray cheese made for desperate men, potato chips, a jar of marshmallow crème, half a chocolate bar, and the saltines.

"Open your mouth, Archie, I didn't drive all the way over here just to watch you nibble on crackers…. like a pregnant woman." A segue made in heaven; Nina smiled and shoved a spoon of soup in the direction of his mouth and managed to push it in. "No brains, I promise. And, no more trash food."

"Hugo brought it over." Archie made a face and reached for her hand and kissed it.

"Let's not get testy over a little bowl of soup. It smells divine," she lied and shoved in another spoonful.

"I notice you're not eating any." Archie stopped to cover his mouth and cough, a dry flu hack that made Nina turn away. The room looked like germs were multiplying in every corner. She could smell viruses or whatever the critters were. Sick rooms always smelled so sick.

"This place looks as bad as you do."

Orderly Archie midst uncharacteristic chaos. He'd torn off his clothes and flung them around the room, willy-nilly. One dirty sock lay over the top of a lampshade. The large table next to the bed was a nest of sickroom props.....a jug of orange juice, aspirin, vitamin C tablets, two kinds of cough syrup, a teapot with tea bags hanging over the side, a stack of paperbacks, fishing magazines, the television remote. A vaporizer hissed in the corner while Mozart twiddled in the background on the stereo. One window blind was cockeyed, the others closed.

"Have you been up at all? Where in the world is your housekeeper?" Nina bent and kissed Archie's broad forehead, damp and warm. She did love him. Even sick, he was a sweetheart.

"Housekeeper? Ran like a rabbit when I told her I was sick. Said she didn't dare get so much as a headache before Thanksgiving. Traitor." Archie pulled the blanket closer to his shoulders and pushed away the last of the soup. He was exhausted.

"You should have called me sooner. I could have taken care of you." Nina yanked Archie forward and punched up the pillows. "How about if I tidy things while we talk. I have somethin' to tell you, darlin'."

Archie had a fleeting moment of panic…he always did when women wanted to tell him something important. It usually WAS important, and he rarely wanted to hear it. My God, what next?

Nina took her patient's temperature, stuck two more pills into his mouth, and left long enough get a jug of fresh juice and bring up the automatic tea maker. She still couldn't tolerate coffee.

Archie acted modestly restored and perfectly content to watch his beautiful mistress work magic. She was more domestic than he imagined. Nadine hated housework. Most likely, Nina required a crew of slaves, too, but he was never privileged to witness the parade.

"Have the boys been to see you?" Nina hung his suit in the closet and tossed the dirty laundry into a hamper in the bathroom.

"Cyrus came over the first day. Brought me three old John Wayne movies."

Nina finished putting things away and returned to Archie's bedside. "I should come over and watch movies with you." She took his hand and held it to her cheek.

"Now, my pretty, what's on your mind?" Archie wanted it over, whatever it was. Giving a woman the green light was akin to laying a mackerel in front of a cat.

Nina rubbed his stubble playfully and said much more quietly than she'd intended, "I'm going to have a baby, Archie. In July." She smiled prettily and sat up very straight, as if trying to make a good impression with her posture.

Archie stared without blinking for a half a minute. Then, his eyes roamed the room, as if a soothsayer might drop from the ceiling with an explanation. When he tried to say 'baby,' his voice croaked and he had to start over. "A baby, you say? That's impossible, Nina." Hadn't she told him she couldn't have kids? Hadn't Hugo told them this too?

"Yes, that's right, sweetheart. But, somewhere along the way, a doctor down in my home town made a big mistake." Nina smoothed the sheet that lay across Archie's big chest. "I'm very definitely pregnant. You're going to be a daddy! Again." She released her finest beauty queen smile.

Life remained complicated. He supposed it would until the reaper grabbed him by the throat, Archie mused as if to soothe his panicked brain. He sat up now, brimming with disbelief and fright. And, a touch of pride too. Maybe this was flu talking. Maybe he was dreaming. He put out a hand and touched Nina's shoulder. She was very real and so beautiful, and he wanted her, sick as he was.

"Honey-bun, are you joking with me?" A part of him, the very young part, wanted this announcement to be true. My God. He must be losing his mind, like Cyrus.

"Not on your life. This tiny bean is real and growing a mile a minute." Nina patted her tummy. She sounded quite at ease with the notion of babies.

"Are you sure WE made the baby? What about Hugo?"

"According to my best recollection, I think you're probably it." Nina kissed Archie's cheek. "I'm not going to put pressure on you; I just want you to know before the world finds out. You're the only person who has this vital information." She sounded to Archie like a female news anchor on TV.

"Hugo isn't stupid, Nina. He might turn tough. Demand blood tests." Archie took a minute to blow his nose. He was feeling worse again. What had he done? This baby thing sounded illegal. Or did he mean indiscreet? Anyway he put it, he was in the soup.

"Don't worry, sweetheart, leave Hugo to me."

Nina watched Archie's face, as if wondering if he might want to claim this coup as his own.

Archie was beginning to feel the primal stirrings of vanity. A father again at 62. By God, he'd put a real feather in his cap, hadn't he? The Old Devils would erect a statue or a shrine somewhere.

"I want you to know, Nina, I may be stunned, but I'm with you on this." Archie heard his own voice but couldn't believe the words. Fever talk. Did he really want to be a father? What about Nadine? She'd kill him. No divorce. Just homicide. Flirtations with Marigold were one thing; impregnating their son's fiancée fell into a new category of philandering. The life-threatening category.

"We'll talk more about this when you're better. OK?" Nina leaned forward and rested her head on Archie's chest.

Archie could still smell the marshmallow crème he'd spilled on his pajamas. He gently rubbed her back and kissed her hair. Could they live together and raise a child? They'd probably have to flee Belmont in the dead of night.

"You're a darling girl. Are you happy or sad? This will change our lives, you know." Archie put a finger beneath her chin and raised her face to his.

"I'm terrified. You know, I grew up in those first five seconds after Dr. Lamb gave me the news."

"I hear it's never too late." Archie pulled her close and wished he could say more.

The next day, Cyrus decided to drive himself over to Archie's after lunch. Betty Hughes had forbidden him to take the car without her, but he told her he was going down to the sauna. What the hell could happen to him on a mile ride to Archie's? He might, a chipper voice inside his head replied, even enjoy himself for five minutes. Cyrus depended on this little voice to make decisions. Otherwise, Betty Hughes and the Docs would take over totally. He had to talk to Arch about Tommy's passing. Jesus, the old sot was really gone. His eyes teared up, and he punched the parking garage button on the elevator panel with an extra wallop.

"Hey, Arch! You still in bed, you old bugger?" Cyrus had let himself in the back door with a key given him years ago. The big house was silent. Too silent. Cyrus stopped in the kitchen for a bag of Oreos left on the counter…his favorite.

"You lazy bastard!" he called out as he mounted the broad curving stairs to the second floor. The big staircase reminded him of his old Tudor house, no longer his but lovingly occupied by Marigold and Parnell. It was safe with them, but he'd never get over losing it. He'd never get over losing Tommy either. Did Archie know about Tommy? He wasn't sure.

Cyrus shuffled into Archie's bedroom waving the bag of Oreos. "Time for lunch and a round of golf," he sang out. Archie was slouched against his pillows. "For a minute there, I thought I was walking in on the old farts slumped over their magazines in the reading room at our villa for the less than spry," Cyrus rattled on. "Dozing and drooling. The two things they do best." Cyrus took off his jacket and threw it on a chair. "Jesus, Archie, you look like yesterday's meat loaf sitting there." He snickered and tossed the cookies onto the bed.

"Oh, shut up. I feel like yesterday's meat loaf." Archie blew his nose and took a sip of warm orange juice. "Does Betty Hughes know you're out?" He smiled. At least he didn't have Nadine pouncing on him every five minutes.

"She thinks I'm sweating in the sauna. I've escaped. Want to fly off to Rio for some fishing?" Cyrus grinned.

"Get me my pants. Over there on the chair." Archie tried to roust himself and got tangled in the sheets. "Give me a hand here. Damned bed. It's a death trap!"

Cyrus yanked at the mess of blankets and sheets and pulled Archie up on his feet.

"Unsteady on your pegs, my lad?" Cyrus teased. "You need a shot of bourbon. So do I, for that matter." He made sure Archie was standing erect and rummaged in the closet for a shirt and some clean underwear. "How about a shower?" he suggested.

"Had one last night. I need to see another room." Archie's head buzzed a little from the exertion and probably the damned cold pills. He'd never take another one, he told himself. His skull felt disconnected from his neck. He pulled on underwear and pants, a pair of old corduroys with thin knees, and accepted the shirt and sweater Cyrus offered him. "How about a cookie?"

Cyrus handed him the Oreo bag, and for a few minutes the two sat on the edge of the bed, munching and taking a breather.

"You know about Tommy?" Cyrus asked as he unscrewed the Oreo and licked off the filling.

"Betty Hughes called. I called Nadine, but she's decided to stay at the spa. I'll go to the funeral with you."

"He finally did it, Arch. Took him a lifetime."

"A good lifetime. He had a boat load of friends." Archie sniffed loudly and unabashedly.

"He wouldn't want us to blubber, you know." Cyrus was trying not to.

"No blubbers." Archie clapped Cyrus on the back. Cyrus thought he sounded more normal, now that he was sitting up and taking nourishment.

"Betty Hughes said she sent Nina over yesterday. Did she feed you properly?" Cyrus knew that Nina wasn't exactly a whiz in the kitchen.

"Some God awful Brussels sprout soup from Ed's Deli. A gastronomic horror." Archie belched a little. But, he looked worried to Cyrus.

Archie said, "Nina told me something that's nearly knocked me on my tail." He made it a point to look directly at Cyrus. "This has got to stay between you and me, you old toad. Or, I'll drum you out of the poker club." He grinned.

Cyrus blinked and gathered his resolve to keep the secret. If he could remember what it was three days from now. He was having a pretty good day, so far. "Shoot. I'm ready."

"We made a baby." Archie ran both hands through his hair causing it to stand on end, rather like Cyrus's. He kept his focus on Cyrus's face, as if to steady his own resolve to keep a clear head.

"Who did?"

"Nina and me."

"You and Nina did what?" Cyrus clutched at Archie's arm.

"We've been having a few matinees together…here," and Archie patted his bed. The cookie bag spilled out a few Oreos, and he took one and popped it into his mouth. "A wee tussle, as Tommy would put it."

Cyrus was incredulous. "You're putting me on. She's going to marry Hugo, right?"

"No joke, Cyrus. Unorthodox behavior by two people who think it's OK to bend the rules. Hugo doesn't know." Archie spoke matter-of-factly. "She was told she couldn't have children. Some kind of medical screw-up."

Cyrus opened and closed his mouth a few times, finding himself without words. Archie and Nina? "What were you thinking?"

"I was thinking I was about forty." Archie ran a hand over the stubble on his face. "Hugo's been neglecting her. Thinks the boot business is more fun, I guess. I always managed to do both. It's all his fault." Archie grinned in spite of himself.

Cyrus started to laugh. "Right. This is a major coup, you know. Cuckolding your own kid, in your own bed. I don't have any stories to top it." Tears trickled from Cyrus's eyes. "You've made my life complete." And, he punched Archie's big shoulder. "So, what are you going to do? You have to think of Naddy! What about Naddy, Arch?"

"I don't know. She'll be mightily pissed. Probably move to the desert forever. I'm all turned around. I wasn't much of a father to Hugo. What the hell do I know about it now?" Archie stood and starting poking through his dresser drawers for socks, which he pulled on with some effort. He slid into old leather boat shoes. "Let's go out for a sandwich."

"Yeah, let's." Cyrus stood and picked up his jacket. "Let's go out and find you a good divorce attorney and a justice of the peace." He giggled again until he felt the urge to pee. "What the hell do you know about babies?"

"This isn't funny. When Nadine finds out, just tell the cops it was justifiable homicide."

"Let me have a pee first. Then, we'll call the cops."

"Why don't we plant that lamp on this table and put the arm chair by the windows." Betty Hughes made her suggestion and then stepped back to visualize it. She was lending Nina a hand reshuffling furniture in the apartment on Thursday afternoon. An armoire from Belle was due to arrive in three hours.

"Might just work." Nina pushed the fauteuil closer to the windows, and Betty Hughes made the lamp exchange.

"I like that better." Betty Hughes smiled approvingly and picked up her teacup.

"So do I. Sometimes I can't put a candlestick in the right place." Nina sat down in the newly relocated chair and put her feet on a tiny footstool trimmed with gold braid.

"I do love that new paintin' over the sofa, darlin'. It makes me think of those Sunday afternoons on the porch with my girlfriends….that would be about a million years ago." Betty Hughes rested in a pale pink silk lounge chair that had big bucks written all over it. Nina was one of those rare women who had a bank account that could withstand her good taste. The Beacon Street flat was spectacular. It had already been chosen as THE place to see on the 'What's New?' spring charity house tour sponsored by the Belmont Women's Club. Nina was still nervous about hundreds of women flocking in and out of the building and possibly getting stuck in the elevator.

Sitting there in the freshly rearranged 'salon,' Betty Hughes didn't quite see Miss Nina as a woman at peace…with herself or with her luscious apartment. Maybe Cyrus was right. Two days ago he'd let her in on Archie's big secret. Cyrus said the news was going to erupt out of the top of his head if he didn't squeal. Betty Hughes didn't believe a word of it. Nina pregnant with Archie's baby? She could fathom a romance, but a baby? Now, sitting there, looking at the 'little mother,' Betty Hughes had begun to reevaluate her initial reaction. She experienced a tingle of excitement. Ooh, what fun! Miss Nina was very definitely a woman expectin'. She just knew it….there was that certain look about her face, a soft glow. Cyrus was right on the money, the old devil, which didn't happen all that often anymore.

"Tell me, Betty Hughes, do you think there's more to Lola Sprigg's murder than meets the eye?"

Betty Hughes's big blue eyes blinked. My, my. Miss Nina wasn't interested in candlesticks and lamps anymore. She said, "Honey, what do you mean exactly?" Betty Hughes didn't want to admit just yet how uneasy she and Nadine were.

"Archie and Cyrus have made offhand remarks. To be honest, I've overheard private conversations which make me think they know more about Lola than they're letting on. And, they're actin' the same way about those old bones in Sandy Hook." Nina shuddered and poured herself more tea from a china pot on the table next to her. "Need a warm up?"

"Sure, darlin', but you sit, I'll get it myself. I could use another one of those yummy cookies."

"What do you think?"

Betty Hughes poured her tea and took two sugar cookies and returned to her pink chair. "To be frank, I've thought all along that the Preacher does resemble Durwood Spriggs. He was Lola's husband. And, all the boys….Archie, Cyrus, the Admiral, Tommy, and Durwood…. were thick as thieves before and after the war."

"So, you think this Preacher Boswell is related to the Spriggs family and nobody wants to admit it because he's such a good-for-nothin'?"

"That's about it. I think those bad ol' boys are coverin' up. I've even thought there might be a connection between the Spriggs's maid, a girl named Sally, and Durwood. Years ago, of course. Could be she and Durwood hatched this Boswell creature and Lola found out and wanted to make things right by givin' him a load of money." There, she'd admitted it all.

"But, why is Cyrus so worried about the bones in Pike's Wood?"

"Cyrus gets in a flap about so many things now. I doubt if he ever knew a big old gimpy legged man who got himself killed forty odd years ago." Betty Hughes waved off this bit of peculiar business and took another bite of cookie.

"Archie says he has flashbacks from the war."

"Oh, yes. They all do."

"Have you told the police about the possible Durwood/ Boswell connection?"

"No, no, no." Betty Hughes shook her head with conviction. "Let Freddy Donovan figure it out, if there's a motive to figure. Poor Lola's gone. If this Boswell killed her, they'll catch him. I can't have Cyrus pulled into a murder case. He'll jump a fence." Betty Hughes smiled. Her Cyrus needed protection more than the world needed to hear his side of the story, if there was one.

Nina remained apprehensive. "What about Archie?" she asked. "He twitches when he hears the word 'bones' or the name 'Lola.' It's scary."

Betty Hughes frowned. She'd long believed that men in big business often ran into shady characters or sometimes hired them for illegal or violent deeds that needed doing. And, Archie was the kind of big man who circulated in many social circles, good and not so good.

"As you know," Betty Hughes went on, "Archie Beresford gets around. Has more influence than the governor and more than a few skeletons in his own closet. He's a hunter, you know. Deer, turkeys, coyotes. Could be one of his big shot corporate pals, one of his huntin' buddies, shot this gimpy-legged guy and they had the accident fixed. Had the poor guy buried, made him disappear. Big money can do that, honey."

Nina nodded. She knew. Her father occasionally hinted at the unsavory practices he'd bumped into through the years. "But, why cover up a huntin' accident?"

"Rich, well-known executive who can't afford bad publicity….then or now."

"Are you saying it might have been Archie?" Nina was leaning forward now, her face pinched with fear.

"I'm not sayin' nothin', as my old Daddy used to put it. Honey, Archie could handle a shift in the way the river runs, if he had to. Don't go worryin' about him. Or Cyrus. That sheriff's more interested in gettin' pie-eyed on Saturday nights than he is in diggin' up dirt on an old corpse with a gold tooth." Nina, she thought, was acting as nervous as a new bride about Archie and with good reason.

"I'm not exactly worried, Betty Hughes. But, I am suspicious."

Betty Hughes thought she'd just wait for Nina to spill the baby beans, so to speak. After all, they were good friends now. Nina would realize that good friends deserved to know the truth before the rest of the world.

"I can ask a few subtle questions, Nina. See if Archie or Cyrus slip up. I wouldn't mind knowin' the truth myself." Betty Hughes popped the rest of her cookie into her mouth.

"Don't forget the Admiral. If you shake him, I bet lots of fascinating things will fall out."

"Lordy, Lordy! The Admiral. He's so darned sanctimonious, he makes my teeth itch," said Betty Hughes. "Of course, the old sailor is a mystery even to himself." There was plenty of time for Nina to confide her own little mystery. Betty Hughes could wait.

And, over a fresh pot of tea and another plate of cookies, that was exactly what Nina did. Betty Hughes made no judgments about Nina's confession. She gave Nina a hug and promised that her little baby secret would be safe with her until they put her into the ground.

13

Farewells

Archie squinted through the blinds in Bathgart's office. A long funeral procession was crawling up Jefferson on its way to Oakwood Cemetery. He and Nadine had plots there, and that was all he wanted to know about it. They'd be burying Tommy at Wanderer's Rest on Saturday. The dear man had wanted to spend eternity in the rolling, stony fields of Ireland, but his wife had quite unexpectedly grown a backbone and insisted that her beloved twiddle his toes in Belmont. Archie could still feel an odd hollow sensation in the pit of his stomach when he thought about it. Jesus, Tommy would have loved his fatherhood story.

Bathgart completed his telephone call, apologized for the interruption, and offered Archie his usual chair.

"I think I'll stand, Doc." Archie was preparing himself to tell Bathgart the entire tale this afternoon, and immediately remembered standing in front of his formidable mother thirty-nine years ago, admitting that he'd been kicked out of Yale.

"Fine. Fire away." Bathgart often adopted a more devil-may-care manner during these sessions. Archie believed the doctor was a bit emancipated these days. A looser goose, as they say. Bathgart had confessed to Archie that he wasn't always clear on who was helping who during these sessions. Archie told him it didn't matter, as long as it was somebody.

Archie plunged right in. "She's pregnant."

The firm, confident, and unapologetic announcement brought a controlled expression of astonishment to Bathgart's round placid face.

"Nina?"

"Yes. Nina."

Archie began to pace. He was sure this dizzying circuit would be interpreted as a desire to flee the scene and the circumstances. Not far from correct, he supposed. He noticed that Bathgart was jotting things in his notebook already. The Doc didn't like tape recorders.

"A serious complication. Does your son know about this?"

"My son thinks his fiancée cannot conceive. Both lived with the same information. A medical misdiagnosis in New Orleans years ago. Or, a miraculous conception?" Archie paused in his trek to look directly at Bathgart and grin. He was discovering, week after week and quite by surprise, that he was giving himself over to this natty man with a markedly disappearing hairline and kind eyes.

"My money is on the medical mistake." Bathgart smiled too.

"So is mine. But…and here's the rub…I'm thinking that maybe I should do the right thing. Maybe Nina and I should get married. What do you think, Doc?"

"I think I'm not the one who can answer that question. But, perhaps we can figure out how YOU might answer it." Bathgart planted his elbows on the desk, a minor bit of body language that told Archie that they'd be getting down to work soon.

"Of course, there is the question of the Old Bones," Archie pointed out gravely. "I could be in serious trouble with the law if the truth ever comes out." His mind flew back to Pike's Wood. So far, Sally was keeping her silence, and the sheriff's investigation had ground to a standstill, in spite of the fact that they'd identified the remains. Who would rebury Buzzy Turk's dry bones after all these years? Perhaps an anonymous donation would secure a decent grave for the old bastard and assuage any remnants of guilt.

Bathgart said he was no longer nervous about the corpse of Buzzy Turk. He said, "A consideration, but we might assume that the case will never be solved after this many weeks and a sheriff who seems to have lost interest."

Archie nodded. "Or, so it seems. Could be it's a trick to get someone to talk."

"Good point. The back woods sheriff might not be sophisticated, but that doesn't mean he isn't crafty." Bathgart turned the page on his notebook. "But, let's focus on the immediate problem and keep the others in the back row, for now."

Archie took a chair across from Bathgart and inclined his torso and head toward him, as if accepting the doctor's challenge to find the answer. Everything would be OK. The Doc was a man who kept secrets for a living.

Archie ran both hands through his hair and prepared to bare his soul once again.

"He would have been sixty-three next week," Lettice reminded Betty Hughes, quite unnecessarily. "Think of that. And none of us thought Tommy would live past forty." She dabbed her eyes, crossed herself, and cast an appreciative glance toward the dim vaulted ceiling of St. Hyacinth's. Tommy had been good at beating the odds.

Lettice and Betty Hughes were seated midway in the gloomy nave with a hard rain pecking at the stained glass windows, their brilliant primary colors striking a discordant note against gray stone walls that seemed to moan with misery. Plaster statues of saints robed in pastels stood guard in their niches while mourners filed into the pews. Few folks in Belmont were unfamiliar with Tommy Delaney or his cluttered liquor store on Third Avenue. Two of Tommy's cronies, stinking of gin and tobacco, slid in behind Lettice and Betty Hughes.

"Tommy's been pickled for forty years; I doubt he needed embalmin'," Betty Hughes whispered. She could have shouted since half the mourners were hard of hearing and the other half would have appreciated the levity. A Delaney funeral always drew a deeply mournful but still highly spirited crowd, as if the grief-stricken felt a need to do penance before the uproarious party that was due to follow the Mass.

"Gracious!" Lettice muttered, "Such a thing to say. Tommy was a darling man. Just a bit too fond of blurred edges and pretty girls."

Betty Hughes ignored the rebuke; Lettice was overly emotional today.

With the approach of Archie down the aisle, followed by Hugo and Nina, Lettice and Betty Hughes made room in the oak pew. Nina in a stylish black hat and a full-length mink coat took a place between Hugo and Archie. Cyrus said he would sit with Duncan and his wife.

"And won't Nadine be sorry she's missed all this?" Lettice hissed over to Archie, once he settled in beside her. "Just to lie around a spa and have her legs pummeled. Such a waste of money."

Betty Hughes smiled. Lettice was funnier than she knew.

"How could she know Tommy would pass on while she was gone, Lettice? The spa will do her good. You should try it."

"On my budget." Lettice rolled her eyes. "Pettibone beach is more my speed."

Betty Hughes's brain conjured up a picture of Lettice in a bathing suit and immediately filed it under 'almost too awful to contemplate.'

"Who will we be burying next?"came a female voice behind Archie. The Beresford contingent turned to see Judith Pardee O'Hara (Jumping Judith), herself a bride of only a few weeks, squeezing in beside her latest husband, a heavy-set man who nodded pleasantly. He, like Nina, was trying to get the hang of Belmont's landed gentry. Judith had already buried three husbands and Nina thought her new one was looking tired. It was generally conceded among the Old Devils that Tommy Delaney had very likely added five years to his life by never pursuing Jumping Judith.

"Could be any one of us," replied Lettice, who always insisted she was unafraid of grim death. Lettice Mulroy was a woman who believed that heaven was a real place paved in gold brick with angels playing harps and cherubs running errands for you. Many of her close friends refused to buy the pearly gates scenario, but Lettice always held fast. She said it was very comforting to know where you were going. Cyrus would say that Lettice woke in the middle of the night with the same terrors they all did. The fear of death, he said, visited everyone. Betty Hughes tended to agree.

Nina could feel Archie's warmth beside her, reassuring and sexy at the same time. She put a little pressure on his arm and he returned it. She had no urge to pressure Hugo's arm. He was in a pout today, struggling, he said, with impending fatherhood…..she had broken the news two days ago. Archie didn't seem disturbed by it. So far, he was behaving like an excited father should behave. He'd sent two dozen pink roses on Thursday and this morning Mr. Foote, Belmont's single taxi driver, delivered a huge box of Hubert's chocolates.

"At least the poor man died in his own bed," Judith whispered loudly into Lettice's back, as she reached for her husband's chubby hand.

"Where did you hear that nonsense?" said Lettice, craning her neck around to look at Judith, who was known for her simple-mindedness.

"Evette told me," Judith answered defensively.

"Next time, get the real story from me." Lettice winked at the newlyweds before turning back to the chancel.

The organist began an overwrought rendition of 'Danny Boy,' one of Tommy's favorites. An instantaneous volley of snuffles, coughs, and nose blowing swept across the church. Lettice leaned toward Betty Hughes and said that Tommy wanted to be buried on the ancestral land, just outside of Dublin. He'd arranged for his casket to be shipped there, she said, but Evette had put the lid on that one. She needed the money for more practical purposes. She was having the plumbing redone.

Lettice amused herself by surveying the pews. She poked Betty Hughes's arm and said, "Who's that woman in the big red hat on the side aisle, crying like a widow." She drew her folded glasses up from their chain and touched them to the bridge of her nose; she rarely put them on all the way.

Nina could feel Archie twist to have a peek. He could be an old hen sometimes.

Betty Hughes squinted and said she didn't know. She said Miss Red Hat looked a good deal younger than the chief mourners. One of Tommy's ladies, no doubt. Lettice sighed. The widow, Evette, sat impassively in the front row surrounded by her seven children and their offspring. After anticipating her husband's demise for more than thirty years, Evette was finding the actual death something of an anti-climax. That was what she was telling her friends.

A middle-aged gentleman familiar to them all and an old friend to Lettice scooted in beside Betty Hughes. Parking was impossible, he hissed. He leaned across to squeeze Lettice's hand. Lettice sniffed and reminded them all that Tommy and her husband, Billy Mulroy, had fought together in the Pacific. Of course, Billy Mulroy had died in the Pacific.

"Nice flowers," Archie said quietly, gesturing toward the customary wired-up arrangements of green carnations and yellow mums in baskets that stood against the chancel rail. The bronze-toned coffin rested in the middle of the display like a half opened book. Tommy's boyish face was clearly visible, its mischievous smirk erased by the undertaker's sure hand. He wore an unnatural pink makeup. Archie pointed out in a deep whisper that the morticians had powdered the bloom from Tommy's nose, a violation nearly as unacceptable as parting his hair on the wrong side. Archie was heard to mutter something under his breath.

"A waste of good money," remarked Lettice, pointing to the flowers. As a widow living on a small pension, she watched her pennies and forthrightly refused financial help from her daughter's rich husband, who was embarrassed that his mother-in-law should live in a cramped apartment and wear the same winter coat year after year.

"More bouquets for Tommy than for Lola Spriggs," put in Archie.

Nina guessed that Archie was actually enjoying the funeral. He'd said it was his first without Nadine, who liked to shush him and forbid him cake at the luncheon afterward. He said Naddy wouldn't have approved of Tommy's death either. Nina wasn't entirely sure that Archie didn't disapprove too. He and the old boys certainly had a 'thing' for Marigold, the Cleopatra of expatriates. Could Archie still fancy her? Nina wasn't ignorant of Archie's reputation or his appetites.

It would have surprised Lettice and Betty Hughes to know that while they were worrying about the lady in the red hat and the consequences of love and lust, Archie Beresford, while buoyed with youthful emotion about Nina these days, had found he'd been jolted into the realm of reality after Nina's announcement of impending parenthood. Archie was suddenly feeling the wear and tear of age and females. The immunity of youth, taken so for granted, started to evaporate when one turned fifty. Archie said age was pursuing him with more urgency these days, and it scared him. His rather vivid imagination had painted the years of middle to early old age as a great plateau, occupying limited real estate, a flat place where you rested, lingered, floated for a short time in a shallow, lukewarm eddy of experience tempered by maturity. Nina said his observations were poetic. He'd replied that here on the great plateau, man was given time to review the past and catch a glimpse of the future. Unfortunately, in Archie's mind's eye, he could see a giant bulldozer parked on the plateau's horizon, as dark and as powerful as a dinosaur, fully prepared to push the unsuspecting over the edge.

Sitting beside Archie Nina felt relatively peaceful between her two lovers, thinking death would always be a futile subject to discuss and especially at a funeral. The end seemed quite far away when she could only think of the new beginning she was carrying around. Then, quite out of the blue, a wave of nausea hit. She took a deep breath and decided she'd better get out while the going was good. Morning sickness apparently had its own time table.

"I feel a bit ill, Hugo," Nina murmured into his shoulder. "I'm going out. Be right back. Don't bother to come." As she rushed out her complaint and instructions, Nina pushed past the others in the pew, leaving Archie looking stricken. She tiptoed quickly up the east aisle and into a small vestibule that accommodated the church rest rooms.

Sensing that Nina might be in some difficulty, Betty Hughes excused herself and slid from the pew and followed Nina up the aisle.

Meanwhile, in the main vestibule of the church, an impressive contingent of mourners swarmed like large sodden rodents, coats rain spattered and stinking of wet wool and moth-balled fur, their buzzing and yapping muted and distorted by the architecture of the building and the sheer number of voices. Most were content to rub shoulders in the icy air of the entrance rather than pack themselves into hard pews too many minutes before the priest arrived.

After finding Nina slightly sick but all right, Betty Hughes had joined her son, Duncan, in the damp vestibule where she remarked that the mourners looked like they were waiting for a reprieve from the deceased. Maybe good old Tommy, she said cheerfully, would rise up and declare that he wasn't dead after all. Duncan, who had no sense of humor, did not find his mother's remarks amusing and continued to scowl.

A good many of Tommy's pals smelled of whiskey and corned beef from the private wake held the night before at O'Reilly's Pub. For the most part, these were Belmont's serious drinkers and devoted Irish. For them, Tommy Delaney's funeral would be a little like their last hurrah too.

"That woman is here," Admiral Moss was sputtering. He pointed repeatedly to a woman in a large red hat. "I saw her go into the church and now she's come out again."

Melvin Moss, in full dress uniform with gold braid and bars, kept track of such things. He was a man who professed righteousness and piety, so much so that he almost begged others to speculate about his more private business. It was thought that the Admiral might suffer from some deep personal conflict. Many found him oddly frightening.

The Armbruster clan, Cyrus, Betty Hughes, Duncan and his irritating wife, were waiting together in a rarely seen display of togetherness. No one had much to say, and Cyrus was insisting that they not take their seats until precisely eleven o'clock. Betty Hughes was perfectly content to watch the crowd.

Once again, the Admiral declared that the red hatted woman's presence at such a solemn occasion was an affront to the devout mourners and to the widow. Those standing around the Admiral found the loud pronouncement amusing, since most knew about the lady in question.

Cyrus announced in his reedy voice that the woman must be the bride! He was leaning unsteadily on a cane after twisting an ankle playing volley ball at the Meadowlark fitness center.

"No, Dad." Duncan hissed. "She is definitely not the bride."

Mrs. O'Reilly, who owned Tommy Delaney's favorite haunt, let out a hoot of appreciation for that little exchange and remarked that Tommy surely would be loving his own funeral.

Cyrus ignored his son's explanation and demanded to know when the wedding would start. He waved his cane at the Admiral and said, "Are you performing the ceremony, my good man?" Cyrus was having an off day.

The Admiral reared back and suggested that Cyrus watch where he was pointing his stick. Cyrus told him to bugger off, that they didn't need any Navy chaplains at a Delaney wedding.

It was at this point that Nina entered the vestibule, just in time to hear the exchange. It would seem that Cyrus and the Admiral were providing the mourners with the necessary diversion. Her stomach was still rolling, and she was grateful for any distraction. She joined Betty Hughes, who offered her another Tums. Betty Hughes was fussing about Cyrus's terrible behavior, saying he had forgotten to take his pills.

Duncan put an arm around Cyrus's thin shoulders and then took time to retie his tie, which, Nina noticed, was dotted with soup stains. Tufts of sparse white hair stood at attention on Cyrus's scalp, making him appear either very alert or greatly alarmed, Nina wasn't sure which, but the old editor did present a touching picture, nonetheless. Betty Hughes sighed and said he'd dressed himself. The jacket didn't match the trousers and he'd forgotten his socks. Nina smiled and said it was OK. Tommy would have appreciated Cyrus's wardrobe choices and that was all that mattered.

Betty Hughes drawled, "Cyrus hasn't uttered a lucid thing all mornin'."

On hearing this, Cyrus turned to her and exclaimed, "Lucid? Terrible name for a woman! Much prefer Lucille, myself." Then, using his cane, Nina watched him lift the back of the skirt of a woman next to him. Betty Hughes turned away to giggle. Nina laughed, so did others. Strangely, the woman never seemed to notice the offense or to feel the draft.

A minute later Nina caught sight of Beatrice Wrenn making a diva's entrance in a magnificent plum cape and matching hat with a dashing pheasant's feather stuck through the crown. She was followed by Isobel Woolsey, sheathed in black cashmere and escorting a timid old woman in a shabby tweed coat. Nina could only assume the elderly lady was Isobel's housekeeper, who was nearly as old as Belmont.

"You don't suppose the old housekeeper and Tommy were chummy years ago?" Betty Hughes whispered to Duncan. Duncan said this was hardly the place to theorize on Tommy's love life.

"Good grief, darlin, Tommy's love life *was* his life. Talkin' about it is like offerin' up a tribute to the old Romeo." Her rebuke was taken in silence by her son. Nina laughed quietly. "Tommy once told me I was the most beautiful woman he'd ever seen," Betty Hughes announced softly to no one in particular, but probably to the Admiral who was closest.

Somehow, in the din of conversation, Cyrus caught his wife's remark and immediately took a serious grip on his cane. Raising his weapon, Cyrus bellowed, "How dare you flirt with my wife, Sir!" and proceeded to whack the unsuspecting and quite innocent Admiral across the shins.

The Admiral yelped in pain and began hopping up and down on one foot, crying, "Get a hold of yourself, you nitwit! There's a dead man in there!"

"Right you are, Sir! The dead man *in there* was the *last* man who winked at my wife!" And, Cyrus stepped forward and poked the Admiral in the chest with his finger.

Mourners let go with peals of laughter. Another classic Delaney funeral!

Never one to shun the spotlight, Cyrus bowed to the crowd while the Admiral stood next to him with one trouser leg rolled up to inspect his bruises.

As if on cue, the church organist began the rumbling chords of the dirge, a somber reminder that it was time to pay their respects.

Duncan firmly escorted his father down the aisle, followed by the family. Admiral Moss located Lettice and pushed in beside her just as the two ancient mourners behind them began to snore. Archie was striding back up the aisle hoping to find Nina. Hugo remained in the pew, uninterested in her whereabouts.

A minute after the Mass started, Marigold and Parnell made a barely noticed entrance and took a back pew. Nina and Archie slid in beside them. Nina recalled the odd rumors circulating….that Marigold had lured the dying Tommy into her bed, only to cause his premature expiration. Such nonsense. Marigold had told her two days ago at a bridge party that Tommy stopped by to see them that afternoon, fell ill, and needed to lie down. As he napped alone on her bed, the Irishman's ravaged heart simply stopped, as if finally finding its peace. For those who liked to believe the worst, it did appear that Marigold had been only too happy to oblige a willing but dying man. The truth was never as amusing, of course.

The Grants knew that Tommy's painless death had nothing to do with seduction. Parnell had advised Marigold to keep the truth their secret. Let the rumors fly, he told her with a twinkle. "These poor souls have so little scandal to feed on these days," he said, "why not give them a gift of it, in Tommy's honor?"

Tommy would have agreed. Wasn't it that saucy, spicy tittle-tattle that kept people going, after all? Parnell was right, Marigold said. He was always right.

After Mass the congregation maneuvered up the aisles as best they could amid walkers and canes and the infirm trying to pilot each other out of the cold church. Many looked in need of the facilities after the lengthy service by Father Mayhew, a new, longwinded priest who'd only known the Delaney family two weeks and kept calling the deceased 'Thomas.' A good many of the older mourners were heard to mutter about who the strange priest was going on about. Had they come to the wrong funeral? This Thomas sounded far too pious for a Delaney.

Downstairs in the windowless church hall, bluish tube lights cast an anemic pall across long tables draped in white, where the Ladies' Altar Society had laid out refreshments. The rich fragrance of brewed coffee and freshly baked chocolate cake beckoned like opium and fought with the faint pungency of damp coats. The real wake, of course, would be that evening at the Knights of Columbus Hall on King Street. Tommy had left a sizable sum for what he had called a proper sending off party.

Nina persuaded Hugo and Archie that she would be content to rest in the car while they paid their respects and had coffee. Archie promised to bring her a slice of cake. Hugo walked back into the church in an advanced pout.

Downstairs in the hall, one of the Delaney grandsons was heard to remark that the priest looked more hung over than the corpse and was promptly rewarded for his humor with a swat on the head from his grandmother, who warned that if he didn't show the proper respect he'd be trotting off home without any dessert.

Muttering 'really, today of all days,' over and over, Isobel shepherded her weepy housekeeper through the throng and finally planted the woman next to Marigold and Parnell before heading for refreshments. The housekeeper looked sheepish and red-eyed from crying and refused to tell Marigold how she knew Tommy Delaney. Marigold admitted to Parnell that her attempt to pry information from Doreen might be shameless, but it was worth a try.

Shunned by a few of the more conservative mourners and greeted cordially by the rest, Marigold chatted with friends, seemingly content to appear exotic and a trifle mysterious, dressed in a fabulous sable coat and a veiled black hat. When pressed for details about Tommy's last hour, Marigold would only smile wickedly behind the netting and say that Tommy Delaney had died a happy man.

14

Second Chances

Archie hurried down Concourse F at Augusta County Airport and searched the crowd for Nadine. According to the arrival and departure board, the commuter flight from Chicago had arrived on time; he'd been on time. So, where was Nadine? He double-checked the scrap of paper in his pocket with the flight number and scheduled arrival. Everything was A-OK.

He pushed his way past a family hugging and kissing as if they'd never see each other again and started back up the concourse, past the T-shirt boutiques, the hole-in-the-wall bars, rest rooms, and the Jiffy Deli that always looked more iffy than jiffy. Maybe she'd sneaked past him and was waiting at the baggage carousel downstairs. Archie was irritated and hungry. He'd missed his dinner.

About a hundred passengers ringed the loop of revolving luggage like anglers waiting to cast lines into a pond, hoping to land the big one. Again, Archie scanned faces, all a bit hazy without his glasses; he'd left them in the car. At the far end of the carousel he could see a female vaguely resembling his wife's body build. She was carrying a large leopard patterned tote over one shoulder and wore oversized gold speckled sun-glasses pushed down slightly on her nose. Nadine wouldn't wear glasses like that, he decided, and the woman's hair was a neon pinky orange sherbet cone. He squinted again at a good view of the broad hips in gold tights, a striped tunic in orange, red, pink, and yellow. His wife wouldn't appear in public in an outfit like that. No loud colors, no metallics, she would insist when the idea of gifts came up. But, high fashion or not, the hips looked familiar. Almost too familiar. Maybe this babe deserved a closer look.

As he wove his way through the tangle of passengers, their hand luggage barking his shins, the children underfoot yipping like dogs, Archie fished in his pocket for a candy bar he thought he'd stashed. The pocket was empty. He approached the flamboyant traveler and called out, "Nadine? Is that you?"

Up close, Archie recognized the unmistakable profile…a firm pointed chin, long, slender nose, and the prodigious bosom of an aging showgirl. "For God's sake," he bellowed, "what the hell have you done to yourself?" Several couples turned to stare at Nadine. One older gentleman whistled softly and then smiled at Archie with great envy in his eyes.

"You don't have to shout, Archie." There was little warmth in the greeting. And, no hello kiss. "And don't call me Nadine."

"Why the hell not? It's your name!" Archie took a closer look just to make sure. He was married to this woman. She'd done something to her face too. False eyelashes, he thought, and green eye shadow.

"My name is Sonja now."

"What the hell are you talking about?" Archie boomed. Several more heads turned. The exchange of information was attracting attention. A good rumpus in the airport lobby, Archie figured, would certainly make time pass more quickly for the poor souls waiting endlessly for their bags. "What have you done to your hair?" Was she trying to look like Marigold? Goodgrief! He took a step back and surveyed this creature for about the fourth time. "Sonja? Are you nuts?"

Nadine (or Sonja) made a grab for a large calf-skin suitcase that was circling in front of them on the conveyor. She hoisted it from the carousel like a stevedore. Archie pushed forward to take it from her, saying, "Here, let me do that. What about your back?"

"My back is fine. I've been working out, Archie." After a minor struggle, the new Nadine relinquished the heavy suitcase and marched off toward the exit carrying her leather cosmetic bag. "Do you have the car?" she called over a shoulder at him.

"Of course, I have the car!" Archie barked back. "Do you think I rode a horse over here?" The man behind him laughed.

Archie hurried along after his wife, the luggage handle grinding into his palm. She always over-packed. From this advantageous angle Archie decided that Nadine didn't look any thinner. Those spa exercise classes (as overpriced as the rabbit food they served) hadn't made a dent in the famous Naddy hips, as Cyrus liked to call them. And the hair! What was she trying to prove this time? This wild spurt of color had to be a dig at him and the forever glamorous Marigold. The desert spa was an establishment of ferment, he'd learned through the years. Nadine or Sonja, or whatever the hell she was calling herself, always came home with screwy ideas about independence and women's rights and leafy vegetables. He'd spend the next two months eating yogurt and beans. Jesus! Why couldn't she just exercise at the health club like Betty Hughes?

Once settled in the car and out of the airport parking structure, Archie brought up the Sonja business again. "Cute joke, Nadine. Goes with your new hair. You had me going there!" Archie chuckled good-naturedly as he swung the big car up the ramp and out into freeway traffic.

"It's no joke, Archie. I'm going to court. I am having my name legally changed to Sonja. I prefer it. Sonja Stein. I am retrieving my maiden name too. I've never liked Nadine. Not even as a child. Sonja is more creative." The new Sonja smiled for the first time since Archie spotted her at the carousel. "I've found my creative side, Archie. At last."

Archie sputtered something unintelligible and thought he might be having a nightmare or acute indigestion. He'd had French fries and barbecued pork for lunch, and nothing since. He should have known better. He turned to the woman who used to be his wife and saw for the first time that her fingernails were two inches long and painted two colors, pink and turquoise. "What have you done to your hands, for God's sake?" He passed a cement truck and then exited the highway for Belmont.

"Aren't they wonderful? To go with my new hairdo. And my life as an artist!" Sonja smiled again, obviously pleased with her decisions.

Archie felt prickles of fear crawl up his arms. A new life? An artist? What was the woman talking about? "What new life?" he asked more calmly. Perhaps she'd starved herself into insanity at that damned spa. Best be soothing and collected right now. Until they were home and he could call Doc Liebermann, a shrink in the neighborhood who was surprisingly normal. Maybe a nice steak would bring her back to her old self.

"I've had oodles of time to think, Archie. If Marigold Woolsey can have a life of fun and creativity...if that's what you want to call those hideous sculptures of hers...then, so can I. I'm thinking of taking an apartment in Augusta and a studio in the Third Ward. I'm going to make pots." She examined the dagger nails with satisfaction in the light of a shopping mall they were passing.

"Pots? What kind of pots? Cooking pots?" Archie was bewildered and intent on driving. He suffered slightly from night blindness.

"Heavens, no. Art pottery. Vessels, Archie. Clay vessels that I intend to sell at galleries in Chicago and New York." Sonja smiled privately. "My pottery instructor at the spa...his name was Kevin...said I was the greatest talent he'd seen in ten years." She pushed the window button and a gust of cool night air slapped them like a damp towel. "Kevin said my glazes were divine. Absolutely divine. Those were his exact words, Archie. And, he's an artist from New York."

"So, why hasn't all this divine talent bubbled up before?" Archie slowed for the curves at the base of the bluffs. The oncoming headlights made it difficult. He should have had 'Sonja' drive. There wasn't a thing wrong with her eyesight.

"Latent development, it's called. But, I fully intend to cultivate my talent. I've already ordered the equipment, and I'll look for a suitable studio in Augusta next week."

Archie didn't like the emphasis on a studio in Augusta. "So, you're moving out after all these years? To make flower pots?" Archie nearly stopped the car.

"Keep driving, Archie, or we'll have a crash!" Nadine braced herself with a hand on the dash. The new fingernails flashed in the street lamps. "Vessels!"

"A crash might make you come to your senses, woman!"

"Don't call me woman, Archie. I absolutely forbid it! I bet you never use that tone and that word with Marigold Woolsey." Nadine pushed the window button again and the night air disappeared. "Think of the advantages.....with a boring wife off in Augusta. You'll be able to entertain Marigold any time. Day or night." She turned to stare at the scenery which was largely shadows and looming dark shapes until they hit the city streets again.

Archie took a deep breath and kept on his path to their house. He couldn't believe what he was hearing. "You actually believe Marigold and I are seeing each other behind your back?" There was that one time, but he didn't think he would admit it now.

"I think what I think. She always preferred you and Tommy. Well, now with Tommy out of the picture, she'll be calling you."

"Be reasonable! I don't want you to move out." Did he really mean that? What had he done to deserve this? There was Nina to consider. The baby. "You know very well that you're happy if I'm happy. Isn't that the way it's supposed to work?" Had that come out right?

"No, Archie. If I believe I'm happy, then I'm happy. It has nothing to do with you."

Nadine's responses were calmly and firmly administered. Had she taken one of those stress management classes as well? All this happiness crap was spa talk. If you put fifty rich women in mud baths and feed them lettuce and herb tea, they're going to come out talking like Nadine….. Sonja.

Archie pulled into the drive, pushed the garage door button, and guided the car into its slot next to Nadine's white Mercedes. Nadine got out, her animal skin tote over one shoulder and her Gucci bag on the other. Her gold tights shimmered in the garage lights. She let herself into the back hall and closed the door. She had not asked about Tommy's funeral.

Archie sat there in the dark a very long time, thinking that if he lived forever he would never understand Nadine/Sonja. Come to think about it, he didn't really understand Marigold all that well either. Or, Nina. The closer he got to females, the more eggshells appeared on the path. Why such mystery? Funny, it was the mystery that drew you to them in the first place, he thought, easily ticking off Marigold's roster of enticements and Nina's astonishing ability to make his knees buckle. But, tonight, he was neither drawn nor enticed by any of them. Just frustrated. And tired of being a man trying to figure out women.

"Why can't you get your landlord to move this stuff for you?" Cyrus shoved a small table out the way with his hip and got a firmer grip on the bigger table.

"Landlords don't move furniture. Where'd you get that idea?" The Admiral hoisted up his end and slowly backed his way down the hall and then halted in front of the second bedroom where the table was supposed to go.

"Now, be careful making the turn, Cyrus. I don't want it all banged up." And the Admiral tilted the old table very carefully while Cyrus followed suit on his end. "You've got to jockey those legs around the door jamb!" The Admiral was trying to pay attention to his end and keep an eye on Cyrus at the same time.

"I'm not ten, you know. I've moved my share of tables." Cyrus puffed out his chest and gave the table a good twist. One leg snagged the molding around the door and took away a big chip of paint.

"Now look at what you've done!" The Admiral almost dropped his end but kept backing up, snorting and grumbling and talking about buying paint and sandpaper.

"Oh, shut up, Mel! What's a little ding? You'd think you were living at Versailles with Marie Antoinette, for God's sake." Cyrus grinned, obviously visualizing the Admiral with a French queen in a castle.

"Oh, shut up, yourself. I bet you didn't carry a stick or a chair when you moved into the Meadowlark." The Admiral and Cyrus set the table under the window.

"What the hell is this place?" Cyrus asked a bit foggily, looking around the room as if he'd never seen it before. Cyrus's grip on reality, the Admiral noticed earlier, came and went in spurts today. But, by and large, the new meds were working wonders.

"My office. I'm putting my computer in here. And, my printer."

"Jesus. What are you? General Motors' accounting division or something?" Cyrus sat down in an old club chair that was always his favorite. It had a slipcover with side pockets, handy for cigars and Snicker bars.

"I'm going to write my memoirs." The Admiral dropped into the other soft chair. The small square room was painted a bright aqua picked out by Lettice and didn't accommodate much, what with the filing cabinets and a big bookcase filled with World War Two volumes. There was one window with a Venetian blind.

"Memoirs?" Cyrus was dumbfounded. "Who in the hell wants to read your memoirs?" He made the pronunciation very la de da French and the Admiral gave him the finger. He preferred Cyrus 'on' rather than 'off,' even if the old bugger was a pain in the ass.

"I've already talked to an agent in New York," said the Admiral. Actually, he'd sent off one letter to one agency and was waiting for a reply. Nothing so far. "I've led an interesting life. My years in the Navy during the war would make a great movie."

"Maybe I should write mine too. I'm colorful….that's what Betty Hughes always says. And, I sure as hell remember more about anything forty years ago than you do." Cyrus wiped perspiration from his forehead with a hankie and giggled. "A movie? That's rich, Mel! My problems will disappear completely if your life ever comes out on the screen." He giggled uncontrollably for a minute. "Who's going to play you in the flicks?"

"There would be a young me and an older me…..I thought Cary Grant might do for the older me. I don't know much about the young actors now days."

"I think Cary Grant is dead. If he isn't, the prospect of playing you will push him off the twig all the sooner." Cyrus laughed and felt an urgent need to go off to pee.

When he came back Cyrus asked the whereabouts of Parnell Grant, who was supposed to stop by for a quick game of cards.

"Visiting Lettice across the hall. He'll be along."

Cyrus announced he could use another 'brewski.' "Let's raid the ice box. Or do you have an armoire you want me to move for you." He pronounced armoire with a French accent and then minced his way down the hall swinging his hips like a mannequin.

"La de da. You're a riot." The Admiral followed quickly; he didn't like Cyrus rummaging in his refrigerator. He always upset things….the

Admiral stored his food in alphabetical order. Ketchup was lined up ahead of mustard and pickles. Milk took a front seat to orange juice.

Ten minutes later, Parnell strolled in. He'd had coffee with Lettice, he said. The old bard of the Riviera wasn't looking too well, the Admiral thought. Thin as silk. He'd taken Tommy's death very hard. The Admiral worried about him.

"Lettice is a lovely woman," Parnell commented as he sat down in the Admiral's tiny kitchen. "Somebody should snatch her up." Parnell sighed, as if thinking about something entirely different. "I'll have a glass of wine while you're up, Melvin."

"Yeah," Cyrus put in. "Mel should snatch up Lettice. Think of the rent you'd save. The two of you could take that big flat on the second floor." Cyrus winked at Parnell.

"Me, marry? Whatever for?" The Admiral fished a bottle of Mogen David from the refrigerator and poured some into a juice glass. Parnell graciously accepted it.

"She's a terrible cook. And, frugal as hell," Cyrus said. "Just what you're used to."

"Lettice and I are good friends. That's all. We share the Sunday paper." The Admiral sat down in a hard kitchen chair and wished this conversation would end.

A half hour later, the three of them were tight and willing enough to howl at every bad joke Cyrus could tell. Cyrus had put together liver sausage sandwiches over his host's objections, and they'd played a few hands of poker, but it wasn't the same without Archie and Tommy. Archie was sorting out something at the boot factory today. Finally, after another round and the last of the Admiral's stale potato chips, Cyrus leaned toward his host and the poet laureate and said, "Do you want to hear the latest?" His head dropped nearly into his lap with laughter. "This'll knock you off your scrawny asses!"

"Get on with it!" the Admiral complained. He hated preliminaries.

Parnell kept giggling for no other reason than the fact that Cyrus had that effect on him.

Cyrus thrust his head across the table and whispered, "Archie's going to be a Daddy." He held himself rigid, like a poised lizard, and kept his eyes on his audience, as if to memorize the moment. "This is the story of the century, my lads. Forget men on the moon; forget computers."

"What do you mean?" Parnell sounded a trifle perplexed.

The Admiral said, "You mean he and Nadine are adopting one of those foreign kids?" His mouth hung open unattractively.

"Holy Toledo! What do you think I mean? You've got to shift into low here." And Cyrus sniggered. "Archie's been having a few afternoons off, if you know what I mean. A few nooners. One or two matinees, if you're not too drunk or too old to remember what those are." He slurped up a good half a glass of beer.

"Who with?" Parnell asked.

"You'll never guess." Cyrus rocked back and forth on the chair until his host told him to cut it out.

"Well, it sure as hell wasn't Naddy, right?" crowed Parnell, rather inelegantly for Parnell Grant. He slapped his thin leg and belched softly.

"Ten points for the gentleman drinking the cheap wine," said Cyrus. "Have another. It's all…relative." He winked theatrically to let them know he was giving them a big clue.

"Relative?" The Admiral remained confused. "Archie doesn't have any female relatives. Except Nadine. It's all boys in that family."

Parnell stared at Cyrus and a sly grin began shaping his lips. "Oh, yes he has. Or will. One's on the drawing board, so to speak. With blonde hair and a sweet Southern drawl." He pounded the table top. "That old dog!"

The Admiral squinted his eyes and screwed up his mouth. A Southern woman? In Belmont? "Betty Hughes?" he blurted out. "Your own wife?" The Admiral gasped a little. Had Cyrus gone round the bend? "That would be a medical miracle."

"Oh, really, Melvin. Use your head!" Parnell shook his head at the Admiral and the Admiral looked hurt. "Betty Hughes isn't blonde!" Parnell sniggered.

"Does the lady have a name?" Cyrus asked Parnell, ignoring the Admiral.

"Miss Nina Dupree, just shortly arrived from New Orleans, comes to mind."

"Bingo!" shouted Cyrus. He stood and executed a silly jig with his arms and legs flapping and bouncing.

Parnell teetered dangerously on his kitchen chair and then toppled over. He sprawled on the kitchen floor, unhurt but dissolved in laughter. Cyrus lowered himself to the cold vinyl while the Admiral pretended to be stunned.

Rising from his stool like a bishop, the Admiral declared the whole thing scandalous. Outrageous! Immoral and quite unacceptable. And he began cleaning up the mess they'd made of his kitchen.

"Unacceptable?" Parnell asked.

"Yes. Archie can't go around Belmont impregnating women who are betrothed to other men. Like his own son. It's incest! That's what it is. Incest!" The Admiral rinsed the glasses in the sink and put away the loaf of bread. They'd eaten far too many liver sausage sandwiches. He'd be up all night with heartburn.

"It's not incest. Hugo isn't married to Nina. And, Archie doesn't do this sort of thing for a living. It just happened." Cyrus rose from the floor, sighed and wiped the tears from his face with the Admiral's kitchen towel. "They were keeping each other company, so to speak. Nina's lonely and Nadine's been off in the boiling desert eating sprouts and flirting with the pool boys."

"They're over twenty-one," Parnell pointed out, unnecessarily. He picked himself up and planted his thin rear on the chair again.

"What are they going to do about this?" the Admiral wanted to know. He wiped off the kitchen table with a bright yellow sponge. "You two have always been too liberal."

"I take it the party's over?" Cyrus remarked sarcastically.

"Yes. I'm tired. And, this news about Archie has me upset." The Admiral finished his chores and herded his guests into the front hall, where he handed out their coats.

"For heaven's sake, both of you," said Cyrus as he wiggled into his jacket, "don't breathe a word about this to Archie or anybody else. It's supposed to be a secret."

"Not for long," Parnell replied, "but, my lips are sealed. He was leaning precariously against the wall and began a slow slide to the floor. "Marigold will love this."

"Ah, Marigold. Has a streak of libertine in her," said Cyrus. "She might just approve of Archie's affair with Nina. And the baby."

"Is Archie going to divorce Nadine?" asked the Admiral.

Cyrus shrugged his shoulders. "He says he loves Nina. I haven't heard Archie say that about a woman in forty years." Cyrus said he envied Archie's new love.

"Love?" Parnell said. "I thought we were talking about sex."

"Oh, do be quiet." The Admiral was familiar enough with new love. He pulled Parnell to his feet.

"You'd better call Mr. Foote," Parnell said. "It's a taxi night."

The Admiral ordered up the taxi. He wanted to be alone.

"It's a soap opera, that's what it is," Cyrus said. "Our life is like 'General Hospital.' Just one damned thing after another." He held up his hand and began ticking off his fingers. "Old bones in Sandy Hook; Lola Spriggs dead in her closet; Archie's matinees with a beauty queen...." At this point he let his thoughts drift away.

"That skeleton doesn't mean anything to us," said Parnell, as he tried to figure out how to turn the door knob. "A local mystery. You don't get many here on the frontier." He giggled again.

Cyrus and the Admiral stared at each other and each one put a finger to his lips, as if to say, not another word. Lucky Parnell. He didn't know about Pike's Wood.

"You're absolutely correct!" said Cyrus, and he took Parnell's arm as they moved through the doorway. "Mr. Foote is tooting his horn."

Parnell and Cyrus tottered down the walk toward the taxi, which was belching fumes and rattling. They were chanting names of soap operas as they crawled into the back seat.

The Admiral closed the door and hurried down the hall to his office where he jotted down some notes. His memoirs had just gained a new chapter. So far, he didn't have many titillating stories to tell, but Archie's seduction of Miss Dupree would be the perfect juicy bit in the publishing game. Archie could relive the whole thing in 'Memoirs of an American Admiral.'

Melvin Moss was most pleased with the title.

"The lame, the halt, the incontinent. Was anyone missing? Except Naddy?" Betty Hughes asked as she carefully placed a silver tray of caviar and toast rounds on the coffee table. It was the canapé portion of the Old Devils' Supper Club, an excuse for sharing a meal and each other's cooking for more than thirty years now. Naddy turned Sonja and Archie were preparing the main course, an Italian recipe straight from the pages of 'Bon Appetit.' Lettice and the Admiral were sharing salad duties, while Marigold and Parnell, newly initiated into the club at the insistence of Lettice and the Admiral, had offered to do dessert. Isobel Woolsey would contribute the wine and said she would be late. The subject of Tommy Delaney's funeral was on the slate for tonight. Two weeks had passed since the Mass at St. Hyacinth's.

Tommy's Irish contemporaries, according to Archie, had caroused into the wee hours at the Knights of Columbus Hall and the adjoining parking lot. Four were arrested for lewd and lascivious, which added just the right touch to the proceedings, according to Cyrus.

"Everybody in town knew Tommy. I wished I had been here," Sonja commented more wistfully than she'd intended.

"Will we end up like that?" asked Parnell, "a gaggle of doddering old fools, bumping into each other, barely able to see and hear and with peeing as our first priority."

"Of course," Archie answered quite calmly. "One must face these things head on and honestly." He stood by the drinks table and made himself a double gin martini. "Why should we end up any differently?" He dropped three olives into his glass.

"One must face the facts of life until the end," chimed in Marigold, who certainly didn't look like she was ready just yet; her face remained unlined, her hands unspotted. She was a marvel, according to anyone who met her. Most thought her prodigious sex life was responsible.

Pouring himself a glass of red wine, Parnell said, "The gang at St. Hyacinth's reminded me of my old dad describing the University Club to a friend. Dad explained that the club was roughly divided into two groups.....those who couldn't pee and those who couldn't stop." Parnell grinned as everyone laughed in a kind of grim appreciation for what was coming. No one wanted to think too seriously about adult diapers.

"Why must it always boil down to faulty plumbing and a loss of wits?" asked Sonja. "Like Isobel's housekeeper in her sneakers?"

Betty Hughes noticed that Sonja had arrived on wobbly pegs, as her Daddy liked to say, and was inclined to be quarrelsome tonight. Generally, Sonja (silly damned name) came back from the spa in a better mood. Perhaps moving to Augusta and starting a career was too much to handle. Betty Hughes's private competition with Marigold had reached a new plateau….. each hoping the other would fail to write another decent novel or play in this lifetime. Belmont had never been quite so full of sexual and professional intrigue. On a subterranean level, Betty Hughes was loving it and wanting to escape all at once.

After fixing a fresh drink, Sonja moved closer to the fire but kept her eyes on Archie, as if he and Marigold might bolt. Actually, Marigold was shunning him tonight.

Marigold rose at that point and poured herself another glass of pinot, taking time to compliment Betty Hughes on a lovely potted orchid bound to a beautiful curling branch. It sat on the drinks table as an elegant reminder of warmer days. Betty Hughes explained that she just kept buying them from the florist, replacing one dead orchid after another. It was the only way she could grow plants. This sounded so silly the two laughed. Betty Hughes sensed a kind of peace rising between them.

"I suppose we could all jump from a tall building when we hit eighty," Cyrus was saying. "Betsy Lamb…a neighbor at Meadowlark… says we should end it before we get gaga and can't make the hike to the roof." He smiled.

"Good grief!" cried Archie. "Dramatic but sick!"

"Crackpot idea!" spouted the Admiral, shifting his weight from one leg to the other, an old nervous habit that renewed itself lately. "A decision based upon female vanity, I should expect." He huffed and puffed and disappeared into the hallway, looking for the powder room. Cyrus excused himself too and headed for the bathroom in his bedroom.

"Oh, who cares the method?" put in Lettice. "What about Cyrus? He doesn't choose to say and do the things he does. Like at the funeral."

"Absolutely," replied Archie, always a voice of sympathy and understanding when it came to Cyrus.

"After the funeral, on the way back to the car," Betty Hughes said quietly, "Cyrus told me he's afraid of turning into a turnip." She couldn't laugh at this.

Archie groaned and stared at the carpet, soft swirls of blue and cream as tranquil as clouds in a summer sky. "Cyrus's descent into hell is just about more than some of us can bear," he said, choking back tears. He dabbed his eyes with a large white handkerchief. "I'm praying for those new pills."

"Well, some people," Marigold pointed out quickly, as if to give Archie time to collect himself, "some people get mean and nasty out of spite…when they get old. Has nothing to do with disease. Isobel's a tyrant and knows what she's doing every minute. Her mother was the same. And, one or two of her sisters. Runs in the family. Except for my dear brother…" Her thoughts drifted off.

"True enough," said Sonja. "Certainly Isobel is a senior, like us, but she'll never get any nicer." Her friends were nodding in agreement. Sonja moved to the windows to watch a fine rain soak the earth. Fallen leaves were turning to mush, and the metallic sky hovered like a heavy pot lid. It was depressing. The desert had been so uplifting. "Isobel's just pulling into the parking lot." She nodded to the scene far below.

The Admiral and Cyrus rejoined them, first helping themselves to appetizers before sitting near the fire.

"Our children think we have lived relatively uncomplicated lives," said Archie. "Hugo says it's just one round of golf after the other."

"Hah! If they only knew, huh, Arch?" Cyrus commented with some vigor and a twinkle.

Archie's heart jumped into his throat again….Cyrus was moving dangerously close to the body in Pike's Wood and the saga of Betty Grable. Or, those days in Florida, the flying fish and the strippers.

"Heavens, what about Lola Spriggs?" Betty Hughes put in quickly. "How many of our children have a friend murdered and left in her closet?"

"Here, here!" replied Parnell. "By the way, I'm leaning toward her son. How about you? I think he needs money and couldn't wait for mama to die." The poet dipped into the caviar and ambled about the room nibbling on his toast round. His own mother and father, he told them, still vigorous, lived alone on a vast country estate outside

Milwaukee. His father still sailed a forty-two foot Catalina on Lake Michigan and drove to the office every day. He was a successful attorney and had a mistress who was sixty-five. Parnell snorted at this.

Just then the bell rang and Betty Hughes hurried to admit Isobel, all done up in mink and carrying two bottles of wine…..the remaining bottles were in the car, she said.

"What a night!" Isobel exclaimed, removing her coat and arranging the damp fur on the back of a chair. "Why do we have these suppers in winter?"

"It's only rain, Isobel. This could be a cool night in April!" Archie handed her a glass of white wine and escorted her to a comfortable chair. "We're just happy you didn't bring your dogs." He grinned.

"I know you hate my dogs, but they have better manners than you most days." Isobel scowled at Archie. They'd been arguing about large dogs for decades. Isobel believed her Irish wolfhounds should be welcome anywhere, anytime. Archie belonged to a more conservative discipline that would have any canine weighing more than his mother banned from galloping down the sidewalk or entering a small café for a drink. Their exaggerations were often entertaining.

"Could be some old farts have done marvelous and daring things nobody knows about," Cyrus was saying to no one in particular.

Isobel said, "What are you talking about, Cyrus?"

Sonja, ignoring Isobel altogether, said, "I think Archie and Cyrus were very naughty boys at Hugo's age." She remained perched on the arm of a chair near the windows, smiling, her carefully penciled eyebrows arched provocatively. No one had commented on her new look or her new wardrobe tonight. The subject was just too touchy. But, everyone turned to look at her now, as if she knew a secret.

Archie jumped quickly into the conversation saying that the Old Devils might have been naughty, but they'd fought in World War II, for God's sake! "Cyrus and I landed on Omaha Beach and lived! The Admiral made it through Pearl Harbor." He was standing now, bringing himself up to his full height, demanding their attention. Cyrus remained seated, content to let Archie defend their honor. "None of our children ever went to war."

"Why this ferocious defense, Archie? We know all of this." This from Betty Hughes.

"We should be reminded from time to time," put in Parnell. "Facing death and horrible injury on the battlefield has no equal here...where the bombs never fell." He raised his glass to the Old Devils.

"True enough," replied the Admiral. "All we've had to worry about since is how to make money and have a good time."

There was a quiet and unanimous concurrence once again before Isobel insisted someone explain what they were talking about. Archie filled her in.

"Growing old is a state of mind," Isobel replied with finality.

"Hell, the Admiral here has been an old fart since college!" Cyrus managed a giggle and so did everybody else, including the Admiral.

"It's my attitude, Isobel, old girl. I decided early on to be an old fart." He giggled too, enjoying the attention.

"Attitude and genetics together," put in Marigold. "If you worry about getting old, you'll probably act old and look it. My mother hasn't celebrated a birthday in twenty years."

"My dad acts like he's forty-five and stays away from the docs," said Parnell.

They loved that one.

"Card playing and sex are the secrets," said Betty Hughes with an elbow in the ribs to Cyrus, who seemed to be keeping up rather well. She ran her fingers down her throat, as if searching for wrinkles or a double chin. "My mother plays bridge nearly every day."

"Sure, who in hell would sleep with your mother?" yelped Cyrus.

"She's still gorgeous, Cyrus Armbruster. Has men runnin' after her every week end at the country club. She's comin' up here in another few weeks. Watch out! She and her maid will keep you hoppin', I would guess."

"The boys in Alabama are running all right…..for the doors!" He bleated like a sheep. Betty Hughes's mother was still trying to find her fourth husband after killing off the first three. "She's Montgomery's version of Jumpin' Judith, for God's sake!"

"Oh, shut up, you old goat. Sex sells books. Keeps my stories alive." She raised her glass to her audience. "Look at Marigold and Parnell…. ageless and spirited. Still stirring up trouble, most having to do with chemistry." There, she'd said it…..out in the open. She was a trifle drunk.

Marigold laughed and so did Parnell. Marigold said as casually as she could, "There are beating hearts in my play."

Betty Hughes sat as still as a frog pretending to be dead. Why did Marigold have to spoil the moment? Was this a preview of comin' attractions?

"Glad to hear it, Marigold," Cyrus responded. "Isn't it about time for dinner?"

"Yes. The roast is roasting," Sonja told him and stood, preparing to leave.

As they all finished their drinks and began to assemble near the coat closet, Lettice declared that men often think a woman half their age will save them.

Archie didn't like the direction of this conversation and hurriedly helped Sonja with her coat, all the while thinking about Nina and the potential devastation in his future. He opened the apartment door and stepped into the corridor

"Who is more foolish," Parnell asked, as he put on her beret and cape, "a woman of sixty dating a man of forty or a man of sixty dating a woman of forty?"

"In our society, women aren't supposed to have fun with younger men." This came from Betty Hughes, who was rummaging in her handbag for a lipstick.

A rumble of agreement moved through the little knot of guests. The rain continued its snap against the windows; a crackle of thunder could be heard in the west. No one was particularly eager to go outside and retrieve the cars in the Meadowlark parking lot.

"Motives and moves like that should remain private," said the Admiral. "It's a completely private bit of folly or good fortune. We're all entitled to take chances after forty. It's another rite of passage." He adjusted his cap and joined Archie in the hallway.

"Archie, ring for the elevator," Sonja said quietly.

Lettice was shocked at the Admiral's comment. He so rarely jumped into these discussions on behavior. Why would he be in favor of a second chance? He didn't often try anything remotely daring. She smiled a little to herself, remembering the silk undershorts. Was he thinking more seriously about their little friendship at the seniors' boarding house? Lettice hurried to catch up with him.

Sensing tension, Betty Hughes said, "Age does peculiar things to all of us." The bickering and commentary died away. She turned out the lights and locked the apartment door.

"Hear, hear," said Cyrus. He put his arm around his wife's shoulders.

"New beginnings keep us young!" cried Marigold, as she stepped into the crowded elevator. "Sonja understands that better than anybody here."

"Second chances are over-rated," muttered Isobel from the back of the car.

"You might think about it, Isobel," said Cyrus, who was in front of her. "Who among us wouldn't like a fresh start, another stab. It could be as simple or as difficult as Betty Hughes rewriting chapter five or act two? Or, you could build a new stable at Woolsey Farms or get a third dog!"

The elevator doors swished open and the gaggle of guests stepped into the lobby, all strangely silent after Cyrus's heady suggestion. They filed out the doors and into the rainy night.

Cyrus was right. Betty Hughes could see it in the faces of her friends. Getting it right was what it was all about, wasn't it? One or two might even sell his soul for the chance. She wondered which two that might be.

15

Playing the Game

"Archie, darling! I won!" The voice had kept its continental seasoning. It was Marigold in a state of great excitement.

Archie sat straighter in his chair and waved Sonja off as she passed the study door. What the hell was the woman going on about? Did she mean that silly play competition? Good God, he'd forgotten about it. He asked cautiously, "You mean your play won?" He tried not to sound surprised, but he was. What the hell did Marigold Woolsey know about writing a play? Close to Nadine's notion of penning short stories. Belmont was going literary. Was everyone balmy?

"Yes, of course. 'Black-eyed Susans' took a first! First prize! Isn't that astonishing?"

"How? I mean, how did you find out?" Archie asked, suspicious now. Was someone playing a cruel joke? He thought immediately of Betty Hughes. She would slip into a long Southern belle swoon when she heard this news. Had Marigold paid off the judges?

"Professor Fitzhugh, head of the committee, called this morning at nine. Very polite and official. He said, in his opinion, the best play won. By far! Hands down!" Marigold fairly squealed with delight and she wasn't a woman who squealed. She generally accepted accolades and compliments with a kind of old world noblesse oblige not often witnessed in Belmont. "Ashbury's theatre department will produce it in April.…one of my favorite months."

"Three cheers, Marigold. We all knew you could do it." Archie had mustered what he thought was the proper exuberance without mentioning Betty Hughes.

"Surprised you, didn't I?" Marigold said, more calmly. "Betty Hughes took honorable mention for 'Cat's Cradle.' Poor darling. Must be quite a let-down for her, a published author and all."

Archie thought he detected a whisper of snottiness in that. He said, "Sounds good to me. Honorable mention, I mean."

"Hardly, Archie. Honorable mention is someone handing you a tacky wood plaque when your colleagues are picking up silver and gold trophies." Marigold seemed to emit a kind of high level 'hah!' with that remark. "Second prize went to Billy MacDuff, a student, for 'Empty Pockets.' Charming title. And, guess who beat our Betty Hughes for third?"

Archie said he had no idea. His head was reeling.

"The Reverend Brightbill at First Presbyterian!" Marigold pronounced the name in a saintly tone. "An extra layer of thick frosting on the cake. The sinister minister, as he was called, had managed to push Betty Hughes into the back row." Her tone remained jubilant.

"Hard to believe, Marigold. Didn't know the reverend wrote anything but bad sermons." Archie was honestly dumbfounded. That oily Bible thumper wrote a prize winning play? It was as inconceivable as Marigold taking first. "I suppose Parnell's taking you to the St. George for a celebratory drinkie?" Archie wondered in the back of his mind if Marigold might be angling for a celebratory drinkie with him…over in Augusta. He was beginning to feel trapped.

"I wouldn't mind celebrating with you, Archie. It's been a long time. I'm feeling quite full of myself, actually!" She laughed gaily, sounding an alarm inside Archie's skull. He needed to free himself from this entire scenario.

"I'm pretty tied up this week, Marigold. Let me give you a call. Again, congratulations! Have to go.…an important call on the other line." And, he rang off.

Archie didn't move for a long time. Another sticky wicket. He didn't want to make an enemy of Marigold…who knew what characters she would put into her next play? He might see himself up on stage ... tricked out in a strange name, bad wardrobe but spouting lines that would clearly identify him to the audience and humiliate him at the same time. Jesus! Females! His wife was into pots; his old mistress into show business and his new mistress into motherhood and acting! How had this happened? Archie put his head in his hands.

When he pulled back into an executive position again, the first thing he noticed was his trophy fish, a bluish lacquered marlin mounted on the far inside wall of his home office. When he and his cronies were in their forties, they would fly off to Miami each winter in search of the 'magnificent flying fish,' that was what they called them. The Hemingways of the Atlantic, Archie and Cyrus and company would go after deep sea fish with flamboyant fins and snouts. It was a safari on water, like bagging rhino and leopard using unspeakable acts of brutality. For a few fleeting seconds, Archie recalled the night Naddy nearly impaled him with one of his frozen walleyes! A new slant on the old flying fish story. He couldn't help smiling.

This macho male bonding ritual that men of his father's generation seemed to need was looked upon as their right as rich men who deserved time away from the pressure of work and family. His own father did it. He recalled vividly a day when he was only thirteen and one of his father's cronies whispered to him as the men waited for the train to Chicago that they would be hunting more than exotic fish down in Florida.....there would be the occasional exotic dancer, he said, giving young Archie a manly wink and a macho poke in the ribs, as if the boy was now privy to the single most important information for his coming of age. Exotic dancers? Archie didn't quite know what to make of that. The older man's secret had left him confused and somewhat disappointed in his father and his pals.

The day after Archie's departure for Florida, he knew Naddy would fly off to New York in search of her own trophies. Nadine's prizes came from Sotheby's and Israel Sacks. She would arrive home with a painting or a Chippendale chair worth twice Archie's escapade. Always keep your eye on the prize, his father had always told him. Year after year. Of course, old dad got himself into hot water eventually. Was Nina his new flying fish, his new prize? He wondered for a few minutes if he might be her prize. Had she bagged him with a baby? Jesus! Hugo was in a dither over the pregnancy. Hugo naturally assumed he was the father. Archie worried that his son might not have the stamina for marriage and fatherhood. And, Archie was left in limbo, not knowing which Beresford male had done the deed. No blood tests were taken. Nina said she did not want to know. The child had created a mystery that promised to go unsolved forever. Archie suddenly realized that his life was filled with maddeningly complicated puzzles!

Archie punched out seven numbers on his desk phone and asked for a man named Harvey in the maintenance department. He told Harvey to stop by his house that afternoon. He had a stuffed marlin he wanted delivered to his son's office at the boot factory. He said it was a gift.

The flying fish was coming down. Naddy would be pleased; she hated it. Archie felt an odd sense of power and relief in that moment. And, he knew Hugo would be annoyed.

Honorable mention? Betty Hughes rolled over. The sheets and blanket were in a twist. What kind of prize was that? A scrap, a bone. They might just as well have shoved her off the platform for the fun of watching her fall.

It was damned embarrassing. 'Black-eyed Susans.' What kind of title was that? A play about four bitchy Yankee females, who sounded suspiciously familiar. Betty Hughes had persuaded O'Neill to let her read Marigold's masterpiece, and he had relented, but only after getting Marigold's permission. Marigold, he said, was thrilled that her old friend had taken an interest. Right.

Betty Hughes sat up, threw off the bedding, and reached for her robe. She slipped into it and out of the bedroom without waking Cyrus. She was a novelist, not a playwright. Why had she nibbled at the theatrical worm in the first place? And, a worm wiggling in the Ashbury pond was akin to fishing for minnows in a mud puddle. What did it all matter? The burning question, of course, was whether or not Marigold Woolsey had actually written the play. Or, had she found a willing drama student in need of extra cash to pen the thing for her. Marigold and her young studs.

In the kitchen Betty Hughes's favorite old cat, Oxy (for oxymoron), opened one eye as she walked past him, curled like a ball of fuzz on his pillow near the pantry. If it weren't two in the morning and if she weren't so damned nice, Betty Hughes muttered to herself, she would dial up O'Neill Spender and demand answers. She would toss that silly love-sick pup on the grill. She poured milk into a mug with Nestle's Quick and put it in the microwave. Well, she would fry him up for lunch tomorrow…because she was so damned nice! He'd gone soft in the head over the glamorous Marigold….some kind of mother figure, she supposed. He was such a sucker for anything Southern… hush puppies, jazz, Southern Comfort, Lady Bird Johnson, and herself included…that she couldn't fathom his interest in an older woman who had lived most of her life in England, France, and Italy. The bell dinged on the microwave and Betty Hughes removed the hot chocolate, wandered into the living room, turned on one light and cuddled up on the sofa. If he admitted that Marigold got outside help, she would wring his neck. And, cut his commission.

The dark apartment wasn't very comforting even with the ticking of the big clock. Cake, she needed cake. This sent her back to the kitchen where a bakery chocolate cake waited in its carton in the cold oven. She carved herself a large slab, vowing to avoid the rest of it.

Actually, Betty Hughes was thinking, just who was in charge of that contest anyway? With the Reverend Brightbill walking away with third, one had to wonder who was paying off the jury? Who was on the jury? After ten best sellers, Betty Hughes was facing public humiliation over a college play competition. This was worse than a bad review in the Sunday papers. She stabbed her cake.

Hardest of all was the truth of it. She loved Marigold's play! It was touching, funny, well-constructed, and entertaining. What else could you ask of a play? She could hardly wait to see it produced on stage. Of course, she wouldn't admit this to Cyrus or Oxy. Or, Naddy, for that matter.

Who was she kidding? Naddy already knew.

To celebrate Sonja's return from the spa and her new identity Archie assembled the gang for dinner on Saturday night. Sonja made her formal big name change announcement to everyone's great amusement (as if orange hair and sequinned fingernails were not enough), and the guests voted to continue calling her Nadine until they actually saw the legal papers. Cyrus offered to accompany her to the courthouse because 'seeing is believing.' Sonja wasn't pleased with their reaction, and to extract the proper revenge for this insult, she was in the process of getting royally pissed on a very expensive Pinot Grigio.

Betty Hughes suggested she come to her senses, that Sonja was a name for ice skaters or foreign tour guides. Lettice declared the new Sonja had spent too many hours in the sauna. The Old Devils wisely kept their wisecracks to themselves when it became apparent that Sonja was truly angry and hurt. When she brought up her plan to rent a studio in Augusta where she would create 'clay vessels,' the short-held restraints fell apart. Cyrus wrote out a check for a hundred dollars as a down payment on her first 'vessel.' Lettice offered to bake cakes for the grand opening. Parnell promised a poem to commemorate the occasion. Sonja accepted Cyrus's check, kissed his cheek, and then stuck out her tongue at the rest of them.

Not satisfied to let the matter drop, and after two more glasses of pinot fit for a White House state dinner, Sonja reflected huskily, "They think we're such bores."

"Who, for heaven's sake?" responded the Admiral.

"The kids. The town. The butcher, the baker," Sonja cried out impatiently. "And our husbands, too, I suppose."

"I have no kids," replied the Admiral, missing the point.

"She means OUR kids," said Archie, suddenly sorry for his wife. They were badgering her. If they thought she had turned herself into a fool or a clown, they would have to change their minds. His wife was nobody's fool. She had simply reinvented herself, the prerogative of any human with a brain and some courage and a fear of getting old too soon. He wisely did not express this aloud. But, hadn't the gang discussed this very thing at the potluck dinner two weeks ago?

"If only they'd known us when we were young!" Sonja fussed in a tremulous voice. "When we were pretty and fun. When we faced big, important things…like war and polio."

Betty Hughes said quite kindly, "The kids know about the bombs and the iron lungs, honey. They've seen the medals and ribbons." She was regretting making fun of Sonja.

"What about OUR sacrifices?" put in Lettice, exhibiting a genuine understanding for Sonja and more than a touch of the grape. "The women who stayed behind." She swayed in her chair, expertly holding a goblet of red wine precisely on the level in front of her, as she might have kept a cup of hot coffee from spilling on a swerving bus. "I worked in an airplane factory and gave permanent waves to my neighbors during the war. Nobody gave me a medal. And, my husband came home in a box." Her eyes grew teary and she sniffed loudly.

"Righto," answered Sonja, sensing a rush of camaraderie. "Who was it who prayed they would come home in one piece? Who was it who marched off to the butcher once a week for a tiny package of meat.... contents unknown."

"And, rationed sugar and shoes," put in Marigold. "Remember those little stamps?"

"How about Beatrice Wrenn's uncle, who came back with his nerves shot to hell," said Cyrus. "I feel damned sad every time I see the sweet man." He sniffed loudly.

"That was the Korean War, Cyrus," put in Lettice. "But, we know what you mean."

"My son thinks I'm a senile fuddy-duddy who can't find my way home from the drugstore," Cyrus added, somberly. "They bombed our hospitals. The guy next to me on the beach in France had his head blown off." His eyes watered again. Then, he impetuously raised his glass and said quite cheerfully, "We did get to sleep with Betty Grable."

"Not that again," chimed in Betty Hughes.

Archie's heart almost stopped. Cyrus was swerving into dangerous territory. He tried to give him a warning look, but Cyrus wasn't paying attention. The Admiral, Archie noted, was on full alert.

"Yes," Sonja interrupted, "what about that girl who made beds for old Mr. Spriggs?"

Betty Hughes poked Cyrus's arm with her fingernail. "I've been meanin' to talk to you about her."

Cyrus got up and poured himself another glass of wine. "Never heard of her."

Archie and the Admiral were keeping their mouths shut.

"She worked in the kitchen and went goofy for guys in uniform." Cyrus grinned.

Archie flashed Cyrus another look. It failed to penetrate. Cyrus was back in the summer of 1945.

"Yes," replied Sonja. "I often wondered why they kept her on. She was boy crazy. I'd bet you another bottle of this cheeky wine that she slept with old Spriggy…the young one, not the old one." Sonja wasn't focusing too well, and Archie could see that nobody else was sober either.

"They didn't pay their help much," said Isobel, who had been quiet all evening. "You know, Sonja, I do love your new fingernails." She smiled and put an arm around her friend's shoulders. "You might have a very good idea here…remaking yourself. Turning over a few pages. Maybe we should all give it a whirl!" And, she laughed enthusiastically and twirled around the room a few times.

The guests were dumbfounded, but giggled and joined in Isobel's burst of enthusiasm for life changes, as she was now calling the transformation.

Archie felt his face grow hot and wished he could drag Cyrus from the room before he blurted out the secrets. Fortunately, the gang had suddenly lost interest in long winded memoirs and ancient misadventures about the war and gone on to embrace Isobel's antics. What a night.

Then, out of the blue, Sonja sang out, "How about dessert?"

On hearing his wife single-handedly turn their guests around to thinking about pecan pie with whipped cream, Archie nearly dropped to his knees. He caught the Admiral crossing himself when he thought nobody was looking. Cyrus just said he wanted double the whipped cream.

Saved again, Archie hissed to the ceiling. The Almighty moved in mysterious ways, and in total silence. Sonja had to be on His payroll. Maybe it paid to eat raw vegetables and swim laps in the spa pool until you wrinkled. And, hats off to Isobel, too, the prissy woman was finally showing a bit of sparkle.

As Archie and Sonja dished up pie in the kitchen, he reminded himself that their very own Betty Grable, sweet Sally, remained cool. She assured him of this every time he drove up to Stone Bank to see her. Not to worry, she would say. The big war was over and so was the little one…. with her cruel father. She would remain forever grateful.

It wasn't long before Lettice was asking Sonja about her clay vessels and how much she was going to charge. Not long after that, Isobel admitted that she'd always wanted to try tights and tunics. Sonja said she wouldn't mind as long as she didn't have to look at too many jungle prints. Sonja had apparently laid claim to zebra stripes as her own signature statement.

Archie cut himself a second slice of pecan pie and marveled at the complexities of age and wisdom and courage and silliness. He thought immediately of Beatrice Wrenn, all done up in purple most of the time. Who was hurt by it? Her peculiarities were good for business. The woman was highly successful and no nuttier than Sonja or Marigold, for that matter. Maybe old Naddy was on the right track after all. Crazy like a fox.

Lieutenant Donovan was getting heat from the chief, heat from the mayor, and heat from the editor of the *Bee* and several other publications. Here it was, a week before Thanksgiving, a few weeks before Christmas and Lola Sprigg's killer was no closer to sitting in the Belmont jail than he was three months ago. The only person who truly understood his predicament was Sheriff Charlie Lemmon, who had all but given up on finding out how and why Buzzy Turk met his end and who had stuffed him into the ground. Archie and Cyrus had heard their sad stories over beers at Billy's more than once.

Archie was sympathetic. Freddy was an old friend, but he did wonder if the Irishman didn't slack off when nobody was on his tail. If he'd been on Archie's payroll, he might have taken a second look at the man's performance record. He might have cracked the whip a bit. The lieutenant's lack of interest in alternative suspects in the homicide was troublesome. What about Lola's gardener? Iffy alibi, stood to inherit. Or, Lola's batty cousin who preferred LSD to seeing straight? Archie kept going back to the cousin, who fancied himself a horticulturist (probably because he saw colored spots a good deal of the time). He and Lola could have quarreled over a cutting from her garden. Cousin LSD could have brained Lola with his own obelisk and forgotten all about it. Lola never owned a marble obelisk. Wrapping and decorating the dead body seemed the act of a misfit killer on drugs.

Freddy was still holding out for Preacher Boswell, even though he had no evidence to support the theory and Boswell had an alibi. Toby Spriggs had two witnesses who swore he was discussing John LeCarre's latest novel at the time his mother was killed.

The Old Devils were not sleeping well.

Maybe it was the way Archie always greeted Nina, as if she'd been gone a month and he'd missed her more than food or water. Hugo wasn't sure what he was thinking or seeing. He just knew something was odd, out of kilter. Right at the moment he was sitting alone in his father's study, drinking a beer, waiting for the usual Sunday football festivities to break loose. It was snowing, which annoyed him for some reason. And, he'd been paddling around in a suspicious stew since Nina announced they were expecting. Like a new song out of Oz. Hugo was calming himself with denial….that he couldn't be the father of this 'impossible' child, that Nina was duping him. Of course, if he wasn't the father, who in the hell was? Several candidates came to mind, but Archie had suddenly moved to the top of the list. A man in his forties, Hugo thought grimly, should not have to imagine a circumstance this devastating.

The last time he and Nina were at the house for an afternoon of Packer football, several weeks ago, Nina sat on the couch between Betty Hughes and Archie. All very cozy. The Old Devils and their counterparts were there, whooping it up, drinking like teenagers and making as much noise. The afternoon was fueled by Nadine's five alarm chili, plenty of beer, and rude insults for the referees and the Bears' quarterback….. another bitterly contested NFL rivalry playing out on the tube. Hugo got the feeling that he was in the middle of two contests.

Was Archie so arrogant that he would make a play for Nina right in front of everybody he knew, including his wife and his son? Hugo first noticed how closely Archie snuggled in next to Nina on the sofa, indulging himself every so often with a friendly pat on her arm or a squeeze of her shoulder during a good play. He didn't miss an opportunity to touch her hand or give her leg a little slap during the excitement. What the hell was going on?

Nina seemed to enjoy Archie's attention. She laughed at his jokes, never pulled away when he touched her. During half-time she brought him a beer and a bowl of chili, for God's sake. Hugo was steaming just remembering. He had never said a word about it. There were rules about these things.

Hugo ran this old football scenario around the track about a dozen times as he slumped in one of Archie's leather chairs. Nina had cooled toward him. He'd cooled toward her too. But, Nina Dupree was still his official fiancée….by society's definition of such things. She was wearing his big diamond. Was she allowed to openly enjoy the company of Archie or any other man who happened to think she was gorgeous…. and there were dozens?

But, cuckolded by your own father? It left Hugo nearly sick. Was there a nice psychological term for this? Some literary expression (possibly in French or Italian) that fully described this ancient Greek dramatic theme? Hugo wanted to bust his father's nose. How's that for Italian? A tiny part of Hugo still loved Nina, he supposed. But, he hated that his great homecoming was now tainted by gossip and giggles…. his fiancée lived in her own apartment downtown…she lunched with Archie……drifted off to art openings and plays with that silly painter from the college with long hair and sandals. He'd heard rumors. The baby would make things worse. Today, he would watch Archie and Nina like a mother watches her toddler in a swimming pool. He would not play the idiot.

The afternoon passed uneventfully…innocent of any suspicious behavior from Archie or Nina. They'd barely come within five feet of each other. As Hugo was driving Nina back to her apartment, he caught a glimpse of her staring out the window. The car was silent, brightened intermittently by a flash of street lamps, the occasional neon shop sign. She looked peaceful and private. Perhaps this state of serenity had to do with pregnancy. Then, just as he was about to turn away, a tiny smile crossed her lips. Sadly, Hugo knew in his heart that it had nothing to do with him.

The Berefords' holiday party always exceeded expectations, sweeping well beyond Santa cookies and egg nog. Sonja did not do anything by halves, according to Betty Hughes, who was describing the annual festivities to Nina, uninitiated in Belmont Christmas customs. Belle and

Beau Dupree were due to arrive in a few days from New Orleans, their first look at the snowy North country. Unfortunately, they would miss the Beresford gala, unlike more than a hundred lucky revelers who had managed to secure a position on Sonja's invitation list. The spacious old house on Washington Circle, one of the grandest of the small town's 19th century palaces, would be swagged and festooned from lamp-post to chimney stack with fresh greens, wreaths and lighted trees in each room. Caterers would be pulling into the drive all afternoon, while a regiment of bartenders and waitresses filed through the back entrance. The Christmas gala stood second only to the Armbrusters' summer Famous Characters costume party, a bit of social rivalry that seemed to amuse Archie and Cyrus more than it did the girls.

"Maybe they had a fight," Betty Hughes was remarking, as she and Sonja, dressed to the nines, stood arranging miniature quiches on trays in Sonja's remodeled kitchen, abuzz with cooks and hired help. Sonja liked to think she was giving the caterers a hand, a silly gesture, Betty Hughes thought. The two ladies were speculating on whether or not Hugo and Nina would make an appearance. The question had arisen earlier in the day when Hugo told his mother he wasn't sure of their attendance. He said Nina wasn't fond of holiday parties, and she was in 'a mood.'

"Frankly, I'm not terribly fond of these seasonal suppers myself," replied Sonja. "But, here I am. Throwing this damned bash every year, like clockwork. People like to come; they call in July to ask about the date. Sometimes you just have to show up or grit your teeth." She popped a quiche into her mouth as if it were a prize for good behavior.

Betty Hughes laughed. "They're not exactly a perfect match, are they? Hugo and Nina." She was well aware of the couple's festering relationship. It was beginning to show.

"Almost as ridiculous as watching me scramble eggs," said Sonja. And, before Betty Hughes could add a salty comment to that, Sonja glided off with the tray, the silk of her long dress swishing against the swinging door.

Betty Hughes sighed a bit, threw a few extra quiches on the tray and followed along. If this were her party, waitresses would be arranging the quiches.

When the doorbell chimed a good twenty minutes into the festivities, Sonja greeted Hugo and Nina as cordially as she ever did. But, when Nina removed her coat, Sonja found herself making unintelligible sounds of shock and disbelief.

"Is that dress what I think it is?" Sonja cried out, her fingers fluttering about her mouth.

"It most certainly is," Nina said, beaming. "I'm expectin'. Isn't that excitin'?"

Sonja thought Nina's smile smacked more of victory than excitement, as if she'd just won a lottery. Or, could it be revenge? Sonja turned to Hugo for a similar show of enthusiasm but found her son wasn't exhibiting the same spellbinding exuberance. He merely nodded and grinned as if his gums hurt.

"Congratulations, you two!" Sonja exclaimed as brightly as she could. "My goodness, this will certainly make a few heads turn, won't it?" She gave Nina a perfunctory hug and another to Hugo, who patted her back, as if in consolation. "Well, well, can a wedding be far behind?" She tried to make this sound airy and nonchalant, but it failed. The order to immediately march, preferably down the aisle, was implicit.

Glowing and confident, Nina took possession of Hugo's arm and said, "We can hardly wait to tell you all." No mention of a forthcoming ceremony.

As Nina gushed, Hugo's face registered a unique kind of pain, his mother decided. Then, Nina and her consort grandly led the way into the living room.

The couple's entrance stopped conversation in mid-sentence. Their timing was perfect. No one breathed for a full minute. Nina's spectacular designer maternity dress told the story in a split second. Then, just as abruptly as voices had been squelched, they rose again in a magnificent crescendo of congratulations and squeals of surprise and delight. Everybody in the room moved immediately into the cheap seats. The stars of the show had clearly arrived.

"I can't believe it!" exclaimed Sonja, hurrying over to Betty Hughes, who was trying not to look too stunned, or to let on that she already knew. Sonja inclined her head toward Betty Hughes's and said softly, "I'd bet my new fur coat Nina put off this little announcement until tonight…. just for the audience."

"And, I do believe we were right about her moods lately," remarked Betty Hughes in her usual sardonic manner. When they'd taken Nina to lunch that week, the little mother had burst into tears three times before dessert.

"You don't think it's a trick, do you?"

"A trick pregnancy? To what end?"

"Nina will think of something. She's so damned radiant, I'm surprised Hugo isn't passing out sunglasses."

Betty Hughes laughed. "Hugo's baffled. Still can't figure out where little babies come from."

Cyrus had just come up behind them and overheard the remark. "Unnerved, I'd say. Poor Hugo's following her around as if she might tip over any minute." He chuckled. "Best Christmas party you've ever dreamed up, Sonie," he said, slapping his hostess on the back. He'd given her a new nickname, loosely based, he said, upon her old one. Actually, they were all lobbying Sonie to take back her old name and to save Sonja for the business world. Sonie had agreed to think it over.

"Where's Archie?" Sonja suddenly asked. She was judiciously keeping one eye on the little mother and another on audience reaction. That third eye, the invisible one possessed by all females (in back of their heads), was searching the crowd.

Isobel Woolsey sidled into their circle and said, "I told Hugo that pregnant women needn't be watched like fish frying in a pan." She made room for Lettice, who was frowning.

"According to Hugo," Lettice told them quite seriously, "this is a miracle child. Supposedly, Nina was never to have children, according to a medical diagnosis years ago when she was much younger."

"Well, well," Isobel jumped in, "maybe the real trick of the evening will be getting the real daddy to stand up."

This remark raised a semicircle of eyebrows and a chorus of cluck-clucks, and Betty Hughes scolded Isobel on her bad manners. Lettice said she didn't like hearing such things.

Isobel didn't seem to care. Months ago, she had predicted the union was doomed the minute Hugo and Nina drove into Belmont that long ago June morning and Nina took a look at their new house, chosen and furnished without her. Hugo must have been nuts to pull a stunt like that in this day and age of the modern woman.

Isobel said, boldly, "And, who cannot question the baby's paternity after watching the two of them. They're rarely seen together."

"Ridiculous!" Sonja protested with little conviction. "You have no cause to say such things, Isobel."

"Just wait and see. Be sure to send me a wedding invitation." Isobel smiled wickedly, a courageous gesture for any guest at a lavish Christmas party, Betty Hughes was thinking, but Isobel could do that.

Of course, no one in the room had conclusive evidence of anything unseemly, except one or two intimates who knew the truth of it. But, be that as it may, there would remain a vicious undercurrent of gossip about Hugo and Nina, as so often happens with private matters between members of a prominent family. Betty Hughes thought it started the day Nina moved into the Beacon Street Arms. Standing there now in the Beresfords' almost too perfect living room, aglow with candle and lamplight, garlanded for the occasion, the old, priceless furniture buffed and smelling faintly of lemon oil, the lovely paintings beckoning to be loved, Betty Hughes could hear mutterings of speculation singing a soft alto beneath the cheery strains of the stringed quartet playing in the foyer. Any scoop with a Beresford connected to it would be fresh fodder for Belmont's gossip mill. And, she knew it would be Hugo who would play the fool.

"Face it, ladies," Parnell Grant was saying with a grin, "Miss Nina's out-maneuvered you this time. Not one of you predicted this. The young beauty from New Orleans is showing us some depth, and, at the very least, a marvelous sense of theatre!" He laughed and said, "Come on, Lettice, I'll fetch you a drink." And, the two wandered off.

"Our little Virgin Mother," remarked Sonja, without smiling. "And, her biggest fan, Mr. Broadway." She nodded toward Nina huddled intimately with Cosmo Freese across the room. "I can't believe this is happening. Hugo hasn't taken any genuine interest in her in weeks."

Betty Hughes suggested they might be reading too much into everything. Lots of engaged couples have a bun in the oven, as Cyrus would put it, before the wedding date is set.

"Even so. Hugo's to blame? He's terrified of children." She sipped her wine as if it might give a clue to the mystery.

"Remember, Nina was told she couldn't conceive."

Cyrus had rejoined them. He said almost too casually, "I think you're barkin' up the wrong tree, girls."

Betty Hughes gave him a look that should have frozen him in place for weeks.

Sonja asked him what he was talking about.

"He's babbling, just pulling your leg. Aren't you, Cyrus?" She stabbed his ankle with the heel of her shoe.

Cyrus blinked and nearly cried out, but said instead, "I think I'll buy the baby a monogrammed sterling cup."

"Good idea, Cyrus. Now, run off and play with Archie."

"Good idea. I haven't seen our host in half an hour." And, Sonja took off, slightly tipsy and wobbly on her spike heels.

Hugo had rarely taken his eyes from Nina since their grand entrance. And, Archie had spent a good portion of the evening watching Hugo. He could see the distrust on his son's face; he was engaged to a woman of surprising unpredictability and complexity, something neither one of them had noticed. Hugo wasn't a man who liked surprises, and Archie knew only too well that the soap opera wasn't over yet. Unfortunately, as one of the principal writers of the script, he remained bedeviled about the ending. He, too, wandered off....in search of a fresh drink.

The baby news hit Miranda Burke of Cat Woman fame between the eyes. If Hugo had known about the kid, he'd obviously never uttered a word about it to her. Mistake number one.

"Hugo, darling," Miranda whispered seductively, as she snuggled into him and then directed his body with considerable strength to a secluded spot near the piano, out of ear shot. "Or, should I say, Big Daddy Beresford."

Miranda offered her lover a chilly smile and noticed that he was perspiring. Hugo was about to pay for his cowardice.

"Don't be too upset, darling," Hugo mumbled awkwardly. "It's as much a surprise to me as it is to everybody else. Nina can't have children." His face twisted foolishly. "Ahhh, eerrr, well, that's what we thought. This is a shocking development. One can barely comprehend!" He drew himself even taller, as if good posture might help his argument.

"*One* can barely comprehend?" growled Miranda. "*One* is trying to keep *oneself* from baring *one's* teeth!" She reached boldly inside his evening jacket and gave his chest a wicked pinch through the starched shirt.

Hugo was close to yelping, and Miranda watched him bite his tongue. "Why did you do that?" he squeaked.

"For lying, you weasel. You boring, impoverished, lovesick weasel."

"Weasel? I had nothing to do with the surprise aspects of this ...ahhh, event." Hugo jammed his hands into and out of his jacket pockets while glancing nervously over his shoulder. No one was paying attention to them.

"Surprise aspects? Is that Bootworks Doublespeak?" Miranda laughed. "Our waltz around the park is over, Hugo. For the second time. There will be no more waltzes, you pitiful cheapskate. I hope Nina and the kid send you stumbling into bankruptcy." She dug a cigarette from her bag and lighted up, against Beresford rules.

"You're dumping me?" Hugo asked unnecessarily, coughing. "You haven't heard my side." His features registered incomprehension, as if he had a side to defend.

"I know what makes babies, you half-wit! Your side is pretty obvious. Good luck, Hugo. You're going to need it."

And, with that out of the way, Miranda marched off in search of the world's driest martini.

In a restless scotch-tainted dream much later that night, Archie heard Nina's soft, accented voice whispering lovely things, like... love is madness, and where have you been all my life? Those old lines. When he awoke to take a Tums, Archie remembered the pretty words; they made him feel better, but not that much better. What did it all mean? Nina had avoided him all evening, as if she didn't want anyone to sniff a connection between the two of them. Hugo had cast a fishy eye toward him a couple of times. Archie had simply offered a hail and hearty congratulations, praying it sounded sincere in the crowd. Nina spent a good deal of time talking with Cosmo Freese, obviously smitten with her. Archie didn't think Nina would want attention from a guy with his track record? Three-time divorce court loser, according to Sonja. Miranda Burke, Hugo's obvious and not very secret mistress, had drunk herself into an early taxi ride home. Perhaps she found Hugo's impending fatherhood too much to take. Signing a marriage contract had rarely kept men faithful. Or, women either. Miranda could still have Hugo on the side, if she worked it right. But, the bigger question for Archie was almost too simple. Was he ready to sit on the couch with one gal, forever? Was he ready to toss poor Hugo to the wolves or to the Mirandas of the world? Would Nina eventually toss Hugo from the scenario, all dolled up in her haute couture maternity dress? Three cheers for Nina, if she did. Hugo would make a terrible papa. Let Miranda have him as a lover. Archie decided that he must appreciate the humor in it all, like Cyrus did. Keep your perspective with humor, old boy, Cyrus kept telling him. Cyrus on his foggiest day seemed to have the best answer. Humor was the key.

Archie chewed his Tums, had a glass of water and crawled back into bed. Sonja, innocent of such matters, had not stirred in her sanctuary across the hall. The house dozed, no doubt relieved and gratified by its survival of yet another extravaganza. And, Archie slept, the dreamless, colorless sleep of a man at peace.

16

Creative Living

Archie wound a red cashmere scarf securely around his neck and stepped into the cold night. He and Nina had just dined at the Yellow Bird Cafe in Augusta's Third Ward, a rejuvenated warehouse district populated with artisans and avant-garde theatres and smart cafes, largely supported by yuppies who thought the neighborhood was cool and they were cool for being there. Ironically, Sonja was scouting real estate in the Third Ward for her pottery studio. Life in the Beresford household had taken on a decidedly Bohemian turn. Archie was feeling more at home with Nina, even with a baby on the way.

As they hurried to the car parked in the angle stalls on Webster Street in front of Cuthbert's Wholesale Florists, Nina reached for his arm. Archie could feel her body shaking against the biting wind. He put his arm around her waist and pulled her close to him. When they reached his vintage BMW, she hopped in and huddled deeper inside her coat.

Just as Archie was about to open the driver's door, his eye caught the prominent hood of a dark blue sedan with headlights on high beam gunning up Webster. He scowled and instinctively edged closer to the side of the car. Damned kids out joy riding! The sedan, he could see, was a 1976 Buick; he'd owned a car like a few years back.

As the Buick approached, it suddenly slowed, stopped, and then backed into the only vacant space left on the street, directly across from his BMW. The Buick idled with its lights still ablaze, the driver a ghost behind the windshield. Archie shielded his eyes with his hand and thought it looked as if the driver were taking aim at him. He put his key in the door lock, but before he could climb in, he heard the Buick revving its engine. He turned to see the old sedan tremble and then lurch forward in a tentative spurt. It seemed to catapult across the narrow expanse of snow powdered pavement! Horrified, Archie flattened himself against the car door.

Like a prehistoric hound on a prowl for its supper, the Buick rammed the rear of the BMW with a mighty metal to metal wallop. The heavy Bavarian automobile shivered on impact but absorbed the blow. Inside, Nina let out a piercing scream.

Archie yelled for her to call the police on the car phone and moved to the rear of the BMW where he could see that the back end remained largely unscathed. It must have been a perfect bumper to bumper crash. The old Buick rested quietly, a trembling, immobile, sputtering beast, coughing from its effort with its crinkled snout nudged indelicately into the rear of the BMW.... giving the show dog a sniff.

Archie called out to Nina to stay in the car. He'd handle everything, he bellowed.

"What the hell are you doing?" he roared at the Buick. "Have you lost your mind?" He moved toward his attacker and banged his fist on the hood.

The Buick remained silent, content to be where it was, catching its breath. Archie stepped back and raised his arms as if to signal surrender. He shouted, "Come out of there!" There was no response, just clouds of exhaust and vapor curling from the back end of the Buick and the BMW. Archie was somewhat afraid to move closer. What if this nut had a gun?

By this time, two couples had stopped to watch the show, and Nina abandoned the relative warmth of the car to join Archie, who was cussing the Buick and waiting for a response. No word from the Buick.

"This is like Star Wars!" Nina said. "A giant alien is out to get us!" She stared at the alien and shielded her eyes from the glare of the head lamps. "Do we know this nut?" she asked Archie. "Why won't he come out of the car?"

Archie said they were going to know very soon and bravely stepped forward to get a closer look through the windshield of the Buick. By God! As he peered inside, he couldn't believe his eyes. It was Hugo hunched behind the wheel.

"It's the kid!" Archie yelled. "Get out of there, you crazy bastard!"

"Hugo? But, that's not Hugo's car, Archie," Nina called out. The wind was tossing her fine hair like silk straw.

"It's him. He's gone around the bend. I'm going to drag him out of there."

Just as Archie's hand searched for the door handle, the Buick backed up and slid neatly into its launching pad across the street, leaving Archie empty-handed and vulnerable a second time. Hugo threw the car into low gear again, gunned the accelerator, and rocketed across the pavement, crashing a second time into the BMW's hind quarters. By this time, Archie and Nina had retreated to the sidewalk. A modest cheer rose from two young men standing a few feet away from them. They'd apparently taken the side of what appeared to be the underdog, the Buick. The other couples were laughing, hanging on, despite the cold. Archie glared at the crowd and suggested they mind their own business. The young people laughed at him.

This time, Archie noticed, the front end of the attack car was sporting a seriously crimped hood and a dead, smashed head lamp. One fender was left to hang like a sock on the rim of a wash basket.

The BMW had taken the impact well enough, but the trunk lid was popped and showed a large dent.

"Damnation!" Archie roared. "What the hell is the matter with you?" He turned to Nina and asked if she'd called the police. She said she had, but no squad car was in sight yet.

Archie began waving his arms and cursing the battering ram crouched behind his own vehicle. Finally, Archie charged the Buick and began pounding on the door.

Nina was furious now and thumped the hood with her gloved hand. "This is Hilda's car, isn't?" she called out. No response. "I know this is Hilda's car, you, you eighth grader!" She informed Archie that Hugo must have borrowed his housekeeper's car. The Buick hadn't moved an inch since the second attack. It rested where it sat, an old animal still licking its wounds.

Archie demanded that Hugo get out and confront them like a man. They could hear the knot of witnesses on the sidewalk giggling and calling out advice. 'Hit him with your shoe, lady!' 'Pull out his windshield wipers!' The advice kept coming, but no one tried to help or interfere. No police cars in sight.

Nina pressed her face close to the glass of the driver's window and peered inside. "I can see you in there. You're acting like a child, as usual."

Very slowly, the driver's window wound down four inches, revealing the top third of Hugo's head.

"To answer your question, no, I have not lost my mind," Hugo thundered back. "And, kindly take your hands off that woman, sir!" he growled at his father.

Archie took a firmer, more defiant grip on Nina's shoulders. "CEOs don't generally ram cars for amusement, my boy. Time to give it up."

Hugo's response was cool, even though Archie could see his son was breathing as hard as the car. "Nina, get into my car. We have to talk." With that, Hugo rolled up the window.

"How do you like that?" Archie fumed. "I'll have the police after you. Damned if I won't! Giving orders. Kidnapping. Damaging property. Creating a public scene. Endangering life!"

"Archie, darling, listen to me. I'll go with him. Don't worry. I'll explain everything to him one more time. He's just not getting it. He doesn't want to be a father." Nina tugged at Archie's coat sleeve and kissed his cheek.

"I don't like it."

"He's angry and hurt and scared. We'll go to my place."

"I'll follow at a safe distance and wait outside."

Nina walked around to the passenger side and climbed into the Buick.

Archie returned to his bruised vehicle and started the engine, ready to follow.

Hugo's wreck rattled and shook but chugged off down Webster with Archie right on its tail. The Buick's left front fender was rubbing the tire and there were odd squeaks coming from the front end. Archie could hear the noise. The Buick was swimming a little as it moved along…out of alignment, no doubt. Archie felt a curious rapport with the Buick, a scarred machine, much like himself, getting slightly out of alignment but not out of gas. Bravo for the Buick. Hugo could go to hell or back to kindergarten.

As he drove along, Archie consoled himself with the fact that Hugo had lost the contest. The two Beresford boys had gone to battle (Hugo, without realizing it), and Hugo's ill-advised fling with an old girl friend had put the crusher on a future with Nina. His old flame had given him the heave-ho a second time. Of course, Archie couldn't be sure if he would end up with Nina either. The woman was taking her sweet time picking a mate. He sometimes wondered if she would ever decide.

As Archie neared the Beacon Street Arms, he felt a little sorry for his son. After all, he'd arrived in Belmont full of hope and big plans for a new future. He'd conquered the catalogue business without batting an eye. But, the boy's grip on romance wasn't nearly as keen or precise as his nose for parkas and hiking boots.…..an ironic twist of fate for a handsome man to face.

Would Hugo spill this little scenario to Sonja? In his bereavement would Hugo seek comfort from his mother? Hugo and his mother were not close. In spite of the heat in the car, Archie shivered. Could it be that the Beresford boys remained up against it, after all of these trials?

Betty Hughes sat in Freddy Donovan's office the following morning; a light snow was falling; the crime business was slow. She could smell Christmas cookies. Freddy kept a big box next to his coffee machine. Up and down King Street old-fashioned lamp posts were festooned with silver bells and red bows. From the second floor window, she could see a Salvation Army Santa standing at the corner with his bell and kettle. And, as usual, it was panic time for her.…she'd put off shopping until the last week.

"It's almost Christmas, Freddy, and I'm still in October." Betty Hughes unearthed an emery board from the bottom of a hand-bag the size of Rhode Island and began to repair a chipped nail. "Have you guys come up with anything on Lola?"

Freddy was sipping tea with lemon (and a drop or two of medicinal whisky) for a bad head cold. "We may never know, Betty Hughes." He pulled out a cigar, stuck it in his mouth but didn't light up. A few seconds later he put the cigar back in his pocket and blew his nose.

"True enough. I keep hearin' a wrong note in there." Betty Hughes finished her nail repair and leaned back in Freddy's battered guest chair. The office needed a complete overhaul. The huge arched windows leaked cold air; the putty walls demanded demolition or new paint; the bleak institutional furniture had died years ago. Freddy's orange, three-legged curb sofa remained the room's main attraction. Betty Hughes wouldn't have sat on it for a thousand dollars.

"What wrong note?"

"Maybe lots of wrong notes, but I haven't figured out the tune yet. Do you know what I mean?" She helped herself to a paper napkin full of Christmas cookies. Diets be damned. It was December. She'd starve her way through January and February.

"So, which wrong note is the sourest?" Freddy closed his eyes and folded his big freckled paws over his big contented stomach. It was theory time again.

"Ahhh. Alibi clinkers maybe? I should know. I dream up this stuff every day."

"Toby Spriggs comes to mind now and again." The cop opened one eye and then both. Then, he narrowed them to make his point.

"And the gardener and Cousin LSD and Boswell, himself."

Freddy leaned forward on his elbows. "You mean triple check the alibis? Put a few sources on the back yard grill?"

"Or, the time honored approach to all investigations......follow the money."

Freddy sighed. It all sounded like a lot of work. "Anything you say, darlin'. First, we'll have a barbeque and then we'll double check the money."

Betty Hughes sighed and ate her cookies. Stirring Freddy Donovan to think and move was a full time job. Poor Lola. Could be she'd be the only person on the planet to ever know who killed her...except her murderer, of course.

After his attack on Archie with the Buick, Hugo convinced himself that he could not and would not be a father. And, he would not be a husband either. Not at his age. And, to do this, he was conveniently placing the blame on Nina… for the pregnancy and for the paternity.

Right at the moment, a mere three days after the Buick attack, Hugo and Nina were standing in the living room of his house in the bluffs. Nina still called it his cave dwelling, which never ceased to annoy him. They were quarreling again. He wanted the baby foolishness to be over, he said grimly. He had a catalogue company to run. And, he wanted the engagement officially broken. Whatever that meant. Their discussion the night of the Buick attack had ended in a terrible row.

"You're up to your neck in lies!" Hugo insisted, holding firm, like Bogey in one of those forties noir films Nina loved so much. Hugo pointed an accusing Bogey-like finger at Nina, currently playing the suspicious dame in the scene. Too bad he didn't have a cigarette smoldering between his lips. "You're tricking me," he snarled. And, with that, Hugo flung his long arms behind his back and began to walk in a perfect circle around the room. The house was chilly; he kept the thermostat turned down to save on heating bills.

"Tricking you? This baby is as real as the nose on your face. We're not indulging in a smoke and mirrors stunt." Nina slipped back into her wool coat and shivered.

"How do I know I'm the father?" Hugo was coming to believe his own argument even more firmly, now that he was forced to defend it.

Nina sniffed loudly at this point. "You are not the man I thought you were, Hugo," she said. "You are selfish and immature. Your behavior is most unbecoming." Nina began following Hugo around the room, in the same tight, neat circle.

"Passing off this child as mine is pretty unbecoming too. For all I know you've been sleeping with Spender, or, or, or.….my own father, for God's sake!"

"That story is old, Hugo. I refuse to respond. Archie is my friend. Always will be. So is O'Neill." Nina put her hands in her pockets to keep them warm. "I should have hired a detective to follow you. Nice cozy shots of you and Miranda Burke at the Blink 'n Nod." She would never divulge her private comings and goings to Hugo after what he'd put her through the last few months. Never.

Hugo stopped pacing. Nina nearly bumped into him; she stepped back.

"You and my father were eating at that café in the Third Ward three nights ago. He takes you everywhere. I know my father. Beautiful, willing women, like you, are just his style. It's disgusting." Hugo stretched his neck high above his collar and began circling again.

"Not as disgusting as your morbid obsession with your father! What about a grown man who borrows his housekeeper's car so that he might destroy his father's automobile and nearly kill two people, simply because he has failed to…*GROW UP!*" Nina was following Hugo again. "Since when is it disgusting to have dinner with a friend."

Hugo stopped again. "Since when do doctors make misdiagnoses like the one you dreamed up?" He wagged his Humphrey Bogart finger at her again.

Nina instantly grabbed the finger and twisted it. Hugo yelped and swore as he jerked his hand away and stuck the sore finger to his lips. "You are a sick woman!" he cried.

"I won't dignify *that* with a response or anything else you have to say, Hugo Beresford! Besides, your father is a lot nicer than you are!" Nina clenched her fists, and Hugo, fearing another attack, backed up in tiny retreating steps.

"I can see how nice he's been." Hugo pointed crassly at Nina's belly. "You're not denying it, are you?" he retorted snidely. "Of course, if Archie fails you, there will always be that has-been actor, Cosmo Freese, waiting in the wings!" Hugo was standing in place now, his arms rigid at his sides. He was ready for all-out war.

Nina narrowed her eyes at him and advanced a few inches, her hands in her pockets, as if she might be concealing a lethal weapon. Again, Hugo retreated and quickly put his hands behind his back, expecting another finger-twisting.

"And, while we're on the subject of chummy….how about you and that slutty Miranda Burke? What about the Greensleeves bar? And, the little rooms upstairs? Didn't think anybody saw you there, huh? I have a witness. I live at the Beacon Street Arms, not underground." Nina tossed her hair and buttoned her coat.

Damnation! What did she know? There were spies everywhere in these pathetic little towns. Hugo hated that Nina had found out about

Miranda, even though the woman had just dumped him and on very flimsy evidence.

"Ah, hah! Even her name makes you twitch." Nina looked thrilled with his reaction. "You've been seeing her since that costume party. Cat woman on the prowl. And, you were only too eager to oblige, weren't you?"

Hugo was speechless now. Nina began to laugh.

"I don't care anymore, Hugo. We're both guilty of gross negligence. We allowed a perfectly lovely romance to disintegrate into acrimony and recriminations. It apparently just wasn't meant to be." Nina shrugged her shoulders.

"You never loved me," said Hugo.

"Don't be silly. You only asked me to marry you so that you'd have a good looking babe on your arm when you waltzed into town after fifteen years. I was your trophy to show off in front of Miranda. Well, here's my trophy." Nina patted her swollen belly. "This little bundle is mine. It's no longer your business. Let the baby be the biggest mystery you will ever have to ponder, Hugo Beresford. Let the whole of Belmont wonder for eternity about the daddy. Frankly, I don't give a damn." Nina pulled a pair of gloves from her coat pocket and put them on.

"You're crazy! How dare you turn this around?" Hugo's face bloomed pink and then red. He felt weak and transparent. Damn, the woman!

"Good bye, Hugo. It was sweet in New Orleans. It has been a disaster here."

Nina did not slam the door.

A snow shower leaked from a metallic sky. By ten o'clock the asphalt streets were slick, and Nina was on her way to Augusta for Christmas shopping and a quick lunch with Cosmo Freese, who was playing Scrooge this season at the Repertory. Ever since his late night phone calls, their friendship had grown. He had offered his counsel and his shoulder, instinctively knowing she needed a friend. Nina saw no reason not to accept his companionship. She was fond of Cosmo. When she told him about the baby, he wasn't shocked, but assured her things would work out. He made no inquiries about the father or her plans. She didn't tell him about Archie.

"Amateurs!" Nina muttered behind a line of motorists driving like children in kiddie cars. She was getting accustomed to maneuvering in snow and ice and decided she could handle all of it like a damned Yankee. The station wagon ahead of her swerved gently, as if its cargo were shifting.

'Nothing ages faster than snow.' These words flitted through her mind, words from Albert Bonnard, her grandfather. He was the only member of the Bonnard family who had ever abandoned the South for the North. He left New Orleans to make his fortune in the meat packing business in Chicago, where he learned about snow and canned hams. Of course, he returned to Louisiana years ago, retired and rich and terribly knowledgeable about Yankees and what goes into cold cuts. He and his Chicago cronies would sit around on the holidays and explain to the ignorant all about Chicago winters and the perils of snow, since they'd lived through every configuration of the stuff and knew its degrees of usefulness and beauty. They did agree that English speaking people could use a few more words for snow; there seemed to be a shortage of precise terms for its various forms. Certainly, Eskimos had done a better job of it, according to one old gentleman from Winnetka, who had studied the subject. Nina wasn't sure about that, but she did know the white stuff no longer scared her half to death.

Of course, man's inability to create a definitive vocabulary had nothing to do with the forces of nature. So, by now, this close to Christmas and out of pure contrariness, Nina supposed, the heavens had released five more inches of fresh powder to mask a graying blanket that had already covered the ground. Whoever was behind the weather was definitely in collaboration with the devil himself and the same big shot who had invented holidays. And, putting a nice clean face on December wasn't going to fool her.

For reasons only a shrink might understand, Nina dreaded the holidays, anything generally noted on calendars and in greeting cards, admittedly juicy settings for movie and novel plots, but in reality pure agony for those who had to witness relatives at their worst 'round the festive table. Aunts and uncles and cousins would show up at Dupree House….it was the biggest house in the family, and Beau had the most money, except his father, who refused to have relatives in his dining room. Sherry and other libations would flow and eruptions of temper would follow, along with tears and reprisals, threats and promises. Ah, the spirit of the season. This year, with the flock so far away, Nina was trying to put it all in a new light. And, just to make sure, she would not have a single bottle of that awful sherry in her apartment. Her parents were flying in and booked into a suite at the St. George. They could buy their own sherry.

Nina waited at a red light behind the swerving station wagon full of wiggling kids driven by a woman very likely on the verge of a nervous breakdown. Nina paid close attention. She could be this driver in another five years. The back end of the wagon was a hive of squirming arms and legs and bobbing heads in parkas and bright colored tights. An occasional flash of pink net and sequins told her the brood was en route to ballet class at Esther Baldwin's studio or a holiday recital at Village Hall. Ballet. She hadn't thought about ballet for ages. A hundred years ago she'd wanted to be a ballerina. Her pale pink satin toe shoes still hung above her bed back home.

Home. New Orleans. Family. She would break the news to her folks the very day they arrived. She dreaded it and felt like a naughty teenager. Belle was expecting mountains of snow, reindeer grazing in the parks, and elves perched on roof tops, certainly not a pregnant daughter. Beau was more familiar with the winter season; he'd play professional football in the snow. He would be satisfied with a few hot toddies in honor of the holiday. She believed he might be more understanding about the baby, too. Nina had to admit that Christmas, pregnant or not, did take on a certain authenticity in the North.

Wasn't this the year she was supposed to run off to Barbados with a bikini in her luggage? Hah! Belle always insisted that major holidays automatically turned women into Supreme Court justices…..dying was the only way out.

Up ahead, the crazed mother driving the station wagon lurched forward and honked impatiently at a slow truck ahead of her. The poor woman should carry a flask of brandy, Nina thought kindly, smiling, and remembering Uncle Jack, who had conquered Christmas by nipping his way through the whole ordeal. 'Hell,' he'd say, (after yet another arrest for driving under the influence on the sidewalk or taking a pee in the park) 'having a snort of brandy makes the hols more civilized.' And, then he would offer the arresting officer a swig.

"I cannot believe it!" cried Belle. "You are pullin' a pitiful Yankee Christmas stunt." She clutched her husband's hand and tried to see the humor in Nina pretending to be pregnant.

"It's no joke, Mama. July fourth is the big day." Nina poured two eggnogs laced with bourbon and sprinkled with nutmeg. Hers was virgin. She handed the silver cups to Belle and Beau, whose arrival an hour ago would be forever branded with her baby news. For a moment Nina allowed her thoughts to drift to Christmases in the future. Where would she and the child be? Belmont? New Orleans? Sunny California? No, New York sounded more fun.

"Honey lamb," Beau said calmly, interrupting Nina's thoughts, "surely you can tell your old Daddy the truth. Are you sick, sweet pie?" He released himself from Belle's grip and came over to Nina where he put his big arms around her. Beau was still the tough, handsome halfback, all done up in an Armani suit.

"Truth be told, Beau, you're going to be a granddaddy. God's honest." Nina took a little twirl in her heart-stopping maternity dress, yards of creamy silk that matched her hair. She grinned at her folks and knew they would come around. They simply required time to polish up their good manners and then take hold of a slightly augmented acceptance of reality.

Belle and Beau shook their heads simultaneously and fell into the soft sofa like twins completing a vaudeville act.

"And, Hugo is unhappy about this?" Belle asked.

"A bit. He thinks I've tricked him." The issue of the wedding would be next on her agenda. It would take some courage. Nina walked over to the fireplace where logs crackled and the warmth of the fire melted any resolve she had made earlier to tell them the whole story.....the Archie part.

"Are you going to marry Hugo?" Beau asked, hopefully.

Nina took a deep breath and said, "No, Daddy. The weddin's off. I'll go this alone." She saw no need to bring Archie into it right now. "Lots of women my age have children and never marry."

"Alone? No weddin'?" Belle gasped. "Up here?" Belle raised her free arm to the ceiling, aghast at every word her daughter had uttered.

"I'm beginnin' to like it here. I have friends." Well, a few. And, a lover.

"Holy smoke, girly," her father exploded. "You should come home! This is no place for you now." Beau slapped his knee hard.

"I'm forty-two. I can take care of myself and a baby. I'll hire a nanny."

"I don't think they have nannies up here, darlin'," said Belle. The full sleeves of her red velvet tunic wafted like bird wings as she gestured.

"I'll send Jessie up to help you," Beau insisted grandly. He was warming to the situation; Nina could tell. It wouldn't be long and the two of them would be taking a suite at the St. George for six months, just to be on hand for the arrival.

"Jessie!" shrieked Belle. "Heaven help us, Beau, the woman's eighty and wouldn't know a diaper from a dishpan. You know very well that Missie Langdon raised Nina until I could figure it out." Belle laughed, obviously remembering her youth and her ignorance. She suddenly sank in the nearest chair and exclaimed, "Blast and damn! I've told five hundred people to expect a big weddin' at St. Timothy's! This is the second time, now. Can't you reconsider the ceremony, honey?"

"Put all your weddin' ideas in storage, Mama. They'll keep. For another time."

Belle groaned with disappointment; Beau poured himself a straight whiskey and his wife another dolled-up egg nog.

Nina said nothing more. It was too bad she couldn't tell them about Archie, because they were going to love him. But, more importantly, she had just managed to jump a high hurdle without falling on her face. She was grateful.

Garlands of plastic pine boughs swung gently across Main street. Lamp posts wore clusters of silver bells. Shop windows winked with lighted trees, overfed Santas, and chirpy looking elves toting toys. These days Nina avoided standing too long in one spot for fear an overzealous Martha Stewart might materialize to fling a wreath around her neck or smear her with marzipan. Christmas was two days away and her parents were out touring Belmont and Augusta, on their own.

A left on Fourth and a right on Oak took Nina into the Tudor Oaks neighborhood, occupied for the most part by well-fixed professionals who preferred classic pre-war brick and stone to aluminum siding and home entertainment centers. Right now, she was on her way to a holiday tea with Marigold Woolsey. Betty Hughes had begged her to come along for moral support. Seeing Marigold's bold hand upon her beloved Tallyho, Betty Hughes declared, might require a strong shoulder to cry on. Oddly enough, Sonja had declined the invitation, saying she had another commitment. Betty Hughes did not elaborate. Betty Hughes and Marigold had patched up their old rocky friendship somewhere between Thanksgiving and Christmas, according to Sonja. Nina was delighted. She hated to see the two on the battle field.

Another pair of eccentrics….Marigold and Parnell….Nina would add them to her notebook of characters, a marvelous catalogue of Belmont odd balls. Cosmo pointed out rather mischievously that Nina, herself, was becoming quite a character….. unmarried, over forty, pregnant, a budding actress from Dixie trying to make it in the North. Not an average resume. Nina said he was exaggerating, even though she had to admit she'd been invited to everything from piano recitals to lavish buffets at the country club by society matrons she barely knew. She was very, very popular this Christmas, far more popular since leaving Hugo out of the mix. But, would she be this in demand next year?

Cosmo speculated that Princess Diana might be similarly situated if she left the prince and the Windsors. The fairy tale marriage of Charles and Diana did sound hopeless.

Before the China tea and poppy seed cake, Marigold took Betty Hughes and Nina on a grand tour of the house. Most of the rooms were finished; one or two were in the final stages of redecoration, their floors blanketed in drop cloths; the only furnishings were ladders leaning into the corners. Nothing had been left untouched by Marigold's vivid imagination. Glamorous continental furnishings filled the opulently ornamented rooms. The spacious house breathed old money and sophistication with crystal chandeliers and gilded mirrors, silvered and shaded sconces, a leopard divan near the hearth, velvet draperies, ravaged leather Italian arm chairs of undetermined age, marble Greek torsos, and exotic nudes posing from marbled and scumbled walls. The house was the very essence of expatriates who knew how to spend their loot.

Back in a small first floor sitting room, Betty Hughes sat down and instantly complimented her hostess. "It's an artistic miracle, Marigold. Your vision and taste are sublime. Of course, we're not surprised. We didn't expect William Morris reproductions."

Marigold smiled appreciatively; she was accustomed to compliments.

"A few too many yards of silk fringe, for some, I suppose," she said without apology, "but, this is my way. I've lived abroad too long to be infatuated with New England tea tables and Cantonese plates." She poured tea and offered her guests thick slices of cake.

"Is Parnell home today?" asked Nina.

"He is at the club, giving a reading at the Seniors' Afternoon Book Club....a new poem about a return to one's roots."

"Speakin' of Parnell," Betty Hughes began carefully, taking out a few seconds to taste the dessert. "Absolutely delicious...light as a snow flake." She took a sip of tea and then went on. "I must ask how he's feelin'. Cyrus is worried that he might be unwell." She let this fall away to silence. "You might think me out of line to ask, but we're concerned. Parnell is so thin."

Nina's thoughts flew to an evening in the Deco bar with Archie where they'd seen Parnell and the Admiral having a drink together. Two aging queens? Was that correct or just nasty? What was Betty Hughes driving at?

Marigold waved one bejeweled hand, as if she knew full well what Betty Hughes was edging up to. It would be Betty Hughes who must complete the last leap by herself, Marigold was saying.

With no explanation immediately forthcoming, Betty Hughes squinted, as if expecting a blow and plowed ahead. "Is it possible that Parnell likes to play with...ahh,... the boys on his own team?" She tried to smile but it was more of a grimace. "Archie heard somethin', mentioned it to Sonja, and she whispered it to me. You know how it goes."

Nina smiled at Betty Hughes's turn of phrase. And, from the expression on Marigold's face, the suspicions about Parnell must be right on the money.

The hostess sighed and fiddled with an enormous emerald ring. "Frankly, I'm surprised it has taken this long for anyone to ask. Darling Parnell, my dearest companion of forty years, my precious friend, my inspiration…" Marigold's dramatic gestures and her full-sleeved kimono nearly upset the footed cake plate.

"Yes?" Betty Hughes responded patiently. It was now up to Marigold to complete the tale.

"Certainly. Parnell is gay. He could be nothing else. Has been since childhood. One is born with it, like red hair or a crooked toe." Marigold acted put out by mankind's ignorance of such matters and science, in general.

"Why the secrecy? He's so open, so free-spirited." Betty Hughes sounded a bit cross. After all, she said, the man is known as a ladies' man, a great lover. How had this come about?

"Our generation, as you well know, Betty Hughes, didn't broadcast this kind of thing. Society's conventions do bear down on us, even on those of us who flout them the most." Marigold reached over and patted Nina's arm. "I hope this doesn't shock you, my dear." She sipped her tea, inhaling the fragrance with relish. "Parnell says he knew when he was two years old and stood in his crib wailing against the pale blue of the nursery walls!" Marigold jiggled with laughter. "How I love that man!"

They all laughed. Only Parnell could have come up with that story. Nina easily envisioned tiny Parnell in a miniature magenta beret stomping up and down in his crib, demanding puce walls.

"What color walls has he here?" asked Betty Hughes with a wink.

"You're naughty," Marigold replied. "His private rooms will be teal and burgundy. Very dramatic, don't you agree?" Marigold paused and then said, "He wants to come out of the closet, you know. Very soon. Isn't that a horrid term for something as old as mankind itself?"

"Come out now?" Nina blurted. "Isn't he sixty-eight?"

"He says it's the modern thing to do, and he's a modern person. He wants to end the deception." Marigold's modest double chin shook with emphasis. "After all, we are who we are."

Nina supposed the man's decision made sense, but there would be those who might scorn him publicly. One or two matrons had offered disapproving comments about unmarried pregnant actresses. Nina would carry her own secret (about the child) for many years, she imagined, not really knowing the truth of it. She was finding the entire mystery absolutely delicious.

Betty Hughes sat quietly, taking stock. She said, "Well, Lettice and Isobel will pass out. And, Sonja? She'll need a doctor. The Old Devils will find it hard to digest. What about you, Marigold? He's your husband."

"Oh, darling, we're not married! That's been our little joke for decades. I think we've pulled it off rather well, don't you?" Marigold ripped off a peal of laughter and then popped more seed cake into her mouth.

"What about Parnell's reputation as a ladies' man? He's supposedly wooed and won every woman over fifty," said Nina.

"A lot of hot air and posturing. Vivid imaginations at work. Parnell's never slept with any of them. He's befriended them, loved them, taken an interest when their husbands have not. And they've had the good sense to keep this marvelous affection private. Parnell's done wonders for nearly every marriage I can think of. Husbands take a second look at their wives when they think another man, a rich man, might have her."

Marigold had a point, Nina thought.

Betty Hughes said, "Parnell was always a good friend to me. But, there was never any suggestion of hanky panky. Frankly, back then, I worried that I'd been left out, that he didn't fancy me." She giggled girlishly.

"He fancies all women, but only in his own way."

"Is he plannin' to announce his preference with a new poem and read it publicly?" Betty Hughes asked with some hesitation. "Belmont might not be ready for this, you know."

"He's scheduled a reading at the university in another few days." Marigold was very matter-of-fact. "We'll throw a party, of course. A grand house warming with the closet doors standing open! The Old Devils will be shocked. And a few others. Dear Admiral Moss will be mortified. Parnell tells me that Melvin wishes to remain in his closet and thinks Parnell should stay in his too. But, one must do what one must do." Marigold stuck a bright blue cigarette into her ivory holder and set it afire.

Betty Hughes gasped a little. "The Admiral?"

"Apparently, the Admiral is the best kept secret in town."

Nina decided that Marigold and Parnell had been snickering at the peasants.

"Why that old puff!" Betty Hughes was stunned. "That's what the Admiral calls men who like men," she explained. "All those Sunday brunches at Lettice's place gone to waste." Actually, Betty Hughes wasn't all that surprised. She just wanted to give Marigold the little dramatic scene she craved.

Nina felt slightly left out of the proceedings. She barely knew Marigold and Parnell.

"What about Parnell's health?" Betty Hughes insisted now.

Marigold didn't respond right away. Tears filled her eyes. A bit of heavy mascara melted onto her cheek. "Parnell is suffering from the new disease....that AIDs horror."

"Oh, no!" Betty Hughes cried out. "Not that? Will he die?"

"He takes a very new medicine. We're praying for a miracle, but….." Marigold stopped.

"I'm so sorry," Nina said. She leaned across and put her hand on Marigold's.

"Yes. Yes," said Betty Hughes tearfully. "A miracle. Let's think only of happy times. Belmont will never be the same, Marigold. It has been altered by your return."

"Bless you, darling. Parnell and I wouldn't have it any other way. To happy times. To freedom, my dears!" Marigold lifted her nearly empty teacup. "And creative living!"

They finished their tea and then prepared to leave. Betty Hughes kissed Marigold's smooth, unlined cheek. Nina decided that Marigold was nearly ageless, probably the result of Swiss goat hormone injections over the years. Was this daring iconoclast with her ropes of precious gems and gold turbans gay too? The world was so confusing these days. If she thought about it all too much it might just push her over the edge. Nina wondered if that was what happened to Cyrus.

17

CIRCLING THE WAGONS

After surviving the Christmas holidays with Archie and Sonja and the Armbrusters, including the cleverest bit of holiday upstaging any two adults (and an unborn child) ever perpetrated on anyone, Hugo was preparing to muddle along until New Year's Eve, always a bachelor's trickiest night. So far, he had remained unscathed after a very brief meeting with Nina and the visiting Duprees at Nina's sumptuous apartment at the Beacon Street Arms…Nina was playfully calling the party 'a farewell to arms' for dear Hugo, meaning she wouldn't be seeing him again. She had insisted they all gather for a civilized seasonal drink. After all, they had nearly become family. Belle and Beau understood there would be no wedding. Just a baby. The Duprees were polite and gracious, but obviously eager for him to drink up and leave at his earliest convenience, which he did after forty-five minutes of listening to Beau's stories about his eccentric old uncles and aunties, all delivered in that relentless drawl. Hugo would never understand why these people refused to speak properly.

With his admirable survival of boring and potentially lethal fetes behind him, Hugo should have been beautifully prepared for anything. But, alas, tough and relatively experienced as he was, Hugo, like his father, had his weaknesses.

The night before New Year's Eve with a powdery snow swirling around street lamps, Hugo stopped at the spiffy St. George Hotel where a modest bachelor party was rounding out the evening in the Bird Cage Bar. An old college room-mate would be marrying on New Year's Day. Hugo had promised to meet Nina around eleven. She said she would be out and about and would deliver a portfolio he had left behind at her apartment.

One of the party guests at the hotel bar turned out to be the wedding consultant, Miss Treu, a pretty young woman from Chicago in town for the event and a guest at the hotel. She and several other young women in the bar had joined the male guests as token bachelor party females, insisting they would not strip dance or jump from any cakes. Hugo was finding Miss Treu charming and even more alluring as the evening wore on. She was regaling the fellows with wedding stories about quavering sopranos built like Viking brides, nervous fathers of the bride who tripped over church pews, priests who recited the wrong names, and the occasional bridegroom who had forgotten to zip up.

The party wound down until Hugo was left with Miss Treu. He ordered her yet another drink and they spent the next hour talking about things other than weddings. When Nina failed to show, Hugo called her apartment and left a message…that he was still waiting at the Bird Cage bar. When he returned to the table, Miss Treu insisted it was time for her to turn in. Her room was on the fourth floor; Hugo offered to accompany her to the elevator.

Miss Treu asked if he might ride upstairs with her; he agreed.

Once alone in the elevator, Hugo and Miss Treu surprised themselves by caving into the most basic chemical reaction since hydrogen met oxygen. Once out of the elevator and in the corridor outside Miss Treu's door, pure lust overpowered Hugo, striking him nearly blind and certainly stupid, and Miss Treu's easy acquiescence did nothing to curb the chain of events that was about to take place in room 402.

 Hugo's eagerness to kiss Miss Treu started it off. He found her just as eager when she returned the favor and began tugging at his jacket, as if to remove it. Hugo experienced the familiar rush of lust, and between the two of them, they unlocked Miss Treu's room door after dropping the key three times. Hugo pulled them both inside where they began stripping off each other's garments with little regard to buttons or seams.

They fell upon the bed and each other with careless abandon, leaving a light burning softly on the dresser and the corridor door open.

Passion of this magnitude, having bubbled for hours, climaxed and subsided and then rose to glorious heights once more with the delirious participants paying little attention to the world around them.

It was at this point that Nina Dupree arrived outside room 402. She had been advised by a bartender that the bachelor party had been moved upstairs. Finding the door ajar and the light burning, Nina stepped inside after giving a few taps to the jamb and calling out "Yoo-hoo."

Neither Hugo nor Miss Treu, otherwise preoccupied, heard the call, and when Nina came upon the couple writhing among the sheets, she could only gasp in horror, thinking she might have come upon an assault…after all, the room was nearly dark; there were no guests sitting around, and the corridor door had been left open. Perhaps this poor woman was fighting for her life!. The result of this encounter was most gratifying for all who heard the story later. And many did.

Soon discovering that it was Hugo Beresford who was naked and heated and wound around the tousled young woman, similarly unclothed, Nina Dupree knew that this was no assault. She let out a wail of disgust like nothing heard before at the St. George and landed a blow to Hugo's head with her Chanel handbag, nicely weighted with the usual accouterments carried by a woman, including a set of keys attached to a heavy brass fob in the shape of a grand piano.

Hugo must have believed he'd been brained with a sandbag and fell off the bed, where he sprawled on the floor, stunned and pathetically vulnerable. Nina shrieked at him again, and Miss Treu, seeing Nina for the first time, immediately grabbed a pillow to cover her more private portions.

Nina debated slugging Miss Treu but decided she would rather have another go at Hugo and did so to the bottoms of his feet with the Chanel bag. Hugo's body reacted with a violent spasm as the blows fell, and he emitted a terrible groan of pain and misgiving. All the while, Miss Treu's sobs of regret and surprise accompanied a shrill monologue recited by Nina, most having to do with boorish sex fiends who attack women in hotel rooms.

The uproar brought a modest crowd to the door and a nervous hotel manager, who had sense enough to throw a blanket over woozy Hugo, still collapsed on the carpeted floor, looking groggy and certainly chilly, as the manager told his assistant an hour later.

It took only minutes to clear the hallway of sightseers and to get Hugo and Miss Treu back into their clothes. Silent, Nina marched immediately to the elevators and exited the St. George without looking back.

Miss Treu quickly packed her belongings and took the stairs to the lobby where she paid her bill at the desk. Wearing dark glasses, she disappeared into the night after telling the concierge she would find another hotel in Augusta. Unhappily, Hugo would never see her again.

Upstairs in room 402 and quite alone now, Hugo sat on the edge of the bed, bone   weary from the fray, slightly dizzy from the blow to his skull (a large bump had risen like a small muffin on his forehead), and wounded with a kind of pubescent shame over the stories that would surely circulate by morning. The flap would be loud and long and humiliating. Beautiful Miss Treu was history, of course. And, beautiful Nina Dupree would go down in Belmont's Anthology of Gossip as the second Hugo Beresford fiancée to give him the boot.

But, as Hugo slid into his loafers and thrust his tie into a jacket pocket, he experienced a wave of relief. Surely, this was for the best. The succulent Miss Treu had shown him the way. She had done him a grand favor. He was born to be a bachelor. What sense did it make to marry? He might remain suspicious of Nina's pregnancy until the end of his days, but he knew their split was the best thing that could have happened. She might have delivered a few severe wallops tonight, but they were wallops of humiliation, not blows of disappointment.

With these thoughts meandering through his head, Hugo felt somewhat better and began to review what he might say to his parents. He put on his overcoat. He would say that he'd fallen, fallen victim to lust and desire and poor judgment. Given Nina's upbringing and Belle and Beau's sure hand on their daughter's life, Hugo was certain that Nina would never forgive him such a public transgression.

He would call Nina after breakfast. No face to face confrontation. Too dangerous. A sincere, abject apology and four aspirin ought to just about take care of the whole mess.

As the Beresford Outerwear king was about ready to leave, he stopped short. Betty Hughes! And, the rest of them...Cyrus, Lettice, Isobel, Marigold and Parnell...and all his old pals from school lined up in his mind's eye. Tonight's fling was disgrace on a new level, a more comic level, perhaps. This tale of humiliation and public embarrassment would never cease to amuse. The number 402, the name St. George, the very words 'wedding' and 'elevator' would forever bring on a flood of leers and rude remarks, that particular brand of hilarity that never dies. It would live on after his death.

With this realization stamped upon his cortex, Hugo skipped less enthusiastically down the rear stairs of the hotel and drove back to his very empty house in the bluffs. Very slowly.

Betty Hughes adjusted her goggles, gave a tug to her swim cap, and then slid gracefully into the pool. She swam the width and returned to the side where Sonja was dangling her legs in the water, still debating the wisdom of diving in from where she was sitting. Sonja was acting a trifle inhibited this morning, another bit of odd behavior from a woman who had experienced a rewarding artistic transformation just a few months ago. The old Nadine had never been a mouse, but the new Sonja had a good deal of spunk when she first returned to Belmont before Christmas. Lately, she had grown listless. Of course, Sonja was no Olympian, but she looked darned good for sixty. She filled out her purple and turquoise one-piece spectacularly, compared to the other Meadowlark 'dolls,' as Cyrus called the resident lady swimmers. Well, the old Naddy hips might still need a little work.

"Hugo sure did add a little sparkle to New Year's Day, didn't he? The whole town's talkin' about Room 402 at the St. George!" Betty Hughes started to giggle. She still had to get the whole story from Nina.

Sonja harrumphed, as only she could, and remained on the edge of the pool. Several women in the changing room had made a few comments about Hugo's fling with the bridal consultant. "Takes after his father! Damned fool. Nobody will ever let him forget this one."

"The fuss will die down, eventually. Of course, Cyrus will never let it go." Betty Hughes laughed and dipped beneath the surface of the water. She loved swimming. When she popped back up she hissed,

"What are we goin' to do about Archie and Cyrus?" She was careful to speak softly; the pool was ringed by the dolls, most of them wearing white bathing caps with leaves and colored flowers glued to the tops. Betty Hughes thought they looked ridiculous; half couldn't swim a stroke. She was satisfied with how she looked, still full-breasted, not much of the dreaded cellulite. Good legs. And, unlike the other dolls, brave enough to wear a two-piece, which had caused a small stir. That was the trouble with Meadowlark…the least little thing caused a stir. She was privately regretting selling Tallyho. She didn't dare tell Cyrus, who had probably hit the nail on the head when he said they had traded a long driveway for an elevator and three hundred neighbors they didn't particularly like.

"What do you mean?" Sonja pushed a few strands of sherbet hair up under her purple cap and slowly slid into the sea green water. "Nice and warm," she said, approvingly.

"They know who killed Lola. That's what. I'm sure of it!" Betty Hughes pushed off again and treaded water a couple of feet from Sonja. Four other swimmers were in the shallow end.

"Remember, voices carry over water," Sonja whispered back. She gave Betty Hughes a warning roll of her eyes. "That Mrs. Spivak is listening."

Betty Hughes threw a warning glance in the direction of nosy Mrs. Spivak who chose to sit on the edge of the pool a few feet away. She collected gossip which she freely disseminated to certain dolls who wouldn't have told her the time without it.

"Let's swim over to the other side."

Sonja lay back in the water and floated like a large Carnival Cruise liner. She gently circled her arms to keep herself skimming the surface. Her aristocratic nose pointed toward the lights in the ceiling; the strong smell of chlorine caused it to twitch every so often. Betty Hughes followed suit.

"Cyrus has let a few tidbits drop. You know how he is.

"What tidbits?"

"Like the Preacher should grab the inheritance and run before the cops arrest him." Betty Hughes reached the side of the pool and clung to the edge. "Duncan says the attorneys are doling out payments from the estate in installments. The big final payment will probably come in April or May."

"The boys haven't any proof. Neither have the cops," Sonja replied, still keeping her ship afloat a foot away from the side.

"Maybe they know too much. Cyrus sounds as if he knows for a fact that the Preacher is guilty. And, this is connected to that wild party after the war. He mumbles 'Betty Grable, Betty Grable' in his sleep."

"Inconclusive." Sonja wasn't moved by the testimony so far. She stopped treading water and gripped the edge. "Archie still talks to Freddy Donovan. He's had drinks with Freddy and that Sheriff Lemmon, who doesn't seem to care if he solves the skeleton case or not."

"Lettice doesn't think the Preacher's the killer."

"Lettice. What would she know? Who then? That screwy cousin of Lola's….the one who thinks LSD is a vitamin supplement?" Sonja snickered and began swimming around and around in tiny circles.

"Here's the other part," Betty Hughes whispered loudly, taking a few seconds to make sure nobody was listening. Mrs. Spivak, she noticed, who weighed a good two hundred pounds, was in the process of taking her position on the end of the diving board. It usually took her two full minutes to actually jump up and down and then jettison into the pool. Her favorite 'dive' was the cannon ball, which created such a tidal wave that the Meadowlark Council had put her pool behavior on their next meeting agenda. "Cyrus said one night at dinner that Archie was making sure Sally had enough money."

"What?" Sonja began an upright treading position. "Sally? Paying her for what?"

"Who knows? He must be meetin' her somewhere."

"Sally would be our age by now. What did you say to Cyrus?"

Betty Hughes took three strokes along the side of the pool and Sonja followed along. "I asked him what Sally needed the money for."

"I can well imagine." Sonja's eyes were dark and fierce now.

"He said, quite innocently, to keep quiet."

"About what?

"He wouldn't say. He came back to normal and started talkin' about the basketball game on Saturday."

"Good grief!" grumbled Sonja. "I'm tired. Time to get out." She swam smoothly to the ladder near the center and pulled herself up and out. She walked quickly to her white plastic patio chair and wrapped a large beach towel around her shoulders. She dried her hands and fished a packet of cigarettes from her bag. As she lighted up, her freshly manicured nails varnished a shiny orange winked in the harsh pool lights. Two of the dolls at the next table frowned and whispered to each other. They disapproved of smoking and didn't much care for Sonja's new look or her new name and artistic demeanor. Sonja had known them for years but wisely refused their company at the pool. She blew her smoke toward the ceiling and pretended an interest in the other swimmers. She had important things on her mind. Like Archie and Sally and sums of cash.

Betty Hughes decided to swim two laps and started out at the shallow end, which was about four feet deep. As she neared the deep end, Mrs. Spivak began her preliminary hops on the board. Betty Hughes looked up to see the woman bouncing up and down like a wet stuffed animal in a particularly dreadful yellow one-piece. Betty Hughes began to alter her course but too late. Mrs. Spivak executed what many observers later that day would call her best cannon ball that season. Her enormous body hit the water like a badly designed spherical mine which exploded on impact. A spray of water erupted twenty feet into the air while the resulting wave nearly swept Betty Hughes and one or two others out of the pool. Betty Hughes held her course, treaded the waves and gulped chlorinated water. As she sputtered and choked, her fiercest desire, besides staying afloat, became an intense need to drown Mrs. Spivak.

As the Human Cannonball climbed awkwardly up the ladder, she managed to cast a self-satisfied sneer in Betty Hughes's direction as if challenging her to a duel of sorts.

Betty Hughes managed a fairly elegant side stroke to the ladder and rose from the water without coughing. Sonja had hurried over to see if she was OK.

"That horrid woman nearly drowned me! Cannon balls indeed! We'll see about that at the next council meetin'." Betty Hughes left a snarl on her face.

The dolls heard every word and started an energetic buzz at their pool-side tables. Betty Hughes dried off and looked around for Mrs. Spivak.

"She's gone," called out one of the dolls. "I'm surprised she didn't lose her suit on that one!" The other dolls snickered.

"You may have seen her last cannon ball," Betty Hughes called back.

"The manager says we're adults and should be able to have fun in the pool." This from one of the older dolls who never entered the water.

"That was before I got here," replied Betty Hughes with a laugh. "I don't think the manager had manslaughter in mind when he said that."

"Go for it," said one of the younger dolls, smiling.

"Well, that was enough to take my mind off Sally and my very own Daddy Warbucks," Sonja said, softly, as she and Betty Hughes headed for the changing rooms. "What are those two boys up to now? You'd think at their age they'd be reliable." Sonja slammed open her locker door, withdrew a clean towel and then headed for the showers.

"Don't worry, Sonja, this time the money and maybe even Sally have to do with murder. Not matinees."

"I have a copy of Betty Hughes's new play. Cyrus, are you listening?"

Cyrus was on the floor of his living room in a warm-up suit with holes in the elbows exercising to an old Jane Fonda tape. He was looping one leg over the other....for thinner thighs, he kept saying.

"Why do you want thin thighs? You're a man, Cyrus!"

"It's the only tape I've got, Arch. So, what? I'll look great at the pool, won't I?" Cyrus giggled and began throwing his left leg over his right and humming along to the music. "How's the new play? Betty Hughes won't let me read it." He did not sound concerned or suspicious.

"I was snooping...just a bit...happened across it on Sonja's desk. Borrowed it and made a copy." Archie was pacing around the living room. Outside, a brilliant sun, a cloudless blue sky, and a light sprinkle of snow had turned a familiar landscape into calendar art. Archie felt like messing it up...throw in a guy fishing for bass. He was ready for daffodils and violets and the golf course. "Apparently, Betty Hughes lets Sonja read her rough drafts."

"Snooping's not a good idea, Arch. Girls don't like that. So, what's it about?"

"We'll have to leave town if it ever gets on stage." Archie sank into the nearest soft chair with a cup of coffee. "Are you paying attention?"

"Yeah, yeah, I'm with you." Cyrus was grinning. He said he loved Jane Fonda.

"We ARE the play. You, me, the Admiral, and Tommy."

"That's real sweet of Betty Hughes to put us in her play. I've never been in her damned books. What's so bad?"

"You'll find out. It's about four guys, like us, maybe a little younger, who bump off a mobster and bury his body in the woods. When the corpse turns up five years later, these guys go crazy thinking the cops are after them."

"Sounds like a hoot!" Cyrus was standing now and lifting cans of cling peaches like weights. "Great for the arm muscles. You should try it, Arch. You're getting soft." Cyrus aimed his eyes at Archie's middle.

"The plot sounds like the adventures of the Old Devils Meet Buzzy Turk, Mr. Fonda." Archie marched off to the kitchen in search of breakfast. He found a box of doughnuts in the cupboard and carried it back to the living room. "Where's Betty Hughes?"

"Exercise class."

"Why don't you exercise together?"

"She can't keep up with me."

Archie was losing ground fast. Why did he try to explain things to Cyrus?

"There's a Betty Grable in the play. Ring any bells? She's the daughter of the mobster and knows how he died. And, there's a second girl. She guesses the secret and tries to blackmail one of the guys. By the way, it's a comedy." Archie bit into a doughnut and sprayed powdered sugar down the front of his dark blue sweater.

"Sounds like a winner, Arch. I think Betty Hughes has a knack for this stuff." Archie and Cyrus had heard rumors about the rehearsals at the college for a production of Marigold's prize winning play. Supposed to be good, and Nina had a part in it. "You're a lucky man. A gorgeous girl who is nuts about you and gets a big part in a new play. And, your wife is still in the dark. Doesn't get much better than that." Cyrus whistled and then stopped the tape. "Enough. I'd rather have a doughnut and a cup of coffee with you, Arch."

Archie sighed. "I'm not laughing. How did Betty Hughes find out about the old bones? How did she find out about Betty Grable? Did you tell?" Archie asked kindly.

Cyrus looked bewildered. "Maybe you told her without realizing it." He grinned knowingly. "We do that sometimes, Arch."

"Hell, could be Sonja figured it out and told the B.H., Sonja, Lettice…they're all asking questions about 1945 and Sally and Spriggy's love life those days. Jesus! They've all but wrapped it up. Except for Buzzy. How the hell did they figure out the old bones? " Archie was nervous.

"What about that baby? Tommy's coming back from the dead just to see you change that kid's pants." Cyrus cracked up and began hitting his knee with enthusiasm.

Archie couldn't help but laugh too. "We won't be laughing if Naddy finds out. Sonja. Damn it, I can't get used to that damned silly name." Archie was worried too about any impending divorce, the splitting up of assets, the reprisals that were bound to catapult his way. Sonja's choice of lawyer could spell more doom than freedom. Was a new marriage really a good idea? Divorcing Naddy after all these years? Jesus, he was bordering on bastard over that alone. Guilt had set in lately in large, black clouds. Bathgart told him to work it out if he wanted some relief. Archie loved Nadine and Nina. His predicament was awesome.

"What are we going to do about the play?" Cyrus asked.

"What can we do?" Archie picked up a second doughnut.

"Admit we've read it and tell her we were disappointed because this play isn't as funny as the first one."

Archie thought about this idea for a minute. "Not bad, Cyrus, not bad at all. Creative people don't like hearing things like that. Could be she'll stuff it in the desk drawer and write something else." He grinned, feeling better already.

"I sure do have a new opinion of Hugo, Arch, after that fiasco at the St. George the other night. What a performance!" Cyrus started one of his long, girlish giggles that usually made Archie laugh too.

"Jesus! He hasn't done anything right since he got back…..except run the company…..that he can do. He'll have to go out of town for his women." Archie shook his head. "The bridal consultant?"

"With the door open?"

The two old friends howled with laughter, taking a father's delight in the comic mishaps of a kid who should know better at middle age.

"Smooth he isn't, Arch." Cyrus gobbled up his doughnut and washed it down with coffee. "Now, how about a little Jane Fonda to go with breakfast?"

Archie drove to Stone Bank early the following morning. He'd had enough of the doubts and questions and speculation about Sally and the Preacher and Durwood Spriggs and Lola's last will and testament. The sky was just taking on the light of day. He walked into the Starlight Café, inviting and warm with the smell of good coffee, fresh cinnamon rolls and frying bacon. He removed his coat, shook off the snow, and hung the coat on a hook by the door.

The turquoise vinyl counter stools were occupied by ten men in heavy jackets and tractor hats. They looked like construction workers stoking up before a long day. There was one booth left and Archie slid in. As soon as Sally caught sight of him, she came over with two mugs of coffee and a plate of fresh rolls. She sat down on the opposite side.

"What brings you up here so early in the morning?" Sally asked. Her nicely ironed aqua uniform matched her eyes. There was a lace handkerchief peeking out of the breast pocket.

"You can probably guess." Archie offered her one of his best smiles. "How about if we start with Durwood Spriggs?" He sipped his coffee and took a big bite of sweet roll. He loved diners, especially at breakfast time in winter. Sally's tinted blonde hair caught the light and shimmered. She was still pretty. Bit of a double chin, a few crows feet, but still pretty.

Sally raised both eyebrows and put down her cup. "It was the picture in the paper, wasn't it?"

"For starters."

Sally poured cream in her coffee and then told Archie the whole story, in a low, easy going voice that spanned the years and took Archie back to 1945. He listened attentively. It was the truth this time.

The bugaboo about the body in the woods wasn't over yet. Archie still had his wife and Betty Hughes's new play more or less sitting in the middle of Pike's Wood. He admitted to Sonja that he'd 'borrowed' the play for an hour while he read it and copied it for Cyrus. He figured Betty Hughes would be flattered they had taken such keen interest in her new line of work. Sonja wasn't thrilled. Archie said he wasn't thrilled with the plot. He and his pals were the main characters. And, he demanded to know who had squealed about the Preacher's daddy.

Sonja immediately turned defensive. She confessed she'd overheard a few conversations that led her to believe the Old Devils were up to their ears in something. But, nobody squealed. She and Betty Hughes had figured out Boswell's connection to Spriggs....that was simple. Boswell looked like Durwood! They had to be related. Betty Hughes had simply used the information she had, tossed in a playwright's imagination about mobsters and blackmail, threw in the mysterious skeleton because it was an interesting news item, added a pretty house maid, a wild party and out popped a new play.

Archie said he didn't think submitting the play as it stood in this draft was a good idea. Sonja told him it was Betty Hughes's decision to make. And, shame on him for reading her private mail and business on her very private desk.

"It was an accident," Archie explained somberly. "We never meant to kill the man."

It was one of those melancholy nights in January that would stretch on and on like a long, straight, boring highway until spring broke through to save them. Earlier that day Archie informed Cyrus and the Admiral that it was time to confess to the womenfolk.

The Old Devils circled the wagons in the Beresfords' living room. Their moment of truth was at hand. They would tell the tale of those infamous three days and nights in the summer of 1945. Cyrus defined the time as seventy-two hours of unrestrained debauchery with a shelf life of a thousand winters. As it turned out, the story lost a good deal of punch when Betty Hughes and Sonja admitted that they'd figured out the parentage of Preacher Boswell. He was the product of Durwood Spriggs and Sally, facts which explained the large inheritance to Boswell and the Preacher's decidedly beady eyes. Those awful beady eyes gave him away.

What the ladies had not figured out, Archie knew, was the sad fact that the Old Devils had been led to believe by Sally Turk for over forty years that any one of them could have fathered the Preacher on that victory party weekend. It was only after Archie's final meeting with Sally at the diner just a few days ago that he had learned the truth himself.

"To get back to the beginning," Archie was saying, "you have to know that Sally Turk's father was a monster who beat his wife and daughter and insisted on loyalty besides." Archie had taken a lecturer's position in front of the blazing fire, nearly intolerable, but he stayed where he was, as if the heat might singe off his great regret or burn a hole in his pants, whichever came first.

"What happened to the wife?" asked Lettice, sidetracking again.

"She finally got the courage to run off with a guy she met in a bar. Sally stayed because she was too scared to leave."

"But, you're telling us that this Sally, the girl you like to call Betty Grable, accused all of you? That any one of you could have fathered the child?" Sonja, for one, was very skeptical. "It seems to me your…shall we say…war-time behavior with this young woman deserves forty years of suffering." She was not amused.

"Sally was a willing participant, Naddy," Cyrus put in quietly. He often forgot her new name. "Granted, we were eager to live it up."

"And, this bastard baby is definitely Preacher Boswell," Betty Hughes declared flatly. "Durin' the past four decades, you all believed that one of you had produced this awful man, this creature with bad teeth and piggy eyes. It was only three long breaths ago that Miss Sally confessed that Spriggy committed the deed." Betty Hughes liked to line up the facts in a tidy row. It came from plotting books.

After looking over at Lettice, the Admiral said, "Try not to get riled. It was war time." Lettice turned her head and stared into the fire.

Archie knew that Lettice wasn't pleased about the Admiral's 'friendship' with Parnell Grant. She'd be punishing him for weeks. The Admiral would have to buy his own Sunday paper. The Admiral, of course, was still steadfastly hiding in his closet….with the door wide open.

"It was that picture in the paper....those tiny black eyes. Positively reptilian." Sonja sounded pleased with herself. Betty Hughes nodded and smiled.

Lettice looked disgusted with the lot of them. She said, "I can't believe your behavior, especially with my dear husband coming home in a box."

The boys tried to look properly chastised, and they were genuinely sorry, but the punishment was nearly over now.

"This Betty Grable," Lettice went on sourly, "was just as devious as the rest of you. She lied to you in 1945 and took your money under false pretenses and made you suffer."

"Of course, who'd want to claim Boswell now?" Sonja declared with a wrinkle of her slender nose. "If he's really the killer, his own mother might run the other direction."

The six of them seated there in that sumptuous room had been friends long before the war and still were. Most of the romances and marriages came well after that fateful victory party. It wasn't as if the boys had cheated on their wives with this Sally Turk. Betty Hughes reminded them of this and suggested they cool off and make peace.

"So, in exchange for a large sum of cash," Sonja was summarizing, "this woman had the child, put him up for adoption, and kept her mouth shut about the baby and her father's death for years and years." Sonja sighed. "Some babe. I think I like Miss Sally rather more than I like the rest of you."

"That's about it," the Admiral interjected. "Except for Tommy, who didn't have any money, as usual."

"Who cares now? Or, who cared then?" Cyrus grumbled.

"Just how was this Buzzy Turk killed?" asked Betty Hughes, eager to get back to the beginning.

Archie stepped away from the hearth and sat down. "We all drove out to see Sally at her cottage in Sandy Hook," he told them. "To discuss the situation. Sally had called Cyrus to tell him she was expecting a kid and needed help. Sally's old man overheard the conversation through an open window. He burst into the cottage and accused us of raping his daughter, for

God's sake! Threatened to call the police. Sally tried to reason with him, tried hard to shut him up. But, Turk pushed her to the floor and kept ranting."

"Drunk as a skunk, he was," the Admiral jumped in.

"Buzzy picked up a rifle that was propped up in the corner," Archie went on, "and started to swing it at us, cutting it through the air like he was warming up a baseball bat. And, then he slowed down and pointed it at me and at Sally and said he was going to kill the bunch of us."

"Dumb bastard," said Cyrus. "Always itching for a fight. Sally showed me her bruises once. He'd broken her arm twice. Fractured her mother's skull once, she said."

"Cyrus lunged at him when he lost his balance a little. A scuffle started we all tried to get the gun away from him. We gave him a shove. He tilted backward and couldn't get his footing again. On the way down, he hit his head real hard on the corner of an iron stove. Dropped like a tree," Archie said softly. "The blow killed him."

The room and its guests sat silent for a long minute.

Cyrus finally said, "We had to get rid of the body. Sally was scared the police would think she did it. Everybody in town knew how mean Buzzy was. We were scared shitless," said Cyrus.

Old images flashed again in Archie's head… the blood on Turk's big skull, the rifle lying innocently on the linoleum floor, the march through the wood with twigs breaking underfoot. He could still feel the enormous weight of the body straining his back; he could still hear the sound of his own heart pounding and the taste of fear in his mouth. The pictures were always black and white, just as they were in his nightmares, and the sounds echoed in his head like reverberating voices bouncing from the walls in an old stone church.

"We carried the body into Pike's Wood and buried it," Archie said. He moved to another chair, away from the others, where he could feel the tension in his muscles lessen, just as the weight of Turk's body had dropped away that night the second the corpse rolled from their arms and landed in its grave.

Betty Hughes gasped. Lettice frowned. Sonja sat as erect as a queen.

"We never figured out this part," Betty Hughes said quietly to Sonja.

"The bones in Pike's Wood," Lettice said emphatically. "It's the skeleton of Buzzy Turk." She looked triumphant, happy to be part of solving the riddle, after being left out.

"Gracious!" Betty Hughes exclaimed. "You've been luggin' this around all these months?" Betty Hughes hurried to Cyrus who was slouched on the other couch.

"Why did Sally lie to you all?" asked Betty Hughes. "Why didn't she blackmail Durwood?" She reached for Cyrus's hand and he took hers eagerly.

"She didn't dare lose her job," Archie answered. "Spriggy wasn't exactly the honorable sort, you know....then or later. Money was tight. Buzzy Turk drank up most of the money Sally could make. She figured she could squeeze a tidy sum from the four of us....more than she'd ever get from the Spriggs family."

Archie scratched his head, still bowled over by what they had done and how long they'd kept the secret.

"Truth be known," Archie continued, "Sally said she and Spriggy had been having a bit of fun together since April. Remember, he came home early for his mother's funeral?"

"Didn't Turk's buddies wonder why he suddenly disappeared?" Lettice asked.

"Sally told Turk's pals....the few he had....that he'd gone off to make his fortune in Alaska. He'd been bragging for months about going to Anchorage where his cousin had a logging business. There was no good reason to be suspicious." Archie was feeling almost lightheaded at revealing the details. "Now, we might have to face the music."

"Sheriff Lemmon isn't exactly Dick Tracy," Sonja reminded him.

The Admiral said almost matter-of-factly, "The Crawford County district attorney doesn't think there's enough evidence to continue the investigation or to prosecute anybody. A friend of mine checked. I think we're off the hook." He sat slightly slumped in a big chair near the fire.

"Will Sally ever tell?" asked Lettice.

Archie shook his head. "No. She buried her past with Buzzy. She said we did her a favor that night, even though we didn't mean to hurt the bastard."

"Are we the only ones to know this story?" asked Betty Hughes.

"Yes. And, we'd like to keep it that way." Archie sounded stern.

"Let Belmont remember you as war heroes," said Sonja, softly, in a rare display of sentimentality.

"Righto, Naddy," said Cyrus. "We were the guys who conquered the French hedgerows! Right, Arch?" He grinned.

Archie smiled too. But, it was an effort. The weight of the years and the sobering facts made him feel a hundred years old. Of course, he was old enough to know that the fatigue and the regret would gradually disappear. The nightmare never would.

"But, we still don't know who killed Lola!" Sonja said, almost too brightly, Archie was thinking.

"Yes, you're right!" put in Betty Hughes. "We still have a mystery to solve." She was definitely bright-eyed over the prospect. Even Lettice looked eager.

"Now, girls, don't get caught up in a police investigation. Freddy Donovan won't like it. He'll thank you for keeping your noses out." Archie tried to sound serious, but he didn't think his tone of voice would keep the ladies away from the case. His head was swimming. Cyrus and the Admiral looked relatively calm and peaceful. How could he impress them all of the serious consequences of dabbling in homicide?

18

Dragonflies

It was one of those perfect days in early May, nearly a year since old Buzzy Turk found his way to the surface. A cloudless cerulean sky stirred itself with a warm, soft breeze out of the southwest, and there wasn't a bug in sight. Freddy Donovan said it was the kind of day that begged to be fished, and he called Archie, who always agreed with him on these things. Archie had been playing Freddy's father for a long time.

Freddy picked up Archie about eight o'clock on Friday morning and insisted on driving. He had a new Jeep that needed breaking in on the back roads that would take them to Horsehead Slough a few miles south of Sandy Hook. Archie said he was game.

With a pack of Pfeiffers rattling in a cooler on the rear seat, the two of them bumped across the Willow Creek bridge and set off down county FF at a speed that would normally bring on a radar car. Archie pretended Freddy wasn't driving and consoled himself with the notion that they'd be cranking along like this for years to come, no doubt picking over the remains of old police cases, solved and unsolved, and boring the pants off of their friends with tales of fishing on the big river. Forgetting for the moment that Freddy was closer to Hugo's age, Archie still pictured the two of them as old men, both with canes, a six pack of Pfeiffers between them on the porch, regaling their grandchildren with stories about the mysterious body in Pike's Wood and the unsolved murder of Lola Spriggs.

"Don't you still get a sick feeling in your gut about that Spriggs case, Freddy?" Archie asked, as they stopped short behind a plumber's van, coming within a hair of impaling the new Jeep on a dozen long pipes sticking out the rear end of the truck.

Archie sucked in his breath; Freddy drove on, unruffled by the close call. "Hell, yes," the Irishman admitted bitterly. "But, no evidence, my friend. And, no other suspects." He lighted up his first cigar of the day as some kind of comfort. "Looks like he got away with murder and will make a tidy profit doing it."

Archie was still mulling bar room gossip at Billy's...to keep forging ahead, beyond Preacher Boswell. He liked the 'follow the money' law of investigation. It pretty much suited the way the world worked. Freddy did too, but Freddy's line of inquiry was always a trifle muddled. Weeks passed and no one seemed to think about poor Lola Spriggs.

Donovan turned off the bridge road and swung on to a patch of asphalt pavement. The road eventually crossed a swampy arm of river and ended up at Iggy's Boats and Bait on the north end of Horsehead Slough. A listing flagpole flying tattered colors marked the spot. He parked beneath the shade of a drooping box elder.

"Well, Charlie Lemmon didn't have any better luck figurin' out who bashed in Buzzy Turk's head almost half a century ago," Freddy said honestly enough. He pushed open the door and stepped into the sunshine. "We've had the usual daffy ducks walk into the station to confess. The D.A.'s sick of the whole thing. He's pretty much closed the case. Nobody gives a damn." Freddy gave his pants a hitch and stuck a Brewers' baseball cap on his head.

"I can understand that, Freddy. A lot of murders never get solved; we might have two of them right here in God's country." He felt lucky.

Donovan agreed and leaned back into the vehicle for more cigars.

Archie laughed. "By the by, Freddy, I hear the lawyers in the Spriggs case have paid out over half of the big bucks already." He struggled into a faded green canvas fishing vest sprinkled with small pockets. "Several million smackeroos."

Freddy hopped down to the gravel speckled ground, closed the Jeep door, and moved to the back where he retrieved his poles and tackle box. "Lucky stiffs. Can't say I can count on any generous rich relatives. My Great Uncle Simon left me his homburg hat and a rhinestone tie pin. Hat's too small and I feel like a girl with the pin stuck into my tie." He laughed and so did Archie. Archie tipped his hook loaded hat toward his eyes and against the blinding sun and slipped on sunglasses.

"I've never inherited a centavo myself, Freddy. My old man spent it all." Archie sighed. "Thank God I know how to make boots and parkas, huh?" He laughed and picked up his gear.

Freddy said they were both very fortunate men and sniffed the clear air, grateful that it was May and still tolerable. He didn't like summer on the river; it turned people sour, he said. Good thing they had spring and fall to temper their tempers, Archie added.

The two headed for the bait shop, a rough, weathered shanty with a big white ice chest holding up the outside wall. They picked up four sandwiches from Iggy's refrigerator case, put more ice in the cooler, and paid the boat rental fee.

The dock was a rickety stretch of gray planks that jutted boldly into the brown river water. Neatly lined up on the packed sand beach were a dozen aluminum rowboats and a few flat-bottomed bass boats with their motors tipped forward in the only example of order at Iggy's.

"Here it is!" Freddy called out to Archie, who was trailing behind with the heavy cooler. The Irishman pointed to a dented craft with 'Orphan Annie' painted on its side in red letters. Freddy settled his little Igloo in the bow and the rest of his gear on the bottom. Once Archie took his seat next to the Evinrude, Donovan shoved off.

Two pulls started the twenty-five horses and they chugged softly into the narrow channel. The peace of the morning settled down on them as gently as the engine putted.

"Did you ever have another go at those two professors who stood by Toby Spriggs?" Archie asked, his mind still unsettled by Lola's death. He was motoring in and around a maze of uninhabited islands that nearly choked the flow of the river. It was hard to tell who would eventually take over the kingdom.

"Talked to them three times. Not much cause to do it again." Freddy popped the caps on the first two beers of the day and handed one to Archie. "What did you have in mind?"

"Nothing much, I guess. He's at one end of the money trail. How about the other relatives who got money from Lola?" Archie finally settled in a secluded cove where they dropped anchor and tossed out their lines. "Any shot in the dark, Freddy."

"Dead ends. We liked the gardener for a bit, but he was at the movies the afternoon Lola was killed. The ticket-seller verified it. Unless he paid off the ticket seller. Pretty far-fetched. I can't see it." Freddy sighed. "Hell, I don't know what I'm doing in this business half the time."

"We all have our dark corners, Freddy." Archie was thinking now about the possibility of divorce court and fatherhood at his age. A very dark corner. He and Nina had never solved that far-reaching puzzle either. Neither one could make a decision, and Archie was having great misgivings about abandoning Naddy after all these years. Nina seemed to agree.

Archie sipped his brew, soaking up the solitude as much as the companionship. A big green dragonfly lighted on the bow, as content as he was to tip his face into the sun. Then, quite suddenly, Archie's mind returned to something Betty Hughes had said and connected itself rather smartly to another time-honored theory. He tinkered with this for about five seconds and began to feel almost light-headed. It all had to do with going backward.

The Irishman threw his line into a fresh spot, and just as the hook dipped into the water, Archie looked across the brown water only to experience a new clarity of vision, a new acuteness of hearing, and an amazing ability to focus. He supposed a writer….like Betty Hughes…. would call it a revelation. Holy Toledo! His head was floating above his body; he just knew it.

"I've had a flash, Freddy!" And, Archie let out a loud whoop, bound to scare away the bass, but he didn't much care. The dragonfly flew off. As if to fuel the stupendous mental process going on in his head, Archie reached into Iggy's brown paper sack and pulled up a bologna and mustard sandwich. He took a huge bite.

"What kinda flash?" Freddy was looking slightly worried. He reached into his pocket and pulled out one of his stinky cigars and stuck it into his mouth, but didn't light up.

"About the Spriggs case."

"Send your flashes over to me, pal." Freddy pulled his sunglasses down on his nose and eyed Archie with renewed interest.

"Could be just a spark, Freddy, but, sparks start forest fires. Silly cliché, but what the hell." Archie smiled.

Freddy squinted into the light. "One beer can't turn a man clever this fast, you old dog."

Archie grinned like Charlie Chan in the movies and felt a tug on his line.

"They sang like canaries, Arch. Can you believe it?"

Cyrus let loose with a drive that arced and then hung in the sky for a good five seconds before it fell to the green.

Archie swung at the ball and nearly repeated Cyrus's grand whack. It happened to be a morning when Cyrus remembered how to play golf.

"It's hard to believe we figured it out up at Horsehead Slough. Freddy finished piecing the puzzle together while I reeled in a very nice bass." Archie howled. It didn't get much better than this.

"How did you figure it out, Arch?" Cyrus hopped into the golf cart, and Archie began motoring up the fairway.

"Betty Hughes and Naddy were talking about looking back, reliving the past….all that stuff the ladies like to hash over when they're feeling old and neglected. You know." Archie drove expertly around a fallen branch blown into their path.

"So what, Arch?"

"So, I thought again about following the money. The beneficiaries were paid sums over a period of months, in three installments. We all know where the money went up to that point. From Lola's estate account to the individuals specified in her will. Real simple."

Cyrus ruffled up his hair and looked agitated. "So….?"

"Hang on. So, why not find out where the money went after that? Check out Toby Spriggs's account. What did he do with his money?"

Archie paused. Cyrus made a keep-it-going motion with his hand. "Donovan checked the bank accounts of Toby Spriggs and his Ashbury pals. They all had accounts in a bank in Augusta." Archie stopped the cart.

"I'm with you, Arch!"

"Bingo!" Archie laughed. "The two professors were unaccountably much richer than they had ever been before. And, Toby's account showed two very large withdrawals after his final inheritance deposit." Archie shook his head.

"How can anybody be that stupid?"

"Maybe you have to be real guilty."

"What happened next?"

"The geography professor sang soprano. His buddy, the econ chairman, warbled alto." Archie hopped from the golf cart and stretched. "After Freddy stuck them under the bright lights." Archie said all of this just happened.

"Toby bumped off his own mother? Jesus! Nasty little kid. And, he paid off his pals to cover for him." Cyrus mopped his face. It was getting hot.

"Toby will be charged with planning and executing his mother's murder. The other two, as accomplices, I guess. They weren't discussing spy novels the night she died. According to Freddy, Toby wrapped up the body and stuck a lampshade on her head just to humiliate her. Not a man who likes women very much. If you get my drift."

"Like I said, nasty little kid."

"Toby claims his mean father drove him to it."

Cyrus spotted his ball not too far from the pin. "You mean parental brutality?"

Archie sized up his next shot. "Could be. Spriggy was a son-of-a-bitch."

"Not much class, Arch." Cyrus stretched out on the green on his stomach to line up his putt.

"You know, Cyrus," Archie said calmly, "I'm kinda glad the Preacher didn't do it!" He watched Cyrus going through his putting ritual.

"Me too," said Cyrus. "Even though we thought he looked guilty as hell." He sank the putt and then replaced the ball where it was and began the procedure all over again. Archie waited. Cyrus liked to do things twice on a good day.

"So, the Preacher's off the hook and so are we. Let Boswell take the marbles and run. He's mayor of Fontana City and king of his little patch up there. A good place for him." Archie watched Cyrus sink the putt a second time, and then, he quickly moved in to play his own ball. Cyrus was mighty fine this morning, very alert, except for the goofy golf. He was taking another experimental drug, Betty Hughes had told him.

"You and Nina off to the justice of the peace any time soon?" Cyrus tugged at Archie's knit shirt sleeve to make sure he had the man's complete attention. "Miss Nina's as big as the clubhouse. Time to get a move on, Arch."

"To be honest with you, Cyrus, my feet are blocks of ice and Nina's wearing socks most days. She says I'll regret the whole thing and hate her and the tot."

"Jitters. Just plain jitters. Imagine starting over with fresh material, Arch. You could raise the kid and make Nina happy and reap all the benefits. You're retired! You've got all the time in the world to make things right." Cyrus headed for the golf cart. Archie knew that he often forgot about Nadine.

That was it. Archie often forgot about Naddy too. The sun was baking them, and Archie hurried into the cart and drove on. Maybe they were all living in a dream world half the time. Fresh material was always tempting, but it was the old material that gave Archie pause. Lately, he just couldn't get over what this would do to Naddy.

Betty Hughes and Nina were enjoying the ministrations provided at Alexandre's the following afternoon.

"I'm tellin' you, darlin'," Betty Hughes was saying to the hairdresser, "it does my heart good to know that Freddy Donovan can figure out a murder case. He caught that twirpy Toby in his evil scheme. Imagine, killin' your own mother." She leaned back in the pink leather chair and let the shampoo girl lather up her hair.

There were mutters of agreement among the other patrons, two ladies in pink smocks having their nails varnished by Alexandre's cousin, Fiona.

"Toby Spriggs has hired Burton Dance as his attorney," Nina said. "Best in the state. They say he could get the devil off with enough money." Alexandre, who was snipping her hair with the precision of a sushi chef, howled. The baby gave her a lovely kick.

"Can you imagine," said Alexandre in his breathless voice and waving his expensive chrome-plated shears, "those three very unattractive boors depositing that kind of loot in accounts just ten minutes from Belmont and using their REAL NAMES!" He whooped. "Solid wood from the neck up!"

"The police and the D.A. grabbed the bank records," said Betty Hughes from the shampoo bowl.

"Off shore accounts, darlings! Off shore accounts!" Alexandre's big brown eyes told his 'darlings' that he knew all about off shore accounts. "It's practically spelled out for you if you read John Grisham." He returned to Nina's blonde tresses.

"The whole thing does read like a cheap novel," said Betty Hughes. She was upright now; the shampoo girl was wrapping her head in a monogrammed rose towel.

The two ladies in smocks nodded in agreement.

"Just you watch," Nina quickly pointed out, "that scene in Lola's closet will be in somebody's next novel." She glanced at Betty Hughes, but Betty Hughes refused to let on she'd heard.

"Frankly, darlings, I would just LOVE to be a mouse behind the bar tonight up at Fergie's Tap up in Fontana City. My bookkeeper tells me that Preacher Boswell's throwing himself a wingding of a party. He's mayor; he's rich; he's free. No longer under suspicion." Alexandre looked at his clients and said, "Too bad he's not my type." They giggled. Alexandre spun around on his expensive Italian shoes. "Maybe if I gave his honor a complete makeover."

The darlings loved it when Alexandre was bad.

By June the country had endured the New Hampshire primary, among others, and hundreds of stump speeches by Dukakis, Bush, Hart and Dole. Movie buffs were duly horrified by a bunny boiling in a pot and had gone home to rethink the allure of a quickie weekend affair. The majority of folks spent the cold winter nights vicariously skating and skiing with the Olympians. Toni Morrison won the Pulitzer, and music fans lost Woody Herman. Irving Berlin burned a hundred candles on his cake, while Thurston Contractors were constructing an up-scale shopping mall in the Williamsburg manner on what used to be a swamp and landfill on the south end of Belmont. Most of this was covered in the *Bee*'s early summer wrap-up column by the editor, Nathan Bombay.

In the Personal Jottings column, it was noted that on Memorial Day Marigold Woolsey announced that famous artist Harry Freese would pose nude for what she was predicting to be her finest work in marble. And, she was working on a new play, a comedy about senior citizens enduring a retirement home. The rigors of high rise living eventually forced Betty Hughes and Cyrus to move out of Meadowlark Village. They purchased Belmont's notorious 'haunted house' on Two Tree Lane, a large stone residence once owned by a lovely old ghost named Maude. Cyrus said the disruption of relocating and the possible strain of living with ghosts and spirits would be easier than staging a coup at Meadowlark. Betty Hughes insisted they'd be safer with poltergeists than they would be with any more chicken croquettes from the Meadowlark kitchen.

Topping this cavalcade of developments was a two-column news item, with photograph, in the June tenth edition of the *Bee* and the *Tribune* (and others) that provoked vivid reactions in the unsuspecting and in one reader in particular.

"Going on Broadway?" Hugo shouted with his chin pointed at the chandelier. He'd been enjoying a leisurely breakfast of eggs and toast in the sunny kitchen of the old coach house he'd purchased from a gentleman who owned the original Moss ancestral home, just several hundred yards away. Recently remodeled to fit the needs of a bachelor CEO, the coach house had been written up in the *'Our Homes'* section of the local newspaper two weeks ago. Hugo's glass house in the hills had developed serious structural problems after a hard winter, and he was forced to abandon it to the elements. He was suing the builder.

This morning Hugo's breakfast companion was a middle-aged estate agent from Bigelow and Jones Realtors, who'd closed the coach house deal and then gone on to suggest one or two other deals of a more intimate nature. She was one of a half dozen women who occupied Hugo's hours outside of Beresford Boots. None had made much of an impression, which was exactly the reaction Hugo wanted.

Startled by Hugo's outburst, the lady from Bigelow and Jones promptly spilled coffee over the comics but bravely asked, "What, Hugo, what?" She was discovering in their brief time together that Hugo Beresford was extraordinarily grumpy for a man of forty-something with very few cares in the world.

"My wife...errr, my former wife...ahhhh...my former fiancée...will be starring in a new play on Broadway in October. If that isn't the absolute pits! That's what it is. Can you believe it? No, of course, you can't. You have no idea. No one has any idea." Hugo flapped the pages of the newspaper as if trying to extricate a moth from inside the pages.

Nina's off-Broadway debut in April had been rewarded with rave reviews. It was discovered that she sang as well as she acted, and no one in New York seemed to mind watching a pregnant soprano prance around the stage. Egads! Nina and her new career and the interminable matter of a fatherless baby due in early July and how it was probably his father's love child, for God's sake, which would make the kid a peculiar kind of relative...a half-brother, he supposed...had given Hugo hives and insomnia. The oddities of birth could drive one into orbit, he thought to himself. He and Archie hadn't spoken in months, not since he accused his father of fooling around with Nina. Good grief, what was happening? He'd been thrust into a ridiculous familial snake pit with Archie and Nina and an unborn Beresford. His mother, busy with her artistic pots business, was acting blissfully removed from all the horrors. And, what about this Cosmo Freese, who had been seen almost constantly with Nina the past few months? Was this actor to be the big winner in the end? There was no divorce on the Beresford family horizon, which meant that Nina was not going to marry Archie. Sonja Beresford, the unsung heroine in the melodrama, many were saying, refused comment on any of the developments in her family, acting as if nothing new was going on. Hugo was generally left limp after going over these lurid machinations of romance and infidelity.

Hugo glanced down at the coffee soaked comics, which his guest was ignoring, and then back to the article in the newspaper sporting a flattering shot of Nina standing next to Cosmo Freese, who was looking a good deal like a natty William Holden. Judas priest!

"Is she famous?" asked the very attractive estate agent with considerable curiosity.

"I certainly hope not! I suppose she will be. It's that damned Cosmo Freese who's responsible." Hugo pointed to the article about Nina's play. "It says here that Freese was instrumental in getting Miss Dupree an audition with the famous impresario, Montgomery Zwick, a long-time New York theatre director. The two worked together on a dozen plays in the last twenty years." Hugo harrumphed loudly. "Cosmo Freese! That...that...actor!"

"He's marvelous, Hugo!" exclaimed his breakfast partner, pouring more coffee and then dabbing unenthusiastically at the soaked newspaper with her napkin. "I saw him last winter in *'You Can't Take It With You'* at the Repertory." She laughed out loud, recalling the performance, and helped herself to a second applesauce doughnut.

"He's a scoundrel!" cried Hugo, giving the page another flap and then handing it over to his guest, who was gesturing for a look. "He's simply after Nina's money. It's as plain as the...the...coffee stains on that newspaper!" Hugo made a face.

"According to this, Mr. Zwick, he thinks your former fiancée is the 'find of the century.' Isn't that something?" The estate agent comically batted her lashes at Hugo.

When Hugo didn't respond, the lady at the breakfast table put down the paper and gave Hugo another good look, as if to ask if Hugo Beresford might still love this Nina Dupree and might just want her back, now that she was close to famous. The estate agent wasn't the kind of woman who wasted her time and talents on rich men pining for their old lovers. She said, "It says here that she is considering another play for the future, a play written by another local talent, Betty Hughes Armbruster, the noted romance novelist turned playwright. It's about four small town guys who kill a mobster by mistake." The agent laughed heartily at this.

"Who would want to see that? Sounds like a Damon Runyon knock-off."

"I think it sounds like fun. Your Miss Dupree looks decidedly pregnant in that photograph. I take it she's unmarried." The agent from Bigelow and Jones seemed to be enjoying her breakfast immensely.

"Well, it isn't mine, if that's what you're insinuating!"

Hugo stormed off to his bedroom to dress. He needed to do something. And he wasn't quite sure what it was. What he didn't need was this Bigelow female who spilled coffee on the comics giving him the once-over at the breakfast table. He wasn't sure he liked her all that much. He couldn't even bring himself to call her by her first name. As a matter of fact, he couldn't remember what it was.

As he pulled on his trousers, Hugo suddenly longed for candied orange slices, the comforting sweet tang of youth, the candy he and Archie loved so much. He sank to the edge of the bed in what felt like a hopeless depression. Was all this misadventure really his fault? He fell back on the rumpled heap of the unmade bed and recalled the warm golden years in New Orleans, the uncomplicated years.... before Nina. Those days wore simplicity like a custom tailored suit. Just peddle the hot pepper sauce and have a good time. No responsibility, no fuss, no worries. No family. From now on, he decided grimly, this would be the Hugo Beresford formula for happiness.

As predicted by Dr. Lamb, baby Nina made her debut on the fourth of July just as fireworks shook Wrenn Park and fractured the clear night sky with explosions of colored stars and bursts of blue-white light. On hand for the production was Cosmo Freese, beaming like a new father, which he wasn't, of course, but a man comfortable with the role and eager to play the part, if he was ever asked.

Hours later, Hugo stopped by the hospital for a tentative peek at Nina and her offspring, so fragile, so beautiful, and so very frightening that he knew instantly that he would be eternally grateful to whatever force of nature or mankind had put an end to his betrothal. Marriage and fatherhood would not be his bag, of this he was now positive. If Cosmo Freese wanted to take over the job, he was welcome to the task. Hugo soon left, thinking more highly of Nina for having accomplished this most remarkable feat...other than finding an acting job in New

York. And, Hugo had to admit, he was far more respectful of Cosmo, too, who seemed to be a gentleman of depth.

The following morning, before Belle and Beau's arrival, Archie and Sonja, Betty Hughes and Cyrus stopped by. Archie held the infant for several minutes before relinquishing the bundle to its mother. Nina saw tears in his eyes and understood. Cyrus cried openly. They stayed long enough to celebrate the occasion with a bottle of champagne smuggled in by Cyrus.

As the four of them were leaving, Nina overheard Sonja say, "Goodness, Archie, the baby looks just like you." The tone of her voice seemed a marvelous blend of sympathy and forgiveness.

Nina couldn't see Archie's reaction, but she was left with a lingering feeling of apprehension for him.

"The Admiral and Lettice are having Sunday brunch together again," Naddy commented, as she bustled about her studio on Commerce Row in Augusta's old Third Ward. "She's apparently forgiven him for staying in the closet, so to speak, and for his friendship with Parnell."

She rinsed her hands at the industrial sink. She'd kicked off her new professional life with a triumphant studio opening that spring.

"Good for them," said Archie, finding the entire gay closet routine tiresome and unnecessary. Let people do what they want or do what they must. Why couldn't the Admiral have girlfriends and boyfriends? Wasn't he, Archibald Beresford, living with a woman with orange hair and a new name? This was 1988, for God's sake. Wasn't he a phantom father, as Cyrus liked to call him these days? An amusing thought in the light of day, but not so at three in the morning when his guilt over Nina and baby felt bottomless. It was weeks ago that Nina suggested they each move on in their own directions. Nina told him honestly and sweetly that he didn't have the disposition for raising a toddler.

Nina was undergoing her own personal triumph. Years of amateur acting in her mother's small theatre had paid off nicely. Cosmo Freese's old theatre pal, director Montgomery Zwick, had auditioned Nina for a part in his new play and was so enchanted by her performance and poise that he immediately offered her a contract. With Cosmo's help, Nina rented a large apartment in New York and hired a nanny. Cosmo said she was now officially launched. He offered to accompany the little family to New York to get them settled and then return to Belmont for the winter season at the repertory. Nina agreed.

Archie could only wish them well. He again offered his help if she ever needed him. But, to his regret, he didn't believe Nina would call upon him regularly. So, the two women in his life were off to the races, as Cyrus put it, and Archie was in the clear.

Archie wandered around his wife's well-lighted work room outfitted with the latest pottery wheels and kilns. Supplies and her clay vessels and *objets d'art* were neatly arranged on wooden racks. Outside the studio a clever orange and pink neon sign glowed proudly… *'The Sonja Stein Studio…Nom du pot,'* as Cyrus had christened the enterprise on opening night. His bride's self-remodeling had been an astounding success, and no one was snickering about her marvelous pots or her new look. She had turned entrepreneur and artiste with amazing speed and aplomb. With her pots selling in shops and galleries all over the country, Naddy had hired sales representatives from New York, Atlanta and L.A. Who would have thought? Archie muttered in amazement several times a day. And, she had capitulated on her name…friends and family could still call her Nadine or Naddy, if they wanted. She would reserve Sonja for business. Archie said he could live with that.

But, as puzzling as it seemed, Archie was finding his spouse to be not only independent but rather nice these days. He was enjoying her company again, a bewildering development after years of indifference. And, he no longer longed for Nina or desired Marigold. He'd acquired a cure without even realizing it. Cyrus blamed it on a Caribbean voodoo hex put on him by Belle Dupree.

"Toby Spriggs's trial starts tomorrow." Archie took a bottle of mineral water from the small refrigerator next to the microwave. A wave of muggy air was seeping through the studio's weathered brick façade in yet another old warehouse reborn and generating high rent. Maybe he should look into the commercial rehab business. He'd realized in the last few months that he was too young and energetic to be retired.

"Awful young man. Takes after his mean-spirited father." Naddy looked properly disheartened. "It's a wonder Mr. Boswell turned out as well as he has. Must take after Betty Grable." She and Archie laughed together at that one.

"And, the Turk case is officially closed. The D.A.'s calling it an accidental death and a burial by persons unknown. Doesn't sound very legal, but nobody cares." Archie began whistling happily. The studio cat, a tabby called Glaze, jumped off the window sill and headed for a quiet corner in the storage room.

"Bravo, darling! You must feel light as a feather."

"Yes, yes. No more nightmares about burying Buzzy!"

Naddy selected a bottle of iced tea for herself and sat down in one of two woven reed chairs fitted with plump orange cushions. She planted her feet clad in pink silk sandals dotted with fake gems on a crate of supplies. Her toenails matched her fingernails, all done up in neon orange. Archie found it all fascinating and strangely sexy.

"I hear Preacher Boswell's bought a huge sheep ranch in Australia and plans to move there. Sit down, Archie. I bought these chairs for the two of us. They're so comfy."

Archie did as he was told. "Sheep? What the hell does he know about sheep?"

"He's rich. He can hire someone who does." Nadine was still good at reducing the obvious to even simpler terms.

Archie stretched out his long legs and kicked off his leather boat shoes. "Sally will never tell, you know. Just in case you have doubts."

Naddy sat silently, just breathing and resting. It had been a busy week. "I hope so. We'll just have to trust her. How's Cyrus doing these days?"

"Sounded pretty good yesterday. He's still on those new meds. Same old Cyrus, happy as a clam in the new house. Talks to the ghosts, of course. Says they're on very good terms. Says he's coaching the old farts at Meadowlark on how to overthrow management and take back the dining room!" Archie snickered. Naddy, he noticed, seemed quite willing to listen to his stories today. "Still bellyaches about Betty Hughes. Says she's moved him into the guest bath down the hall. She's tired of sharing the sink. Anyway, to take his midnight pee now, he tells me, he must first negotiate that big armoire in the hall that sticks out like an elephant's hind-end. Showed me his big toe, where he cracked it on the corner...as black and blue as a boxer's eye." Archie howled. He still prayed every day for Cyrus's miraculous recovery. He couldn't imagine life without him.

Nadine giggled too and then sighed. She'd always liked nice Cyrus stories. "I've been thinking, Archie, about my name, my new name. Sonja. I am enjoying it so much. Just knowing I own it for the business world, my serious side. I feel like a new person. I am a new person."

Archie's body slammed into automatic alert. He began listening to his wife with great care. What was coming next? Jesus, the terror a woman could strike in a man's heart with those three little words... 'I've been thinking.' "Are you going to change it again?" he asked cautiously and yet casually.

"Heaven's no! Sonja is perfect. Sonja Stein! My name is my new identity. But, I've

been thinking about *your* name, Archie."

Nadine was beaming and gesturing energetically, as if stirring the cosmic dust before

releasing a new brainstorm. Her plump arm loaded with silver bracelets jingled like far-eastern chimes.

"Mine?" More terror.

"Archibald Beresford. Really, darling. It's *so* old-fashioned. *So* stuffy. *So* last Thursday, don't you agree? I've been thinking you should have a new name." Naddy took a long pull on her iced tea.

Stuffy, old-fashioned Archie Beresford sat motionless and speechless. Would this desert spa madness ever cease? The dangers of the creative spirit were vastly under-reported by the press, he was suddenly realizing. Inventive minds were hell on the blood pressure. Why hadn't the *Tribune* or that silly *Belmont Bee* ever printed articles about creative minds? What the hell was *Time* magazine's health editor doing these days?

"Archie, are you listening?" Naddy was asking rather sharply.

"I'm listening." Archie wasn't sure he could feel his feet.

"I think we should call you...Milo!" Nadine looked instantly radiant and threw up her arms as if directing a concert band. "Milo Beresford! Isn't that marvelous? It's so sophisticated. So...romantic. Don't you think? Milo, are you listening to me?"

THE END.